"Eloqu   he
and p   d.
tragic NOV 1 2 2004   an
is an   —*The Times-Picayune* (New

"This touching, elegantly written tale aptly describes love and fr
amid the terror of contemporary war." —*The Dallas Morni*

"A finely drawn story of love and friendship and of finding one's way
in the world through both success and heartache . . . [Lee] imbues his
characters' surroundings with authenticity while creating prose that
is so smoothly readable that it pulls the reader in and through to the
novel's final, reluctantly turned, page."   —*The Denver Post*

"*The Canal House* is an action-packed, erotically charged novel that
spans the globe. All three central characters are extremely strong and
Mark Lee's novel uncoils like a spring from the innate drama of their
razor-edge lives."   —*The Age* (Australia)

"Makes you feel like a member of the press corps."
—*Seattle Weekly*

"There's a deft density to the prose and the satisfying smack of authenticity, particularly on working, traveling and living in Third World
countries. Lee is brilliant at capturing a whole culture in a paragraph,
and devastating on the range of 'types' among expatriates and their
diffidence and rootlessness."   —*St. Louis Post-Dispatch*

"Dear Mark, The Pulpwood Queens Book Clubs of Louisiana and
Texas (10 chapters strong) are so excited about   FIC Lee
book was mesmerizing and I became truly lost i

is reporting in daily on what they thought of reading your novel. I knew this would be a winner for book club discussion."

—Kathy L. Patrick, founder of The Pulpwood Queens book club

"Four stars." —*Detroit Free Press*

"Moving from war-torn Africa to London, then back to violent East Timor, a war correspondent falls in love with an aid worker but discovers it isn't just war threatening their romance; her ex-boyfriend remains in the picture as well." —*USA Today* (Summer Reading pick)

"Intensely compelling . . . Engaging . . . The model for this sort of novel is Hemingway, and Lee honors this tradition with a brisk narrative, excellent character development, and a powerful sense of place and struggle. It's perfect summer reading."

—*Dear Reader* (newsletter for the Square Books
Constant Reader Club, Oxford, MS)

"Exciting and touching." —*The Roanoke Times* (Virginia)

"*The Canal House* takes the reader to far-away and troubled places and tells the story of four people whose lives are forever changed by their experiences with violence, disaster, and even treachery. While there is plenty of action, the real story—the story of a photographer so divorced from his subjects and from life that he cannot be said to be fully alive—moves with telling subtlety toward a gripping denouement." —Robert Bausch, author of *The Gypsy Man*

"Lee spans three continents, mixing high-stakes suspense with erotic intrigue . . . A gripping storyline, rich with detail, shaped by a traveler who has talked the talk and walked the walk."

—*Kirkus Reviews*

"An experienced foreign correspondent, [Lee's] knowledge of the perils and challenges of that life comes across most powerfully in this somber and elegaic novel. . . . There's no denying the eloquence and terror of Lee's vistas of contemporary war . . . they have the breathless immediacy of battlefront reporting."   —*Publishers Weekly*

"Creates a powerful aura of realism that will forever alter your perception of the news."   —*Booklist*

"For an excellent read look no further than this account of epiphany, corruption and contemporary politics. . . . Lee clearly knows his locations and a great deal about aid organisations, journalistic scoops, and human suffering and need."   —*Canberra Times* (Australia)

The Canal House

The Canal House

Mark Lee

A HARVEST BOOK · HARCOURT, INC.

Orlando   Austin   New York   San Diego   Toronto   London

Requests for permission to make copies of any part
of the work should be mailed to the following address:
Permissions Department, Harcourt, Inc.,
6277 Sea Harbor Drive, Orlando, Florida 32887-6777.

www.HarcourtBooks.com

First published by Algonquin Books of Chapel Hill,
a division of Workman Publishing

Library of Congress Cataloging-in-Publication Data
Lee, Mark, 1950–
Canal house/Mark Lee.— 1st Harvest ed.
p. cm. — (A Harvest book)
ISBN 0-15-602954-5
1. War correspondents—Fiction. 2. British—Foreign
countries—Fiction. 3. London (England)—Fiction.
4. Women physicians—Fiction. 5. East Timor—Fiction.
6. Uganda—Fiction. I. Title. II. Series.

PS3562.E35455C365 2004
813'.54—dc22   2004046550

Text set in Sabon

Printed in the United States of America
First Harvest edition 2004

A C E G I K J H F D B

FOR MY MOTHER

With thanks to: Wendy Belcher, Robert Cook, Jenny Darling, Liam Kelly, Therese Kosterman, Pat Lau, Joan Marble, Don Miller, Kathy Pories, and especially Joe Regal.

Nicky

1   LOVERS' WALK

I once read the diary of an Englishman who was trapped at the South Pole in 1914. After their ship was frozen into the ice, he and his companions survived for two years on seal blubber and boiled penguins. On several occasions they almost starved to death. The men became obsessed with food and considered themselves experts on its preparation and consumption. Huddled in their canvas tents, they spent hours describing favorite meals and imaginary banquets. They debated the right way to cook trout, and two men had a fistfight over the proper use of clotted cream.

I offer these facts as an oblique defense for my own obsession. Like those lost explorers, I'm a starving man. For most of my life I've never been in love, but I think about it often and consider myself an expert on its various complexities. I watch for lovers on the street and in restaurants. I've become a collector of jealous glances and lingering kisses, capturing the moments of others and storing them in my memory.

I was watching one afternoon at a dusty refugee camp in northern

Uganda when Daniel McFarland and Julia Cadell first spoke to each other. I saw nothing in that encounter, but they met in England a few months later and fell in love. This time the collector was collected. Even now I'm trying to understand the faith and desire, the large ambitions and small compromises, that brought the three of us to our final moment together.

A FEW YEARS AGO, a powerful earthquake hit southern Turkey. I was a photographer on contract to *Newsweek,* so the magazine flew me to Istanbul and I hired a taxi driver to take me south to the city of Adana. When we finally got there, I discovered that only a few hundred people were dead. The earthquake was a disaster for the people who lived there, but as far as *Newsweek* was concerned it wasn't a major story.

Normally I would have taken a few hundred shots and returned to London, but this time I was forced to stay. My photo editor, Carter Howard, said that a canine search-and-rescue team from Missouri was being flown to Adana by the U.S. Air Force. He wanted pictures of a golden retriever named Cliff finding people lost in the wreckage.

While waiting for the dog, I wandered around the collapsed buildings and took photographs. I prefer 35mm film to digital, but there was no easy way to develop negatives or send them out. The digital camera made it easy. I'd shoot a disc, download everything onto my laptop, then hook up to my satellite phone and send the images to London.

I was sleeping at the home of an Armenian tea trader. Every morning I would roll up my sleeping bag, eat a few candy bars, and go look for rescue crews. Almost everyone in Adana was wearing surgical masks to filter out the dust and germs. Street vendors sold perfume to block the smell of uncollected garbage and I sprinkled a French product called Illusion on my mask. Sniffing the scent of roses, I wandered past piles of shattered concrete and twisted rebar, the collapsed remains of factories, apartment buildings, and mosques. The streets of Adana were clogged with bulldozers and trucks. Bodies were stuffed into plastic bags and laid out in rows in the middle of the soccer stadium. By noon my clothes and skin were covered with white dust and there was a salty, foul taste in my mouth.

Cynicism is an occupational necessity in my profession; it's like the chloroquine you swallow in a malaria zone. You can still get the disease, of course, but the bitter little pills hide your symptoms. The trick is to take your photographs and get out before the medicine loses its effectiveness.

Unfortunately, I stayed too long in Adana and the cynicism wasn't working. The destruction of the city and the grief of its survivors clung to me like the dust from the shattered buildings. The grief became a physical sensation, a hollowness in my stomach and a weakness in my bones. I woke up wondering why this disaster had happened and what purpose it served in some divine scheme. My weakness, my confusion, stayed with me as I wandered around and met the earthquake victims. Most of them carried objects saved from the wreckage: a photo album, a vacuum cleaner, two green parakeets in a little brass cage. The sky above us was clear and blue, but the air was dusty and it distorted the light.

I began to worry about Cliff, the golden retriever. Covering the floods in southern China I learned that rescue dogs got depressed when they found nothing but dead bodies. Their handlers would have to bury a few living people under a pile of leaves and branches so that the dogs would feel encouraged enough to keep working. That's what I needed— a fake rescue to help my morale—but it wasn't going to happen.

The soldiers stopped finding survivors after the third day, but they kept on searching. Late in the afternoon on the fifth day I found a rescue crew pulling away chunks of concrete at a partially destroyed medical clinic near the river. A soldier screamed at me in Turkish, then English: "Go back! Go back! Many dangerous here!" And I could see that part of the second floor was about to collapse.

I turned away from the wreckage, and N. Barbieri, the Italian photographer who works for Reuters, slipped past me and scrabbled over the chunks of concrete. Nina started out using only her first initial so that the Italian newspaper editors would think she was a man. Other photographers called her the Rat, because she was small, fearless, and had close-cropped black hair. Since there aren't a lot of photographers covering international news, we all know each other. We drink together and travel together, but that doesn't mean we're friends.

The Rat stopped for a moment, then glanced back and asked, "You going in there, Nicky?"

"Forget it." The danger of the situation didn't bother me; I had simply had enough of Adana. I took a quick shot of the building's shattered facade, then trudged back home to my bag of chocolate bars.

Five minutes after I left, N. Barbieri took a great photograph, a finalist for Picture of the Year. The Rat was standing on the edge of the second floor, shooting downward, when they discovered a dead mother, embraced by her unconscious but still living, four-year-old son. Both are covered with a white dust. The Turkish soldiers stand back, amazed, like the shepherds who have just found the babe in the manger.

I had made a mistake, but I didn't know it yet. A day later I gave up on the dog and bribed my way onto an army truck going north to Istanbul. I checked into the Sheraton and spent two days taking baths and ordering room service. By the time I returned to London, the latest edition of *Newsweek* was being sold at Heathrow. The earthquake mother and child were on the cover and the photo credit was N. BARBIERI/ REUTERS.

Standing in front of the airport magazine rack, I felt tired and ashamed. I hadn't missed the shot because of equipment problems or bad luck. That afternoon in Adana I had lost my photographer's faith: the certainty that if you go forward, always go forward, the picture will come to you.

I rode the underground into the city and checked into the Ruskin, a two-star hotel across from the British Museum. Alex, the Greek night clerk, smiled when he saw me and we had the usual exchange.

"Welcome back, Mr. Bettencourt. Where have you been?"

"Up, down, and all around."

"Take lots of pictures?"

"Truckloads of them."

"*Newsweek* wants to talk to you." Alex handed me a piece of fax paper and I unfolded it inside the tiny elevator that groaned to the second floor. Carter Howard had sent me a short but ominous message: *Spiked you. Ran Reuters. Call for appointment.*

I don't normally go to expensive restaurants unless someone else is paying, but I had gotten into the habit of treating myself to one good dinner when I returned from an assignment. That night I took the underground to Touraine, a French restaurant in Chelsea. Touraine is at the end of a dark street and has a small sign over the entrance. When you reach the door, you think that no one could possibly be there; then you step inside and find that the place is filled with customers. After David, the owner, led me to my table, I ordered a bottle of Vosne-Romanée wine and some grilled mushrooms. I worked my way through a bowl of fish soup, sautéed chicken with braised leeks, veal *à l'ardennaise,* an herb salad, and pears poached in red wine. A meal like that can overwhelm your doubts and make you feel satisfied with the world, but images from Adana still lingered in my mind. I drank three glasses of cognac, paid the outrageous bill, and took a taxi back to my hotel.

I GREW UP IN MODESTO, an agricultural city in California's San Joaquin Valley. A huge sign arches over the main street downtown and it proclaims four words: WATER, WEALTH, CONTENTMENT, HEALTH. Even when I was a child, I knew that I was different from my parents and their friends. I wanted to live in a place where people didn't talk about property taxes and gas mileage.

I won a Nikon camera playing poker during my sophomore year at college, began to take photographs of the football games, and quickly discovered one of the key pleasures of being a photographer: It gives you an easy excuse to slide into other people's lives. You're there, part of the action, and yet the camera gives you a busy shield to insulate yourself from what you're seeing in your viewfinder.

When I first started out, I didn't know how to take a good picture, but I lacked three qualities that can inhibit a young photographer:

dignity, shame, and fear. After graduating from college I moved down to Los Angeles, bought a police scanner from Radio Shack, and drove around the city looking for car accidents and other disasters. I would shoot two or three rolls of film, then drop them off at Associated Press and the local newspapers.

Eventually the *Los Angeles Times* printed my photo of a Latina mother weeping as her son was zipped into a body bag. At the edge of the photo they printed my name: NICKY BETTENCOURT—FOR THE TIMES. I didn't feel proud at that moment, but more real, more substantial. I suddenly realized why fifteen-year-old kids climbed over barbed-wired fences and shimmied up concrete supports to spray paint their tags on freeway overpasses.

I began working for the major wire services and had a weekly feature called "Out of the Frame" in a local alternative newspaper. I would search out the bloodiest possible car accident, then photograph what was happening a few feet away from the paramedics—a little boy eating a snow cone or a cop picking his nose. The managing editor said it was "postmodern ironic" and my name was put on the masthead.

When the Bosnian civil war broke out, I sold my car, got some press credentials from the *San Francisco Examiner,* and flew to Sarajevo. I had never traveled in a foreign country, didn't know any language other than English, and had never covered a war. Three days after my arrival in Bosnia, I found myself huddled in a foxhole near the Serbian lines, sharing a bottle of wine with Dieter Getz, the Austrian photographer. Aside from his photos, Getz was famous for his long blond ponytail and the pull-on-a-condom T-shirts he bought in Thailand.

"This job is very simple," Dieter told me. "When there's gunfire, the journalists, the soldiers, and the aid workers all fall to the ground."

"Okay."

"Yes. Okay. Okay." He mocked my American accent. "But when there's gunfire, we shooters stand up to take the picture. That's the difference, Nicky. That's who we are."

• • •

I WAITED UNTIL the next morning, made an appointment to see Carter at three o'clock, then took the elevator down to the dining room in the basement. The Ruskin is a dump, but it's one of the few hotels in Bloomsbury that doesn't have American college students staying there during the summer. There's something depressing about eating an English breakfast with a group of nineteen-year-olds from some Midwestern university.

It was a warm August day so I walked over to the *Newsweek* offices on Park Street, a few blocks east of the American embassy. I went upstairs to the third floor where Ann Weinstein, the young assistant photo editor, was scanning negatives into her computer.

Ann glanced at Carter's private office. The door was closed. "We used Reuters for the quake."

"Yeah. I know. That's why I'm here."

"Don't lie and say you weren't at that building."

"Maybe I wasn't."

"Carter adjusted your color levels on his computer when I was in Cornwall for the weekend. You took a photo of a Turkish soldier wearing a red emergency vest. The same man is in Barbieri's picture."

"I wouldn't have lied," I told her. But maybe I lied when I said that.

"Carter!" she shouted. "Nicky's here!"

Carter Howard was in his fifties, an elegant man with thinning hair who'd lived in London for the last eight years. He used to be a photographer, but he made the transition to editor when he fell in love with a young British artist named Jonathan Campbell. I'd never been invited to their row house in Kensington, but I'd heard about their herb garden and the immense studio with a skylight.

Whenever I dropped by the office, Carter liked to plug in his kettle and make tea. That afternoon he just stood there wearing his custom-made shirt and pleated trousers. Carter had picked up a slight British accent from living in London and he called me Nick-o-loss, dragging out the last syllable.

"Welcome back, Nicholas. I haven't been out of my office the entire day. What do you say we take a walk through the park?"

"Sounds good to me."

Carter pulled on his suit coat and I followed him downstairs. As we wandered up Alford Street, Carter described his attempt to grow antique English roses in a shady part of his garden. We took the pedestrian passageway under Park Lane to Hyde Park and stopped in front of a fountain. At the center of the fountain was an elaborate sculpture of a naked couple either dancing or falling through space while a bunch of cherubs surrounded them. Carter turned west and led me down a gravel pathway beneath some oak trees. The fountain was dedicated to lovers and the pathway was called Lovers' Walk.

A little boy and girl were running across the park grass, trying to get a dragon kite up into the air. It could have been a good photograph, but I turned away from the shot and looked down at Carter's polished wing tips. "Nice shoes," I told him. "You always wear nice shoes."

"New York isn't happy with you, Nicholas."

"New York can go to hell. They weren't walking around Typhoid City, waiting for a goddamn golden retriever."

"That's your job."

"I sent out over four hundred shots—with captions. Some things didn't go right and Barbieri got a better picture. You're a photographer. You know how it is."

"It's not just the earthquake photos. They've been complaining about your stuff since you came back from Nigeria. These days every photographer with a sat phone and a digital camera can send us pictures five minutes after they press the button. You're competing with every other shooter in the world."

"I know that, Carter. I've met them. They're all twenty-six years old with tattoos."

"News organizations don't want full-time employees or even contract photographers. If you expect a paycheck from *Newsweek*, then you're going to have to provide images that are consistently unique."

"I've risked my life for this goddamn magazine. You know that's true."

"I'm on your side, Nicholas. There's no reason to get angry. Maybe you're just tired, burned out from the traveling. If you want, I can transfer your contract to the Washington Bureau. Life is a lot easier there, just one long photo op."

I imagined myself standing in a pack of photographers, taking shot after shot of the president in the Rose Garden. What every photographer wants is that unguarded moment when a person's defenses are down and you can capture an image so intimate that it connects with anyone who sees it. But successful politicians have learned to conceal their emotions in public. Working in that world would be like photographing wax dummies.

"No. I don't want a job like that."

"All right. It's your choice." Carter stopped in the middle of Lovers' Walk and looked around at the green fields of Hyde Park and the rush-hour traffic grumbling up Park Lane. "Do you know an American journalist named Daniel McFarland?"

"Sure. He was the one covering the fighting in northern Iraq after the Gulf War, and then he worked in the Balkans. We were in Bosnia at the same time, but we never actually met. I used to see him drinking with a bunch of Polish photographers at the Café Metropole. Wasn't Victor Zikowski killed working with McFarland?"

Carter shrugged and resumed walking. "McFarland has a five-year contract with the *Daily Telegraph,* but he also does features for the *Washington Post.* John Scofield deals with him quite frequently."

The *Post* was owned by the same parent company as *Newsweek* and they shared offices on Park Street. Scofield played squash every Wednesday with Carter, and I could tell they had discussed my awkward career.

"So how does McFarland connect with me?"

"Four months ago a group of tourists were kidnapped from a game park in northern Uganda by some guerrillas called the Lord's Righteous Army. They're led by a local prophet, Samuel Okello."

"I've read about him. He kidnaps children from the villages."

"The Red Cross, the Ugandans, and our State Department have tried to contact this group, but they haven't succeeded. The British sent in military advisers to help the Ugandan army, but the guerrillas killed twenty-three of their soldiers in an ambush. One of the hostages is a librarian from Madison, Wisconsin. Little kids are tying yellow ribbons to a tree on her front lawn. It would be a wonderful story if a journalist could track down Okello and interview him."

"And McFarland wants to try?"

"He thinks it's possible."

"Who's going to pay him to do it?"

"He'll sell the story to the *Washington Post* and the *Telegraph*. We'll get magazine rights."

"And I'd be the photographer?"

"Exactly. McFarland takes a few risks, but he's been very successful. There's a good chance he can pull this off."

In our business "takes a few risks" meant "he's completely insane." I didn't know if Carter thought he was doing me a big favor, but the situation was obvious. Daniel McFarland was looking for a photographer because everyone else had turned him down. If the Lord's Righteous Army had already kidnapped some tourists, it would enjoy capturing some foreign journalists. We might find Samuel Okello's camp, but we wouldn't be able to leave.

"Do you want to go to Uganda? I told New York that you'd spent a lot of time there during the Rwandan civil war."

"I spent three days in Kampala, then crossed the border at Kabale."

"Sounds like you're an expert."

Carter glanced at me, waiting for my decision. Whenever there's a big choice in life, it's usually no choice at all. I hesitated for a few seconds, then turned and walked back to the cherubs. "Do I get expenses?"

"A plane ticket plus fifteen hundred dollars."

"When do I leave?"

"First, you've got to fly down to Rome. McFarland wants to meet and see if you can work together."

"I can work with the devil, given a limited time frame."

"McFarland isn't exactly the devil. But John says he's very intense."

"In other words, he's crazy."

Carter took out a handkerchief and flicked some dust off his shoes. "McFarland will bring you to the picture, Nicholas. You just have to take it."

2   THE ITALIAN SUIT

I walked Carter Howard back to his office, then caught a bus going to Bloomsbury. It was too damn depressing to sit in my hotel room so I walked across Montague Street to the British Museum. Most of the tourist groups were being herded toward the Elgin Marbles. I threaded my way through a crowd of Japanese high school kids, entered the Egyptian collection, and headed for the ground-floor gallery and the Shabaka Stone.

The stone is a chunk of black basalt that's named after the pharaoh Shabaka who founded the Twenty-fifth Dynasty. It's said to contain a complete account of the creation of the world, but someone carried the stone away from the ruins of Shabaka's palace and used it to crush grain. A hand-sized divot was chipped out in the center of the stone and little channels radiated from that like the rays of the sun.

Sitting on a bench, I stared at the faint hieroglyphics rubbed away by some Bronze Age miller. I knew why Carter had hooked me up with Daniel McFarland. Journalists are like gamblers eager to rub up against a winner at the dice table. If Daniel McFarland had the luck to get a good story, then perhaps he could pass it on to me.

I made a reservation on Alitalia and flew down to Rome the next morning. Ann Weinstein had printed off some of Daniel's old clips and I read them on the plane. There were two kinds of feature articles about the Third World: "Why? Oh, why?" and "Fancy that!" Daniel had come up with a different approach, a point of view that told the reader "These are the facts. What are you going to do about it?" During the Gulf War he had been one of the few journalists to report on the Kurdish uprising in northern Iraq. His article about the Kurds' retreat to the Turkish border was nominated for a Pulitzer Prize. Daniel never placed political statements in any of his writing, but he explained how each army had acquired the guns and bombs used to kill civilians. When you read one of Daniel's articles, you always felt uncomfortable —and a little angry—about what was going on.

I changed my money at Leonardo da Vinci airport, then took the train into the city. *Newsweek* wasn't paying for the trip so I checked into a cheap hotel near the Stazione Termini. I took a shower, killed a few cockroaches, and tried to contact Daniel McFarland at his three phone numbers. Carter said that Daniel had a home in the countryside north of the city, but the phone rang forever and no one picked it up. The second number was linked to an office answering machine so I left a message there. The final number was for a cell phone, but I kept getting a perky recording in Italian.

I went to a trattoria in the old Jewish Ghetto and ate two bowls of oxtail soup. When I returned to my hotel, the night clerk bowed slightly and called me *dottore* as if I were a classics professor who had arrived to study the ruins. Signor McFarland had called and requested that I meet him at the Stampa Estera for lunch.

I had been there for a news conference a couple of years ago and remembered that it was near the main post office. It was a club, run by the Italian government, for the foreign journalists working in Italy. I took the subway to the Spanish Steps the next day and strolled past the tourists, the North African street hustlers, and the *carabinieri* dressed in their dark blue uniforms. A flock of pigeons rose up into the sky and I took a picture for the hell of it.

I found the small building that housed the Stampa Estera and went upstairs. The first floor lobby had a few saggy club chairs and a well-stocked bar. I told the elderly bartender that I was looking for Daniel McFarland and he pointed to the dining room where several people were eating lunch. I'm a confident man behind the camera, but this was a job interview. I took a deep breath and walked into the room.

When I last saw Daniel at the Café Metropole in Sarajevo, he had a two-week beard and wore blue jeans. Now he was clean-shaven and dressed in a well-cut Italian suit without a necktie. His brown hair was still long enough to show that he wasn't a corporate journalist worried about his mortgage and pension plan. There was an intensity about Daniel, a way that he watched your eyes and listened to your words that was somewhat intimidating. You knew right away that he was one of those people who burn brightly as they move through the world.

He got up from the table and smiled. "Nicky Bettencourt."

"That's me."

"Daniel McFarland." We shook hands. "How was the flight?"

"Short."

"Where are you staying?"

"Hotel Centro. Near the Termini."

We both sat down at the table. "Carter said you were in Bosnia for a while."

"Yeah. I knew a photographer who used to work with you."

"Who's that?"

"Victor Zikowski."

Daniel looked away and poured some wine into my glass. "Bosnia was tough on photographers. A few months after Victor was killed, I was working with Tommy Boyle and he got hit in the neck with a chunk of shrapnel. The wound messed up his vocal cords. Now he talks like a frog."

A waitress came over and gave me a menu. "Stay away from the fish," Daniel said. "The lamb's okay, but it varies. I recommend the *spaghetti alla puttanesca.*"

"*Puttanesca.* Whore's style," I said. "The perfect dish for a photographer."

I thought that we were going to have a private meal together, but a Slovenian journalist and a reporter for a Brazilian newspaper joined us a few minutes later. Daniel ate lunch at the Stampa Estera two or three times a week and anyone who showed up was welcome at his table. It didn't take me long to realize that most of the people eating with Daniel didn't exactly have a real job. They were stringers, squeezing out a living with an occasional article for a newspaper in Finland or a Catholic magazine in Ukraine.

Whenever Daniel ate at the Stampa Estera, he bought the endless *fojetta*s of wine that the waitress set down in the middle of the table. Everyone was supposed to pay for his own meal, but the bill magically became smaller for the hungry-looking Moroccan reporter and ex-Pravda correspondent with the frayed shoes. Daniel had realized that many of the older journalists hanging out at the Stampa were walking encyclopedias of valuable information. We talked about many things that afternoon, but I remember a long discussion about the Golden Triangle: the opium-producing region in Laos, Thailand, and Burma. The Slovenian journalist and a Frenchman who joined us later had traveled through the area and Daniel was relentless with his questions: How did you get there? What was the best way to hire a guide? How do you offer a bribe to a Thai soldier? Information was received and filed, ready for future use, but he was also funny and charming, and I began to feel a little jealous. Some people can strap on ice skates and glide through social situations while people like me are flailing their arms and grabbing for the rail.

The kitchen stopped serving lunch at four o'clock. The other journalists left and Daniel ordered a double espresso. "What's this story about?" he asked. "Hostages, right? Game parks. Northeast Uganda. The Lord's Righteous Army."

I had drunk too much wine and was feeling fuzzy around the edges. "Why are you asking me? I thought you knew all about it. You told everyone in London that you could find Samuel Okello."

"I said it was possible." He set down the little coffee cup with a sharp click. "As I recall, the hostages were British and American—"

"And one German."

"Good. I can sell the story to a German newspaper, along with the *Post* and the *Daily Telegraph*."

I followed him upstairs to the third floor where they kept the mailboxes and a soundproof room for TV interviews. Several people greeted Daniel, but he didn't stop to chat. He led me into a long, narrow room crowded with ten steel desks, each one rented by a different journalist. Daniel's was piled with stacks of old newspapers and manila envelopes stuffed with clips of old stories. An answering machine was attached to the phone and the little red message light blinked frantically.

Daniel sat down at the desk and motioned for me to grab a chair. What I wanted to do was go back to my hotel and take a nap, but I sat down. First he pulled up a background story from the *New York Times* archive, then he took out his PalmPilot and began to call newspaper and magazine editors in Germany.

Successful journalists are experts in charm and duplicity. Charm to get people to answer your questions, duplicity since you discard the opinions of the person you've interviewed and write your own version of what happened. Daniel also used charm and duplicity to multiply his income. Without agreeing to anything specific, he convinced each editor that he shared his or her vision of the world. When Daniel talked to the German editors, the German hostage was a crucial part of the article. As I sat there listening, he sold different versions of the same story to the *Frankfurter Allgemeine* and two magazines.

Between phone calls, he sent e-mail requesting payment for previous articles, then played back his voice mail. The first message was from an Italian woman with a cultured voice. I didn't understand much Italian —aside from ordering food in restaurants—but it was obvious that she wanted to see him.

"That's the Contessa," explained Daniel as he phoned another editor. The Contessa left a half-dozen phone messages that were interspersed with the voices of Daniel's various contacts and two calls from his London banker. She was passionate, then angry, then weeping, and finally shouting. Her last message was short and very formal. She gave a time in English and hung up.

I still didn't know if we were going to Africa. "If you want to look at my past work, I've got an envelope of photographs back at the hotel."

"That's not necessary. I accessed *Newsweek*'s archives and looked at your shots. Some of them are pretty good, Nicky. I liked that picture of the severed arm you took in Rwanda." Daniel shut down his computer. "You and I are going to a party at the Contessa's tonight. Did you bring any clothes to Rome?"

"I'm wearing them."

"Okay. We can deal with that." Daniel unlocked a desk drawer. He took out some one-thousand-lira notes and stuffed them into his right pants pocket. A larger wad of ten-thousand-lira notes went into his left pocket. "Let's go."

I didn't want to attend a party, but it felt like part of the job interview. Out on the street, Daniel lit a Turkish cigarette and led me over to the Piazza San Silvestro. About twenty cars were parked in a tight group near the central fountain. An old man wearing a stained overcoat was leaning next to a Ford Fiesta. It looked like he was waiting to steal something. Daniel bowed slightly, called him Signor Posteggiatore, and gave him some money from the one-thousand-lira pocket. I could see that the old man was a "space finder" who spent his time finding spots for illegally parked cars. He returned the bow, pulled a rag out of his pocket, and limped over to an Alfa Romeo Spider. The red sports car was splattered with mud and trash was stuffed behind the two seats. As we got in, the old man wiped the headlights clean and explained how he had defended the car from thieves, policemen, and all the fiends of hell.

Daniel started the engine, gunned it a few times, and then we were off, circling once around the piazza and heading down a side street. He drove like a dying man searching for a hospital, racing through every gap in the traffic and occasionally driving with two wheels up on the sidewalk. We stopped briefly for a traffic cop who was defending an intersection and Daniel turned to me. "You can't hesitate around here." The cop lowered his arm. Daniel shifted gears and mashed the accelerator.

It was about six o'clock, but the sky was still blue and pink clouds glowed on the horizon. Slipping through the traffic, we crossed over to the Trastevere district on the west side of the Tiber. The buildings were three or four stories high and the streets were even narrower—it reminded me of Greenwich Village. Daniel hit the brakes and turned down an alleyway, which opened onto a small piazza.

He walked over to a shop with a tailor's dummy in the display window, but I didn't follow him. Although I wanted the job, I didn't see why I had to jump through this particular hoop. Daniel had charmed the older journalists at lunch. That wasn't going to work with me.

"What's the problem, Nicky?"

"I'm not buying new clothes just so I can go to a party."

"Let them make you a suit. If you aren't happy with the result, I'll buy everything back from you."

"We're not the same size."

"Don't worry about that." Grabbing my arm, he opened the door and dragged me into the shop. There weren't any customers there, just an older man with a walrus mustache. He was sewing a cuff on some trousers while he sat crossed-legged on a wooden table.

"*Buona sera, maestro.*"

"Ahhh, Daniel!" The tailor embraced Daniel as if he were his long-lost son. They stood there jabbering for a while, then the tailor shouted some names. His family lived over the shop and they started descending the back staircase. There was the tailor's wife, the plump older daughter, the skinny younger daughter, and the tailor's teenage son. Daniel greeted them all—kissing the men and squeezing the women's hands. He said something in Italian and everyone turned around and stared at me.

My grandparents were Portuguese and I'd inherited their black curly hair and brown eyes. I had assumed I was going to get taller when I reached puberty, but it didn't work out that way. I have short legs and I could lose some weight. I hate people looking at me and I especially hate people taking my photograph. When I rented a tuxedo for my sister's wedding, I looked like a dwarf waiter.

Now the whole damn family was staring at me and discussing my body. They got into a loud argument about my shoulders and Daniel had to intervene. The tailor kept circling me, measuring me with his tape and murmuring in Italian.

"What the hell is he talking about?"

"He says you're an interesting challenge."

"That's a nice way to put it. Just tell him to sell me a suit and we'll get out of here."

Daniel translated what I said and everyone laughed. The tailor scribbled some instructions on a piece of paper and gave them to his son. The young man hurried out of the shop and I heard the whine of a motor scooter speeding away.

The younger daughter went upstairs for a few minutes, then came back down with a bottle of Frascati wine and a pair of gray wool pants.

"Italians admire English gentlemen," explained Daniel. "So that's the style we're going for here. You'll look conservative, but elegant."

"This is bullshit."

"Have some wine, Nicky. Sit back and enjoy it."

I tried on the pants and the tailor pinned up the fabric in various places. When he was done he tossed the pants across the room to the older daughter and she began altering them on an antique sewing machine. The tailor's wife brought out another bottle of wine along with a suit coat. It looked all right without alterations, but the fitting lasted an hour. Everything was discussed endlessly. The cuffs. The pockets. The lapels. More wine.

Daniel filled up my glass, joked with me, and complimented the tailor. An Italian would have said that Daniel was *gentile*—kind or polite —but the word meant much more than that. Daniel was graceful. He could make you feel better about yourself and eager to display your best qualities. I envied him, but I hadn't forgotten about the photographers he'd worked with in Bosnia, one dead and the other talking like a frog.

It was almost nine o'clock in the evening. I tried on the pants, a new shirt, and the suit coat. A scooter screeched to a stop outside and the tailor's son ran in with a silk necktie and pair of shoes. I got completely dressed and the older daughter smiled at me. She moved back a wood panel and all of a sudden I was looking at myself in a full-length mirror.

I looked good, almost handsome, for the first time in my life. You couldn't tell that I had stubby legs. My extra weight made me seem solid, not sloppy and fat. I wondered if my life would have turned out differently had I looked like this in high school.

"*Grazie*," I whispered.

"*Prego*," the family answered. They all looked tired and proud, like they had scaled Mount Everest with a pair of scissors and some thread.

I saw Daniel in the mirror, standing behind me. "*Grazie infinite*," he told them.

The younger daughter brought out some grappa and poured it into little brandy glasses. I handed over my credit card while Daniel gave a separate tip to each of the tailor's children. The money was folded over once, then slipped into each person's hand like a gesture of friendship. It was the first time I ever realized that there was a graceful way to pay your bills.

Everyone shook my hand and complimented me, and then we were back out on the street and squeezing ourselves into the Spider. I was half drunk from the wine at the tailor shop or maybe I hadn't sobered up from lunch. The alcohol blurred the streetlights and softened all the edges of the buildings.

"You satisfied, Nicky?"

"I guess so."

"Good. Let's go to the party."

Daniel drove just as fast at night as he did in the daytime, but there were fewer cars in the streets and he was able to glide through most of the intersections. The warm night air swirled around us as we cruised back across the Tiber. Another Alfa Romeo passed in the opposite direction and the driver honked his horn. Shifting gears, Daniel explained that the single male driver was an *Alfista,* that we were *Alfisti* and that if we encountered a pair of beautiful Italian women in a Spider they were *Alfiste.*

"What if they're not beautiful?" I asked.

Daniel shifted again and cut in front of a Fiat. "They have to be. It's a tradition."

On our left, the Castel Sant'Angelo glowed with light. Its round walls and the towers of the inner castle made it look like an enormous cupcake. I began seeing photographs everywhere. Two lovers stared at some illuminated ruins. A drunk old man was doing a little dance on the sidewalk. A black cat perched on a white marble wall. I felt happy at that moment, or maybe it was just the grappa. Everything seemed possible if we just kept moving—perhaps we would even meet some *Alfiste.*

We turned off the *corso* and entered the narrow streets of the old city. The tires bumped over cobblestones, and I felt like the buildings were moving closer and closer together, forcing us into alleyways not much wider than the car. Finally Daniel parked near some trash cans. We got out of the car, walked past a church and through an archway, and then we were standing on the southern side of Piazza Navona. People were sitting at outdoor tables and a small band was playing a waltz.

"Is there going to be food at this party?"

"Of course. It's Rome."

Daniel strolled over to one of the large buildings circling the piazza. A burly doorman with a squashed nose stood in front of a steel and glass door. He recognized Daniel and waved us inside. The elevator operator was a tough little guy and I could see a shoulder holster beneath his suit coat. He guided us into an elevator that looked like a birdcage and pushed down the lever. We went up slowly, the elevator squeaking and shivering, until we reached the top floor.

The Count's coat of arms was hanging on the wall of the vestibule. I guess it was real and historical, but it looked like a plaster-of-paris movie prop. Pop music was blasting from a stereo inside the apartment and Daniel had to knock twice before the Sicilian maid answered the door. She smiled at Daniel, whispered something in Italian, and he gave her a few bills.

If I had come there alone I would have been tentative, cautious, trying not to knock anything over until I met the host. Daniel charged down the narrow hallway and led me into a dining room filled with antique furniture. Platters of fruit and vegetables were spread out on a central table along with plates of pastries and a giant clamshell filled with iced shrimp.

I grabbed a chocolate-dipped strawberry and stayed close to Daniel as we entered a living room filled with guests talking, drinking, laughing loudly. There was a pig's head floating in a Plexiglas box in one corner of the room. Directly across from it, in the facing corner, was a billy goat's head.

"What the hell is that?"

"Art. It just arrived a couple of weeks ago."

A little brass plaque was mounted on the wall, midway between the two boxes. It gave the name of the artist and the title of the installation —*Fama e Fortuna.* "So which one is Fame and which is Fortune?" I asked.

"I don't know, Nicky. Take your pick."

As I followed Daniel through the living room, I realized that both women and men glanced at him as he passed. I remembered taking photographs of two British actors who found themselves in a play with a Siamese cat. Because the audience never knew what the cat was going to do, they ignored the actors and watched the animal move across the stage. Daniel's body, the way he carried himself, had the same degree of unpredictability. There was a restlessness within him, an energy, that was barely contained.

Daniel and I passed through some French doors and stepped out onto the patio. Darkness. Stars. Directly below us was the piazza; the tourists and the waiters and the Italian schoolgirls linked arm in arm circled slowly around Bernini's Fountain of the Four Rivers. A three-quarter moon had risen above the city. It glowed with a soft gold-colored light, like an old Roman coin that had been pulled from the earth and placed on a black velvet cloth.

"You've brought a friend, Daniel."

I turned away from the city and faced a dark-haired woman in her forties. A well-dressed older man stood next to her.

"Mr. Bettencourt is a fellow journalist." Then Daniel introduced me to the Contessa Something or Other and her husband, the Count. Having listened to the Contessa shout and weep on Daniel's answering machine, I had figured that they were lovers, but here she was, talking to us like we were guests at a family picnic. I realized why Daniel had dragged me to the party. If he had showed up alone, his affair with the Contessa would have been more obvious. I was camouflage in a new suit.

The Contessa had good cheekbones and a strong nose. She had probably been a great beauty ten years ago, but now she had one of those unnaturally smooth faces that comes from too much plastic surgery. Her eyes were focused on Daniel and when he lit her cigarette, she touched his hand and pulled the match a little closer.

The Count and I were both dressed the same way: two British gentlemen. While we stood on the patio, he checked out what I was wearing. He disapproved of the camera bag slung over my shoulder, but his eyes lingered on the lapels of the suit coat, my shirt collar, and the burgundy-colored necktie. When he nodded slightly to himself, I was pleased. If he was the fashion inspector, then I had just passed the exam.

"How fortunate that you've brought your camera," the Count said. "Michael Cesare is our guest of honor tonight. He has come to Rome to sing at the Baths of Caracalla."

I must have looked confused because Daniel provided a quick explanation. "Cesare is an opera singer. The Teatro dell'Opera has a summer season at the Roman ruins."

The Count looked annoyed. "He is not just an opera singer. He is the most significant tenor of this new generation."

"We have other guests of honor," the Contessa said. "The Texans."

Her husband sighed. "Ahhh, yes. The Texans."

"They look very lonely tonight." The Contessa grabbed my hand and pulled me away. "Come with me, Signor Bettencourt. You must talk to them."

She slipped her arm through mine like we were two schoolgirls down in the piazza. I turned my head and my lips grazed her hair.

"You are working with Daniel?"

"Maybe."

"What does that mean?"

"We might be traveling to Africa to cover a story."

Her arm tightened slightly. "He didn't tell me this. He never tells me anything."

I saw the Texans right away—two balding guys with their wives. They stood together in the middle of the living room like cattle facing a pack of dogs. They looked nervous and a little scared.

"Signor Garvey, Signor Price, this is Signor Bettencourt, an American news photographer."

"Glad to meetcha," said Price. Maybe the Contessa was right—the Texans were lonely—because everybody wanted to shake my hand. I met Tom and his wife, Arlene, Vernon and a woman whose name I immediately forgot. She was short, with big hair, and giggly.

The Contessa drifted away and talked to one of the servants. I chatted with the Texans. Vernon and Tom owned a motel chain called the Gold Star Inns. In the last few years they had bought controlling interest in a cruise-ship line and a resort in the Bahamas.

"Then Arlene here, she's the reader, bought a couple of books about an American lady who lived in Tuscany. I didn't think too much about them, either way, but Arlene said they've sold hundreds of thousands of copies."

Vernon nodded. "I read the books and figured that lots of people would like to have the same kind of experience without the hassle. One of our attorneys got in touch with the Count and he started sending us faxes."

"The Count is going to guide people around Tuscany?"

Arlene looked amused. "Of course not. He owns a village there."

"An entire village?"

"The whole damn thing," Tom said. "Lock, stock, and barrel."

"We figured that we'd put in some detached units there. Gut out the existing homes and install American plumbing, central heating, and satellite TV. Everything first rate. People could come for a week or two months."

"Where would the villagers live?"

"We'll keep 'em around, of course. They'll be the employees. But it will be a controlled environment. No cars, just electric golf carts."

I stared at them, impressed and appalled. "And the villagers said they'd go for this?"

"Hell, yes. All the young people there want a good job. That working on the farm stuff gets old real fast."

I excused myself, grabbed a glass of champagne from a tray, and drifted into the dining room. Everybody was talking about the two heads in formaldehyde. Apparently the Count had just bought them from a young British genius for ten million lire. The pig had pale skin with blue veins, like a human, and its eyes were closed. I asked one of the servants if the pig was Fame, but he didn't speak English.

Perhaps I should have been angry with Daniel for using me to conceal his love affair, but the new suit changed everything. Although I didn't know enough Italian to flirt with the women, several of them smiled at me and I smiled back. Usually I feel like I'm sitting in the cheap seats watching other people perform in an endless play. But with my Italian suit I was up on the stage—not in a big role perhaps, but definitely part of the story.

Daniel and the Contessa had disappeared. The Count didn't seem to care. Around midnight Michael Cesare showed up with his entourage. The opera singer was a big man with a small blond ponytail. He demanded a special drink that included lime juice, cold tea, and a raw egg. The Count scurried in and out of the kitchen trying to find all the ingredients. It was difficult to figure out who was sleeping with whom, but one thing seemed clear: the Texans were going to lose all of their money.

I was drinking more champagne and eating my third plate of shrimp when the Contessa cornered me. She looked angry.

"You think that your friend is loyal, but that is not true. He only cares for his work."

"Daniel isn't my friend."

"Good. I would not travel to Africa with him. He is a cold man. *Un egotista*. If you get sick or injured he will leave you there."

The Count approached us and pointed to my camera bag. "You," he said as if I were a plumber who had just shown up to fix a leaky faucet, "take a picture of me and Michael Cesare."

"Why?"

"Our photograph must appear in my friend's newspaper."

"Then get one of their guys to do the job."

The Count jabbed his finger at the breast pocket of my new sports coat. "I order you to do this! *Immediatamente!*"

I was going to tell the Count to go to hell when Daniel stepped in front of me and spoke in a soft voice. "What's the problem, Nicky?"

"I don't want to take their picture."

"Why not?"

"I'm a news photographer. That's what I do. I'll risk my life to take a picture that's important, but I won't do it just to pump up somebody's ego."

Daniel nodded, but he didn't move away. "We're guests, Nicky. We've eaten the man's food and drunk his wine. If you don't want to do it, then give me the camera."

He reached out and held both my arms as if to keep me from falling. I knew that he was going to take the picture, regardless of what I said. What the hell, I thought. Don't want him touching my equipment.

"All right," I told the Count. "Go over there and hug your buddy."

The Count turned gracious and charming. He hurried over to Cesare, threw an arm around him, and they both grinned like schoolboys. I raised my camera, took one step to the right to get the pig's head in the frame, then took the picture.

Daniel whispered something to the Contessa and she laughed loudly. He coaxed me out of the apartment and led me down a marble staircase. I was still annoyed that he had maneuvered me into taking the picture.

"What's the problem?" I asked. "Why did we have to leave?"

"You're drunk, Nicky. Time to go home."

"How come the Count lets you screw his wife?"

"That doesn't concern you."

"If we're going to work together, then we've got to be honest with each other. I want to know what's going on so I can evaluate the risk. I'm not going to get killed like Victor Zikowski."

Daniel spun me around on the landing and slammed me against the wall. "That's the second time you've mentioned him. Are you making a point, Nicky? Trying to tell me something?"

"Maybe."

"It was his idea to go up that road and I went with him. Victor knew how dangerous it was. We both took the same risk."

I was too drunk to come up with a reply so I let him drag me out into the square. It was dark and the crowds had disappeared. An old man stood by one of the fountains and played a sad song on an accordion. Somehow we made it back to the Spider. I closed my eyes and leaned against the door as Daniel started the engine.

I assumed he was going to drop me off at the hotel, but when I opened my eyes again we were speeding north on the Appian Way. The road was very narrow and bumpy. Garden walls and pine trees lined both sides and it felt like we were trapped in a tunnel. No road signs. A faint glow came from the car's instrument panel, but it was difficult to see Daniel's face. All I knew was that we were driving as fast as possible toward some unknown destination.

• • •

I WOKE UP AT DAWN, still sitting in the car. My muscles were stiff and I felt sick to my stomach. A flock of sparrows were perched on the hood of the Spider. I lurched forward and they all flew away.

The car was parked on a hillside somewhere in the country. Peering through the windshield, I could see an oak tree and a clump of thornbushes. My hand found the door handle. I got out, took two steps, then felt ill and sat down on some gravel. Daniel had left me here. God knows where he had spent the night. After a few minutes of fighting with my stomach, I closed my eyes and lay on my side.

Footsteps crunched across the gravel, and I felt the shock of cold water splashed on my face. I sat up, sputtering, and an old woman carrying a red plastic pail began screaming at me in Italian. She was less than five feet tall, dressed in black with white hair slipping out from beneath her kerchief.

"I'm sorry, ma'am. But I don't know what you're saying. If you could just talk a little slower . . ."

She tapped her forefinger on her head to indicate that I was crazy, then turned away from me and took a path that led up the slope to a gray stone farmhouse. A patio was at the front of the house and it was covered by a latticework intertwined with grapevines.

I stood up, still wobbly, and saw Daniel come out of the house carrying a silver coffeepot and some cups. He bowed slightly to the old woman. She pointed down the hill and delivered a few more comments, most likely about my sleeping habits and moral degeneracy.

My new pants were covered with dirt. Burs and stickseeds clung to my suit coat. Slowly I followed the pathway up the hill. I passed one terrace dotted with olive trees, then a second terrace supporting a large vegetable garden. When I reached the arbor I found Daniel sitting at a wooden table wearing a Bob Marley T-shirt, torn blue jeans, and running shoes.

"Coffee?"

"Please."

He filled a cup with hot coffee and mixed in some evaporated milk. The sticky, sweet milk usually made me gag, but that morning it softened the harsh taste of the coffee and helped settle my stomach.

"Where the hell are we?"

"North of Rome, near the village of Bracciano." Daniel made a circular motion with his right hand, taking in the farmhouse, the olive trees, and the vegetable garden. "This is my home."

The old lady came out with more coffee and banged the pot down on the table. She spoke to me in Italian, not shouting this time, but giving me lots of advice.

"Nicky, I'd like you to meet La Signora. She lives in another house farther up the hill."

"*Buon giorno, signora.*" I smiled, but the old lady kept talking.

"She thinks that you slept on the ground last night and is afraid that this habit will give you tuberculosis. La Signora's brother used to get drunk and sleep on the ground, and that's how he died."

"Tell her I'll never do it again."

La Signora accepted my apology and brought us a tray of food. She laid out two loaves of hard-crusted bread, a jar of blackberry jam, a bowl of black olives floating in brine with cloves of garlic, a basket of figs, a chunk of prosciutto, and some whitish yellow *caciotta* cheese.

I went into the house and washed my face and hands beneath the faucet at the kitchen sink. The water was cold and smelled faintly of limestone. I dried myself off and took a look around. The house had a flagstone floor and plaster walls. A propane refrigerator, stove, and water heater were in the kitchen, but there were no electric lights. Baskets hung from hooks in the ceiling and they were filled with garlic, onions, potatoes, dried red peppers. A photograph of the pope wearing a cowboy hat and chaps was taped to the wall over the sink.

The kitchen opened up to a living room with a stone fireplace that was big enough to cook a pig, a saggy couch, a leather easy chair, and a coffee table with stacks of old magazines and paperback books in several languages. One doorway led to the bathroom, which contained a toilet and a rusty bathtub. A second door led to Daniel's bedroom where I saw shelves with music CDs and more books.

The farm wasn't connected to a power line, and light came from candles and kerosene lanterns. Daniel's laptop was on the coffee table along with a satellite phone and a short-wave radio. The house looked like a comfortable place to live, but something felt wrong. When I came out of the bathroom I realized that there wasn't a single memento in the house. No Masai spears from Africa or silk prints from Thailand. No faded pictures of mom and dad in a sailboat or a snapshot from a ski trip to Austria. If Daniel McFarland had a personal life, it didn't show.

But then I glanced into the bedroom and saw a framed photograph hanging on the wall over the dresser. Wrong again, I thought. Maybe it was a picture of the Contessa lying topless on the beach in Capri. Daniel was still outside, talking to the old lady. I slipped into the room, approached the photograph, and for a moment I stopped breathing.

It was a black-and-white photo of Daniel and Victor Zikowski in what looked like Bosnia. They were walking down a muddy road together. Knit caps. Heavy jackets. Someone must have said something funny or maybe they had just survived another confrontation with the Serb militia. Daniel was smiling and Victor's mouth was open as he laughed.

Why had he placed this here? The photograph was probably the first thing Daniel saw when he woke up in the morning. Was this a guilty man's daily penance, like a priest whipping himself for past sins? Or was it merely proof that another man was dead and he was lucky enough to survive?

I went back outside and sat at the table. "How you feeling?" Daniel asked.

"Slow."

"Have some breakfast. La Signora always makes enough for five or six people."

He put a plate in front of me and I started to eat. The sun was floating up from the horizon like a bright orange balloon but we were sheltered within the arbor. I mashed up some of the olives and made a sandwich. After my second cup of coffee and some prosciutto, I began to feel better.

That morning in the arbor, Daniel appeared more relaxed and less calculating. Bracciano was his home. While I ate breakfast he passed me dishes and went inside to find some butter.

"Carter Howard told me one thing about you," Daniel said. "A couple of years ago you were covering a demonstration in Trafalgar Square. Then the police moved in and people started fighting."

"Right. I was sitting on top of one of the bronze lions, taking pictures. And some kid started bashing me on the head with—"

"With a cricket bat?"

"Did Carter tell you that?" I smiled. "It was just a piece of plywood that was used to make a protest sign."

"But you didn't do anything? You didn't jump off the lion or stop the kid from hitting you?"

"I hadn't found the picture yet."

Daniel nodded and poured some more coffee. "So what do you think about when you take a photograph?"

"If I'm moving I don't want to trip and fall on my face."

"Other than that."

I mashed some olives on a slice of bread. "Sometimes it's just a job. Take the shot and go home. But usually I'm trying to capture an image that carries its own energy. A good photograph is almost radioactive. You're flipping through a magazine and suddenly you see a picture that burns its way into your brain cells."

"Have you ever shot a picture like that?"

"Once or twice. I'd like to do it all the time."

Daniel stopped talking and we sat there listening to the cicadas. It was still early in the morning and the sun was at a low angle. The atmosphere filtered the light and it felt soft and warm. At the north edge of the farm, I could see a dirt driveway and a windbreak of cypress trees. The south property line was a hedgerow of thistles and blackberry bushes. The slope led past the two garden terraces to a steep ravine and beyond the ravine were rolling hills covered with dark green vegetation.

Daniel finished his coffee and brushed the crumbs off his jeans. "If you want, I'll give you the tour."

"Okay. Just don't ask me to pull weeds."

La Signora's one-room cottage was at the top of the hill, near the road that led to the village. Directly below the cottage were rows of grape-vines, the tendrils curling around rusty wire stretched on fence posts. Daniel inspected the grapes and mentioned La Signora's homemade wine. "It tastes awful, but she thinks it's delicious," he said. "Don't hurt her feelings, Nicky. If she pours you a glass, try not to spit it out."

As we ambled down the slope he explained that the Lazio region was the home of the Etruscans, a cultured civilization that was eventually conquered by the more practical Romans. During the Renaissance, various papal princes owned most of the land and this hillside had been a pasture for some of the horses raced at the Palio up in Siena. The farmhouse was for the horse trainer and his family.

After the property became available, it took Daniel two years of negotiations to arrange the deal. He moved in, installed the propane tank and a septic system, then went away to cover the fighting in Bosnia. When he came back he discovered that La Signora had left her son-in-law's home in the village and moved into the gatekeeper's cottage at the top of the hill. The old lady had swept out his house, watered his garden, and harvested the olive trees. One night a carload of locals had showed up to steal Daniel's furniture. La Signora stood at the front door and screamed at them, reciting the names of their parents, aunts, and uncles going back three generations, every possible dead ancestor who would be dishonored by this shameful act until the burglars took their crowbars and drove away.

Daniel helped La Signora in the garden whenever he was home. The wet terrace was the one closest to the house. There were rows of zucchini and tomatoes, green beans and garlic, and an herb patch with mint, sage, basil, and oregano. Flowers grew around the border of the garden—white and pink mallows, irises, daisies. On the lower dry terrace, Daniel had planted olive, fig, and hazelnut trees.

It was getting warmer. The sun burned a hole in the sky while pale yellow butterflies fluttered over the dead grass. Daniel covered his sports car with a waterproof tarp and then we followed a dirt path down the slope to the ravine. A little stream trickled around brown and gray boulders, then passed beneath a collapsed stone bridge.

"This is my Roman bridge," Daniel said. "It's about two thousand years old."

"You own it?"

"It officially belongs to the Department of Antiquities, but they don't seem to know it's here." We stepped off the road, walked through the grass for a while, and paused near the foot of the bridge. It had been built with bricks and blocks of sandstone. Everything was straight-edged and organized in the Roman manner, except for the broken section and the rubble in the stream.

"It was constructed by the Roman army for the legionnaires. They'd land on the coast after fighting in some foreign country, then go to the springs at Viterbo to get healed. When everyone had rested, they marched down to Rome."

I sat down on a chunk of white marble. "Sounds like a good system."

"It's always worked for me in the past. These days, it takes me longer to recover."

"Stop flying around. Become a bureau chief."

Daniel watched the bees circle around a patch of wild mustard. "We're paid to be witnesses, Nicky. Lots of journalists write about the center of the picture, but some of us need to see what's going on in the corners."

"You're an idealist."

"Not at all. I don't believe in politics, religion, faith, hope, or charity."

"But you believe in a good news story?"

"Yes. Exactly. A good news story—with pictures."

Daniel turned away from the bridge and headed back to his farmhouse. When I didn't get up, he stopped at the edge of the road and waited for me. If Daniel had just assumed that I was going to travel to Africa, I would have told him to find somebody else. But that morning he looked tired and a little desperate. For some reason, he had to leave this beautiful place.

"Come on, Nicky. Let's go."

I waited for a few seconds. Then I stood up and followed him.

3 THE DAY AND NIGHT BAR

I flew back to London the next morning and told Carter to authorize
a check for my expenses. I don't carry a lot of clothes when I'm traveling, but I make up for it in film and photographic equipment. I have
nine cameras, but I store them at a shop near Shepherds Bush Green.
Over the years I've developed a theory that the more equipment you
take, the fewer pictures you shoot. After changing my mind a few
times, I decided on an Olympus digital and my favorite Nikon with
three extra lenses.

Daniel arrived a few days later. We picked up our visas and took the
tube to the *Daily Telegraph* offices at Canary Wharf. We met a sleek
young editor named Jeremy who took us downstairs to a bistro for
lunch. All the editors in the room were sipping Chablis or Margaux,
and Jeremy ordered quiche Lorraine. He mentioned the *Telegraph*'s
web site eight times, then told me to get "good visuals" in Africa. The
drink-a-pint-and-sweat-a-story days of Fleet Street journalism were
definitely fading away.

Later that afternoon, we stopped in at the *Newsweek* offices. Carter brewed some tea while Daniel was talkative and charming. On the way back from the men's room, I caught Ann Weinstein putting on lipstick and brushing her hair before she entered Carter's office. It didn't seem like the beginning of a flirtation. There was something about Daniel's presence that made everyone want to stand a little straighter and become part of whatever he was planning.

IF YOU'VE NEVER worked with a reporter before, you try to find out about them as you travel to the story. After the third glass of wine, people begin to talk about their marriages or how much they hate their job. I asked Daniel a lot of questions on the flight to Nairobi, but I got very little information. He had two younger sisters. His father had been a supply sergeant in the air force and the McFarland family had moved to a new post every three years. When Daniel was a junior in high school, his mother discovered that she had liver cancer. Sergeant McFarland refused to take care of his wife, and Daniel had to nurse her. Daniel was the only person in the hospital room when his mother died, and then the family fell apart like a defective piece of machinery. His father got transferred to Alaska, the two sisters went off to live with an aunt, and Daniel was on his own.

He'd brought along a half-dozen tapes for his cassette player so I did manage to learn about his musical tastes. All great musicians, he explained to me, had recorded a handful of pure moments in which they connected to something powerful. Usually they were searching for that moment, but sometimes it just came to them accidentally during one performance when a special song or the people they were playing with pushed them to a different level. They were still themselves, with the same desires and frustrations, but during that time the music floated clear of them and became an independent creation.

"Sounds interesting," I told him. Perhaps I looked skeptical because throughout the flight, Daniel kept taking off his earphones and slipping them over my head.

"Do you hear that?" he asked. "Right now. That?" I had to admit it was some wonderful music—a trumpet solo by Miles Davis followed by a Puccini aria sung by Maria Callas—but I could never hear the moment. It was like someone trying to talk to you about God.

At Kenyatta airport we hired a taxi. Nairobi National Park stretched out on one side of the highway and suddenly we were in Africa. In the distance I could see herds of zebras and gazelles clustered around a water hole. It was dry season. Two girls wearing pink dresses filled a plastic jerrican in the road ditch. A *matatu* roared past us, crammed full of passengers, their faces pushed against the glass.

We checked into the New Stanley Hotel in the center of the city. It's the kind of place where the towels are frayed and there's always a black beetle waving its antennae at you in the shower stall. The next morning I went downstairs to have breakfast at an outdoor café. I watched the city buses and Peugeot hire cars challenge each other as they roared up Kenyatta Avenue. Africans hurried to work, pushing past schoolboys wearing white shirts and blue shorts. Backpackers from some blond country stared at the café bulletin board while two Japanese businessmen sweated over their omelets. The Kikuyu waiters, old and proud, considered it a badge of honor to ignore me as long as possible.

I ordered a pot of tea and a basket of *mandazi,* the little semisweet doughnuts they serve all over East Africa. Maybe I should eat healthy food, but all rules are suspended when you're working. As I popped a *mandazi* into my mouth, Daniel threaded his way through the tables and sat down beside me.

"I'm going to see if I can find the local *Newsweek* stringer. I'll meet you at the hotel around four o'clock. We'll go over to Reuters and talk to Matt Vickery."

"He's the bureau chief?"

Daniel nodded. "I knew him in Bosnia, but I haven't seen him for two years. Matt was doing an article about the fighting in Algeria when his car hit a land mine. He was badly burned and almost didn't recover."

"Why is he still working?"

"What else is he going to do? The management at Reuters felt they owed him a favor because he got injured on assignment. When he requested the East Africa Bureau, they gave it to him."

I spent the morning looking for Maloprim, the backup malaria drug you take with chloroquine, then returned to the hotel and slept. Daniel knocked on my door around four and we strolled over to the Reuters office on Moi Avenue. Car exhaust and charcoal fires diffused the light and added a brownish haze to the sky. Nairobi feels like a small town; you can walk through the central area in about fifteen minutes. The architecture is a mix of glass skyscrapers, clunky Victorian mansions, and functional concrete block buildings. With each visit, the city seemed to become shabbier and more crowded. I saw a few more prostitutes in bright red dresses, a few more street boys selling Makonde wood carvings, a few more young mothers whispering, *"Mzungu, mzungu,"* as they shifted their babies to their hips and extended their hands.

The Reuters East Africa Bureau was on the fourth floor and a young Indian woman wearing a blue sari sat at the desk in the reception area. The glass door on the right led to an equipment room filled with printers, radios, and sat phones. I could see two African journalists working in a small office on the left.

"Good afternoon. We're here to see Mr. Vickery."

The young woman turned and spoke to us with a precise British accent. "Mr. Vickery is not seeing anyone."

"I'm Daniel McFarland. I talked to him on the phone this morning."

"And he agreed to meet with you?"

"Of course. That's why we're here."

"I'm Miss Patel, Mr. Vickery's assistant. He did not inform me of this appointment." She looked carefully at Daniel as if he was trying to trick her, but then she got up and slipped through a third door.

We waited a few minutes until Miss Patel returned. "You are Mr. Vickery's friend?"

"We worked together in Bosnia."

"But you have not seen him since his accident?"

"No. I haven't."

"You are quite fortunate. Mr. Vickery is having a good day."

She opened the door and I followed Daniel into a shadowy office. All the lamps had been switched off and the only illumination came from the thin strips of afternoon sunlight that glowed through the Venetian blinds. A rolltop desk was shoved against the wall in one corner of the room and a dark shape sat in a high-back leather chair. I couldn't see Matthew Vickery's face, but I heard his voice, thin and raspy, like a man who had walked all day without water.

"You have to count the bodies. That's part of the job. You drive out there and count the bodies before they swell up and villagers bury them."

I closed the door behind me and the room got a little darker until my eyes adjusted. Lights glowed on the buttons of Vickery's telephone. A black cord led up to a headset.

"I don't care how you get there. Walk if you have to. Pay someone to carry you all the way from Kinshasa. And don't try to fake the story because I've got an instinctive sense for fiction. The AP will go to that village. Agence France-Presse will count the bodies. And if what they file is substantially different from your article, then I'm going to hire another stringer."

The doctors in London had transplanted skin from Vickery's back to his burned face, and the surface was uneven and scarred. A baseball cap covered his bald head. Black pants and a white cotton shirt hung loosely on his body like a skeleton wearing clothes.

"Do you like your job, François? Or let me rephrase that: do you like my checks? Of course you do. I'm not paying you for rumors from the *matutu* drivers or the official twaddle from some government minister. I'm paying you to count the bodies and decide who won the battle. *Comprenez-vous?*"

Vickery hung up on his caller and swiveled his chair toward us. "Hello, Daniel. Who's your friend?"

"Nicky Bettencourt. I'm a photographer for *Newsweek*."

"I know who you are. When you worked for Reuters, you took a good shot in Rwanda. A severed arm lying in the middle of the road."

"That was a long time ago." I stepped forward, then realized that Vickery's right hand had been transformed into a bird's claw—the thumb lost, the other fingers bent slightly and fused together. Embarrassed, I lowered my own hand while he watched me.

"As you can see, I've been dipped in fire. All the base metal has been burned away." Vickery hit another phone button. "Miss Patel, could we have a pot of tea and some digestive biscuits? The chocolate-dipped ones, if they're still available."

Vickery pointed out some folding chairs and we set them up near his desk. I glanced at Daniel. His face showed neither disgust nor sympathy. He stared at Vickery as if the bureau chief was going to perform a magic trick.

"What do they say about me in London?"

"That you're working here."

"Do they think I'm doing a good job? That's why I wanted to see you, Daniel. To get the gossip, find out how I'm perceived."

"No one said anything negative."

"Nor should they. I'm still sending out an enormous amount of copy." Vickery gestured with his injured hand. "I've got two or three stringers in every country and I can talk to them by phone twenty-four hours a day. I send them into battle, cheer them on, listen to the guns firing. It's like moving pieces around a chessboard."

Someone opened the door. A patch of light appeared on Vickery's cheek. With a clatter of dishes Miss Patel walked in carrying a wooden tray with a teapot, cups and saucers, and a dish of little round cookies. She placed the tray near the edge of the desk and poured some tea for her boss.

"Do you find Miss Patel attractive, Daniel?"

"Yes."

"Would you like to sleep with her? I'm quite desperate to, but I have a few physical deficiencies. My dream is for Miss Patel to take a lover and then allow me to watch her perform certain acts."

Miss Patel's lips tightened slightly, but she mixed in the cream and sugar. "That will never happen, Mr. Vickery."

"Never say never, Miss Patel. Look at my own life. An infinite variety of joys and humiliations are possible in this world."

Miss Patel retreated out the doorway with a swish of her sari. Vickery made a harsh sort of gasp that resembled laughter. Daniel poured two more cups of tea.

"Don't worry. I can say anything to her. You can, too. She's a college graduate and there are no jobs for college graduates in this town. She's lucky I hired her."

"Tell me about the kidnapped tourists."

"I see you haven't changed, Daniel. Fun and games in Rome, but hard work in the field. Do you even like being a journalist? I wonder."

"What are the chances of finding the Lord's Righteous Army?"

"Virtually nonexistent. And if you do find them, they'll kill you."

"Sounds like a promising story."

Vickery raised the cup to his lips and slurped some tea. "The kidnapped tourists were bird-watchers. Can you believe it? Apparently Kidepo Valley National Park is a prime spot to view large raptors so they flew up there on a chartered plane from Entebbe. Bird-watchers are bloody insane. They all have lifetime lists of the species they've seen. The more birds on your list, the more sex you get at bird-watcher conventions."

"How did they get captured?"

"The group spent a night at Apoka Lodge, then two armed park rangers and two drivers took them out in Land Rovers. About ten kilometers from the camp, the Lord's Righteous Army ambushed them. The guerrillas killed both rangers and one of the drivers, then chopped off the right hand of the surviving driver and sent him back to tell the world."

"Was that unusual?"

"You mean chopping off the hand? Not really. It's Samuel Okello's trademark, like Mickey Mouse or the Coke bottle. I think he bases it on biblical law. The Book of Leviticus."

"Is that all you know about him?"

"He was the top student at his Christian school, formed a religious youth organization, then got a two-year scholarship to attend Southern Methodist University in Texas. When he came home to preach in Kitgum there was friction between the members of his Acholi tribe and the southern tribesmen running the government. Okello got whipped by the district police for leading a protest so he took his parishioners and fled into the bush. He wants to take over the country and set up a government, with him as the supreme leader. In the last few years he's moved north to the Sudanese border."

"Are the hostages still alive?"

"A few herdsmen have seen them. They all look the worse for wear, but Okello hasn't killed them—yet. He's been getting weapons from the Sudanese army because the army hates the Ugandan government. Sudan is the obvious channel for a deal, but no one has attempted it. I guess Reverend Okello makes his own rules."

Vickery picked up another cookie and shoved it in his mouth. The room was as hot and airless as a storage container. Sweat trickled down my neck, but Daniel looked comfortable.

"I do love chocolate-dipped digestive biscuits. They're one of my few remaining pleasures, along with codeine pills and porno tapes." Vickery laughed again. "You know I can't cry anymore? Something's wrong with my tear ducts. When I go outside I have to put drops in my eyes."

"So how do we contact Okello?"

"It's not possible. Several journalists have flown up to Kidepo park, but no one's crazy enough to go out into the bush. This is a lost cause, Daniel. Waste of time and money."

I saw myself returning to London without any photographs. "But we're here," I said. "We've got to do something."

Vickery smiled as if a trained dog had just jumped for a ball. "There's a backup story at a refugee camp near the game park. Not as sexy as hostages and severed hands, but someone might run it. I assume you've heard of Richard Seaton?"

Daniel and I both nodded. Seaton was the Englishman who owned the Riverside Bank. He had started out installing ATM machines on street corners, then took control of several regional building societies. There was a great deal of outcry when Seaton began sacking little old lady tellers, but he countered with an inspired ad campaign: "I Bought

My Home with Richard." You'd see some real-life family in their new house purchased with a loan from the Riverside Bank and Richard would be there, digging up the garden or kicking a soccer ball around like a favorite uncle. There was always one bit at the end where someone would give Richard a baby with a soiled diaper or offer him a towel to dry the dishes. Seaton would raise his eyebrows slightly—he was, of course, a very wealthy man—but then he'd smile, because he truly was part of your family. The ads became so popular that Seaton gave speeches during the last election.

"Mr. Seaton is making a transition from capitalistic exploiter to world philanthropist," Vickery explained. "He's started his own relief organization called Hand-to-Hand. Catchy name, don't you think? He's sponsoring a refugee camp near the border for the Sudanese forced out of their country by the civil war. His girlfriend, Dr. Julia Cadell, is running the operation. I've heard that she's damn good looking, but she might be the real thing. She's also worked in Bosnia and Sierra Leone."

Daniel shook his head. "I'm not interested in relief work."

"Seaton is actually going to be at the camp for the next few days. I got a fax from his London PR firm giving me his schedule. It's an easy story, Daniel. Write your own headline. BRITISH BILLIONAIRE FEEDS THE HUNGRY or, for the tabloids, DICKY DOES GOOD. Nicky can take a photo of the Great Man looking concerned as he holds a shriveled black baby in his arms."

Daniel glanced at me. "Nicky hates celebrities, and I hate articles about famine relief. It's always the same article."

"Emphasize the pain and tears. People in America and Britain always feel better about themselves when they can read how miserable everyone else is."

"I'm going to find Samuel Okello."

"Be my guest. If I were you, I'd fly to Kidepo park and start looking for people who've lost their right hands."

We finished our tea and left a few minutes later as Vickery began dialing his stringer in Zambia. It felt good to escape from that airless room. Daniel said he wanted a drink and we took a taxi down to the Day and Night Bar on Latema Road.

True to its name, Day and Night was open twenty-four hours a day. I'd heard rumors that the front door hadn't been closed in thirty years. Because of fights, the bar was surrounded by a wire cage. Two enormous bouncers strutted around with clubs thrust in their belts. The whole place smelled like spilled beer and bad plumbing, but there were friendly whores, dancing drunks, and a jukebox blasting out love songs in Swahili.

We pushed our money through a slot in the cage, got two bottles of White Cap, and retreated to the back room. Daniel gave one of the bouncers a few shillings, and the man told the working girls and hustlers that he'd knock out their teeth if they didn't leave us alone. For a few minutes we just sat quietly at our table and let the energy flow around us. There was a Somali girl there, probably about fifteen years old, with dark skin and seashells knotted to each braid of her hair. I figured that she probably had AIDS and was going to die in a few years, but that evening she was full of life and didn't care. Clutching a bottle of *changaa* —the local bootleg liquor—she danced around the tables, and the seashells clicked together as she moved her hips. She was a good photograph, but I didn't want to play the tourist and pull out my camera.

"Matt had a Lebanese girlfriend when I first met him," Daniel said. "It looked like they were going to get married."

"I guess he's changed."

Daniel drew an invisible pattern on the table with his forefinger. "I'm not going to end up like that, Nicky."

"Everybody wants to get off the train at the right moment, but for some reason we stay on too long."

I finished my beer and went over to the cage to get two more bottles. Some drunks started fighting, but I managed to dodge them without spilling anything. Daniel looked a little more confident when I returned to our table.

"I've gotten enough background today," he said. "Tomorrow we'll fly to Uganda."

"Have you figured out what we're going to do if we actually find Samuel Okello? I don't want to get killed."

"Don't worry, Nicky. Everything's negotiable. You know that."

I heard the soft thud of a club landing on someone's back. A woman shouted in her tribal language and a bottle hit the wall. Both of us turned to watch as the bouncers hunched like rugby players and pushed three people out the door.

WE WENT BACK to the airport the next morning and flew to Uganda. Daniel sat in an aisle seat, checking a list of names in his leather notebook. I gazed out the window and watched as the yellowish brown colors of the Kenyan savanna disappeared and were replaced by a tropical landscape. The airplane's shadow glided across the earth, and we passed over the northern edge of Lake Victoria. There were little whitecaps on the waves and I saw two fishermen sitting in a narrow boat. The plane banked to the right, landed at Entebbe airport, and taxied to the small terminal.

One of Daniel's lunchtime companions at the Stampa Estera had given him the name of a local driver used by journalists. A big man wearing a satiny blue shirt was waiting for us on the tarmac when we got off the plane. He deftly separated us from a group of German tourists, then smiled and shook our hands.

"Good morning, gentlemen. I'm Winston Kanyara. Please, come with me."

Winston knew every police officer and customs official at the airport. He told jokes in English and three tribal languages, handed out free cigarettes and a few small bribes. Five minutes later, we were out of the terminal and sliding into the back of Winston's ancient Mercedes-Benz. "Once owned by a general," he explained. More cigarettes were distributed to a trio of young soldiers carrying assault rifles and then we glided away from the curb.

The dashboard had been turned into an altar with an ivory cross and a plastic statue of a black Virgin Mary. Instead of the Christ child, a tiny lightbulb burned in her arms. Tropical air flowed in through the open windows as we traveled past small farms and an occasional coffee plantation. Wild orchids were growing in the road ditch and there were stick-and-wattle huts with rusty sheet-metal roofs the color of dry blood. Every mile or so we encountered an old woman or a child sitting on the roadside with something for sale—a bunch of plantains or a pile of yams, two AA batteries or a single bottle of beer.

Winston drove with one elbow on the window frame. He looked happy that he had two paying clients and that it was such a pleasant morning. "What is the nature of your article?" he asked. "Our country's economy? The national parks? This terrible AIDS disease?" He guided the Benz around two long-horned African cows standing in the middle of the road. "Perhaps you might want to interview our country's contestant in the Miss Universe Pageant. She's quite pretty."

"We want to interview Samuel Okello."

Winston looked disappointed. "This is not possible, Mr. McFarland. Okello is a crazy man. He steals children and teaches them how to kill."

Daniel opened up his notebook and studied his list of names. "Nicky and I will look for someone in Kampala who has contacts with the Lord's Righteous Army. In the meantime, I'd like you to find a pilot that can fly us up to Kosana refugee camp. There has to be someone there who has met Samuel Okello and knows how to find him."

Winston extended his right hand and touched the Virgin Mary's plastic feet. "Miss Uganda is a much better story. She's a princess from the kingdom of Toro, a Catholic, and virtuous—or so I've been told."

"We'll go to the Parliament building first, then we'll talk to some aid workers who have been in Okello's area."

Kampala was built on a cluster of low hills and there was enough rainfall during the year to keep everything green. Bamboo grass and jacaranda trees grew everywhere and the vegetation softened the hard edges of the modern glass-and-concrete buildings. Thousands of people were out on Kampala Road that morning, heading to work or to the open-air market. Ugandans from a dozen different tribes mixed with the Nubians from the north and the Tutsis from the south. These days there was a separate tribe of those dying with AIDS. Both men and women had the same appearance, slender and frail, their clothes hanging on their bodies. They drifted down the sidewalk, often with a small child to help them along.

We left our bags with the desk clerk at the Speke Hotel, changed some money at a Forex bureau, then walked over to the Parliament offices. We talked to the Ugandan members of Parliament who came from the northern area that had been ravaged by the Lord's Righteous Army. No one knew how to contact the guerrillas, but some of the office staff were related to the kidnapped children. Rummaging through their desks, they pulled out First Communion photographs of little girls in white dresses and black-and-white snapshots of boys wearing their school uniforms. If you see these children, let us know, they told us. We pray for them every day.

I asked for permission to take pictures, then moved my chair to an angle slightly out of the subjects' sight line. I took my time and tried not to make a lot of noise. Sometimes I thought that I never actually saw anyone unless I was trying to get a photograph. Most people wear a public mask when talking to strangers, but then suddenly they lower their eyes or tighten their lips and their face changes and you see something real.

My ambition had placed me in this situation, but when I started taking pictures all that had to disappear. Successful photographers blend into the scenery. You try not to frighten dogs and babies. You instinctively know where the light source is while your eye searches for an image with something interesting at the center. Since you've spent your life watching other people do things, you can anticipate their movements. A good photograph is rarely the first thing you see in your viewfinder. It's the moment that's going to occur a few seconds later. As I watched, a Ugandan woman held up a photograph. I raised my camera when she kissed her forefinger, then squeezed the shutter when she touched the image of her lost daughter.

Late in the afternoon we ended up at a bar on Kampala Road that was run by the wife of an Italian aid worker. We sat outside at white plastic picnic tables and Daniel bought beer for the young reporters who wrote for the *New Vision,* the government newspaper. Most of them believed that Okello had moved north into Sudan. No one had seen the hostages for several months. It was rumored they were dead.

Winston's Mercedes-Benz pulled up to the curb and he got out with a young white man and a Ugandan wearing a green ranger's shirt. Daniel bought one more round for the journalists and I followed him over to another table.

Winston made the introductions like a diplomat. "Gentlemen, this is Paul Rosen of the World Wildlife Fund and Tobias Magazi from the National Parks Service. They're flying up to Kidepo park and could possibly take you along."

Everyone shook hands and Daniel ordered more beer. I found out later that Paul Rosen's father owned 30 percent of a large corporation in the States. Instead of living off his trust fund, Paul had flown his air-plane to Uganda and started an antipoaching task force with Tobias. The two friends were in their twenties, good looking and energetic, filled with plans to save the world.

"We need your help," Paul said. "It would be great if we could get some coverage in the *Washington Post.*"

"I'm not in the helping business," Daniel told him. "Neither is Nicky."

"Of course. We understand." Tobias leaned forward in his chair. "But this is a big story. People in America and Europe will be very interested."

"The Sudanese army is crossing the border to kill elephants," Paul said. "They're using grenades and assault rifles."

"This is happening in Kidepo park?" Daniel asked.

"They're killing animals in the park and in the area around it. If you fly up there with us, you can see what's going on. Nothing will change unless we get some coverage in the international press."

"We came to Uganda to do a story about the Lord's Righteous Army."

"Forget about Okello," Tobias said. "He's either dead or up in the Sudan."

"Maybe we need a backup article," I told Daniel. "Editors like stories about large mammals."

Daniel nodded. "If you can show us Sudanese soldiers crossing the border and killing elephants, then I'll write an article about it. Take us up to the Kosana refugee camp and we'll be in the area for a few days if something happens."

Paul glanced at Tobias and smiled. They had been hunting for journalists and now they had captured two of them. "Sounds like a plan," he said. "I'm flying there tomorrow to deliver a valve for their broken water pump."

THERE'S A PROBLEM with young idealists—they wake up too damn early in the morning. Paul Rosen called my room at seven and announced that he was leaving from Entebbe in two hours. I pulled on my clothes and hurried downstairs to the dining room where I ordered the Speke Hotel's famous banana breakfast: banana pancakes, banana bread with whipped banana butter, fried plantains, and little finger bananas soaked in rum. I was starting to turn yellow when Winston arrived with his car. Daniel had given him some money to buy canned food and crackers at the marketplace. We packed everything into our traveling bags and headed for the airport.

Paul's Cessna 210 was parked on a side taxiway. While Daniel got out and talked to Tobias, I sat in the backseat and tried to digest my breakfast.

"Did you sleep well?" Winston asked.

"Fair enough."

"The Lord's Righteous Army is not a good story. It would be better if you both traveled west to the Toro."

"I don't want to meet Miss Universe, Winston. Maybe she's beautiful and virtuous, but she won't like me. I'm just the guy taking her picture."

"Toro is my home. We could stay with my uncle, drink beer, walk around and see the gorillas. Things are quiet in the mountains, but very beautiful. The water is clean and clear, and we can go swimming without harm."

"Sounds wonderful. But we've got to go to Kosana."

Winston reached forward and touched the black Virgin Mary. "When I dreamed last night, I saw Mr. McFarland lying dead on the ground. Someone had shot him."

I hesitated for a few seconds, almost convinced of the danger. "I'm sorry, Winston. Daniel is flying north and somebody's bad dream won't stop him. If he goes alone, he'll probably do something crazy. If we travel together, I can hold him back a little."

Tobias walked over to the Mercedes and tapped on the window. "Wake up, Nicky! It's time to go!"

The Cessna was a modified four-seater with a large storage area in the back. They'd loaded several boxes of food and I counted fourteen plastic jerricans of gasoline for the ranger vehicles at Kidepo. It was a flying Molotov cocktail, yet Paul didn't look worried. He was re-arranging the gear when I approached him.

"How much do you weigh, Nicky?"

"About two hundred pounds. Maybe a little more."

"That puts us over the weight limitations, but it's not a big problem."

"Get rid of some gasoline."

"They really need it. Truckers don't want to carry supplies to the park because of the Lord's Righteous Army. Every since the kidnappings, we've had problems getting supplies."

"So the plane's too heavy?"

"Technically, yes. But we've done it before. After we take off, everything will be all right."

I studied Paul's confident smile and silently cursed my own stupidity. For some reason, I kept putting my life in the hands of optimists. Paul tied down everything in the storage area and we squeezed in. One of the jerricans must have been leaking because I could smell gasoline. Paul told jokes over the radio to a Ugandan in the control tower named Boniface, then taxied the Cessna to a patch of gravel at the end of the main runway.

Hot, humid air pushed through the little windows. I was sweating. Tobias sat in the front passenger seat, next to Paul. He glanced back at me and grinned. "Don't worry, Nicky. We had more weight last year taking off from Mombasa."

"But it's hotter today," Paul said. "So the density altitude is higher."

"What's that mean?"

"If we were in Iceland, this would be easy."

The Cessna began moving slowly down the runway. Daniel rolled up his shirtsleeve and scratched a mosquito bite. He looked like he was sitting on a bus in London. "You take your chloroquine, Nicky?"

"No."

"I thought you did."

"I mean, yes. I took it. Yes."

Paul watched the air speed indicator and began calling out numbers to Tobias. "Thirty-three, forty, fifty. Damn."

We were already halfway down the runway and not even close to taking off. My stomach grumbled. Shouldn't have eaten all those bananas. Faster. A little faster. Then, about ten feet from the end of the runway, Paul pulled back the yoke and the plane rose into the air. Within seconds, we dropped back down about twenty feet and I heard the landing gear ripping through the tops of the tall reeds at the edge of the lake. Before I could panic, the Cessna glided back up again. We made a slow, wide turn, like a barge in sluggish water, and headed north.

Paul's mother had sent him a package of kosher food for Passover. When we reached two thousand feet, Tobias handed us a box of macaroons, then spread peanut butter on matzo crackers. It was loud inside the Cessna. Whenever we hit turbulence, the plane bounced a little, as if we were driving over a low hill.

Below us were small farms and coffee plantations. I could see the light green fields of plantain and cassava surrounded by the forest. A plume of smoke rose from a solitary fire as we passed over a small village, its metal roofs glimmering in the sun.

I brushed the matzo crumbs off my lap. We cut across the western edge of Lake Kwania and the landscape changed into a vast savanna, dotted with red termite hills and acacia trees. You could see the bare red lines of earth from cow tracks that split apart like capillaries and recombined at water holes. The cattle milled around the muddy water: white bulls and brindle cows, their long horns jabbing up at the sky. Dust boiled up from the back wheels of a truck racing down a dirt road.

When we began to see wild animals, Paul and Tobias argued about the population of various species. Paul swooped down to check out large herds of spiral-horned kudu and Grant's gazelles. Frightened by the plane, the animals fled through the tall grass. The herd seemed to flow like a stream of water, rippling and changing course with every obstacle.

Red volcanic hills appeared near the boundary of Kidepo park. Surrounded by the flat savanna, they looked vaguely artificial. It was a harsh region with large areas of bushland thicket that could easily hide a guerrilla army.

We flew over the little white cottages of Apoka Lodge, where the six tourists had stayed before their kidnapping, and Paul zigzagged across the massive game park looking for signs of Sudanese poachers. As we headed northeast and approached Kosana, Tobias began to tease his friend about an Irish nurse named Ellen who worked at the camp. Apparently, Paul had flown her around the park a few weeks ago. They had landed in some isolated area and had had a picnic in the middle of Eden. It wasn't quite clear what happened after that.

"Did she get a sunburn?" Tobias asked. "I've heard that red-haired women are very sensitive to the sun."

"We put on sunblock."

"Any mosquito bites, Paul? I hope they weren't in sensitive parts of the body."

"We were there to see the flora and fauna."

"Yes. Of course. Her flora and your fauna."

Paul reduced power and the plane descended a few hundred feet. "There's Kosana," he said.

When I looked down, I saw more than two hundred tents in the middle of a grassy plain. There were bright blue plastic tents and olive green military tents, all of them arranged in little clusters that were linked by a spiderweb of footpaths. A dirt landing strip had been set up about a half mile from the camp and a silver airplane was parked near a clump of thornbushes.

"That's Erik Viltner's Super Cub," Paul told us. "I guess Richard Seaton hired Erik to fly him up from Nairobi."

"And Seaton is the doctor's boyfriend?" Daniel asked.

"You mean Julia? Yes. She's in charge of the camp."

We roared over the tents. Paul banked the plane to the left and for a few seconds the sun blinded me. Trains and planes and taxi rides had brought us to this place, but I still had no idea how we were going to find the Lord's Righteous Army.

Julia

4   KOSANA REFUGEE CAMP

The night before I left for Africa, Richard asked me to meet him at
Sage, a new restaurant in South Kensington. He was late, but I'd come
to expect that. Richard generally ignored the constraints of time. He
had become so successful in his twenties that for the last fifteen years
people had waited for him, waited so patiently that he had become
used to their forbearance. Lateness added urgency and drama to his
daily schedule; it pushed him forward into each new situation.

I had brought along two books in my bag, Langewiesche's *Sahara
Unveiled* and the new edition of Harcourt's *Tropical Diseases*. While
the waiter brought a glass of Sauvignon Blanc, I looked around the
restaurant. That night I realized that all of Richard's favorite restaurants had certain similarities. He liked new places, open for one or two
years, with lots of light and glass, and young food servers wearing long
white aprons. The food itself wasn't that important, something light
and low fat, presented attractively. He hated any place with dark rooms,
heavy chairs, marrow bones, and elaborate desserts.

I loved going to restaurants because I was such a bad cook. I was in awe of flaky pie crusts and light soufflés, though waiters and waitresses made me uncomfortable. I always felt passive and trapped at the table, smiling politely while some stranger brought me a plate. I wanted to stand up and walk into the kitchen, gossip with the cooks and the busboys, see what kind of fish was in the refrigerator.

I was reading about new treatments for malaria and drinking my second glass of wine when Richard's phone calls began to arrive. The bald headwaiter was like a military courier, delivering one folded piece of paper after another. During the last year, I had managed to hold on to the last shreds of my independence: I didn't live with Richard when I was in England and I refused to carry a cell phone. Neither choice was practical, but I wanted to keep a thin demarcation between our two lives. Richard carried a satellite phone and something called a Black-Berry that allowed him to read his e-mail in the bathtub. "You can always switch it off," he explained, but I didn't want to be bothered. When I was away from the telephone, I was out, couldn't be reached, and would be back sometime later. So now, instead of talking to me directly, Richard's messages were conveyed through the headwaiter. Mr. Seaton had left his office. Mr. Seaton's car was turning onto Brompton Road. Mr. Seaton was less than five minutes away.

Finally, Richard appeared in jeans and a camel-hair jacket. He dressed like a student or a young lecturer, in clothing that always looked slightly rumpled. Carrying a shopping bag, he followed the headwaiter over to the table. Richard wasn't famous enough to get immediate recognition from the public. But as he walked across the restaurant you could see people registering the thought Oh, that's the man on television. What's his name? Seaton. Richard came forward in a rush, leaned down and kissed me on the cheek. "Julia, darling. I am sorry. Late again."

"This wine's quite good," I said, closing the book. "You should try it."

"Bring us a bottle," Richard told the headwaiter, then reached into the bag and came up with a present tied with gold ribbon. "I got something for you," he said. "Little going-away gift."

It was a leather Gucci toiletry case about the size of a purse. Inside were thick, frosted glass bottles filled with shampoo and hair rinse, and special 45 SPF makeup for the African sun. I knew that Richard hadn't gone into a store and purchased it himself. His employees handled virtually all the practical details of his life—the dog-walking, shoe-polishing, chip-the-ice-off-the-windscreen moments of drudgery. I could tell that the gift had been chosen by a woman who had given a great deal of thought to what she would require in the middle of an African refugee camp.

"Do you like it?" Richard asked.

"Yes. It's marvelous. Just what I needed."

Of course, I didn't need any of it. Over the years I'd learned to boil my necessities down to two traveling bags: my Practical Bag, for medical equipment, travel documents, and money; and my Personal Bag with a toothbrush, one hairbrush, a mosquito net, an ankle-length cotton dress for meeting officials, four T-shirts, two pairs of pants, a sweater, underwear, and a few books. There wasn't enough room for the Gucci case in either bag. I would have left it in London, but Richard noticed everything. At some point, he would realize that the case wasn't in my tent. If it wasn't there, then it was the wrong gift, and Stacy or Jennifer or any one of the other young women who smiled at me whenever I dropped by Richard's office might suffer career damage for the rest of her life at the Riverside Bank.

I ended up taking my sweater out of the Practical Bag and forcing the case inside. It annoyed me to have to think about the sweater, carrying it along, not losing it on the plane flight to Kenya, but the moment I crossed the border into Uganda all minor problems were blasted away by the immediate situation. That was one thing that outsiders didn't understand about working in a refugee camp. Yes, you were going to a place where people were sick and starving, where nothing worked and you might be in danger. But everything was simpler there: you never thought about how you looked and what you should wear, you never had to deal with rush hour and overdrafts at your bank, there were no hospital administrators criticizing how much time you spent with a patient. There were so many ambiguities back home, so many compromises. Life was difficult at a refugee camp, but easier, too.

The only thing I really needed to bring along was the blue toothbrush I had purchased before I left for college. It was worn down and completely unusable, but I always made a point of placing it next to my cot or my sleeping bag. I didn't own a flat back in London or a house in the country, didn't have furniture in storage or something permanent to return to. My mother once said that home was where your heart remained, but I carried my heart with me and I kept it fairly well protected. Home was where I placed the toothbrush and where I turned out the light. And now, of course, home included a Gucci toiletry case.

OUR CAMP WAS SET up in the middle of a savanna plain dotted with termite mounds and thornbushes. Kosana had once been a destination for the migrating tribes that lived in the area, marked by a dead acacia tree and a well with watering ditches for cattle. The well went dry about two days after I arrived. We set up the tents, drilled our own wells, and waited. After a week or so, small groups of refugees appeared on the horizon. The dust and heat distorted the air and people seemed to emerge from the earth, then grow larger as they came closer. When they reached Kosana they would stop at the outskirts of the camp, like shy children who had just arrived at a birthday party. I would walk out and invite everyone to share our food and shelter.

The refugees were Karamojong, a general name for the six subtribes that lived in the border region between Sudan and Uganda. They were a tall, slender people with dark black skin. The women wore ragged clothes and copper bracelets that clicked together whenever they moved their arms. They smiled at me but didn't meet my eyes. Whenever I turned around quickly, I saw them staring at my clothes and hair. I obviously wasn't a man, but I wasn't what they considered a woman. A third sex, perhaps, a good witch with the power to save their children.

The male Karamojong also thought I was strange, but they were so proud and imperious in their manner that it was difficult to know what they were thinking. Most of men were naked except for the *shuka* cloths they draped over their shoulders. I recall some pop psychologist saying that we wore clothes to impress and dominate each other, but there was nothing more intimidating than a naked man, two meters tall, with a rifle slung over his shoulder. But though the Karamojong were harsh to their enemies, they indulged their children. All the adults played with them, touched them, spoiled them completely as if antici-pating the pain of their adult life.

They were dependent on their cattle, following the herds across the grasslands and protecting them from lions and raiders. The young men sang songs to their favorite cows and decorated their long, curving horns. I had brought two Irish nurses with me, both of whom had grown up on farms. One afternoon, Fiona was talking to an elderly Karamojong man about his life back in the Sudan. "My father had cows, too," she said. The old man didn't seem to understand her En-glish so she made two little horns with her forefingers. "You know. Cows." Fiona smiled and mooed, the sort of thing you'd hear from a genteel Irish Guernsey grazing on a green hill.

"No moo," the old man said. And then he made a deep bellowing sound that seemed to come from deep in his body, the sound of bride price and feasting, the sound of a dying tradition.

For the most part, the Karamojong hadn't gotten involved in the civil war between the Muslims of northern Sudan and the Christians in the south, but a new general had come to power in Khartoum and decided to create a "wall of fire" surrounding his country. Mirage jets began dropping napalm on the cattle herds, and the Karamojong in Sudan fled across the border to Uganda.

The Gucci toiletry case seemed exotic and out of place next to all this, as if one of the Karamojong, naked and carrying his rifle, had ap-peared in the middle of Oxford Street. The case stayed beneath my folding cot and it began to make me feel guilty in the morning. I told myself that I should at least use the shampoo and hair rinse, but our shower was just a bucket on a pulley. It seemed completely awkward to place the frosted glass bottles on the red mud. I thought about using the makeup; the idea of putting it on in that heat was more than I could bear. Besides, there were so many other things that needed my attention. Someone was dying or being born. We were running low on antibiotics. One of the Ugandan soldiers who was supposed to be guarding the camp was swaggering around looking for available women, and the Karamojong men were ready to stick a knife through his ribs. Most days I was busy and occupied and there were times when I felt as if part of myself was disappearing, dissolved into the general need.

It was the white season in East Africa. The grass was brittle and dry, and the earth was cracked open as if gasping for water. After the sun went down, the wind blew east from Kenya. In the daytime, when the ground warmed up, the wind changed direction and came from the northwest so that it seemed as if it pushed the refugees across the border. The tents shuddered and flapped like a fleet of sailboats. Wind picked up the red dust and swirled it around the camp. Dust was in the bottom of our sleeping bags and in the toes of our boots. It got into the cooking pots and I could taste it in our food. Three days before Richard was to arrive, I went to the toiletry case to get some nail scissors and discovered that the glass bottles and the makeup were covered with dust. I hadn't opened the case since London, but dust had forced its way through the brass zipper and settled in a faint red haze on the bottles. It smeared when I touched it with my hand.

WE ARE CONNECTED in large ways by a web of small decisions. I wanted to think that I had guided the direction of my life, but so much of what happens seems to be governed by coincidence and chance. Twelve hundred people were living at Kosana because I got a phone call and went to Cambridge for a conference and accidentally met Richard Seaton. At that time I was on contract with the British Department for International Development. I worked at a Sierra Leone hospital for three weeks at a time, then returned to London for a week of rest. There was no reason to take a lease on a flat so I was staying with my friend Laura in Islington. I had just fed her dog and was thinking about ordering take-away curry when Charles Hart called, a classmate of mine from medical school. Charles had worked in Rwanda after the genocide, but it had all been too much for him and he had gotten typhoid. Now he was a consultant for private foundations involved with international aid.

"Hello? Julia? I heard you were back from somewhere."

"Sierra Leone."

"God. That's a disaster zone. What did I read about it in the *Times*? The Little Boys' Army?"

"The Small Boys Unit. The Revolutionary United Front kidnaps them and gives them assault rifles."

"Sounds hideous. You're in Freetown, right? How's it going?"

"There's supposed to be a peace agreement, but it doesn't mean much. The war lords are still in charge of the countryside. We've just gotten a power generator at the hospital. The petrol supply isn't reliable, but I'm hopeful."

"You always are." Charles laughed as if he had gone beyond that and finally become an adult. "Look, we're having a foreign aid conference at King's College and I want to put you on a panel. Do say you'll come. Lots of wine and good food. It'll be a little holiday."

I didn't like conferences, but I wasn't doing anything that weekend. Laura was traveling to Scotland with someone named Roger who shaved his head and designed nightclub lighting systems. I could have called up my friends Susan and Michael and gone over to their flat for dinner. But they'd gotten married that summer and were buying furniture together. I was happy for them, but I wasn't in the mood to see their settled life.

"All right," I told him. "I'll be there." I packed my one good dress and borrowed a pair of shoes from Laura.

Cambridge hadn't changed much, just a few more gourmet restaurants on Sydney Street. The conference had the usual mix of participants: a few young aid workers who had actually touched starving people but didn't want to mention it, plus aid administrators from the government and international NGOs who didn't know much but did most of the talking. After the first two hours, Laura's shoes began to hurt my feet. The welcoming speeches were a tepid flood of murky sentences with a few real words floating along by themselves. Mumble. Mumble. *Hunger.* Mumble. Mumble. *AIDS.* I began to wish that I was back at the flat, eating chocolate and watching *Roman Holiday* on television.

My panel was supposed to discuss emergency medical relief aid. I spoke for a few minutes, answered some questions, and didn't make a complete fool of myself. Afterward I got ready to slip away. I thought I could change my shoes and take a walk along the river. There'd be willows reaching down to the water and, perhaps, some swans. I had unfastened my name tag and reached the hallway when someone called my name.

"Excuse me? Dr. Cadell?"

I turned. A man in his early forties, blond, with pale blue eyes, was smiling at me. He wore a tweed jacket and carried an expensive leather portfolio. Some sort of academic, I thought, the sort of person who reviewed books for the *Guardian* and gave end-of-term parties at which the students actually had a good time.

"I was impressed by your comments, Dr. Cadell. I'm sure it was difficult to run a clinic in Sarajevo."

"It was a challenge, but I enjoyed that. Relief work is medicine without the nonsense."

"Listen, I—oh, I should introduce myself—I'm Richard Seaton. Charlie Hart is a friend of mine. He thought I could learn a few things this weekend."

"I see. Have you?"

"Yes. It's all been rather informative, especially hearing your remarks. I wondered if we could have a drink together. Tea. Or something stronger. Whatever you want."

"Thanks, but actually, I was going to take a walk."

"Brilliant. I'd like to get out of here for a few hours." Richard smiled again. He was very sure of himself without being overbearing about it. "I've always hated schools and seminar rooms. Chalkboards make me sneeze."

I changed my shoes and we took a taxi to the River Cam and walked through the Backs. I've always liked rivers. It's not just their sound and the damp smell and the birds, but the feeling that a river is going somewhere; if you just pushed your boat off from the shore, the rushing water would carry you away. I never thought of a destination in these daydreams; it was the sense of escape that inspired me.

I began thinking how I'd describe Richard when I saw Laura on Sunday. He was in that special category she called a CSM: a clever, single man. Single was an assumption on my part—Richard never mentioned a wife—but the cleverness was quite evident. I didn't have to explain everything to him. If I described the outline of an idea, he immediately grasped the whole, and the conversation could move forward, skipping and dashing along with a quick rhythm.

"Do you ever want to quit?" he asked. "How do you keep working when all these terrible things are happening around you?"

"It's a discipline," I said. "It's not easy at first, but you train your emotions." I told him that I still remembered my first patient who died, an old woman at the hospital in Bristol. I had been devastated by the loss, felt guilty and miserable, but gradually learned how to distance myself from what was going on. It was better for the patients if you were able to stay objective, but sometimes it just wasn't possible. I had another shock the first time I worked abroad, in Pakistan, and watched a little girl die of cholera. That was even worse because I could have saved her had we been in England. Her death was hard to accept—it took me several months to adjust to the shortages and lack of equipment.

"You do everything you can," I told Richard. "And sometimes, it's just not enough."

We took another taxi to Trumpington Street and had lunch. I was probably one of the few people in Britain who didn't know that Richard was the famous "I Bought My Home with Richard" who owned the Riverside Bank. My ignorance about his celebrity must have amused him. He seemed pleased when I insisted on paying for my share of the lunch.

I asked Richard about his background, but I could tell that I was getting the edited version. He'd grown up in Chelmsford. He was a businessman and worked in London. Mostly we discussed international relief aid. Richard wanted to know what kind of organization I'd create if I had unlimited money and support. We drank a bottle of wine and I told him all the plans I had been thinking about for several years. I talked a bit too much, but Richard kept nodding sympathetically and taking notes. When I mentioned a recent government report on aid, he made a dismissive gesture. "I don't worry much about politics," he said. "I'm results oriented." Apparently, he had decided that helping refugees was a good idea and now he wanted to find the most efficient way to do it.

We got back to King's College in time for the cocktail party and Richard went off to find two more glasses of wine. I was pinning my name tag back on when Charles Hart sat down on the couch beside me.

"So you've met Richard?"

"We spent the afternoon talking. Or, rather, Richard asked questions and I blathered on."

"That's wonderful, Julia. I'm very pleased."

"He's some sort of businessman. He wants to get involved with refugee aid."

Charles looked amused. "Dearest Julia, you've spent far too much time overseas. Don't you know who he is?"

"I guess not."

"He's the Richard Seaton who owns the Riverside Bank. You just spent the day with one of the wealthiest men in Britain."

Embarrassed, I tried to remember what I had said about medical aid. When Richard came back with the wine, he seemed to know that I had learned his identity. Suddenly, he acted distant and somewhat wary. As we talked, Charles tried to get Richard involved with an international conference on hunger. Richard said he'd think it over, then announced that he had to leave.

"You're not staying for dinner?" Charles asked. "We were going to put you up at the head table."

"Sorry, but I'm catching a helicopter back to the city. I've got to prepare for some meetings tomorrow morning."

Charles said he'd send brochures to the Riverside Bank, then rushed out of the room to change the seating arrangements. Richard turned to me, shook my hand, and didn't let go.

"A pleasure to meet you, Julia. You've given me a lot to think about."

"Yes. Well, I do hope it all made sense."

"I'll contact you in a few days," he said. Then he left.

Laura told me that men like Richard never called you back. "It wasn't a date," I told her. "We talked about infant dehydration."

"Steamy sex in an automobile, infant dehydration: it's all the same to them." Laura had recently broken up with a wealthy Saudi graduate student who turned out to have two wives. "They say they'll call, swear they'll call, but they never do."

I had stayed away from relationships for the last three years. If I was in a war zone or a famine area, I was there to save lives. Getting involved with another person seemed irresponsible, even though the after-hours social scene at the relief camps was as active as Club Med on a Saturday night. There's nothing like the presence of death and disaster to encourage love affairs.

But I couldn't stop thinking about Richard and our conversation. He was intelligent and perceptive and interested in helping others. When Laura saw Richard's bank commercial on television, she shouted at me to come downstairs. I resisted the first time, but later that night I gave in. Sitting on the couch, I watched Richard paint a house with some pensioner in Scotland.

"Is he that handsome in real life?" Laura asked.

I watched the commercial. Richard was walking away from the old man. He stopped and glanced back at the house with a satisfied smile. "I guess so."

"I'm sure they put makeup on him and style his hair before he does these commercials."

"Not really. He looked basically the same."

Laura was wearing her black silk kimono with the embroidered dragon on the back. She turned toward the phone and wiggled her fingers as if casting a magic spell. "Call. You will call. Do it, or be cursed."

A week later, a big man with reddish hair showed up at the flat. I knew right away that he was ex-military or some kind of police officer. There was an aggressiveness in his manner that suggested a familiarity with violence and power.

"Morning, Doctor. I'm Billy Monroe, Mr. Seaton's assistant."

I smiled, but I didn't invite him in. "Is there something I can do for you, Mr. Monroe?"

Billy evaluated me for a few seconds, then handed over a large manila folder. "My phone number is in there," he said. "If you want to contact Mr. Seaton, call me."

I went back inside and brewed a pot of tea before I allowed myself to open the envelope. Then I began to read. It contained photocopies of legal documents that created a nonprofit organization called Hand-to-Hand. I was listed as the executive director and Richard as chairman of the board. There were sketches for a hand-clasping logo and checks for a bank account with ten thousand pounds in it.

I put everything back in the folder, took a walk around the park, then came back and called Billy's number. A minute later, I was talking to Richard at his office. "You didn't ask me," I said.

"This is what you wanted, isn't it?"

"It is, but—"

"Then it's done. I can assure you that it didn't cost me anything to set this up. I've got solicitors sitting around all day with nothing to do. If you've changed your mind and don't want to run an organization, then I'll cancel it out."

"But you assumed I'd say yes."

"Not at all. I only knew we'd have this conversation. But now it's a real choice, isn't it? Not just talk. Not just a possibility. So tell me, Julia. What do you want to do?"

MOST PEOPLE WOULD have been ecstatic if a wealthy man had appeared on their doorstep and announced, Yes, all your good deeds have been noticed, and now we're going to create your dream. But I've always been suspicious of anything that seems too easily achieved. Why did Richard want to get involved with refugees? He didn't seem very idealistic and he certainly wasn't religious. Perhaps he was doing this as an act of pride, like a patron who wanted his name on a concert hall. I usually don't care why people decide to help others, but I had to wonder how Richard Seaton would deal with failure or, worse, a controversy.

Though I was supposed to be executive director of this new organization, I doubted if a man like Richard could resist the desire to be in control. And what was the nature of our own relationship? Was this his way of courting me? Was Hand-to-Hand the sort of indulgence that rich men bought for their lovers, something a bit more elaborate than a boutique in Knightsbridge?

"For godsake, just take it!" Laura told me. "He's giving you what you want."

"It might not work out."

"Nothing ever works out, Julia. But we do it anyway."

In the end, I offered a compromise. I didn't want to be the executive director, but I would set up and run the first refugee camp. Richard hired a bookkeeper and a secretary; then the research staff at his bank began to monitor guerrilla wars and natural disasters. While we waited for the right opportunity, I continued to shuttle between London and Freetown.

The president of Sierra Leone had campaigned with the slogan "The Future Is in Your Hands," so the rebels decided to chop off the hands of everyone they suspected of having voted. I was in charge of the clinic at Connaught Hospital and my first week there had been somewhat harrowing. The patients lay on straw pallets in the corridors, frail, exhausted, terrified. I wasn't prepared for the number of children who had been raped and mutilated. It seemed as if the country was determined to release its fury on those least able to defend themselves.

The hospital was a large cavernous building with rocket holes in the south wing. There was a stench from a broken sewer pipe and a half-burned garbage pile that smoldered in the courtyard. One night the power failed, and as I walked through the shadowy rooms with a candle I felt like I was living in a distant age. The patients were grateful and there was a pleasure in helping them. But my most popular idea was the organization of a rat squad. We'd march down the hallways with homemade brooms and the rats would flee in front of us, scrambling over the patients, making little squeaks and leaping through the air. There were shouts and whistles, the laughter of the chase, and then a wave of rats would scurry down the central staircase to a courtyard where a fifteen-year-old boy named Morgan would beat them to death with a shovel.

I'm scared of rats, but I pretended to be positive and confident. Most of the time, I could get away with it, but down in the courtyard, when I counted up the bag like a gamekeeper and handed out little rewards, a few of the rats would start moving again and crawl toward me. I would talk quickly then and step back to the staircase, trying to keep the scream from exploding out of my throat. At night, I would return to my blue toothbrush at the British military compound and go through my little rituals. A shower, if possible. If not, a sponge bath. Then I'd light a mosquito coil and sit on my cot with a flashlight and spend twenty minutes or so with a book that had nothing to do with my life. If I was relaxed enough, I'd lie down and search through my memory for a pleasant image, usually from my childhood. At the beach, perhaps, lying on the warm sand. Or on a lake in a rowboat, drifting through some flowering lily pads.

Two months after I met Richard, I finished my three-week interval and got back on the plane to London. I was recovering from dysentery and still felt tired and feverish. All I wanted was a bath and a bed with clean sheets, but Billy Monroe was waiting for me in the arrival area. "Mr. Seaton thought you might want a ride," he said.

It was a crucial point in my relationship with Richard, but of course he wasn't actually there.

I could have said, Thank you very much, but I'm taking the train. It would have been easy to give up the momentary comfort and to deflect

Richard's world. But at that moment I wanted to get into someone's car and have him handle everything. My weariness and Billy's air of authority were a potent combination. I smoothed back my hair and handed Billy my bag as he led me out of the terminal to a Mercedes-Benz. A black plastic container was in the backseat.

"What's this, Billy?"

"Hot towel. Mr. Seaton likes them after a long flight."

I unscrewed the top and found a moist towel, scented with lemon. I ran the towel across my face, amazed at how wonderful it felt.

"Just drop it on the floor when you're done," Billy told me. "Someone will pick it up." Aside from that, Billy didn't say anything. He drove me to Laura's flat. Richard, he said, would call in a few days.

Laura suggested I buy a new dress and get my hair cut. I was tempted at first, but resisted. "This is a professional relationship," I said again. "We spend all our time talking about relief work."

"He's going to be sitting across the table from you, Julia. You might as well look attractive." She stared at my forehead; I'd hacked off my bangs with some surgical scissors when a lock of hair kept falling in my eyes.

"I don't like dressing up for people."

"Then dress up for yourself. You're in London, not in some awful war zone."

In the end, I did get my hair cut, then bought some heels and a cashmere sweater. Laura said I looked good, but when Richard showed up a day later and took me to a restaurant, he talked entirely about Hand-to-Hand. When he dropped me off, he got out of the car and shook my hand at the door. I tried to act as if that was all I'd expected, but I did start to wonder what exactly we were doing. "Take care of yourself," he said. I studied his face; it was friendly, not passionate. "The British aid coordinator in Freetown says you take a lot of risks."

And he doesn't take enough of them, I thought. I was halfway up the stairs to Laura's flat when I realized that Richard or one of his employees must have called Sierra Leone while I was there to make sure that I was all right. I was in Richard's thoughts, touching him in a distant sort of way.

In my twenties, I'd believed that anyone doing relief work had to be a better person than a rich man who owned a bank. These days I knew the international aid world and could see it clearly. Most of the top UN people were career builders, oblivious to the people they were supposed to be serving. They spent their time in guarded compounds, faxing off memos and adding up their mission allowance. The British soldiers training the army were professionals who had worked all over the world, but over and over I'd met aid workers who were there because of a failure back in their own country. In Freetown, no one would know about their bankruptcy or recent divorce. They drove down the crowded streets in their air-conditioned Land Rovers and complained about the Africans during Friday night drinking hour at the British High Commission. I'd met two saints in Sierra Leone: a Dutch doctor who worked near the border and a French woman who had started a program to provide prosthetics for people mutilated by the war. But saints, real saints, were quirky, difficult people, indifferent to anything aside from their calling. I wasn't a saint. It was much too lonely.

When I returned to England, I expected Billy to be waiting for me at the airport, and I guess that was the turning point. I stayed with Laura but went out with Richard every night I was in London. It was just so pleasant to be in his world. When we saw a play together, the playwright would join us for drinks afterward. When we went to a restaurant, the chef would come out to recommend a special dish. Once, I mentioned a book I had read about in the *Times* and the novel was delivered to Laura's flat the following afternoon. On the title page the author had signed his name and written *For Julia, who has good friends.*

That week a photograph of Richard and me appeared in one of the London tabloids. We had just attended a fund-raising dinner where an aging rock star played his guitar. The news photographer caught us walking out of hotel. I have a silly grin on my face and look startled by the flash of the camera. Richard is right beside me, raising his hand like a policeman as if to protect me from the intrusion. When I saw the photograph I thought, This isn't me. The grainy black-and-white image didn't match the vision I had of myself. No one would allow the woman in the photograph to deliver a baby or remove a bullet from someone's chest. Invite her to dinner, of course, but keep her away from scalpels and forceps.

Laura was always awake when I came home. "Did you sleep with him this time?"

"No."

"Did he kiss you? Put his hand on your leg? Anything like that?"

"Not at all. It isn't that way."

"It's always that way. Eventually."

"We're not wildly emotional with each other and I like that. Things are emotional enough at the hospital."

One night after dinner, Richard finally kissed me. A delivery truck was parked in the middle of the street, so Billy stopped the car at the corner and Richard walked me down the sidewalk to Laura's flat. He took my hand which startled me. Richard had only touched me a few times, guiding me through a crowded restaurant or helping me with my coat. When we reached the door, he stopped and pulled me closer. I knew that he had decided to kiss me; perhaps he had been considering it for several days.

The kiss itself was firm and precise, without a hint of doubt. When it was done, he squeezed my hand and let go. "I admire you, Julia. You're very important to me."

The excitement of the kiss, the giddiness of it, came afterward as I climbed upstairs to the first floor. The next morning, two dozen roses arrived and Billy called to ask if I would accompany Mr. Seaton to a weekend party at his friend's estate in Kent. I flew off to Freetown, and when I returned I found Laura in the living room surrounded by open packages.

"I *am* sorry," she said. "It's all clothes, from Richard, for that party you're going to. I inspected the first package, then I had to look at everything."

Richard or Billy or some employee at the Riverside Bank had discovered my shoe and clothing sizes. There were wool pants for hiking through the forest, sweaters, shirts, and a little black dress for a cocktail party. I called up Richard that night while Laura rolled her eyes in the background.

"Do they fit?" he asked.

"Yes, I'm sure they do, but it's too much," I said. "I don't feel comfortable being given all these things. It's a bit overwhelming."

"I'm sorry, darling. I know you don't have time to shop."

"I'm keeping the dress, but I'm sending the rest back."

The weekend in Kent turned out to be a political gathering. Our host was a cabinet minister and most of the other guests were connected to the government. They gossiped about who was up or down and talked about Public Opinion as if it were a simpleminded giant who needed to be coaxed down the right road. Two experts from London were there to give lectures on monetary policy, with slides. I nodded and smiled and spent most of my time with the wives, more intelligent but less powerful than their husbands. On the second day they began to tell me about Richard's former girlfriends, who all seemed to be actresses or television personalities. "They weren't suitable," said one of the wives. "Not like you, dear."

Richard looked happy as we traveled back to London. "Let's go to my place," he said and Billy glanced up in the rearview mirror just to confirm the statement. Richard put his arm around me. "Is that all right with you, darling?"

"Yes," I said and leaned into him.

It was very late when we reached Richard's house in Highgate and he led me upstairs to his bedroom. A coal and wood fire was burning in the fireplace and it felt magical that everything had been planned for us, that someone was anticipating our needs. Richard looked nervous after he closed the door. He circled the perimeter of the room. "Is it warm enough, Julia?"

"Quite warm."

"Would you like some music? A little more light?"

"Wait here," I said, and when I came out of the bathroom Richard was in bed.

I can't remember much about what it was like to make love to Richard though later it felt as if we had accomplished something. We were together now. We were lovers. In the dim light I could see Richard's pale eyes evaluating me as we lay there without speaking. The fire had burned down to dark red coals. A mantelpiece clock ticked softly but never chimed the hour.

"Do you want a drink, Julia?"

"No. Not now."

"Or some food? It's no trouble, really. There's a man downstairs, on duty."

"I'm all right."

He put on a bathrobe, then sat beside me on the bed. "Those people in Kent liked you. Everyone thought you were very impressive."

"They're somewhat deluded," I said and laughed. "All that political talk made me sleepy."

Neither one of us mentioned love, but I decided that didn't bother me. My emotional life had always been haphazard and foolish. My past relationships had been flimsy little sailboats that could never withstand a longer voyage on deep water. Now that I was with Richard, my life felt easier. We were going to be partners, working together toward the same goal.

The next morning Richard told me that he had to eat breakfast with some American bankers. "The house is yours," he said. "Make yourself comfortable. Order some tea."

He kissed me lightly as he left the room. I lay in the Queen Anne bed, warm and relaxed beneath the silk coverlet. Frost was on the outer windows, but flowers were in a vase on the night table and I could smell the faint, sweet fragrance of jasmine. I felt protected at that moment, safe. I realized that I didn't quite know where the frayed blue toothbrush was at that moment, but there was a new one waiting for me in the bathroom. When I got dressed and went downstairs, Billy Monroe appeared in the dining room. He said good morning and, for the first time, called me Julia.

• • •

AFTER THE CAMP was organized, Richard flew to Nairobi and took a charter plane to Kosana. I couldn't image how he would react to the dust and the sick children and the black flies buzzing around the tents, but he was friendly with everyone and he even tried to learn a few phrases of Swahili. Erik Viltner had brought two coolers filled with ice, so we had fresh meat and cold beer for dinner. Richard and I shared the same tent and he noticed the Gucci case. Before he arrived, I had dug a little hole in the ground to pour out some of the shampoo and half of the makeup.

Richard zipped open the case, inspected the little bottles, and smiled. "So you actually used this."

"Yes. Although not all the makeup. It has been very busy here."

"Wonderful. I'll have my staff send some refills from London."

A few days later, Paul Rosen's airplane roared over the camp. Paul had called on the radio a day earlier and said that he was flying up from Kampala with a connector valve for the broken water pump. I left the medical tent and walked to the landing strip. Paul and Tobias got out of the plane, followed by two other men. I could tell that they were journalists. The photographer was short, plump, and sweaty. He raised his camera and took a few photographs like someone who had once worked in a war zone; the photographers I knew in Bosnia had always gotten a quick shot the moment they arrived in case they had to jump back in the car and flee. The reporter was tall and had unruly hair. He was wearing sunglasses and I couldn't see his eyes, but I noticed how calm he was, not smiling nervously the way most people acted when they first came to a refugee camp.

As I approached the plane, the photographer took two pictures of me, which I still have. The first is from a distance and all you can see is that I'm a woman with a sun hat surrounded by a half-dozen Karamojong children. A casual observer might decide that the children adored me, but of course that wasn't true. There was very little to do in the camp and I was like a walking television show, a never-ending source of amusement. Billy carried an Uzi submachine gun and had an even larger group of children following him around.

In the second photograph, you can see that I'm frowning slightly. I liked Paul and Tobias, but I've always been cautious around journalists. Most of them only spend a few hours in a relief camp, then trivialize our work into little vignettes of brave doctors and sick babies. If you were tired and said something emotional, they smiled and wrote it all down. Later, if I was unlucky enough to read the article, they usually got the facts wrong. It was better not to tell them much of anything.

Paul and Tobias had started to give out candy to keep people away from the airplane propeller. It had become a popular ritual during their visits to the camp. Tobias pulled some lemon drops out of a paper bag and began to toss them to the children. They laughed and held up their hands.

"Good afternoon, Julia," Paul said. "You look quite wonderful today."

"Aren't you supposed to say that to Ellen?"

Tobias laughed. "He's practicing his lines."

Paul reached into his flight bag and pulled out a brass-and-steel fixture about the size of a child's hand. "Some men give women chocolates. Others give roses. I bring more sophisticated presents."

"How thoughtful of you, Paul. I've always loved connector valves."

Paul turned to the journalists. "This is Nicky Bettencourt and Daniel McFarland. They work for *Newsweek* and the *Daily Telegraph*."

I shook hands. "Welcome to Kosana."

"This is a fairly large camp," Daniel said. "How long have you been here?"

"About three months."

"There was nothing in this area until Julia arrived with her trucks," Tobias said. "She organized everything."

"I'm fortunate to have a very good staff."

"Especially the nurses," Paul said. "Is Ellen around?"

"Ellen is sterilizing instruments right now. You can't take her flying. Not today. I need her for inoculations."

"Don't worry. We'll just say hello."

Paul and Tobias wandered off together while I was left with the two visitors. I decided to pass them off to Richard. "I assume you're here to interview Mr. Seaton," I said. "He's probably over in the staff tent."

"We can meet Mr. Seaton later on today," Daniel said. "Right now, we're looking for people who've had contact with the Lord's Righteous Army."

"You're writing an article about Samuel Okello?"

"That's right. Has anyone in the camp ever met him?"

"Most of the people here are Karamojong, but we're also sheltering thirty-one persons from the Acholi tribe who had to flee when Okello burned down their villages."

"Can we talk to them?"

Three Karamojong children stood a few feet away, staring at us and sucking blissfully on their lemon drops. "I don't suppose it would do any harm," I said. "We put the Acholi families in five tents next to each other. They're all farmers. Fairly conservative. They don't like the Karamojong."

It was about three o'clock in the afternoon. The Karamojong women were boiling the day's cornmeal over fires made of twigs and thornbush. The Karamojong men stood separately, staring at the horizon. More children followed us as I led the two Americans through the rows of tents.

Nicky raised his camera and took a few more photographs. I knew that he was looking for dramatic shots, but the images couldn't show what was really going on at Kosana. A news photo of a hungry child drinking a cup of milk wouldn't tell you who was giving out the food, where the money came from and if there was going to be any food three days later.

I walked them over to the tents where the Acholi farmers were living. All of them had seen their homes destroyed by the Lord's Righteous Army, and they looked dazed and fragile, as if they had been in a car wreck. I explained that these two men were journalists working for an American magazine. The Acholis were shy at first, but then they began to tell their stories, how the guerrillas had killed their families, burned their crops and their houses. And though I knew all this, it was painful to hear it again. Daniel wrote down their names in his notebook. "Did you ever see Samuel Okello?" he asked, and everyone shook their heads.

Daniel took off his sunglasses and I watched his face as he talked to the people in the tent. There was an intensity about him, an ability to ignore the confusion, which reminded me of a trained physician in an emergency room. I couldn't help noticing that he was attractive in a rangy sort of way. But something about him made me nervous. I had the feeling that he always held back, his true emotions protected and concealed—the same qualities I most disliked in myself.

Daniel closed his notebook and we went into the second tent. I had moved Isaac, a ten-year-old orphan, into this group, hoping that he would form an attachment with one of the four women there, but Isaac was so troubled that the other Acholis refused to talk to him. Now he'd taken his blanket and draped it over a length of string, creating his own private shelter. I had a broken water pump and a shortage of tents and four new cases of tuberculosis, but I all I could think about was Isaac. I had failed to help him.

I knelt down beside the little tent and pushed back the folds of the blanket. "Hello. How are you feeling, Isaac?"

He didn't answer, but he crawled out of the tent. Isaac wore shorts and a torn T-shirt and carried his most valuable possessions: pink flip-flop sandals. At first, he had reminded me of a little old man. Then I looked into his eyes and saw nothing; they were as flat and expressionless as two brown stones. Isaac had seen his parents killed and it was quite possible that he'd been forced to pull the trigger.

"We just got a shipment of oranges and we're giving one to every child in the camp at five o'clock. Do you like oranges, Isaac? I'll save the biggest one for you."

Isaac considered the oranges for a few seconds, then crawled back into his tent. I turned away from Nicky and Daniel so they wouldn't see the expression on my face.

"He speaks English?" Daniel asked.

"Yes. Sometimes. Isaac's father was a schoolteacher. The Lord's

Righteous Army killed his parents and probably forced him to be a soldier. Somehow, Isaac escaped and wandered into the camp about two weeks ago."

We went outside and they scrutinized a three-meter-high steel tower near the tent. A video camera powered by a photoelectric panel was mounted on the tower. Other towers were placed around the camp. I hated them.

"What's that?" Nicky asked.

"It's one of Richard's ideas. You really should go and talk to him."

"Maybe later," Daniel said. "I'll stay here and ask some more questions. What are you going to do, Nicky?"

"Wander around aimlessly."

"If you'd both excuse me, I need to fix a water pump."

I headed back across the camp. Nicky tagged along, his camera bag bumping against his hip. "I thought you were going to wander aimlessly," I said.

"Aimless people like to follow decisive people."

"It's a facade, Mr. Bettencourt. I just react to the current problem."

"It's a good facade, Dr. Cadell. You do it well."

KOSANA WAS COMPLETELY dependent on the two water wells drilled by the Kenyan firm that had helped us set up the camp. The well pump on the northern edge of the camp was still working, but the southern pump had been disabled by sand. If the northern pump broke down, the next available water was a border outpost about eighty kilometers away. Possibilities like this forced their way into my dreams and woke me up at three o'clock in the morning.

I got the toolbox out of the supply tent and Nicky followed me over to the broken pump. Kneeling beside the machinery, I took a wrench and began to remove the coupling.

"I don't suppose you know anything about water pumps?"

"I can fix a broken camera, but that's about it," Nicky said. "If there's a real problem, you should talk to Daniel. I've seen him adjust the timing on his sports car."

"They didn't offer a repair class when I was studying medicine. Wish they had."

"Where did you go to school? London?"

"Bristol. I was going to be a pediatrician."

"How did you get into relief work?"

"It was sort of an accident. I went to Pakistan during the summer with Save the Children. It was only supposed to be for three months, but when the contract was up I couldn't make myself leave. I've worked for Médecins Sans Frontières and a few other NGOs, but this is the first time I've been in charge of the entire operation."

"Congratulations."

"Thanks. But all that means is that it's my responsibility to fix the pump."

Nicky kept moving around me, the camera shutter clicking rapidly. "What about the illustrious Richard Seaton? Why can't he help?"

"That's enough questions—and photographs. Put the camera away and make yourself useful. Hold this hose steady while I turn the wrench."

Nicky looked embarrassed and lowered his camera. Well, that's good, I thought. At least he had a degree of self-consciousness, perhaps even a sliver of morality.

In fifteen minutes, the pump was working. A thin stream of water began to fill up one of the empty oil drums. The pump drew up liquid in pulses and the pencil-thin spurt of water reminded me of a cut artery.

"Can I take another photograph?"

"Just one."

I walked over to the northern well and turned off the pump that had been running nonstop for the last three days. After that we walked to the medical tent where Fiona and Ellen were trying to organize a group of Karamojong children for inoculations. One of the nurses would get four or five children to stand together, but the line would dissolve and they would dart about, whistling and calling to each other like little birds. Finally, Peter and Tobias appeared carrying eight boxes of oranges and the children clustered around them.

Daniel stood to one side having a conversation with Steven Ramsey, the other physician in camp. He was an American who had worked for several NGOs and I had been forced to hire him as a last-minute substitute when another doctor had a relapse of malaria. Steve was lazy and unreliable, the kind of doctor who got into relief work because he couldn't find a position back in the States. Now he was talking to Daniel, probably telling him that inoculations were a bourgeois artifact of the industrialized world.

The refugee children didn't have enough fat and muscle in their arms so Fiona injected the first boy in a fleshy part of his hip. Tobias handed him an orange and the boy tossed it into the air. Within a few minutes, the oranges were rising and falling through the air, little globes of bright color. The children pushed forward to receive their shots and no one cried from the pain. I glanced at Nicky and he looked happy, switching cameras, then moving around to get different angles on the scene.

Richard came out of the staff tent. Billy stood on one side of him carrying his Uzi while Erik Viltner, the bush pilot, stood on the other. Daniel shook hands with Richard in a formal way, as if they were two Victorian explorers meeting on the shores of the Nile. The oranges flew higher and some children began to dance, and the sun blazed bright in the sky.

RICHARD KNEW HOW to handle journalists. Daniel told him that he had come to Kosana to find the Lord's Righteous Army and Richard nodded yes, of course, quite so, then acted as if he hadn't heard. He told Billy to arrange a spare tent and insisted that our guests spend the night. After Peter and Tobias flew back to Apoka Lodge, Richard proceeded to give the two Americans another tour of the camp. He pointed out the medical tent, the trucks, and the water wells, then went into the supply tent and showed them our battery-powered computer.

"I suppose you've seen the towers scattered around the camp. Each one has a digital camera that feeds into this tent. The images are sent out on a sat phone to the Hand-to-Hand web site. You can sit at your computer in the safety of your home and see refugees being fed and children's lives being saved. Right now, we only have the live feed, but my staff is going to introduce a choice bar next month. If you click it with your mouse you can instantly contribute twenty, fifty, or one hundred pounds."

Daniel studied the image on the computer monitor. "So you show them what their money is used for."

"Yes. But it's more than that, really. We're trying to develop an emotional link between our donors and the refugees. In previous generations, people gave money to charities because they believed in God or the vicar told them to do it. That doesn't work anymore. People don't respond to moral imperatives. They need personal connections."

"Too bad there aren't any dogs," Nicky said. "I spent a week in Turkey waiting for some rescue dogs to show up. Dogs and cute babies. That's the way to go."

"We're not making a Hollywood movie here," I said. "Richard just wants to show what happens in a relief camp."

Richard was oblivious to Nicky's sarcasm or my annoyance. He concentrated on Daniel, trying to win him over. "No, this isn't a Hollywood movie. But the success of reality-based television in Europe and America has showed me that people do want a dramatic, true-life story. In the future, we might train our local staff to carry around video cameras. People can watch at home and wonder if a certain refugee will live or die. They can click their mouse and save a life, for a small contribution."

The sun was going down when Richard finished the tour. "Want a cold beer?" Billy asked the visitors. "Still on ice. Straight from Nairobi."

We all went to the staff tent and ate curry rice mixed with canned chicken. There were two tables and benches where everyone ate together, telling jokes and drinking the beer. After dinner, Daniel moved down the table and began to talk to Ellen Reagan. Ellen was twenty-five and still innocent about journalists and their questions. Every relief camp had a few scandals that needed to be concealed. There had been a minor disaster two weeks ago when some Karamojong left the camp and crossed the border into Kenya to steal cattle. If a reporter decided to publicize this incident, I would have to fly to Nairobi and sit in a government office while some bureaucrat scolded me like an angry headmaster.

I sat down beside Ellen and forced a smile. "Is Mr. McFarland asking you too many questions?"

"No," she said, clearly enjoying the attention. "We're talking about my family's village. Mr. McFarland has visited Carrick on Shannon. He even remembered the name of our pub there."

"I'm sure that Mr. McFarland has visited a great many places."

"I've never been in this area of East Africa," Daniel said. "What do you think about Kosana, Ellen? Do you like it here?"

Ellen chatted about the camp. The children were wonderful, but it was very hot and dusty and Mr. Monroe had killed a snake that slithered into her tent. I watched Daniel stare at Ellen's Celtic cross earrings and the anxious, fluttery way she moved her hands. Throughout the conversation, he would turn his head slightly and glance at me.

Finally Ellen got tired and left the tent. Daniel looked straight at me as we faced each other over the table. I felt like we were two gamblers ready to play cards with each other.

"So why are you doing this?" he asked.

"Doing what? Running an aid organization?"

He nodded. "I'm trying to fit you into one of the six categories of relief workers."

"Is this a theory of your own, Mr. McFarland? You must explain it to me."

"There are the obsessively religious. They pass out Bibles to starving people. There are the benevolently religious. They feed the natives first, then hope they'll ask for Bibles while they're eating. There are the professional aid workers who are in it for the money or because it looks good on their résumés. Then there are the cowboys . . ."

"Aren't they usually American?"

"Cowboy aid workers like to speed around the desert in new pickup trucks and drink cattle blood with the Masai."

I found myself smiling. "There are also cowgirl relief workers."

"The fifth category is the confused or the incompetent—people who don't know what to do with their life so they decide to play God in a Third World country."

"I don't want to be God, Mr. McFarland. It's too much responsibility."

"The final category of relief worker is quite rare. It's the idealist who sees things clearly. That might be you, Dr. Cadell. Or perhaps not. There's a certain professional air about you."

"Cynicism is not a substitute for knowledge. Though for the misguided it can seem that way."

"You're right. I'm frequently misguided. But I did manage to find out that a group of Karamojong warriors got food rations from your organization, then crossed the border to steal cattle from the Turkana tribe."

"Did Dr. Ramsey tell you that?" I asked.

"I don't reveal my sources."

"Are you going to put that in an article?"

"Nicky and I came here to find the Lord's Righteous Army. I'm not really interested in writing about relief aid. The editors want pity or heroism. Usually, they cut the paragraphs where I try to give an explanation."

I checked my watch and got up from the table. "I'm sorry. I've got to turn off our water pump. We don't have enough petrol to let it run all night."

Billy and Erik sat across from Nicky at the long table teaching him how to play a card game called Danube. Richard sat at the other end talking on his sat phone to someone in London. "Yes, we're in the banking business," he said. "But we're also in the information business. You're not exploiting the potential here."

I slipped through the mosquito netting and stepped outside. Kerosene lanterns were burning in the medical tent and the staff tent, but the rest of the camp was dark. The motor on the repaired water pump was as noisy as a lawn mower and I headed toward the sound. I switched on my flashlight so that the Karamojong would know that I was passing through. Some of the men had been brewing homemade beer from the maize we gave them, but everyone respected the graceful fiction that no alcohol or weapons were allowed in the camp. There was an unspoken agreement that I wouldn't search the tents and the refugees wouldn't publicly break the rules.

Two girls were filling up plastic bottles when I reached the southern well. I touched their heads. They giggled and disappeared into the night. Kneeling beside the water pump, I felt around for leakage, then killed the motor. Silence came instantly. I switched off the flashlight, stood beside the four steel drums and saw the moon reflected on the surface of the water. Thousands of stars were visible in the sky in different shades of blue or yellowish white, each point of light glittering separate and distinct. I could hear the Karamojong talking in their tribal language and the quick, hard snap of someone breaking a branch for a fire. After eight years of working in relief camps, I still felt the strangeness of each assignment. Here I was in Africa, under the stars, and it was all quite amazing. I skimmed up some water to drink and saw the moon ripple and shimmer before me.

I switched on the flashlight again and cut across the camp to where the Acholi farmers were staying. A woman was recovering from a throat infection and I stopped by her tent. Moses Sebana, a farmer in his sixties who always carried around a Bible, came out to greet me.

"How's Christina?"

"Very good, Dr. Cadell. There's no more fever and she's sleeping."

"Did Mr. McFarland ask you questions today? Was that all right?"

Moses hesitated, and I felt as if he was considering his next statement. "Mr. McFarland said very little to us, but he spent a long time with Isaac."

"Isaac doesn't speak to anyone."

"He sat beside the boy for an hour and said nothing. Then Isaac came out of his tent and looked at him. When I came back, they were talking."

I went into Isaac's tent. It had the pungent odor of sweat and urine. Everyone was asleep, but they woke up when the flashlight beam cut across the canvas wall. "I'm sorry," I whispered. "Everything's all right. Go back to sleep." I stepped around the bodies to Isaac's private shelter. The boy came out with his hands raised to shield his eyes from the flashlight. I switched it off and sat down on the dirt beside him. The other people in the tent shifted around and whispered to each other. A man began to snore.

"Isaac, I hear that you talked with Mr. McFarland today. Was he a nice man?"

Silence.

"What did you talk about?"

Isaac said nothing.

"Did you talk about Samuel Okello and the Lord's Righteous Army?"

I decided to wait for his answer. Four or five minutes passed before the boy spoke in a soft voice.

"I show him where they are."

"Okello's army?"

"Yes."

"Why would you do that? It's very dangerous."

Another pause, then the child's voice. "Wristwatch."

"Mr. McFarland is going to give you his wristwatch?"

"Yes."

"Well, that's interesting." I reached out and touched the boy's shoulder. "Good night, Isaac. See you in the morning."

I stepped around the sleeping bodies and pushed through the tent flap. Marching across the camp, I held the flashlight in front of me like a sword. I felt especially angry, not because I liked Daniel McFarland, but because he had made me notice him. There was something about him, some quality of his appearance or personality, that had pushed its way into my thoughts.

Back at the staff tent, Billy had just won a card game from Erik and Nicky. Richard was still on the phone and Daniel was writing in his notebook. I approached the table and stood next to him.

"Mr. McFarland, I want you out of this camp by tomorrow morning.

You can use our radio to contact Paul Rosen or a member of the staff will drive you over to Kidepo. Do anything you want. I don't care. But be out of here by nine o'clock."

Daniel stared straight at me with a blank expression on his face. He wasn't intimidated or regretful. I felt like a railway stationmaster who had just told him to take another train. "I understand," he said quietly. "We'll leave as soon as we can."

"There's something going on here," Richard said to the person in London. "Stay at the office. I'll get back to you." He switched off the phone and raised his eyebrows. "Is there a problem, darling?"

"We have a little boy in the camp named Isaac Adupa. He saw his parents killed by the Lord's Righteous Army, and then they kept him as a recruit until he managed to run away. Isaac is traumatized, of course. But Mr. McFarland doesn't care about that. He only cares about his bloody story. Mr. McFarland talked to Isaac when I wasn't there. Tempted him with a wristwatch. And now Isaac has agreed to lead him back into the bush to find Okello."

Daniel's face didn't change. I realized that he had spent his career being threatened by people who didn't want him writing articles. Nothing I said was going to bother him; he was a professional acrobat who could fall without injury. I glanced around the tent. Nicky looked surprised. Erik Viltner was grinning as if he was going to tell us that the exact same thing had happened to him a couple of years ago on a safari with two Dutchmen. Billy watched Richard, waiting for a clue about how to react. Richard turned to him and shook his head slightly. It was a small gesture, an acknowledgment that Daniel was a tough journalist and part of the men's club or something macho and awful like that.

Daniel got up from the table. His voice was calm and unemotional. "I'm sorry that you're angry, Dr. Cadell. But I want to make it clear that I didn't threaten Isaac."

"I suppose that's your idea of ethics."

"As far as I know, the boy has stayed in that tent for the last two weeks. He hasn't gone anywhere or spoken to anyone. The other Acholis act like he has a disease. Maybe the boy is traumatized, but I don't think you or your staff have done anything about it."

"Are you an instant expert about refugee children, Mr. McFarland? How clever of you to walk around the camp for a few hours and talk to a few people, then decide what we should be doing here."

Daniel walked over to the tent opening. "The only thing I know is that Isaac wanted to guide me. It was his choice."

And then he was gone, slipping through the mosquito net and leaving me with my anger. Billy laughed softly and tossed down his cards.

"Well, that was our surprise for the evening. Is this a problem, Mr. Seaton? Should I do something?"

"That's not necessary," I said. "He'll be gone tomorrow."

Billy grinned at Nicky. "Doesn't look like you knew about this."

Nicky shrugged his shoulders as if to suggest that it wasn't an important issue.

"McFarland is crazy," Billy said. "Do you really want to walk off into the bush with a ten-year-old boy as a guide?"

"Right now, I'm going to bed. Thanks for dinner."

Nicky got up from the table. He seemed uncomfortable that everyone was staring at him and I could tell that he hated to be the center of attention. Richard pushed the redial button on his phone.

"Is everything all right, Julia?"

"No. It's not."

"Best to move on, darling. Don't let it bother you."

I wanted to shout at them for going on with their business and playing their card game. Instead I walked outside and went over to the medical tent. The lamp hanging on the front pole had attracted hundreds of insects and they fluttered and hopped and flung themselves foolishly at the light.

Nicky
〰️

5 THE MOTHER TREE

The camp's power generator had been switched off. In the moonlight, the tents appeared more substantial, like little huts constructed out of blue-gray slate. It was late, but the Karamojong refugees called to each other from the shadows. A few people were clapping out a complex rhythm that reminded me of the schoolyard clapping game girls played when I was growing up. I tripped over a few ropes, then found our tent and went inside. Daniel wasn't there and I wondered if he had decided to change his plans. Julia was right; it was dangerous to take Isaac back to his kidnappers. We should forget about the Lord's Righteous Army. It was safer to do an article on the elephants in Kidepo park.

I pulled off my clothes and crawled into my sleeping bag. It smelled like someone else's sweat, but I was glad that I had a place to sleep. I lay there for a few minutes until Daniel slipped inside the tent.

"Where'd you go?"

"I talked to Steve Ramsey. He's going to sell us some blankets and water bottles for our journey."

"Does he know that Julia is angry?"

"Ramsey doesn't like Dr. Cadell. She caught him smoking hashish before going into surgery. Now he wants to quit and get another job."

"You should have told me about the plan, Daniel. This kid has combat shock or whatever you want to call it and we're forcing him to go back into the bush."

"It's his choice. I'm not forcing him to do anything."

"He's ten years old. What if we meet Okello and he decides to kill Isaac because the boy ran away?"

"I'll do all I can to protect him."

"All I'm saying is that . . ."

"I know what you're saying, Nicky. But I've decided to take this particular risk. For you, there's only one relevant question. Are you going to come with us or not?"

I stared at the darkness and tried to make a choice. We had traveled thousands of miles to find the hostages and Samuel Okello. If I backed out, I'd have to return to London with a bag full of excuses.

"So?" Daniel asked. "What's your decision?"

"I'll come along."

"Good. We'll leave as soon as possible in the morning."

Daniel's cot creaked as he got undressed and wiggled into his sleeping bag. Within a few minutes, his breathing was slow and regular. I stayed awake. Somewhere in the camp, a woman began weeping. She said the same words in her tribal language, over and over again, but no one seemed to answer her.

WHEN I WOKE UP the next morning, Daniel acted like we hadn't argued at all. Sitting on the cot, he sorted through the articles in his canvas traveling bag. "All I'm carrying is my phone, water, food, and a blanket. We'll leave everything else here."

"I wish we could rent a Land Rover."

"Walking is good for you, Nicky. You'll see the countryside."

"If Isaac gets lost, that's all we're going to see."

I would have paid fifty dollars for a cup of coffee that morning, but

I figured that we wouldn't be welcome at the staff tent. Daniel unpacked the food Winston had bought for us in Kampala marketplace. We had crackers and canned sausages for breakfast.

It was cold outside the tent and the wind was blowing in from the east. Some of the Karamojong had started a fire and they were cooking cornmeal. The older men wrapped their *shuka* cloths around their shoulders and stared down at the flames as children ran back and forth, tossing twigs and dead leaves into the pit. The smoke and the cold gray sky made all the colors look muted, as if they'd been worn down by the wind.

Trying to avoid Julia, we circled the edge of the camp to Steve Ramsey's tent. The doctor sat on a folding campstool in his underwear. He was trimming his toenails with a pair of surgical scissors.

"Still want the supplies?"

"Yes. We're leaving right now."

We followed Ramsey into his tent. Three army blankets were stacked up on his folding cot along with six plastic bottles of boiled water.

"All this for a hundred dollars."

It looked like Ramsey had stolen everything from the supply tent, but Daniel paid without bargaining. Quickly we rolled up the blankets and distributed the water bottles between our two bags. We stuffed our extra equipment into a nylon storage sack.

"We're leaving this here," Daniel said. "If we don't come back in a week, it's all yours."

Billy and Erik were waiting for us when we came out of the tent. A squad of Ugandan soldiers was officially in charge of the camp, but I wasn't about to argue with a professional thug like Billy.

"You two going off into the bush?"

"Looks that way," Daniel said. "Is there a problem?"

Billy smiled like a genial bartender. "Mr. Seaton isn't concerned about Samuel Okello. However, if you decide to write about Mr. Seaton's leadership of Hand-to-Hand, we hope that it's a positive article."

"People are hungry and you're feeding them."

"Exactly. Well said, Mr. McFarland." Billy pulled out a business card for the Riverside Bank and handed it to Daniel. "We're flying out this afternoon so Mr. Seaton wanted you to have this. Give us a call if you make it back to London."

"I'll do that."

"If you meet up with buffalo, especially a solitary male, stand still and don't make a sound," Erik told us. "Anything else—lions, cheetahs, hyenas —just shout and act crazy. Carnivores stay away from crazy people."

"Great," I said. "Sounds like the New York subway."

Billy made a point of shaking our hands, then we hurried over to the area where the Acholi refugees were living. Isaac stood alone beside one of the tents. He held his pink flip-flop sandals as if he was waiting for permission to put them on.

"Morning, Isaac," Daniel said. "You ready to go?"

The boy stared at us with those dead eyes of his. It looked as if every possible emotion had been squeezed out of him. "I'm ready."

Standing to one side, I was the first person to see Julia approach us. It was still cold, and she wore a sweater along with her khakis and work boots. I've photographed a fair number of relief workers and I've learned how their faces change because of the job. The first time they encounter a war or a famine, they look startled and somewhat scared. After six months, their faces begin to relax and they seem aware of problems even before they happen. After two years or more, many of them become cynical and bored. They spend their spare time calculating the total per diem paid by their aid organization. But a few relief workers remind me of Giacometti's sculptures: they look as if they've been cut and chipped away until only their essence remains.

Julia was just moving into this third stage, but it was too early to tell which way she would go. She came toward us with a long-legged confident stride. In fact, stride was a good word to describe her. She didn't seem to be afraid of anything.

"I want to talk to Isaac."

"Of course." Daniel stepped away from the boy and crouched in the dirt. He took out a cigarette, cupped it in his hand, and tried to light a match in the wind. I knew that he wasn't going to argue with Julia.

Although Daniel wrote about wars, he disliked confrontation. It wasted time and diverted him from his constant movement forward.

Julia turned to Isaac and smiled brightly. "I just had a wonderful idea, Isaac. I know you wanted Mr. McFarland's watch. That's why you agreed to be his guide. But look . . ." She unstrapped her own watch and offered it to the boy. "You can have mine. It's yours if you don't go with him."

Isaac examined Julia's face, then glanced at Daniel. What was he looking for? I wondered. How would he make his choice? Julia obviously cared about Isaac. She wanted to save him and it showed. Daniel was cold and expressionless, but I could see that Isaac was far more comfortable with that lack of emotion. Julia's compassion was not part of his world.

Isaac dropped his sandals and stepped into them. "I'll go with Mr. Daniel."

Julia's lips were pressed into a tight line. I expected her to start arguing with Daniel, but she turned to me. "I think it's obvious that this expedition with Isaac wasn't your idea. Stay here and you can go back to Nairobi in our supply truck."

I felt ashamed for a few seconds, but that emotion was pushed away by a surge of anger. I could have lectured her about the responsibilities of journalism, but that would have been a lot of words piled up over the truth. Last night I had accepted Daniel's plan because I needed to please my employers and I didn't want to look like a coward. Sometimes I think all men are still six years old, daring each other to kick a dead snake in the middle of the road.

"I'm going with them."

Julia shook her head and turned away from me. She touched the boy's shoulder. "We'll be waiting for you, Isaac. You can always come back here." She glanced at Daniel one last time and walked away. A gust of wind passed through the camp and smoke drifted through the gaps between the tents.

• • •

ISAAC STROLLED OUT of the camp and we followed him. The boy's flip-flops made little slapping sounds with each step. As we crossed the rocky strip of dirt that surrounded Kosana, I felt like we were on a beach, approaching a vast ocean. For a few hundred yards we stepped around patches of weeds and thornbushes; then we were lost in the grass. The thick yellowish stalks brushed against my chest and shoulders. A flock of doves rose up from the earth.

Isaac had only a general idea about where we were going. The path of crushed grass divided several times and veered off in different directions. At each juncture the boy stopped and checked the horizon, then took the path that led to the morning sun. After a half hour of slow progress, he led us up a crumbly dirt slope and paused at the top. We looked down at a riverbed about thirty to forty feet wide. During the rains it would be filled with a surge of muddy water from the surrounding hills, but now it was a dry channel of reddish sand and lichen-covered boulders. Instead of forcing our way through the grass and thickets, we were going to follow this natural pathway.

"Where are we going?" Daniel asked Isaac.

"To the mother tree."

"What's that?"

Isaac shook his head. Couldn't explain.

"How far is it?"

The boy shook his head again.

"How many nights' sleep?"

"One night. Then a little farther."

Daniel took off his watch, pulled a piece of twine out of his pocket, and threaded it through the strap's buckle. He tied the ends of the twine together and formed an improvised necklace with the watch as a pendant. "Here you go," he told Isaac and slipped the loop over the boy's head.

Isaac touched the watch cautiously, then held it up and stared at the second hand ticking its way around the dial. Satisfied, he nodded and sighed. It was the first time I had seen the boy show any sort of emotion.

"Is that what you wanted?"

"Yes, Mr. Daniel."

"Wear it under your shirt and people won't take it."

Isaac led us down into the riverbed and we followed it north. By eleven o'clock it was hot and sweat flies began to swarm around us. Isaac walked carefully, picking his way around the boulders. He never seemed to get tired or thirsty.

The sun rose higher in the sky and the shadows darkened. We rationed water, trying not to drink more than one bottle per hour. I started to get worried when we finished the third bottle, but then we found a mud hole with a few inches of water on the surface. We filled the bottles and dropped in iodine tablets, but the water still tasted like rocks and sand.

Larks and warblers darted in and out of the brush. A gerund gazelle with a long slender neck nibbled on a thorn tree, then ran away when we stumbled into view. The riverbed narrowed to about twenty feet across and the boulders got larger. We scrambled over rocks, knocking off pieces of lichen. I slipped twice and banged my knee. When we came around a bend two miniature deer were hiding in the thicket on the right bank. They were dik-diks, so small and delicate that they seemed to come from a gentler place than the rest of the world. I stared at them, forgetting to take out my camera, but then Isaac made a noise and they disappeared into the grass.

Daniel called a halt around four in the afternoon and we spent the next few hours pulling dead branches from trees for a pile of firewood. We camped on a patch of sand near the shelter of two boulders. I dug a pit with my hands and lit a fire as the sun went down.

The cicadas had been chirping all day long, but they got louder at nightfall. Their sound reminded me of a heartbeat, something steady and physical that came with its own rhythm. Birds called from the darkness and a pack of wild dogs greeted each other with a high-pitched yittering sound.

Some people pay thousands of dollars so they can fly to Africa and sit by a campfire under the stars, but sleeping outdoors always makes me nervous. If you take away our guns and cars and drop us into the middle of the wilderness, we become scrawny little apes with no fangs or claws to defend ourselves. Forget about art and philosophy; we're lunch.

"The fire's big enough, Nicky."

"Just one more branch."

"A bigger fire isn't going to make a difference to a leopard."

"That's what you think. All the leopards I know are very impressed."

Isaac was already asleep, wrapped up in one of the army blankets. I sat close to the fire while Daniel leaned against a boulder. Instead of worrying about the Lord's Righteous Army, I started to plan the perfect victory meal for when we got back to Rome. For the first course I wanted *straccetti con rughetta,* strips of young beef cooked in arugula. No. I'd order *saltimbocca,* little chunks of veal skewered with pro-sciutto and sage.

"She was really angry."

I shifted around and looked at Daniel. He sat with his knees up and his head back against the rock. "Who are you talking about? Julia?"

"I can never understand what motivates people like her. Julia's not a missionary or a Bible thumper. Maybe Richard Seaton gives her a big salary, but I don't think she's doing it for the money either."

"And she's pretty, too."

Daniel took a stick and stirred up the fire as if Julia's appearance was the ultimate annoyance. "She made it sound like I had flown to Kosana looking for somebody like Isaac. Believe me, I would have hired an adult if I could have found one. You saw those Acholi farmers. They're terrified of Okello."

"Maybe we should be terrified, too. I really don't want to get my hand chopped off by some fanatic."

"There's always a risk, Nicky."

"All I'm saying is that I don't like dealing with prophets or visionar-ies, especially if they have their own army. People who talk to God are dangerous. I prefer a sleazy police captain who accepts bribes."

• • •

IT WAS A LONG, uncomfortable night. I got up to put more wood on the fire and heard an animal moving through the grass. Whatever it was made a quick huffing sound like an asthmatic breathing. The animal crept closer; then the sound faded away.

I started itching when I lay back down on the sand and realized that the blankets Ramsey had sold us were infested with fleas. I could feel them crawling beneath my clothing, searching for a soft patch of flesh.

The next morning all three of us had welts on our skin. We ate crackers and jam for breakfast before continuing north up the riverbed. I asked Isaac how far we had to go and he mumbled something about the mother tree and kept walking. It felt like we were going uphill. There were fewer places to find water. I was hot, then shivery, and it was hard to swallow. As I stumbled forward I began to fantasize about the White House job that Carter Howard had mentioned during our walk. Once I became part of the press pool I could rent an apartment in Georgetown and buy some furniture for the first time in my life. All I had to do was join the pack of photographers and learn how to shout: "Over here, Mr. President! Over here!"

Isaac saw something and ran forward. When we finally caught up with him, he was standing on the riverbank next to a pair of baobob trees. They looked like two pieces of broccoli planted in the ground. The larger of the trees had two branches that curved around a smaller trunk that grew from the base. It reminded me of a parent embracing a child and then I realized this was the landmark we'd been looking for—the mother tree.

Grass was crushed around the tree and there were patches of ash left over from fires. "Did Okello come here?" Daniel asked Isaac.

"Not Okello, but the archangels and the seraphim. They would stop here after they attacked a village."

"Can you lead us to the main camp?"

Isaac grasped the watch hanging around his neck as if he thought we were going to take it back. "I don't know. They went different ways."

"How far is the main camp?"

"I don't know."

"Screw this, Daniel. If we leave the riverbed and start wandering through the grass, then we're definitely going to get lost."

"We'll stay here and build a fire," Daniel said. "If Okello's men are in the area, they'll see the smoke and track us down."

I sat down at the base of the tree, took out my Swiss Army knife and opened a can of sausages. Daniel built a fire and worked hard to keep it going. The wind pushed the plume of smoke off to the west, a dirty gray line smeared across the sky.

I wandered around the area and found Isaac down in the riverbed. He was building a little fort with sticks and boulders, just like I used to do when I was a boy. I took a few pictures of him working, then put away my camera and picked up a stone. "Want some help?" I asked. He didn't tell me to go away so I figured it was all right.

We started working together, but neither of us spoke. I don't know how to deal with children in general, and war victims like Isaac are in their own special category of pain. There was nothing I could say to him that would take the images of death and killing out of his head, so I stayed quiet and carried rocks. After two hours of labor we had built a little stone house with some branches for a roof. Isaac and I sat inside it together, peering out one of the windows and watching the smoke from Daniel's fire drift past the mother tree.

"So who are the archangels and the seraphim?"

"The archangels are the commanders. You become a seraphim when they give you a rifle."

"Were you a seraphim?"

Isaac nodded and turned away from me. He looked tired and defeated, like a lonely old man.

"Want some chewing gum, Isaac? I think I have a few sticks in my camera case."

The boy crawled through the door and walked away. I sat in our little house for a while, hoping he'd come back, but the game was over.

I WOKE UP the next morning, ready to argue with Daniel. There was no more food and it was difficult to find water. Time to go home.

Daniel vanished into the grass for a few hours, then came back. It was nine o'clock in the morning. He picked up his bag and slung it over his shoulder. "All right," he said. "Let's get out of here."

"I thought you might want to stay."

"I'll go to the edge of the cliff, Nicky. But I won't jump off. If you do that, you can't write anymore."

We left the mother tree and headed back down the riverbed toward Kosana. Daniel moved slowly and he kept glancing around him as if, somehow, the thornbushes and boulders would provide him with a new plan.

We found a muddy patch of ground but no water. When we started walking again I saw something moving through the grass on the right side of the riverbank. We stopped walking as four guerrillas emerged from the undergrowth and pointed their rifles at us. The tallest man was about nineteen or twenty years old. He had dreadlocks and a scraggly beard and wore a ragged blue T-shirt and military pants.

The other three guerrillas were small, shoeless boys with bits of dry grass in their hair. Each carried a Kalashnikov assault rifle and a panga knife. The boys had thrust their knives in their belts, but the tall man wore his in a leather scabbard slung around his neck. Everyone looked hungry and intent, like a pack of hyenas that had just found a limping gazelle.

Isaac stood very straight, his arms at rigid angles, and stared at the tall man's rifle. I licked my lips and tried to look confident while Daniel stepped forward.

"Jina langu Daniel. Jina lako nani?"

"I speak English," said the tall man. "Better than your Swahili."

"I'm Daniel McFarland. I write for British, German, and American newspapers. This is my partner, Nicky Bettencourt. He takes photographs for the newspapers."

The tall man motioned his rifle at Isaac. "And this is the traitor who brought you here."

"Samuel Okello wants to talk to us. We've traveled thousands of miles to see him. He will punish anyone who harms our guide."

The tall man looked startled when he heard Okello's name. He turned to the three seraphim and spoke in their tribal language. The three boys lowered their rifles but kept their hands on the trigger guards.

"If you want to walk to our camp, then we must blindfold you."

"There's no reason to use blindfolds. We're journalists, not soldiers. We've come from London to write down the Prophet's words. You shouldn't make him angry."

The tall man looked frightened. He seemed to think that Samuel Okello might appear in front of us and punish him for making the wrong choice. The three seraphim kept glancing over their shoulders, waiting for the command to shoot, but the tall man snapped his jaw shut so that it made a faint clicking sound. He raised his rifle and motioned to the grass.

"I am the archangel Piramoi. If you're lying to me about the Prophet, all of you will be killed."

Piramoi led us, single file, out of the riverbed and down a narrow path. The three seraphim were behind us, whispering. I was too tired and thirsty to be scared. My camera bag and travel bag kept bouncing against my legs, and I wanted to throw them away. Isaac walked in front of me with his head bowed like a criminal going to his execution. Every time the path split into different directions, Piramoi knelt down and searched for a small stone that had been hidden in the grass. The sun was falling toward the horizon. We followed it west for several hours; then the marker stones guided us northeast. I was about to sit down and refuse to go any farther when we climbed a slope to a plateau dotted with trees. We pushed through the grass and bumped into a pregnant teenage girl sitting in the doorway of a thatch-roofed hut. She stared at us as if we had just arrived from Jupiter, then jumped up and followed the procession.

The trail led us past two other huts and a long brick building with empty windows. I found out later that the brick building had once been part of a British military outpost. Samuel Okello was wary of government scout planes so he hadn't cleared away the tall grass and thornbushes. Every structure was covered with thatching that blended in with the surrounding countryside.

The crowd around us became larger. Most of them were boys carrying rifles, but there were a few girls looking dirty and scared. Two vehicles were parked beside the building: a Toyota Land Cruiser with a UGANDA PARKS insignia on the door and a blue van that probably had been stolen from some *matatu* driver. Grass had been bound in sheaves and tied to the roofs of both vehicles.

Piramoi went inside the building. Another archangel came out a few minutes later and demanded our passports and travel bags. I managed to keep my two cameras, but an older seraphim grabbed my sun hat. A hat was worth something in the bush, but my cameras were completely useless.

We stood there for twenty minutes while the seraphim stared at us as if we were rare beasts that had been driven out of the grass. Finally, Piramoi and two other archangels came out of the house and everyone stopped talking.

"You go with the others," Piramoi said to Daniel.

"What about Reverend Okello?"

"That is the order. You stay with the others." And he led us through the camp to a stick and thorn enclosure that had once been used as a cattle pen. The seraphim pulled the branch back and Piramoi motioned us forward. Inside the enclosure were two thatched-roof shelters that reminded me of beach cabanas. Six people sat in the shade on straw mats.

A young man with a blond beard and ponytail ran over to us. "Deutsche?" he asked. "British? American?"

"American."

"You're from the embassy?"

"No, we're journalists."

The young man looked disappointed. Without speaking another word, he turned away from us and walked over to his companions. "Not from an embassy. Not from the Red Cross. Journalists."

• • •

DANIEL AND I went over to the shelters and met the hostages. We sat down and began to talk while Isaac stayed apart from us. All the hostages had suffered from malaria and dysentery. They'd been wearing the same clothes for the last four months and their shoes were falling apart. Most people assume that they're going to act like a hero in a situation like this, but illness and malnutrition had worn them down. They had exchanged their life histories, told every story twice, and there was nothing more to say. Now they spent their time lying on the straw mats, waiting passively for their ration of millet porridge.

Michael and Nora Barrow were from a suburb of northern New Jersey. Michael was a phone company executive who had spent most of his life giving orders, but now he'd become confused and frightened. His wife, Nora, was a nervous woman who noticed the slightest change in the daily routine. If they replaced the guards or fed them with different bowls, she concluded that Okello was getting ready to kill them.

Ray Stokes was a short, feisty man in his sixties who ran a garage in Oxford. His wife, Livy, had become depressed, but Ray was the chief optimist of the group. He had convinced himself that American spy satellites had found Okello's camp and that SAS commandos were about to attack in stealth helicopters.

Joseph Henning was a German record-shop employee in his thirties who had traveled around the world for several years. Although he had lost weight, he was stronger and in better shape than the older hostages. Nora Barrow was suspicious of Joseph because he knew a little Swahili and occasionally talked to the guards.

At the beginning of their captivity Okello had intimidated the hostages with his power. They were kept blindfolded for several days, then forced to watch one of the archangels execute a twelve-year-old girl. When some of the soldiers returned to camp with amputated hands, Okello placed a basketful of them in the hostage compound. A line of ants had flowed like a tiny black river beneath the thorn wall and across the dirt to the basket.

Eventually, Joan Siebert, the sixth hostage, picked up the basket and gave it to one of the seraphim. "Tell the Prophet that we've had this long enough," she said and the guard obeyed her.

Joan was a small woman in her seventies, a librarian from Wisconsin who had cashed in one of her retirement funds to come to Africa. She was calm and practical, and the other hostages usually followed her lead. During the last few weeks, Joan had started to have physical problems. Her pulse was low, her hands and feet felt tingly, and she got dizzy whenever she stood up.

"I haven't been sick for almost forty years," she told us. "That is, if you don't count a hip operation. Being sick is not the way I see myself. I wake up every morning and decide that I'm going to be all right, but my body doesn't seem to be listening."

"I'm sorry," Daniel said. "We didn't bring any medicine."

"Did you bring any books?" she asked.

"Nothing but food and water."

"It's been difficult to deal with Mr. Okello, but my major problem is boredom. We just sit around all day. There's nothing to do and no one wants to talk anymore. Lately I've been making a list of my ten favorite books. I argue with myself whether a particular novel should be number three or number five."

"What's your first choice?" I asked.

"*Sense and Sensibility.* No illustrations. With a sewn binding."

MILLET PORRIDGE WAS served to us around five o'clock and the hostages went through little rituals with their bowls and spoons. Daniel and I had been talking ever since we met the hostages; this was the first time I was able to sit alone and analyze the situation. We were prisoners. Okello was crazy. And there was no indication that they would release us.

Daniel ate his food quickly, then lit one of his Turkish cigarettes and paced around the enclosure. By now I knew that he didn't smoke very often, only when he was tense or trying to figure something out. I caught up with him and we walked together.

"So what do you think?"

"It's difficult."

"Is Okello going to meet with us?"

"You can't predict much of anything, Nicky. You know that."

"Humor me, will you? Say something positive."

"They're feeding us. If they had decided to kill us in the next few hours, they wouldn't give us food."

"Is that the best you can do?"

"There are no miracles. I only believe in the reality in front of me."

I went back to the shelter and finished my porridge. All the hostages had a different technique. Nora Barrow ate her ration very slowly, letting the food dissolve on her tongue. Ray Stokes divided his porridge into sections and ate bits of it over a three-hour period.

I knew that Daniel was trying to be honest with me, but I would have appreciated something a bit more optimistic. That afternoon, I decided that everything was dependent on the size of the photograph. You could take a picture of a little boy playing with a ball, then expand the frame to his angry parents who are trying to turn him into an angry adult, then expand the frame even larger to include the nice teacher who's going to say something inspiring or the little girl who is going to grow up and fall in love with him. And you could keep doing that with your photograph, making it larger to bring in the good things or larger still to include all the misery and pain. Daniel was right, of course—there were no miracles—but I wanted a bigger lens.

THE RED SUN burned its way into the grass and stars began to come out. As it got dark, you could only see the silhouettes of the hostages, but they kept talking about that day's ration and Okello's plans.

"Are you all right, Mr. Bettencourt?" Joan asked quietly.

"Call me Nicky. Okay?"

"What's the name of the little boy who brought you here?"

"Isaac."

"Was he forced to be a seraphim?"

"Yeah. They killed his parents."

"What Okello and the others have done to the children is very evil. I've prayed but can't forgive him." Joan's voice was very faint, almost overcome by the noise of the cicadas. "I'm not able to find that mercy in my heart."

Daniel and I hadn't turned Isaac into a killer, but we had used him to find this place. Piramoi had said that Isaac was a traitor. The threat stayed with me and maybe that's why Daniel also looked worried. He kept pacing around in the darkness while everyone else lay down on the mats and tried to sleep. At some time during the night, Daniel came over and joined us. Much later, Isaac got cold and lay beside me. I could hear his breathing, feel his small chest moving in and out.

The next morning, Isaac went back to his spot at the edge of the shelter. Joan called his name, but he ignored her and stared dully at the thorn barrier. Daniel was up and moving around, only this time he wasn't smoking a cigarette. "The next twenty-four hours are crucial," he said.

"What do you mean?"

"You and I have just arrived here. We're a new part of the equation. If we stay too long, Okello will see us as another two hostages. We can't let him think that way."

"So what are we supposed to do?"

Daniel studied the barbed-wire entrance to the enclosure. Two young guards stood on the other side with their rifles. "Let me handle this, Nicky."

"Go ahead. Be my guest. Just don't do anything crazy."

About an hour after sunrise, Piramoi and two boys came into the enclosure with our bowls of millet and everyone lined up to get their share. When Daniel received his bowl he glanced at it contemptuously and tossed it on the ground. Piramoi looked shocked that anyone would throw away food, but before he could react Daniel passed through the open entrance and headed toward Okello's house.

"Come back!" shouted Piramoi. "You must stay here!" He ran after Daniel while a dozen seraphim came out of their huts, shouting and waving their rifles. Standing beside the entrance, I watched Daniel walk about twenty yards, then stop in front of a wall of seraphim. He was arguing with them, not shouting, but speaking calmly. Then he turned around and headed back to the enclosure as if he had just completed his exercise for the day. The hostages and I gathered around him when he returned.

"What did you tell them?"

"I asked for an interview."

"Okello won't talk to you," Michael Barrow said. "I've only seen him three times."

"I've met with Okello on two occasions," Joan said. "The first time we discussed food. The second time was when Livy was very sick from malaria. You can talk to the man. He's capable of a rational conversation. But you must never hesitate. He's very skilled at seeing other people's weaknesses."

"They're coming!" shouted Ray Stokes and we stood up as the seraphim pushed open the barbed-wire gate.

Piramoi and three small boys marched in, carrying rifles, and the archangel motioned to Daniel and me. "The Prophet wants to see you now."

We walked slowly across the camp to the house where Okello lived. I took out one of my cameras and glanced at Daniel. "Should I say anything?"

"It's not necessary. Try to get a photograph, Nicky. But don't make it a big production."

About fifty seraphim were sitting in the dirt around the brick house. Using this children's army, Okello had managed to terrorize half the country. I'd like to say that I felt sorry for them, but at that moment I was just scared. The children showed no emotion on their faces. They didn't smile or whisper or nudge each other.

We stopped about ten feet away from the house. Piramoi shouted something in his tribal language, then the Reverend Samuel Okello stepped through a doorway. I had been expecting someone bearded and wild looking, a sort of African John the Baptist, but Okello was a clean-shaven little man who wore a green Sudanese army uniform. His eyes were the most intimidating thing about him. When he first stared at me, I wanted to meet his eyes and challenge him, but there was such coldness there that I found myself looking down at my shoes.

"Good afternoon, Mr. Bettencourt." He handed the passports to one of the archangels, who returned them to Daniel and me. "Welcome, Mr. McFarland."

Daniel bowed his head slightly as a sign of respect. "It's an honor to be here, Reverend Okello."

"I knew you would come." Okello's voice was clear and precise, and his English had a slight American accent. I remembered Vickery telling us that the Prophet had studied at some Texas university. "I predicted this several months ago."

"It's been difficult to find you," Daniel said.

"No matter. You made the effort and God guided you here. I knew that once we captured these foreigners in the game park everything would change. Now the leaders of the world want to hear my message."

Okello didn't sound angry and I wondered if I should take a photograph. I glanced over at Daniel, but he ignored me.

"We've come a long way to interview you, Reverend Okello. Your words will be published everywhere."

"Are you the right messengers or were you sent by my enemies? There could be another reporter on his way. Someone who would report my words clearly."

"As far as I know we're the only journalists in the area. Isn't that right, Nicky?"

"Yeah. We're the only people who wanted to come here." I gripped the lens of my camera, but I didn't raise it up for a shot.

Daniel reached into his shirt pocket and took out a ballpoint pen and notebook. "Reverend Okello, you are obviously a great leader. But some people have criticized you for taking children away from their families. How would you answer them?"

"Their parents were wicked," Okello said. "I have become a new father and mother for these children."

Daniel asked another question and the Prophet launched into a long answer that included a half-dozen biblical quotations. Other journalists might have softened their questions, but Daniel didn't back down. Weren't you whipped by the police, Reverend Okello? Didn't you burn down a school? I wanted to shout at Daniel, That's enough, don't push it any further. But he kept going. I raised my camera a few times, but I didn't have the nerve to take a picture.

Finally, Daniel slipped the notebook back in his pocket. "We're honored to meet you, Reverend Okello. Now that we've heard your story, I can repeat your words to the rest of the world."

"Or you could corrupt my message. Distort it."

"That can't be true," Daniel said. "You predicted our arrival. Your power has brought us here."

A few of the children shifted around in the dirt and Okello glared at them. If he denied that we were the correct messengers, then it might undermine his own prophecy.

"That is correct. I did summon you here. Which is why I will allow you to leave. Speak to your government. Tell them that we will give up the hostages for food, medicine, and weapons. Contact us through the military outpost at Jubba."

"We need the boy to guide us back to Kosana."

Okello gestured with his right hand, indicating that Isaac was a trivial matter. "Take him."

"And we need to bring Joan Siebert as well. Her pulse is very weak. She might die if she stays here. If you release her, America and Britain will see this as the act of a powerful man. They'll be more inclined to start negotiating for a trade."

The Prophet considered this argument and everyone was quiet. Slowly, I raised the camera, but I didn't bring it up to my eye. Judging the angle by experience, I squeezed off two quick shots. The camera shutter sounded incredibly loud, but no one reacted. A bead of sweat trickled down my neck.

Okello nodded and flicked his hand. "She may go as well."

The Prophet returned to his hideaway and two seraphim came out with our water bottles and blankets. They had decided to keep Daniel's sat phone, but we weren't going to hang around and try to get it back. Back in the thorn enclosure, the hostages weren't happy that only Joan was leaving. "I think we should all stay together," Ray said. "We need to show some solidarity."

"This is going to help everybody," Daniel explained. "After Okello gives up the first person, he'll want to trade the rest of the group."

The hostages began to argue, but I thought up a distraction. I told Joseph Henning that he should write a letter to his family and we would pass it on to the German embassy in Kampala. The moment Joseph started writing, everyone else wanted the opportunity and then they argued about who would use my pen.

When all the notes were written, we left the enclosure with Joan and Isaac. A situation like this was a good time to take photographs. Everything is fluid, in motion, and no one concentrates on following the rules. I shot quickly. A desperate-looking girl. A half-naked little boy, clutching a rifle. And then we were out of the camp and hurrying down the trail. We followed Piramoi back to the mother tree. As we entered the dry riverbed, the archangel stood on a boulder watching us, like he wanted to come along. I figured that working for a murderous psychopath wasn't a job with a long-term future.

"Good journey," he said in English.

"Good journey to you."

Daniel walked with Joan while Isaac and I were a few steps behind. The boy kept looking around him. "Did you see the Prophet?" he asked.

"Yeah. He talked a lot."

"Are they going to kill me?"

"No. Everything's okay. We're going to go back to Kosana and see Dr. Cadell."

Isaac relaxed a little bit and Joan began to talk to him as if he had just wandered into her library back in Wisconsin. The boy didn't answer her, but she pretended they were having a conversation. Joan asked Isaac if he had ever seen a lion. "They're very beautiful animals. Don't you think?" she said. "But the male lions are so lazy. Their wives do most of the hunting."

As the day went on, Joan began to get weaker. She felt dizzy and had to stop every ten minutes. Finally we reached our old campsite and opened up a can of tuna. After eating, Joan went to sleep and the rest of us sat there, staring at the flames.

"Is Mrs. Joan going to die?" Isaac asked.

Surprised, I looked across the fire. "No, Isaac. She's going to be fine."

"But she's very sick."

"Joan is tired and she needs some decent food. When we get back to Kosana, Dr. Cadell will make her feel better."

A few minutes later Isaac went to sleep. Daniel was concealed within the shadows, but I caught a glimpse of his face when he leaned forward to toss some wood on the fire. He didn't look happy about getting the interview.

"Isaac is worried about Joan," he said. "I guess that's a good sign."

"She made an effort to talk to him today."

He stared at the fire for a few minutes. "I pushed it too far, Nicky. I wasn't thinking about what could happen."

The next day started badly. Even with sips of water and deep breathing, Joan couldn't walk five feet without getting dizzy. Daniel and I tried to bring her along in a fireman's carry, but I tripped on a root and almost fell. After an hour of slow progress Daniel told Joan and me to wait beside a boulder. He walked off into the bush with Isaac, then they came back with two saplings they had turned into poles. We made a stretcher with the blanket and our shoelaces and then continued toward Kosana.

Joan was in pain, but Daniel distracted her with questions. Where were you born? What did your parents do? As we maneuvered the stretcher around rocks and bushes, Joan told stories about her teenage years. In high school, she'd dated a boy named Gordon whose family owned three lumber mills. Joan's mother and her friends expected her to marry Gordon after he graduated from Princeton.

"Everyone liked Gordon," Joan said. "But he was never *serious* about anything. That year I was on the debate team and that's where I met Henry."

Henry's father owned a shoe store and his mother worked in the county clerk's office. Henry drove a grocery delivery truck after school, but he read three newspapers at the library and knew the capital of Bolivia. Joan and Henry debated against capital punishment and they won four competitions together. One morning Henry invited her to the Snow Ball, the school's big Christmas dance, and Joan accepted. She liked the fact that Gordon was jealous and her friends were horrified. Her mother announced that Joan had just thrown her life away.

A week before the dance Henry had an accident with the delivery truck and ended up in the hospital. Gordon appeared at Joan's house carrying a bouquet of roses, and in a moment of weakness she agreed to go with him to the Snow Ball.

We laid the stretcher down and rested. Isaac crouched beside Joan and listened to her story.

"It was a beautiful dance. The decoration committee had rented one of those mirrored balls and little flashes of light whirred across the walls. I was dancing with Gordon and he was talking about how this was the best car and that was the best golf club and if anyone didn't own the best, they were a fool. Right then I realized that Gordon was a nice boy, but that was all he was ever going to be—a boy pretending to be a man. So I said good-bye and asked one of the chaperones to drive me to the hospital. It was long past visiting hours, but I didn't care. Wearing my white dress, I swept down the hallway and started looking for Henry." Joan paused and drank some water.

"Was he all right?" Isaac asked.

"He was fine, Isaac. Just a few broken bones. Three years later we got married and we were very, very happy."

I WAS WORRIED that we'd miss the pathway from the riverbed to Kosana, but Isaac found it easily. Most of the Karamojong came out to meet us when we reached the camp. Richard and Billy had already flown back to Nairobi. Julia stood near the medical tent between Steve Ramsey and the two Irish nurses. She shook her head as if she couldn't believe that we had survived, then stepped forward and took Isaac's hand.

"Welcome back, Isaac. It's good to see you again."

"Dr. Cadell, this is Joan Siebert," said Daniel. "Why don't you take a look at her and make sure that she's all right."

Daniel and I took turns having a bucket shower. When we dropped by the medical tent, the two Irish nurses were there with Joan. They had given her a sponge bath and she was lying on a cot with an IV tube in her arm. Isaac sat beside her, eating a bowl of oatmeal.

"Tell them I'm all right, Daniel. They're treating me like a feeble old lady."

Fiona came over and checked Joan's pulse. "You're not feeble, Mrs. Siebert. But you do need to rest. Dr. Cadell says that your heartbeat is irregular and you've got very low blood pressure."

"The only thing I really needed was a bath. Isaac had a bath, too."

The boy nodded and raised his spoon. "They gave me soap."

"Lavender soap. It smells quite wonderful."

THAT NIGHT WE HAD a celebration in the staff tent. Julia had decided to call me Nicky, but Daniel was still Mr. McFarland. She kept glancing at Daniel, waiting for him to talk about his triumph. Instead he sat quietly at the table and ate dinner. I was the one who told everybody about Samuel Okello and the hostages. Fiona touched my hand twice and said that I was intrepid. After we had eaten some freeze-dried sponge cake, the nurses and Ramsey went back to their tents.

Julia sat down next to Daniel and began to question him about Isaac. Did he talk about his family? Were any of his friends at Okello's camp? If I had written everything they said it would have sounded like a normal conversation. But there was an intensity between them, an awkwardness in their exchanges. Both of them had the power to make the other one nervous. I sat between them, feeling like I was in one of those mad scientist movies with a charge crackling through the air.

When they had finished talking about Isaac, Julia went around the tent, picking up dirty plates and silverware. I was about to say good night when she put down the dishes and approached Daniel.

"Mr. McFarland, I'd like to apologize to you."

"That's not necessary."

"Joan Siebert might have died if you hadn't brought her here. She was severely dehydrated. And Isaac is talking. He still hasn't recovered from his trauma, but he's much improved."

I had the feeling that Julia didn't apologize very often. She waited, expecting Daniel to accept her concession, but he wasn't in a gracious mood.

"It was wrong to risk Isaac's life," Daniel said. "I made a mistake using him as a guide."

"That's true, Mr. McFarland. But the result was positive."

Daniel stood up and slipped his notebook into his pocket. "Thank you for the dinner and all your help. I think you're doing a great job here."

He walked out of the tent, disappearing into the darkness. Julia looked irritated. "Mr. McFarland can be a very annoying person," she said.

"You're right about that."

"Is he still angry with me? Is that it?"

"I don't think so."

"How does he act back home? Is he always this rude?"

"He doesn't seem to have much of a personal life."

"Does he have any friends, Nicky? Are you his friend?"

"Not really. But we're working on it."

I TOOK A LANTERN back to our tent, loaded my cameras, and cleaned the lenses. Daniel showed up an hour later and sat on his cot. We looked at each other and smiled. Almost anyone can climb a mountain. The trick is to climb down.

"I talked to Paul Rosen on the radio," Daniel said. "He's flying to Entebbe tomorrow. There are four seats in the plane so he can only take Tobias, Joan, and one other person. It's your choice, Nicky. We can stay together or flip a coin to see who leaves. Whoever goes down first will hire a charter plane and send it back to Kosana."

"I've done my part of the job," I said. "You've got to write the article and send it out from Kampala. I'll give you the disc from the digital camera and you can transmit those photos. We've met Samuel Okello and freed a hostage. It's news."

"Are you sure you want to stay here?"

"I'll take more pictures and annoy everyone."

PAUL FLEW IN the next morning and the staff walked out to the airstrip. Joan embraced Isaac and said that she would send him some books from America. I pulled the disc out of my pocket and gave it to Daniel.

"I don't know if they're any good."

"You got a picture of Okello. That's the main thing." Daniel smiled and touched my arm. "We should do this again."

"No more walking," I said. "That's my only condition."

The plane raised a cloud of dust as it taxied away from us, then took off and disappeared into the blue. Julia looked relieved that Daniel was gone. "Well, that's over," she said in a proper British manner. "Back to work."

I spent most of the day in my tent, drinking water, sleeping a little and reading some old magazines I borrowed from Ramsey. An hour before nightfall, Julia came in looking worried.

"I just got off the radio. Paul's airplane is eight hours overdue at Entebbe. No one seems to know where they are."

"They crashed?"

"It doesn't look good, Nicky."

I followed her outside. One of Hand-to-Hand's computer camps had been set up near my tent; it buzzed and clicked and panned back and forth on its little steel tower.

I stood beside the tent with my hands in my pockets while Julia looked up at the sky. And the world expanded around us, past the tents and the grass to a dark horizon.

6 THE CONVENT

I stayed near the camp radio for the next twenty-four hours and listened to the news about the search for the missing travelers. Several pilots retraced the route from Entebbe to Kosana, but the Cessna had completely disappeared. In the morning an airplane flew over the refugee camp and I ran out of my tent, half expecting to see Paul waving from the cockpit window. Instead, it was Erik Viltner.

I walked over to the runway while he taxied to the camp. When Erik climbed out of the cockpit, he saw me and frowned.

"Your friend was with Paul?"

"That's right. Has there been any news?"

"Nothing." Erik glanced up at the sky as if a neon message would suddenly appear in the clouds.

"What are their chances?"

"They have the plane and the radio. Even if Paul was forced to make a landing, his radio should still operate."

"Unless it was a bad crash."

Erik touched one of his elephant hair bracelets for luck. "Paul was a very good pilot."

I returned to the camp and found Julia in one of the medical tents. She had just delivered a baby and Fiona was washing it off in a basin.

"I'm flying back to Entebbe airport. Erik wants me to pick out the landmarks we passed on the way up."

"Good luck. Maybe they just had mechanical problems and had to make an emergency landing. Paul could do anything with that plane." Julia tried to look optimistic, then gave up and pulled off her surgical gloves. "Of course, we probably should have heard from them by now."

"Have you told Paul's girlfriend?"

"Ellen's crying in her tent. She won't come out. If there really was a crash and Paul is dead, I might have to send her home." Turning away from me, Julia tossed the gloves into a pail and began to scrub her hands. "When I began working for Médecins Sans Frontières, a French doctor told me that you should never like anyone you meet at a relief camp. You should never admire another person or allow yourself to care. Because chances are your new friend will die or go away or you'll lose them somehow."

A lock of hair fell across Julia's forehead and she pushed it away. I could have told her the truth at that moment—that I was worried about Daniel—but pride held me back. I already knew that you weren't supposed to care about the people you met in relief camps or anywhere else. I saw myself as a master of that particular discipline while most people were still learning the trade.

"Maybe they're right."

"Yes. It's possible." Julia turned away from me and picked up a basin filled with surgical instruments. "Who's next?" she asked Fiona.

"The twelve-year-old girl with shrapnel in her leg."

"Yes. Of course. Did you check her this morning?"

"She's hypotensive. Febrile. Looks shocky."

"Did you talk to her? Was John there to translate?"

"She said she doesn't want to lose her leg. If she has no leg, she's useless and no one will ever marry her."

Julia hesitated for a moment, then poured off the disinfectant. She picked up two scalpels, a steel probe and tweezers, and carefully placed them on a sterile bandage. I knew what she was thinking—save the life in front of you, concentrate on the routine. "Well then, we'll have to try very hard."

Isaac was waiting for me when I left the medical tent. He looked happy and I figured that no one had told him about the crash. Daniel's watch was still hanging from the twine around his neck.

"Are you going away in the plane?"

"That's right."

"Will you see Mrs. Joan and Mr. Daniel?"

I should have been ready for a question like that, but I felt like I'd just been punched in the chest.

"I'm going to see them in Kampala. We planned to have dinner together." I slipped on my sunglasses so that the boy couldn't see my eyes. "You're a good friend, Isaac. You guided us all the way."

ON THE WAY BACK to Entebbe, Viltner pointed at landmarks and shouted questions: Do you remember this lake? What about that mountain? I looked out the window at the countryside and saw nothing but dry grass and an occasional village. It seemed as if the Cessna had been absorbed by the landscape. When we reached the airport two bush pilots were waiting there to ask questions. They told me that Paul Rosen's father was flying in from New York on a chartered jet.

After spending the night in a small hotel near Lake Victoria, I decided to return to London. Everyone in the Cessna was probably dead and I didn't want to be there when they found the bodies. I took a flight to Kenya and started drinking little bottles of vodka the moment the plane left Nairobi. I hadn't known Daniel very long and I was surprised how much his death bothered me. It was only when we were flying over North Africa that I admitted the truth to myself: I admired Daniel and hoped we could become friends. I hadn't made many friends since I'd left Los Angeles. It was easier if I just did my job.

I remained in my seat when we reached Heathrow airport and was the last person to get off the plane. Carter Howard and John Scofield, the *Washington Post*'s London bureau chief, were there waiting for me and the first thing Scofield said was, "Do you have pictures?"

They drove me into London. Streetlights. Taxis. A blond girl on a billboard telling me that "paradise is a plane ticket away." When we reached the office Ann Weinstein took my film and developed the photographs from my Nikon. I gave the story to Scofield, then did a phone interview with a *Newsweek* reporter in New York.

"Is that all the film you have?" asked Carter. "You only took two rolls?"

"There's another roll in the camera, but that's for the *Telegraph*."

"But you don't work for them."

"Daniel does. He's on contract."

Scofield turned to Carter Howard and rolled his eyes slightly. Go ahead, he seemed to be saying. Tell your employee that we want an exclusive.

"Don't give me any crap about this," I said. "Daniel's my friend and I'm going to file his story."

I left Park Street an hour later and took the underground to the *Telegraph* offices. Daniel's young foreign editor was on vacation, but I found an experienced rewrite man named Stubbs. He sent my film downstairs, then interviewed me and turned my mumbled replies into a coherent article. When that was done we went to a pub and Stubbs ordered two pints of bitter.

"This is all quite unfortunate," he said.

I shrugged my shoulders but didn't speak. Quite unfortunate.

"Mr. McFarland was the real thing. He always focused on the facts, the little details. He understood the beauty of a simple declarative sentence."

The clerk at the Ruskin Hotel gave me the noisy room near the second-floor toilet, but I flopped on the bed and slept for a long time. When I woke up, I bought copies of the *Telegraph* and the *Washington Post*. Both papers gave a front-page position to the hostage story with a sidebar about the lost Cessna. I ate four bags of potato chips and drank four whiskeys at a pub, then went back to bed.

The phone began ringing, but I felt like I was swimming through an underwater tunnel, trying to find a patch of light that would lead me to the surface. I breathed deeply, opened my eyes, and then it was morning again and the phone near the bed was still ringing.

"Yeah?"

I heard Ann Weinstein's voice, bright and cheery. "He's alive."

"What?"

"Daniel's alive. It's a miracle, really. Everyone else died in the crash."

I pulled on some clothes and hurried down to the *Newsweek* offices. All they could tell me was that Daniel was at a rural clinic and that Paul's father was flying north in a private plane. Throughout the day there were random particles of news, mostly from the World Wildlife Fund office in Kampala. We learned that Paul Rosen had discovered a group of Sudanese soldiers butchering an elephant and when he had swooped down to investigate, the plane had been hit with a rocket-propelled grenade. Daniel had broken his forearm and several ribs but was in fairly good condition. He had been flown back to Entebbe and taken to Nsambya Hospital in Kampala.

All of us sat in Carter's office waiting for Daniel's phone call. We expected him to sound tired and sad, perhaps a little fragile, but ready to tell us his story. When he didn't call by eight o'clock London time, Ann contacted Nsambya Hospital. A nurse told her that Mr. McFarland had paid his bill and left the hospital.

During the next twelve hours, Daniel had gained access to a computer and a phone. He wrote one article about his interview with Samuel Okello and another about the Sudanese and the plane crash. All the publications he had contacted before leaving Rome were sent both articles. Daniel didn't attach a personal note or any other indication that he had recovered from the accident. John Scofield contacted the New York desk, then called a German editor at the *Frankfurter Allgemeine*. No one had actually spoken to Daniel. After completing his job in a professional manner, he stopped sending messages.

It was a slow news week and Daniel's articles got a fair amount of attention. In America, the media focused on Paul Rosen's death. In

Europe, the German government threatened to shut off aid to the Sudan unless they allowed the United Nations to conduct an independent investigation.

If Daniel had been in New York or London during this period, he could have easily become a fifteen-minute celebrity. Instead, he stayed hidden and the media forgot about him. Magazine articles about Paul Rosen began to appear a few weeks later. I read about his wealthy family, prep school, Yale, and an attempt to play professional tennis. Paul had gone through a nightclub period in New York before a trip to Africa had inspired him to work for wildlife conservation. The articles reprinted one of my photographs of Paul and Tobias standing beside the Cessna.

The American embassy in Kampala said that as far as it knew Daniel McFarland had left Uganda. I assumed that he had returned to Rome because someone had gone to the Stampa Estera and picked up his mail. Everyone sent Daniel letters, faxes, and e-mail, but he didn't respond. His Italian cell phone had been switched off and the answering machine on his desk at the Stampa Estera was disconnected. It began to feel like he had died along with Paul and the others.

I sent faxes and e-mail to the U.S. State Department, but no one there wanted to negotiate with the Lord's Righteous Army. Finally I called the German embassy in Khartoum and talked to the commercial attaché. Using his contacts with the Sudanese military, he'd made a deal with Samuel Okello and exchanged two truckloads of food and medicine for the hostages. The moment they were set free, the American secretary of state held a news conference and tried to take all the credit.

The people who couldn't contact Daniel called me. It was painful to talk to Paul Rosen's mother and Joan's eldest daughter. They wanted to speak to the person who had spent the last few minutes with their relatives. Was Paul happy? Did he mention his family? What did Joan say before the plane crashed? I mumbled my condolences and promised that I'd pass on their questions to Daniel.

Even Richard Seaton called, twice. He wanted to talk to Daniel and was curious about why he had disappeared. "Does he need medical care, Nicky?"

"I don't know. Probably."

"How about a psychiatrist? I know a good one here in London."

"If I see Daniel, I'll mention it to him."

"If you know that he's actually in Rome, call Billy and he'll make all the arrangements. You can fly down there in my jet."

CARTER OFFERED ME an easy assignment—taking photos at a war crimes trial at The Hague—but I turned him down. I had to know if Daniel was all right so I took a short vacation and flew down to Rome. I left messages on Daniel's answering machine at Bracciano, but he didn't return my calls. Not knowing what else to do, I went to the Vatican and stared at the *Pietà* with the other tourists. Later that afternoon I dropped by the Contessa's apartment on the Piazza Navona.

I had to wait in the lobby for about twenty minutes until the doorman let me go up. Wearing a silk bathrobe, the Contessa stood in the doorway and blew cigarette smoke in my direction.

"I don't know where Daniel is, Mr. Bettencourt. He hasn't called."

"He was in a plane crash in Africa. Three people died."

"Yes. Some British friends of mine read about it in the newspaper. Perhaps Daniel is alive. Perhaps he is dead. When selfish people disappear, no one really cares."

I looked down at her red toenails and little green sandals. "If you see Daniel would you tell him that I'm staying at the Hotel Centro."

"I'm not going to hear from him and you won't either. Don't waste your time, Mr. Bettencourt. Go home, if you have one."

Eating dinner that night, I decided to rent a car and go out to Bracciano. I didn't know exactly where Daniel's farmhouse was, but I thought I'd drive around and ask questions. When I got back to my hotel, a phone message was waiting for me: *Domani. A mezzogiorno. Convento Santa Maria dei Sette Dolori.*

"Who called? Was it Mr. McFarland?"

"It was a man, *dottore*. But he did not say his name."

"And I'm supposed to meet him tomorrow afternoon at a convent?"

"*Sí, dottore*. It's in the Trastevere district."

"What's a man doing at a convent?"

The desk clerk gave me a big smile. "I don't know. But he speaks very good Italian."

After a bad night's sleep I drank a double espresso with four lumps of sugar and crossed the Tiber at the Ponte Sisto. It was early autumn and the rains wouldn't arrive for another month or so. The Tiber had a muddy brown color and the leaves on the sycamore trees were curling up at the edges like thin pieces of paper. Strolling through the narrow streets of Trastevere, I found the tailor's shop that had transformed me, for one night, into an English gentleman. The same dummy was in the window with the same dusty bolt of cloth.

I walked west on the Via Garibaldi, a narrow cobblestone road that curved up the slope of the Janiculum Hill. On the left side of the road there was a small courtyard filled with Fiats and a few scooters. The church of Santa Maria dei Sette Dolori looked like a shabby Gothic castle with bars on the lower windows. I could see that plaster had once covered the brick facade, but most of it had fallen off hundreds of years ago.

The building had three marble archways framing wooden doors. Two of the doors led into a shadowy church. The third door was about twenty feet away and I assumed that it led to the convent. I knocked once, twice, then waited for several minutes. Finally the door creaked open a few inches and I encountered an elderly nun the size of an eight-year-old child.

The nun saw the camera hanging from my shoulder and assumed that I was a tourist. "*No ingresso,*" she said firmly and tried to shut the door on my foot.

"I received a message at my hotel. A man said—"

"*No ingresso!*"

"I'm looking for Daniel McFarland."

"Ahhh. Signor Daniel." The little nun smiled as if I had said some magic words. She opened the door completely and gestured for me to come in.

I followed her into a covered walkway surrounding a garden. All the doors were open and I could see into the nuns' rooms as we passed them: a narrow bed set in the wall of the cubicle. A writing desk. A crucifix. A single chair. My guide glanced back to make sure that I was following her, then led me through the colonnade and into the garden. Generations of visiting relatives had left potted plants and flowers that had been placed in the courtyard's moist soil. It was a jungle of mismatched plants, the kind of place where marigolds and tomato vines fought a murky battle with calla lilies.

I smelled Daniel's cigarette first. The little nun led me around a ficus bush and we found him sitting on a marble bench. Daniel had cut off the long brown hair that had looked so stylish at the Contessa's party. His left forearm was in a cast and there were stitched-up cuts on his face. He looked tired and shaky, like a soldier who had survived an artillery barrage. After ten years of covering wars without a single injury, it seemed as if all the pain and confusion of those experiences had finally touched him.

Daniel stood and shook my hand. "Hello, Nicky. Good to see you again."

"What the hell are you doing in a convent?"

"Smoking." He sat down on the bench and I joined him. "Actually, I've been living here for the last two weeks. I don't like Bracciano these days. It's too exposed and there's too much sunlight."

"So you just knocked on the door and the nuns let you move in?"

"When I came back from Africa I made a contribution to the order's hospice. The mother superior asked if I wanted the nuns to pray for me, but I told her I'd rather stay here for a few weeks. It's worked out all right. They've gotten used to having me around."

Some leaves rustled and the nun reappeared with a white saucer. She placed it on the bench, smiled again, and left us alone. Daniel already had a saucer filled with ash. The nuns probably believed that all American males spent their recreational time smoking cigarettes and staring at tropical plants.

"You all right?" I asked.

"Not really."

"Want to tell me what happened?"

"I don't know if it would make any sense, Nicky. I'm a little confused right now."

I didn't say anything and we both sat quietly on the bench. There's one good thing about working in the so-called Third World—it teaches you how to wait. I had once spent several weeks in Kinshasa, waiting to take a ferry up the Congo River. First the boat's engine exploded and then our captain was arrested for stealing a truckload of flashlight batteries. Every two or three days there was a new disaster, but the third-class passengers held on to their little patches of the deck. We weren't going to leave Kinshasa, I thought. Not today or even next year. Then, one bright morning, we cast off lines and headed up the river.

It was getting dark in the convent garden. Pots rattled in the kitchen as the nuns prepared supper. I wondered if we were going to sit there forever and decided that the convent wasn't a bad place to spend eternity. All I needed was a cushion for the bench, some decent caviar on Melba toast with grated onion and a squeeze of lemon. Maybe a bottle of chilled white wine.

"All of us have different assumptions about the world," Daniel said. "They might be real or they might be illusions, but it doesn't really matter. We believe in these stories, these little fantasies. They help us deal with our jobs and our personal desires. But sometimes, you're caught up in a storm and then you see everything in a new way. What are you supposed to do, Nicky? How do you get normal again?"

"Don't worry about that. Just talk to me."

7 BOMA MISSION

When Daniel climbed into the Cessna with Joan Siebert, he assumed that they were going to fly south to Entebbe. Paul Rosen had a different plan. He still wanted to prove that Sudanese soldiers were crossing the border and killing animals in Kidepo park.

"I'm going to fly over the park one more time," he said. "It won't take long."

"And what if we don't see anything?" asked Daniel.

"Then I've got to coax another reporter to come up here."

Daniel thought that Joan would be upset about the detour, but it didn't appear to bother her. As they flew west over the park, Tobias kept pointing out different species of vultures and hawks that were riding the thermals. Joan borrowed some paper from Daniel so she could write down their names.

"I still love Africa," she told Daniel. "It's important that you put that in your article. There's nothing wrong with looking at chickadees and robins back home, but they can't compare to a black-winged vulture."

A week earlier three adult elephants and a calf had wandered out of the park. They were still protected by Ugandan law, but Paul was worried about them. He passed low over a patch of thorn trees and found the water hole that the elephants had been using. Within a few minutes, they saw the calf alone, running across the savanna. The calf's trunk was extended and he looked confused.

"There!" Paul pointed west to some black specks floating in the air. They flew closer and the specks became vultures circling over a kill. Paul went lower and Daniel saw five men wearing tan uniforms standing next to an army truck. They were butchering three adult elephants with axes and knives. The area around the carcasses was dark where blood had been absorbed into the ground.

"Do you see that?" Paul shouted. "You're a witness!" He banked the plane hard and turned it around while Tobias fumbled in his backpack for a camera. As they passed over the soldiers a second time, several men ran to the truck to get their weapons.

They took another hard turn in the sky. Now Tobias was ready with the camera. The Sudanese began firing as they approached, but Daniel assumed that the plane was flying too high to be damaged. There was a sudden booming sound and the entire plane began to shake and rattle like a freight car that had gone off the tracks.

"Something hit the propeller!" Paul shouted. "I'm cutting power!"

He turned off the engine. The shaking stopped, but the plane began to glide downward. It was very quiet. Only a few seconds had passed, but time seemed to stretch like a bowstring pulled by an archer. Paul switched off the fuel, the magnetos, the lights, and the radio. "Prop the doors open," he told them.

Tobias opened the door on his side, removed his shoe, and forced it into the crack. Daniel opened the other door and wedged a sweatshirt against the hinge. He glanced back out the window and saw that they had dropped lower. Paul aimed the Cessna toward a flat patch of ground near a dry river.

"Seat belts on. Brace for a landing."

Daniel glanced over at Joan Siebert. Her initial panic and surprise had disappeared. She seemed to realize that they were going to die. Daniel remembered how much she had wanted to see her grandchildren again, but she nodded slightly as if to tell him, Yes, we'll be all right. He looked out the window one last time and saw that boulders were scattered across the landing site.

"It's no good," Paul said. Daniel didn't know if he was talking to himself or Tobias. "No . . ."

They landed hard, the plane skittering across the ground. The left wing hit a boulder and was ripped away. There was a grinding sound and the Cessna flipped tail first up into the air.

DANIEL SNUBBED OUT his cigarette and stopped talking. We sat there for about ten minutes watching a bird flutter around the garden. Church bells rang in the distance and another set of bells answered.

"At the last moment, right before we crashed, I reached out and took Joan's hand. When the plane flipped over I could feel her fingers being pulled away from me. And then something happened, Nicky. Something I still don't understand. I've spent most of my life writing about various incidents, summing it all up in a few words. But it's difficult to describe this experience. It was—it was overwhelming."

Daniel shook his head and looked away. "When I was a little boy my mother and I went out shopping and it started to snow. We were waiting for something, a bus or a taxi, and it was getting cold, so my mother drew me into her long wool overcoat and sheltered me there. It was warm and safe inside the fabric, but I could look out at the snow drifting down onto the parked cars and the sidewalk. That's sort of how it felt after the crash, but it was much more powerful. I was held and protected but still part of the world."

WHEN DANIEL WOKE UP, his left arm was in a splint and his chest hurt. He heard a creaking sound, voices, then he opened his eyes.

A soft whiteness surrounded him. It took him a few seconds to realize that he was naked and lying beneath a sheet on a narrow bed, protected by a mosquito net. He moved his legs slightly. The net was pulled away and a thin Ugandan woman looked down at him. Daniel saw that he was in a small room with white walls. Sunlight glowed through a narrow window. Daniel wanted the woman to say something, tell him that he was all right, but she left him alone. He closed his eyes for a while, and when he opened them again the woman had returned with a Ugandan priest.

The priest was a short man in his sixties. He wore old-fashioned horn-rimmed glasses, very large, that magnified his dark brown eyes. The priest stared at Daniel, not as a challenge, but as a means of communication.

"Good afternoon, Mr. McFarland. Can you hear me?" The priest spoke carefully, enunciating each word, as if English wasn't his day-to-day language.

Daniel moved his lips, but no sound came out. The priest nodded to the thin young woman and she sat down on the bed holding a plastic bottle attached to a tube. She slipped the tube through Daniel's lips and squirted a small amount of water into his mouth. "Again," the priest said, and she repeated the procedure two more times.

"I'm Father Timothy Lokali," the priest said. "You're at Boma Mission, about a hundred miles from the town of Kitgum."

"Where are the others?"

"Can you swallow a pill, Mr. McFarland? We have three sleeping pills left in the dispensary. I'll give you one, if you think you can get it down."

He handed a red pill to the woman. Before Daniel could protest, she slipped it into his mouth and gave him another squirt of water. "Thank you, Ann," the priest said and the young woman left the room.

"You've broken your arm and a few ribs. I'd like to see if there's more serious damage." The priest stood near the end of the bed. "Can you wiggle your toes, Mr. McFarland? Good. Now push your foot up slightly against my hand. Excellent. Can you move that arm? I've put a splint on it, but it will require a proper cast. We're out of plaster around here. It's near the end of the month so we're nearly out of everything."

Father Lokali removed a stethoscope from a side pocket in his cassock, listened to Daniel's heart, and took his pulse. The red pill was dulling the pain and making Daniel feel sleepy, but he tried to keep his eyes open.

"What happened to the others? Where's Paul Rosen?"

"The three other people in the plane are dead. Tomorrow I'll take some men over to the crash site. We'll place the bodies in coffins and bring them back here."

"The Sudanese army shot them down. I need to call people in Kampala."

"There's no telephone here, Mr. McFarland. I've sent a boy to the district police headquarters in Kitgum. Right now, you need to rest."

Daniel wanted to stay awake, but his eyes kept closing. "It's not fair. They shouldn't have died."

"We've prayed for them."

"It's not fair."

Daniel slept for fourteen hours. When he woke up, it was morning and a gasoline engine was running somewhere outside the building. He forced himself to push back the mosquito net and sit up. A plastic bottle filled with water was on the floor and he sat on the edge of the bed, taking little sips and trying to readjust to the world. The bed was a crude construction of rope and cast-off pieces of wood with a thin cotton pallet. There was a clay chamber pot near the wall. Daniel stood up, felt dizzy, and sat back down immediately. Take it easy, he told himself. Just take it easy. He used the chamber pot and shuffled back to the bed as the thin woman entered the room.

"Good morning, Mr. McFarland. I'm Ann Gawara. Do you remember our conversation yesterday?"

"A little bit. I'm at a mission."

"Boma Mission, near Kitgum."

"There was a priest."

"Father Lokali. He left this morning and went down to the crash site." She placed Daniel's clothes on the bed and he covered himself with the sheet. "We've washed your clothes. Here's your wallet and passport. Your shirt was ripped so badly that we've given you another."

"Thank you."

"I've brought you some *ugali*—cornmeal porridge. Shall I feed you or can you feed yourself?"

"Let me try it on my own."

She gave him the bowl and left the room. The porridge had a bland taste and gritty texture, but eating it made him feel stronger. Ann returned a few minutes later with a cup of milk. It was still warm from the cow.

"Who runs this mission?"

"Father Lokali."

"Are you trying to convert people?".

She smiled for the first time. "Oh, no. None of that. Boma Mission is for people who have AIDS. They come here from all over the country."

"Why are you in the middle of nowhere?"

"Father Lokali started the mission in Kampala and the church gave him this place. It used to be a seminary, then it was abandoned. We have fields here to grow food and grass for the cattle. Once a month, our truck goes down to Kampala to get supplies and more patients."

"Are you a nurse?"

"No, I'm a patient. I have AIDS, too."

Daniel had always been confident in his ability to come up with a serious comment or a witty remark; it was an occupational skill. But that morning, sitting in the little room with the bowl on his lap, he didn't know what to say.

"Are you strong enough to walk?" Ann asked. "Perhaps I could show you around."

She helped Daniel get dressed. He placed his good arm on her shoulder and they walked outside. Boma Mission was a collection of about twenty dormitories constructed with bricks made from the local clay. Each building was painted a different color. Purple. Scarlet. Lime green. Ann mentioned that a Muslim businessman donated paint to the mission and that Father Lokali thought different colors were more cheerful.

About two hundred men, women, and children milled around the dirt courtyard while a portable water pump filled a steel barrel. Everyone stared at him, and a few men bowed their heads and nodded sympathetically. It was obvious that the plane crash had been a major topic of conversation.

AIDS patients were everywhere, skinny and fragile looking. Several had rashes or boils on their faces and arms. It surprised Daniel to see so many children. As they walked through the courtyard, Ann explained that many of the people who came to Boma Mission had already lost other family members to the disease and they wanted their children to be in a safe place when they died.

"And what do you do with them?"

"If they have surviving relatives and they want to return to their village, our truck takes them home. Most of them stay here. We have a little school. The younger children help the patients and the older ones take care of our herd. One of the cattle boys saw the plane crash and found you."

A tall man was distributing nystatin tablets for throat infections, but Boma Mission lacked any kind of AIDS medicine. Father Lokali had taken a two-year nursing course in Italy and could handle basic medical problems. A local doctor with a motorcycle visited the mission every Wednesday.

"We have some support from the United Nations and the Canadian embassy. The Canadians give us medical supplies, but we usually run out near the end of every month."

Daniel started to feel woozy in the hot sun so he returned to the room and went back to sleep. When he woke up, it was late in the afternoon. Two little boys stood in the doorway, watching him as if he was a strange animal. Father Lokali entered the room a few minutes later and sat down on the chair.

"I'm afraid we were unable to retrieve your belongings from the airplane. Everything caught fire after the crash. The three bodies were badly burned, but we placed them in coffins and brought them here."

"I think we got hit by a rocket-propelled grenade. It destroyed the propeller."

"And you're a journalist? I looked at the visa form folded inside your passport."

Daniel told the priest what had happened. He got through the story fairly well, but when he described the crash he started crying. Father Lokali sat beside Daniel and put an arm around his shoulder. Finally, Daniel got control of himself and pulled away.

"I'm sorry," Daniel said.

"For what?"

"I don't usually cry."

"How unfortunate for you." Father Lokali stood up. "One of our patients is about to die. I'll have to leave here in a little while."

Daniel tried to talk about the plane crash but became frustrated when he couldn't explain what had happened to him. "Why was I the one who survived?" he asked. "What's the explanation?"

He waited, expecting some kind of pronouncement, but Father Lokali didn't answer him.

"So? What do you think?"

"I think you'll have to figure this out on your own."

"You probably believe that it's all because of God."

"We are his creation, but I don't expect others to feel the same way."

"I don't believe in God or religion. The whole thing doesn't make sense."

"Before I became a priest, I was in love with my cousin, Hannah. And, of course, I loved my parents and they loved me." Father Lokali stood in the middle of the room and smiled. "To love another—simply, purely—gives us a small glimpse of what it means to love God. We make up reasons in our mind to love a person. We say, 'She's very pretty' or 'He speaks well.' But it's all nonsense, of course. There's an impulse within us, a movement in our heart, that pushes away the questions and simply wants to be. To believe in God is to become a lover."

A little boy entered the room and spoke briefly. Father Lokali nodded and the child went away. "It's time for me to go."

"May I come with you?"

"If you wish."

Daniel and the priest walked across the dirt courtyard, where women were serving beef stew and cassava. Several children were holding two or three bowls in their arms. They carried the food back to family members who were too weak to line up for supper.

"How many of these children have AIDS?"

"I can't tell you exactly. Probably about a third of them."

"And they'll die in a few years?"

Father Lokali stopped near a dormitory that was painted sunflower yellow. "Yes, they're all going to die. Unless an inexpensive cure is discovered and someone pays to have it brought to Uganda."

"How are you able to believe in God?"

Father Lokali smiled. "How are you able not to?"

"If God exists, then why does he let all these people suffer?"

"Ahhh yes, the pain-and-misery question. A healthy, white American is going to tell me how terrible life is."

"You can't deny it."

"I know all about misery, Mr. McFarland. I'm an expert on the subject. For example, there is a horrible rumor in this country that you can get rid of AIDS by sleeping with a virgin. Some of these little girls were raped and infected when they were seven or eight years old. And that's just one particular evil. Poverty and sickness is everywhere. I see it every day. And yet, even in the worst situation, when there is no reason to care for anyone but oneself, I have encountered love and faith and sacrifice. Why waste your time trying to prove, once again, that the world is a dangerous place? Of course life is dangerous and cruel. A more interesting question is, Why does compassion always assert itself? Why does it always survive?"

They entered the yellow building, a long, narrow room divided into four sections with blankets hanging from ropes. A young woman lay unconscious on a straw mat in the northern corner of the room. There was an ugly rash on her neck, and her body was so bony and slight that she reminded Daniel of the marble skeletons placed on some of the Renaissance tombs in Rome.

Ann squatted beside the patient and waved a palm-leaf fan to keep the flies away. When she saw Father Lokali, she went over to a shelf and picked up a plastic box. She took out a purple cotton stole with crosses embroidered on the ends and draped it around the priest's neck. Father Lokali opened a small cylinder of holy oil and knelt beside the young woman. He dabbed the oil on her forehead and prayed, then anointed her hands and prayed again.

When Lokali was finished, he leaned over the woman, almost like a lover, and whispered something in her ear. The woman's eyelids fluttered open and she gazed up at the ceiling. Her pupils were black and very large, as if she had just stepped out of a dark room. Her eyelids closed again. Lokali whispered a third prayer. A few minutes later, the woman's body relaxed and seemed to grow heavier. Daniel could see it become an empty vessel, no longer filled with life.

Father Lokali stood up and handed the stole to Ann. While he visited the other patients in the dormitory, Daniel went outside. The sun had set ten minutes ago, but the sky was filled with light. Strips of pink and orange glowed on the horizon, and every tree seemed like a distinct creation.

Father Lokali left the dormitory and approached him. "Her name was Mary Bukoba. She worked as a prostitute in Masindi. A very hard life. When she first came here, she taught the children a funny song about a man who got drunk and married a crocodile. I can still hear some of them singing it when they walk around the mission."

"How can you stay here? Don't you get tired?"

Father Lokali ignored the question. "You're a lucky man, Mr. McFarland. It's movie night. We only do this once a week."

They returned to the dirt courtyard as it began to get darker. Thousands of stars appeared in the sky and a three-quarter moon glowed brightly above them. While the patients and their families set up benches and chairs in the courtyard, Father Lokali explained that the Canadian embassy had given the mission an old television and a VCR. During the last few years, they had acquired three videos: *The Little Mermaid,* a Hong Kong martial arts film called *Fists of Fury,* and a British instructional tape, *Training Your Dog.*

"*Training Your Dog* is the favorite by far," said Father Lokali. "That's tonight's movie."

The weakest patients were placed on straw mats and someone would sit behind them, holding the patients' upper bodies in their laps. Other patients used rattan chairs or sat on the benches. Daniel squeezed himself onto the bench closest to the television, wondering how they were going to run the gear without electricity.

When everyone was settled, a young woman, a man in his thirties, and a fourteen-year-old boy walked into the courtyard carrying a bicycle attached to a small power generator. Everyone applauded after they connected the generator to the television and the VCR, and the boy made a mocking bow.

The young woman was the strongest and healthiest person at the mission. She had broad shoulders and an enormous head of hair. It was her job to power the bike, creating enough electricity to run the television. She climbed onto the seat, hitched up her tight skirt, and began to pedal furiously.

The video played without sound. First you met seven dog owners and their pets at what looked like a British community center. The trainer, a formidable-looking woman who wore gray tweed, taught the dogs basic commands: heel, walk, run, stay. Periodically the camera would cut to one of the owners' houses where the trainer would solve different problems with their pet.

The man in his thirties spoke English and provided the voices for the trainer and the owners. He had decided that the trainer talked like a crazed drill sergeant and all the owners were idiots. The fourteen-year-old boy, who had the cocky smile of a class clown, had come up with seven different voices for the dogs. Each dog seemed to be motivated by one of the deadly sins, such as sloth, gluttony, and lust.

Daniel had watched famous comedians at nightclubs and in the movies, but he had never seen anything funnier than the two performers at Boma Mission. Many of their routines had evolved over the last year and Daniel was told that new material had been developed for that night's show. The conversation between a sexually starved Pekinese, who liked to rip furniture, and his plump owner was so hilarious that one of the patients fell out of his chair laughing. When the owners and their dogs ran around in a circle at the community center, the mission comedians improvised appropriate comments as each pair trotted past the camera.

Halfway through the film, Daniel remembered that a young woman had just died and her body was still lying in a building less than twenty yards away. Most of the people around him were going to die within the next two years, and Paul, Tobias, and Joan had perished in the plane crash. All this was true and yet he was laughing. Everyone was laughing.

It was hard to sleep that night. Three of his ribs were cracked and whenever he coughed, it felt like a bone was jabbing into his right lung. Daniel thought about the plane crash and all the things that had happened afterward. He had a fantasy that he would go to sleep, then wake up and his unpleasant memories would be gone forever.

In the morning, he stood in line to get his bowl of *ugali* and a cup of milk. The cattle boys were driving the herd out of the thorn-walled corral. There was a lot of dust and shouting, but they seemed proud that they had such an important job.

Daniel learned from Ann Gawara that there were definite rules at Boma Mission. Do your fair share of work. Unmarried men and women in separate dormitories. No fighting. Alcohol was only allowed on Friday nights when they drank some homemade beer made from millet. Everyone was allowed to fill up their bowl with beer and it caused a lot of singing.

Father Lokali was fairly disorganized and things got done only because Ann and two older women took charge of the food and the nursing. A mechanic named Gabriel was responsible for the mission truck and now he was in Kampala picking up more patients and supplies.

While Daniel ate his porridge and cleaned his bowl, he watched Father Lokali. The priest never seemed to have a casual conversation. Whenever he spoke to anyone, even the children, he concentrated on them completely, as if they were the most important person in the world.

Daniel heard the sound of a truck engine and saw red dust rising up from the northern road. By now, Father Lokali's messenger had reached the outside world and someone official was coming to get him. He returned his bowl and cup to Ann and went back to his room. A few minutes later, Father Lokali appeared in the doorway.

"The police are here from Kitgum. The district captain wants to talk to you."

They walked back outside. The policemen had arrived in a Land Rover and a pickup truck. They were parked near the blue dormitory, next to three plywood coffins.

The district police captain was only in his twenties, but very stern and proper. There were creases in his blue uniform and he carried a swagger stick. Daniel spoke to him briefly, answered a few questions, and the captain went off to give orders to his men.

Father Lokali stood beside Daniel as the policemen picked up the first coffin.

"Thank you for everything," Daniel said. "You saved my life."

"Your life had already been saved when the boys found you."

Daniel coughed a few times and tasted blood in his mouth. He didn't want to leave the mission. It felt like the plane crash was merely a prelude to a more terrible danger.

"You've got to tell me what to do."

"Go to Kitgum and give a full statement to the police."

"I mean, what do I do now that I've survived?"

One of the patients approached with a problem, but Father Lokali shook his head slightly. He wasn't finished with Daniel.

"When I took my nursing course in Rome, my language teacher had us read the *Divine Comedy*. Just inside the gates of hell, Dante has placed those people who lived neither for good nor evil, but only for themselves. Because they believed in nothing when they were alive, they are lost forever in shadows. They follow a flag back and forth, back and forth, over a dark plain, never finding comfort, never finding the right way."

"So pick sides and make a decision."

"Yes. Exactly." Father Lokali looked pleased. "The moment will come to you, as it does to all of us. Then make a choice, without hesitation."

The police took Daniel to Kitgum and Paul Rosen's father arrived there a few hours later. When Mr. Rosen learned his son was dead, he cried and pounded his fists on a table. He wanted words of comfort, an explanation for what had happened, but Daniel didn't know what to tell him. Daniel had always been able to come up with the right phrase for any situation, but now his mouth felt dry and the words seem to stick to his tongue. Back in Kampala, he sent out his articles from the American embassy, then got on a plane to return to home. The journey made him feel even more disoriented.

When he got back to the farm, Daniel took some pills and slept for a couple of days. His broken bones seemed to be healing, but he felt restless and sick to his stomach. He drove back to Rome, withdrew half his savings, and wired it to Father Lokali's friend at the Canadian embassy in Kampala. That made him feel good for a few hours, but the restlessness came back again. He began to wonder if the wrong people had died in the crash.

"THAT'S WHEN I started living here at the convent," Daniel said. "I thought it would help me being here, but I'm even more lost than in Africa. I feel different, Nicky. I feel changed. How can I go back to work and pretend like nothing has happened? Maybe I should stop being a journalist and do something different with my life. Maybe I should sell Bracciano and give everything away."

"Don't make any quick decisions," I said. "You survived a bad accident. It takes some time to recover."

"We don't have enough time. Not really." Daniel turned and stared at me as if I could help him. "So what am I supposed to do, Nicky? Can you tell me?"

8 AT BRACCIANO

I didn't know how to answer any of Daniel's questions. Instead, my first reaction was to get him out of the garden and buy him some lunch. A few blocks away from the convent, right off the Piazza Santa Maria, we found a restaurant with only four tables. No one greeted us when we arrived so I went into the kitchen. A massive woman wearing a white smock was there, drinking wine and glaring at a dead rabbit lying on a chopping board. I had the feeling that the rabbit had somehow offended her sense of dignity.

Using my fractured Italian, I said that *il mio amico* was feeling somewhat *precario* and that he required a meal that would give him *ottimismo* and *coraggio*. The cook fired off a lot of questions, most of which I didn't understand. Finally she asked me if Daniel was suffering from *un amore interrotto*.

"*Si, signora.*"

The cook took a bottle of white wine out of the refrigerator, handed me two glasses, and pushed me back into the dining room. She served us stuffed mushrooms and onion soup, then homemade ravioli. A few more customers came in, but she kept bringing us dishes. Fried cod. Rabbit stew in a thick cream sauce. A spinach salad. Baked pears sprinkled with brown sugar.

I kept filling Daniel's wineglass and distracting him with questions about obscure countries like Uzbekistan or Chad. The food, the wine, and my constant chatter pulled Daniel back into the present and he began to relax. We got up from the table around five, sedated from the feast. The cook came out from the kitchen and scrutinized Daniel like a doctor who had just performed surgery. She pinched his cheek, gave us a parting shot of grappa, and sent us on our way.

Outside the restaurant I tried to act casual. "You know, I've only visited your farm in the summertime. What's it look like in the fall?"

Daniel hesitated for a few seconds, but the fried cod and the grappa, the talk of old news stories, and the bright blue truck roaring past us kept him from walking straight back to the convent garden.

"It's beautiful, Nicky. It really is. Why don't you come out and see?"

The Alfa Romeo was parked behind the convent. Daniel said good-bye to the little nun and we drove out of the city. That evening, we didn't speed down the road and Daniel actually glanced at the landscape. The country air was cold and smelled like pine trees.

I STAYED AT BRACCIANO for fifteen days. It was a relaxing vacation, even though it involved two of the things I hate most in this world —waking up early and gardening. Usually La Signora marched in around seven o'clock in the morning and started banging pots on the stove. She treated Daniel with firm affection, as if he was a difficult farm animal that kept breaking out of his pasture. One morning she was cleaning up the breakfast dishes while Daniel played a Louis Prima CD on the portable stereo. As Prima sang "When You're Smiling," Daniel took La Signora's hand and danced with her in the kitchen. The old lady laughed and twirled around on the stone floor. For a moment I could see her fifty years ago, breaking hearts at a village dance.

On a typical morning we planted the trees that Daniel had bought for a few thousand lire at the government nursery. He would drive over to the nursery, place the plastic buckets of two or three saplings on the floor of the Alfa, and lean the slender trunks against the passenger seat. Back at the farm, he'd carry the trees down to the ravine and plant them near the stream to fight erosion. La Signora handed me a pick and shovel, then pointed to the ground between the terraces and the cypress windbreak. You. Go. Plant trees.

The volcanic soil was rock hard, packed down by centuries of over-grazing. It took me several hours to dig what I thought was an accept-able hole, but La Signora said it was too small. When I objected, she harangued me in Italian, most of which I didn't understand. I kept dig-ging, hacking away at the soil, until she finally murmured, *"Bene, bene,"* and dumped two baskets of mulch into the hole. In all, I planted three oaks and two cherry trees. I got a blister on my left hand, but I had to admit it felt good to look down the slope at my small accomplishment.

We usually finished work around noon, then ate the big meal of the day. I took a nap on the couch while Daniel sat in his bedroom and played CDs. He was searching, always searching, for those moments of pure music. Now he was obsessed with the early recordings of Louis Armstrong and I had to listen to repeated trumpet solos from "Tight Like This" and "Potato Head Blues." I knew that Daniel was thinking about the plane crash when he abandoned Louis Armstrong and put on Bach's cello suites. I felt as if I was living with someone who had just been released from prison. The sun was shining and La Signora was singing in the kitchen, but sometimes Daniel would sit in the arbor and stare at the dirt driveway as if he was waiting for the police to take him away.

In the late afternoon Daniel helped La Signora with the wet garden while I took my cameras and wandered down the hill. I forgot that I was a shooter for two weeks and spent hours photographing the tex-ture of the stone on the Roman bridge. Leaves were falling and the countryside was brown and dark gold. I'd look up and see a huge flock of swifts surging across the sky.

At night we'd cook up some pasta or roast a whole chicken on the spit in the fireplace. Daniel bought his wine from a barrel at a local farm and he kept it in old scotch bottles with screw-top caps. We'd drink a fair amount, then play chess or gin rummy. It was during these games that I learned a few more facts about Daniel's past. After his mother's death when he was eighteen, he bought a car and began to drive around the United States. He spent two seasons running a chair lift at a Utah ski resort and worked for a traveling carnival that toured the West.

Eventually he'd ended up in Washington, fighting fires for the state forestry service. After one particularly tough job, when he and three other men were caught between fire lines, he returned to the camp covered with soot, sat down on his bunk, and wrote about the experience. "I just wanted to tell the story," he said. "I wasn't doing it for money or because I wanted to be famous. I thought, if I wrote down all the facts, I could understand what happened."

An editor at the *Seattle Times* read the handwritten submission, ordered some photographs, and printed the entire five-thousand-word article. When Daniel dropped by to pick up his check, the editor told him that he was wasting his time digging fire trenches, that he should take a few journalism classes and start writing for the newspaper. Within a year, Daniel was a general assignment reporter for the *Times*. It seemed incredible that he could get paid to drive around the city and ask strangers questions. Like a priest or a doctor, he had the right to step around the strip of yellow emergency tape and enter into different worlds.

"I didn't know what I was supposed to do with my life and I thought . . ." He paused for a second and took another sip of wine. "I believed that, if I asked enough questions and talked to enough people, I could get some answers for myself."

"But that's not true?"

"No." He finished off his wine and got up from the table. "I've asked thousands of questions, Nicky. And I don't know one damn thing."

Daniel was quieter, slower, more deliberate. For the first time in his life, he was cautious about the future and regretful about the mistakes he had made in the past. I know that he wrote letters to a half-dozen people whom he had angered for some reason. Three of the letters were returned unopened and two people wrote back, accepting his apology. His chief enemy, the AP bureau chief in Moscow, sent a long e-mail with a great many exclamation points and capital letters. He hoped that Daniel would step on a land mine in a war zone and suffer a painful death.

I was the follower and Daniel was the leader in Africa, but now the relationship had changed. Daniel had lost his psychological armor, the proud confidence I had seen before the accident. I felt older than him, almost protective in an odd way. He was like a sick man whose defenses were down, susceptible to any infection. He was safe at Bracciano, but I wondered what would happen once he left this sanctuary.

Gradually I began to coax Daniel back into his responsibilities. I encouraged him to pay his bills and send messages to his editors. He told everyone that he was recovering from the plane crash and that he would return to work in a few months. Using Daniel's computer, I checked my e-mail and found a message from Richard Seaton: *Newsweek says you're in Italy with Daniel McFarland. How is he?*

I wrote back a chatty little note: *Daniel is okay. He just needed some rest and relaxation. Beautiful weather here.*

There were immediate consequences. The next day a red pickup truck came through the gates and rolled slowly down the driveway until the driver found us digging a hole for a pine tree. The driver got out wearing the brown uniform of an overnight delivery service. Inside a manila envelope was an engraved invitation to a black-tie fund-raising party at Westgate Castle, Richard's country estate near Gloucester.

Along with the invitation was a letter from a Miss Hedges, obviously some kind of social secretary. In a neat and precise cursive she informed us that there was also a house party that weekend for Mr. Seaton's friends. Richard wanted to know if Mr. McFarland and Mr. Bettencourt could arrive at Westgate on Thursday afternoon.

Daniel jabbed his shovel into the ground, then studied the invitation.

"It must be strange to own a castle. I wonder if Billy Monroe is in charge of the drawbridge."

I reached into the manila envelope and found a second letter written on cream-colored stationery.

Dear Nicky and Daniel: Richard says that he's invited you both to the house party. I do hope you can come. Yrs. Julia Cadell.

That was all. Nothing personal. But when I handed the letter to Daniel, he read it several times. "She's left Kosana."

"Looks like it."

"I guess she isn't mad at me anymore."

"She apologized to you. Remember?"

"I wasn't graceful about that," Daniel said. "I wasn't graceful at all." He stared at Julia's letter as if her spidery handwriting could provide more information. "Want to go back to England, Nicky?"

"I'm tired of planting trees. I think I'm ready for hors d'oeuvres."

9   WESTGATE CASTLE

I went back to Daniel's tailor, got measured for a tuxedo, and flew to
London that weekend. As soon as I arrived Carter Howard sent me
north to photograph a plane crash outside of Edinburgh. A Boeing Air-
bus had been transformed into shards of burning wreckage scattered
across three acres of muddy pasture. I took about three hundred shots,
but *Newsweek* only used the one of a constable placing a woman's shoe
into an evidence bag. I kept fantasizing about owning a farm like Daniel
and growing something that wouldn't take a lot of work—wildflowers,
maybe, or mistletoe. I didn't know anything about farming, but I was
getting tired of photographing disasters.

When I returned from Scotland I hung around the *Newsweek* offices
for a few days and did an Internet search on Richard Seaton. I had assumed that Richard was created in the poor-boy-makes-good mold, but
that wasn't really true. His father was a solicitor in Chelmsford and
Richard went to a public school—although not one of the famous
ones. While a student at Oxford, he had leased and installed an ATM

machine at the town bus station near Gloucester Green. The rest of his banking empire seemed to flow from that one act.

Until he met Julia, Richard was famous for dating beautiful women in the actress/model category. Searching through the computer archives of the British tabloids, I found several news photographs of Richard in a tuxedo standing next to actresses wearing dresses that contradicted the laws of physics. He seemed to prefer women who had slept with members of the British royal family. This preference led to a memorable tabloid headline: DASHING DICKY RECYCLES ROYAL REJECTS.

I found one feature article in the *Guardian* where Richard mentioned that he had met Julia during a Cambridge symposium on refugee problems. Last year, they had been photographed together at a charity event. When Richard became more involved with humanitarian organizations even the tabloids began treating him with respect. It wasn't Dashing Dicky anymore, but BANKING MOGUL RICHARD SEATON AND DR. JULIA CADELL AT OXFAM DINNER.

Daniel flew in on Thursday morning with my new tuxedo. I tried it on in my hotel room; then we got a taxi and went to Paddington Station. Our train rumbled slowly through the long, shadowy hall and then we were out and moving beneath a gray October sky. We passed council flats, gas works, parking lots and factories, little brick houses, each with a TV antenna attached to the chimney.

A doctor in Rome had cut off Daniel's cast and removed the stitches. His hair had grown longer and he superficially resembled the same person I had met at the Stampa Estera. But Daniel held his body differently and his tone of his voice had changed. There was a dreamy intelligence about him, a preoccupation with other thoughts that made him seem like an absentminded mathematician. Before the plane crash in Africa, Daniel would have had his ticket ready. He would have known exactly when the train departed from London and when it arrived in Kemble. Now he smiled and fumbled through his pockets when the conductor came up the aisle.

After a short stop in Reading, we passed through a flat farmland with rolled-up cylinders of hay. I stared at the brown stubble on the fields and a red fuel can that would have been the center of a photograph. After we changed trains in Swindon the landscape became hilly and strips of forest appeared. Sheep grazed in the distance, little spots of white dotting the dark green grass.

Kemble was a neat and orderly town with signs directing you to the Cotswold Hills. Billy Monroe was out in the train station parking lot, leaning against a Jaguar sedan. He wore new jogging shoes and a blue warm-up suit. In Africa he had carried a submachine gun, but there were laws against that in Britain. Billy looked relaxed and friendly, as if he was the real host of the party.

"Good to see you two again." He winked at Daniel. "They said you were dead, but I knew you weren't. You're too much of bastard, Daniel. Just like me."

"We should form a club, Billy. Get a special tattoo."

"Already got mine."

We got into the Jaguar and roared out of the parking lot. Billy swore at every shuffling pensioner who forced him to use the brakes. We left the town in about five minutes and began racing down narrow country roads lined with hedges. Billy switched on the car's tape recorder and French techno-pop boomed out of the back speakers.

"This is a bit more comfortable than Kosana," Billy said. "Wasn't that the fly-specked asshole of the world?"

"What's going on at the camp?" Daniel asked.

"Most of the younger Karamojong ran off to steal cattle, but we're not sharing that news with the contributors. A reporter from the *Times* flew to Africa with us on the second trip. He wrote a damn good article and the photographs were even better. There was a nice one of Mr. Seaton holding a sick child in his arms."

"Why did Julia leave?"

"Because of the banquet on Saturday. We're going to raise a great deal of money for Hand-to-Hand. Mr. Seaton hired two new doctors and they're in charge of the camp. They finally sacked Steve Ramsey. I would have gotten rid of that wanker a long time ago."

We came over a rise in the road and saw a gray stone castle in the distance. It sat about halfway up a large hill. A pine forest grew on the slope behind the castle and two parts of it curved around both sides of the building like the flanking wings of a green army. The car bumped across a cattle grate and entered a farmland area divided by walls and more hedges. An apple orchard was on our right, the bare branches of the trees outlined against the sky. Across the road a flock of sheep grazed on the grass surrounding a solitary beech tree. A bearded old man carrying a shepherd's crook saw the Jaguar and touched the brim of his hat.

"Lonely job," I said.

Billy looked amused. "It's not what you think."

"What do you mean?" Daniel asked.

"Mr. Seaton invited you here as friends so everything you hear and see this weekend is off the record."

"Of course. We're not working on a story." Daniel glanced at me and smiled. "Just don't ask Nicky to take any celebrity photographs."

"Nothing ends up in any kind of newspaper."

"You've made your point," I said. "Daniel and I are on vacation."

"All right. I'll accept that as a promise. And promises are very important to me." Billy downshifted the car. "Now, to answer your question, the shepherd is an actor named Charlie Drayton. I hired him for the weekend. The landscape designer thought that sheep would look picturesque for the party guests so we rented a flock and trucked it in from Wales. Charlie worked in one of the Riverside Bank television ads. He doesn't know one bloody thing about sheep."

"But he looks good. Nicky wanted to take his picture. Didn't you, Nicky?"

When I nodded, Billy looked pleased. "It's all in the details. Minding the details is why Mr. Seaton is a successful man."

The car passed between two stone pillars and followed a tarmac driveway up the hill. The castle was really a collection of buildings—a square tower at one end, a round tower near the middle, and then a great hall with three floors of arched windows. Everything was connected to a gray stone manor house that had a steep slate roof. Four triangular pennants flew from the corners of the square tower and each one displayed the advertising logo of the Riverside Bank.

"Who built this?" Daniel asked.

"Henry the Eighth. At least that's what we tell the American tourists when they show up with their cameras. Actually it was thrown up around 1860 by a crazy bugger named Robinson who loved reading Walter Scott. He pissed away a fortune building the place, then fell off one of the towers and broke his neck. The previous owners were going to turn it into a health spa, but Mr. Seaton bought the property and did a complete renovation."

We crossed a bridge over a dry moat, passed through the barbican, and entered the front courtyard. We got out of the car and Billy told us to leave our luggage in the trunk. As we followed him around the corner of the great hall, he pointed out the heating vents concealed by shrubbery and an ancient-looking pump house that contained the feeder lines for fiber-optical cables. "All modern. Everything modern," he kept saying, as if we didn't believe him.

Crossing the back lawn, we heard the sharp whack of a tennis racket hitting a ball and approached a red clay court. Richard and Julia were playing tennis against another couple. Since Kosana, I had held images of Julia in my mind. I remembered her inoculating the refugee children and washing blood off her arms in the medical tent. It was jarring to see her in a completely different setting. She wore tennis shoes, sky blue tennis shorts, and a white sweater.

A middle-aged butler stood next to a portable serving table crowded with bottles of water and fruit drinks. His head swung back and forth like a metronome with each volley of the ball.

A young couple sat together on a wooden bench. The man was in his thirties with the rumpled appearance of an undergraduate. The blond woman beside him wore a let's-go-tramping-across-the-moor skirt-and-sweater set. Engrossed in the tennis match, they both leaned forward with a perkiness that reminded me of college cheerleaders. Whenever someone on the court scored a point or made a good save, they shouted encouragement.

Another guest in his late sixties stood a few feet away from the young couple. The man's brown suit and sweater vest were shabby and stained. His thinning hair failed to conceal his bald spot. He looked like an unemployed hotel clerk who had accidentally been invited to the party.

Julia saw us and waved. The ball flew back over the net and she continued playing. The other couple on the tennis court had more experience working as a team. They were in their late fifties but in good shape, as bright-eyed and sleek as otters. The man had pale skin and reddish hair that looked like a wave about to break. His wife was small and strong, an aggressive player.

The volley between the two couples became fairly intense until the small woman hit a backhand that bounced between Richard and Julia.

"That's enough. You're too good for us," Richard said.

Still holding her tennis racket, Julia passed through the gate. "Hello, Nicky. Hello, Daniel. It's wonderful to see you both again." Julia and Daniel glanced at each other, then looked away. It was that same awkwardness I'd seen between them in the staff tent at Kosana.

Richard joined us and shook my hand. "There you are. Glad you two made it. I promise, no Righteous Armies this weekend."

Wallace, the butler, served drinks while Richard introduced us to the other guests. The sleek couple was in the current government. George Riverton was the international development secretary, the politician who had supported Hand-to-Hand's first effort in Uganda. His wife was named Jacqueline, but everyone called her Jax. She worked in the foreign office and I remembered seeing her on various television talk shows.

The young couple was also involved in politics. Malcolm Barthorp was the MP for a West London suburb. His wife, Connie, raised their children and organized pocket gardens in poor neighborhoods. Both the Rivertons and the Barthorps laughed at Richard's jokes and nodded when he spoke. They had obviously decided that Richard had some sort of political future and they were eager to become his supporters.

The man in the shabby brown suit stayed away from the introductions. Suddenly, Richard swung around and gestured to him. "And this is our good friend, Digran Petrosyan."

I had heard Digran's name before, but I couldn't recall why. I glanced at Daniel—Help me out here—then Connie stepped forward and grinned. "Isn't it exciting to have Mr. Petrosyan here? Richard got him out of prison six days ago."

"Actually, Jax and the foreign office had quite a lot to do with it," Richard said. "I just provided some moral support."

"And your jet," Malcolm said. "Don't forget the corporate jet. You got him out of Armenia before they changed their minds."

Political prisoner, I thought. Older man. And then I remembered. Digran Petrosyan was the world-famous poet and candidate for the Nobel Prize. When he called for a peace agreement between his country and Azerbaijan, the Armenian government sent him to prison. During the last few years, he had been a poster boy for the Amnesty International crowd.

The poet nodded to Richard and Jax. "I thank you," he said with a whispery voice. "I thank everyone for their assistance."

Everyone smiled politely. I felt sorry for the guy. A week ago he was sitting in a cell staring at a crack in the wall and now he was at Westgate Castle with Richard's butler hovering behind him. When deep-sea divers come up too fast, they get the bends.

We finished our drinks and crossed the lawn to the manor house. Julia turned to Daniel as we walked together. "Richard said you were in Italy."

"Yes. I own a small farm there."

"And you actually grow things?"

"Olives. Vegetables. Nicky helped me dig up three sacks of onions."

Richard left the Barthorps and caught up with us. "The party on Saturday is a fund-raiser for Hand-to-Hand, but up until then we can have some fun. Wallace will show you to your rooms. Drinks at seven. Dinner around eight-thirty. You're welcome to come pheasant shooting with us tomorrow morning."

"Think I'll sleep in late," said Daniel.

"I used to hunt when I was younger," I said. "We'd drive out to my uncle's ranch."

"You'll find this a bit more organized." Richard turned to the butler. "Wallace, find a jacket and boots for Mr. Bettencourt and tell Quinn we're adding another gun."

The butler led Daniel and me upstairs to our rooms in the west wing of the manor house. Recessed lights in the hallways illuminated a series of eighteenth-century paintings. A man holding the reins to a dappled horse. Two bare-knuckled prizefighters posing in a field.

"Nice place," I said.

"The whole building was gutted like a fish," said Wallace. He had a strong northern accent. "Pulled out the innards. Stuffed in something new."

My room was small, but it had a view of the castle's herb garden. Richard's elves had already brought my suitcase up from the Jaguar. The bathroom was decorated with framed prints and lots of Italian tile. The mattress on the bed was firm enough to bounce a coin yet the rest of the furniture was cracked and faded. I inspected a mirrored armoire, an easy chair, and oak shelves crammed with turn-of-the-century agricultural books. A pewter mug filled with white roses was on the side table along with photographs of people from the 1940s and 1950s.

After using the bathroom, I noticed a full-color photograph on the wall. It was a picture of the room. Same bed. Same book shelves. No, I thought. That's not it. There was only one window in my room, but a pair of windows in the photograph. A little brass label at the bottom of the frame read THE PRIORY. KILKENNY, IRELAND.

Then I realized: Richard, or someone working for him, had bought up the entire contents of a room in Ireland and installed it, intact, at Westgate Castle. It was as if a natural history museum had set up a reconstructed hut from the Amazon basin. Lots of people collect antiques, but having the photograph in the room was something new. Did Richard think his guests would be interested? Or was it simply a demonstration of his wealth and power, the fact that he could grab a little fragment of the world and make it appear anywhere he wished? Staring at the photograph, I realized that Daniel, the Armenian poet, and I had been collected in exactly the same manner.

AROUND SEVEN O'CLOCK I walked down the hallway to see Daniel. A framed photograph of his room hung on the wall and I wondered if his furniture had also come from the house in Kilkenny. Daniel was wearing one of his Italian suits and an ivory-colored shirt with an open collar. He looked like he was going to sit outside at a café and order a glass of wine.

"Want to get a drink downstairs?"

"Sure. In a few minutes." Daniel stepped into the bathroom and combed his wet hair. He moved quickly as if our new surroundings had awakened him from a long sleep. "This is a very strange place, Nicky. It's like a stage set with real people bumping into the scenery. I can't see Julia living here."

"Well, she does. At least for this weekend. Maybe her room is a re-creation of a medical tent in northern Uganda."

"You think she's happy here?"

"All this is Richard. If you pick the man, you get the castle."

We went downstairs and found a maid lighting candles. She led us down a long hallway to a frosted glass door with rubber seals around the edges. The door made a faint whooshing sound when she pulled it open. Daniel and I passed through an anteroom warmed by an electric heater. We pushed open a second door and entered a conservatory with a twenty-foot ceiling.

The glass-walled room was filled with potted trees and flowering plants. Overstuffed couches and chairs had been brought in from another part of the house. Digran Petrosyan, the Rivertons, and the Barthorps were already there, talking to each other like old friends. Billy Monroe stood in one corner behind a wooden serving cart filled with bottles of wine and liquor.

We walked over to get a drink and he gave us a benevolent smile.

Although Billy was making drinks for the guests, he didn't act like Wallace or the other servants. This might have been Richard's party, but Billy felt connected to what was going on.

"How are your rooms?" he asked. "Everything satisfactory?"

"Very nice," I said.

"You have any problems, anything you need, just talk to me. Whatever you do, don't bother Mr. Seaton. He's got a lot of things on his mind this weekend."

I ordered an Irish whiskey and Daniel asked for Campari and soda. After we got our drinks, I followed Daniel over to a potted palm tree where Digran Petrosyan was talking to Connie Barthorp, the MP's wife.

"I just asked Digran if he was ever tortured in prison. He said—"

"I wasn't." The poet looked like his teeth hurt.

"But other people were. He could hear their screams." Connie rattled the ice cubes in her glass. "Isn't that horrible?"

The glass door opened, and Richard and Julia entered the room. She wore a black dress and her hair was coiled up at the back of her neck. If I had brought along my camera, I would have raised it at that moment.

Daniel ignored them and focused on Digran Petrosyan. "Do you regret being let out of prison?"

The poet looked startled, as if Daniel had just read his mind. Connie Barthorp shook her head. "What a horrible thing to say! Mr. Petrosyan was in a dreadful situation. It took three international petitions and a personal appeal from the prime minister to get him released."

"If you don't mind, Mrs. Barthorp, I can speak for myself." Digran stood a little straighter. "You must understand that I would not have survived another year in prison. It was very cold and dirty and people were dying of typhoid. But, in another way, I do regret leaving the place. When I was alone in my cell, I was aware of everything around me. I could look at a spider and see the world."

"But aren't you grateful that you're in Britain among friends?" Connie asked. "At least, you said that earlier."

"Yes. Very grateful."

"Being released must have been an enormous surprise."

"Not really. When they moved me to the new cell, I was allowed to hear the warden's radio. I listened to Mrs. Riverton's interview on the BBC."

"You heard Jax? On the radio? Oh, you should definitely tell her that. She'll be thrilled."

Before Digran could object, Connie linked her arm in his and led him across the room to Jax Riverton. I glanced at Daniel as he pulled a petal from a flowering cherry tree.

"How did you know he didn't want to get out of prison?"

"It's obvious, Nicky."

"It wasn't obvious to me."

"Digran isn't comfortable here. He used to be a poet and now he's a foreign-policy success."

Richard and Julia had split up and were standing in different areas of the conservatory. Holding a glass of white wine, Julia left Malcolm Barthorp and approached the cherry tree. She smiled at both of us, but her eyes lingered a bit longer on Daniel.

"Is everything all right?" Julia asked. "If you don't like your own room, Wallace will move you to another one."

"Who gets the round tower?" I asked.

"No one. Richard has his office there."

"How's the water pump at Kosana?" Daniel asked.

Julia touched her gold necklace. The relief camp was thousands of miles away. "It could be broken again, but there's nothing I can do about it. I'm a doctor with no patients. My only responsibility these days is to be charming to our friends and donors."

"You're doing a very good job."

"You think so? It's strange to see you and Nicky here. I feel like you two should be covering a story."

"Billy gave us our instructions," I said. "Everything that happens this weekend is off the record."

"So I can say anything I want to you?"

"Yes," Daniel said. "Anything at all."

Julia glanced up at the branch of white cherry blossoms hanging over our heads. "I don't know what I think about having these plants here. It's cold and dark outside, and yet here's a cherry tree waiting vainly for bumblebees that died two months ago." She glanced at me. "Is it beautiful or pathetic, Nicky?"

"I don't know."

"The flowers are beautiful no matter what season it is," Daniel said. "It doesn't change anything because it's October."

"But they shouldn't be here," Julia said. "It's silly and artificial."

I heard a beeping sound and Billy took a cell phone out of his pocket. He talked to someone, then announced that dinner was being served and led us down a corridor to the Great Hall. The dining room was massive; it had a vaulted ceiling, a fireplace that was big enough to roast a Volkswagen, and a long stained-glass window. There were place cards written in a graceful cursive. Richard and Julia sat at opposite ends of the table, like the king and his consort. Daniel and I were placed beside Julia. Jax Riverton was to my left.

Sitting among this grandeur, it was comforting to be served such a mediocre dinner. Richard was a man who concentrated on the details, but I guess he wasn't interested in food. The tomato bisque tasted like spaghetti sauce. The lamp chops were stringy and tough, and the broccoli had been boiled until it was limp. The wine, however, was excellent, and Wallace kept bringing out new bottles.

I hate being in a social situation without my camera. I never know what to say or what to do with my hands. Perhaps Julia sensed my uneasiness because she ignored her dinner and made an effort to talk to me.

"Is it strange to be back in England?" she asked.

"Not particularly. I don't have a home to come back to, just this hotel near the British Museum."

"It's getting harder for me to make the transition from a relief camp. The moment I get off the plane at Heathrow, it feels too noisy and frantic and there are too many advertisements. People are always complaining about the most ridiculous things." Julia leaned forward and lowered her voice. "George Riverton talked for fifteen minutes about how he got the wrong seats at Wimbledon."

"Sounds like a tragedy."

"I can't see you getting annoyed about anything, Nicky. You seem like a calm person."

"I just watch and take pictures. I don't risk as much as you."

Julia shook her head. "I should risk a lot more. There's always something extra you can do, another step in the right direction."

The broccoli was taken away and I hoped it would have a dignified funeral. We were served a rubbery custard, and then Wallace brought out a bottle of twenty-year-old brandy, crackers, and a large chunk of Stilton cheese that looked like a piece of rotting firewood. I dug out some cheese with a silver spoon and smeared it onto a wheat cracker. It was rich and well aged, easily the best part of the meal.

Jax Riverton sipped some brandy and decided to acknowledge my existence. "So tell me, Mr. Bettencourt—did you see Richard save the child's life?"

"What child?"

"In the *Times* article it said that he found a sick little girl at the relief camp and gave her some kind of transfusion that saved her life."

"That must have happened when I wasn't there."

"You sound skeptical."

"No. I'm sure Richard did save her life. That's easy to do at a place like Kosana."

"It doesn't seem easy to me. Even the *Times* reporter was impressed. The photograph was marvelous."

"If you're hanging out with starving people, there are lots of opportunities."

"Have *you* ever saved someone's life, Mr. Bettencourt?"

"That's not my job."

"I see. Rather than doing something about the suffering, you just stand there and record it."

When Jax turned away, I grabbed the Stilton and dug out another chunk with the spoon. Richard was telling everyone what he thought about the euro and I pretended to listen, nodding or shaking my head at random points in the monologue. I eavesdropped on the conversation between Daniel and Julia. From what I could gather he had asked Julia what she would do if she quit relief work and she was trying to answer him. Julia had read quite a few books when she was traveling around Africa. Most of these favorites were kept at her aunt's house in Windsor and Julia wanted to buy a house in the country with a lot of bookshelves.

"That's what I dream about. Bookshelves and a good view at sunset."

"Sounds like an achievable goal."

"Mind you, it has to be my own view and my own shelves."

"Would you stay in England?"

"I can't tell you that. The fantasy only goes so far."

Richard was talking about the euro rising or falling or flying out the window. Pouring some more brandy, I lost part of the conversation.

"So what do you want, Daniel? To be famous? Win the Pulitzer Prize?"

"That wouldn't change anything."

"Do you want a bigger salary? Most of the journalists I know are always talking about their salaries."

"I've never really thought about money. I've always had enough to get by."

"You must want something. Most people do."

Daniel was quiet for a moment, but I didn't dare glance at him and let him know I was listening. "I want . . ." He paused again, then spoke with complete certainty. "I want to live a good life."

"What do you mean by that?" Julia asked. "Buying a home like the people in Richard's television ads? Playing golf? Eating chocolate?"

"I do like to eat chocolate and I own the farm in Italy. I'm afraid I don't know much about golf."

"Golf or something like it? Is that what you mean?"

"I want to understand the consequences of my actions. That's all I can really tell you. During the last few weeks, I've been trying to find a new way to live. I don't have any answers, only the desire."

At the end of the table, the talk had turned into a consideration of international relief aid. Richard spoke a little louder, trying to draw everyone into the discussion. "In Britain, if there's a flood or a train wreck, we don't send out a twenty-three-year-old Oxfam volunteer wearing a T-shirt and sandals. It should be the same procedure in foreign countries. The work needs to be done by professionals."

"But that twenty-three-year-old girl and others like her encourage popular support for foreign aid," George said. "Professionals are politically isolated."

"That's why Hand-to-Hand is going to create a different paradigm. Using the Internet, our contributors will be able to interact with the staff and help pick the country we'll be working in."

Daniel drank some brandy, then lowered his glass. "So the professionals will do the work, but the amateurs will tell them what to do?"

"Not totally. But we want them to be emotionally connected to our activities. There are constant moments of suspense and drama in any relief camp. Will this person live? Will that person die? Using the digital cameras we've set up in the camp, we can create our own story."

"That could lead to panda-bear relief work," Daniel said.

"I beg your pardon?"

"Panda bears are cute so people want to save them. If you're dependent on an audience reaction, won't your contributors prefer situations where the starving people are appreciative and photogenic?"

Malcolm reached for the brandy. "Which is why no one gives a damn about the Somalis. Nasty group of people."

"I care," Julia said. She was trying to be polite so her voice wasn't loud or confident. When no one reacted, she said it again. "I care if they live or die."

"Well, of course you do. That's your job," Jax said. "But George is talking about the rest of us. Public opinion."

When Wallace removed the cheese, the dinner was over. Malcolm and Richard went into the library for another drink, but everyone else drifted off to their rooms. I could see Julia watching Daniel as he headed up the staircase. I wondered what she had thought when Daniel said he wanted to live a good life. I'm sure Jax Riverton and the others would have smiled if they heard that phrase. It sounded like something a sensitive friend would say walking home from a college party.

A few years later, the friend would become an arms dealer or a public relations consultant defending the oil companies in Nigeria. Or perhaps something not so dramatic at all—just an assistant executive something or other who had a favorite TV show and washed his car on the weekends. That was what happened to most people. Not a good life or a bad life, just an ordinary one.

I realized that everything was different if you took Daniel's statement seriously. Idealists are dangerous to themselves and the people around them. If you truly wanted to live a good life, it was a revolutionary act. I could admire someone like that, but I knew that I'd never make such a choice. It bothered me to think that people would be staring at me and criticizing my decisions. If you want to be a saint, you have to risk looking like a fool.

I went upstairs to my room and took off my suit coat. When I hung it up in the armoire, I heard the Rivertons passing in the hallway.

"Panda-bear relief work," George said. "That was somewhat witty."

"I don't know why Richard invited those two."

"They're witnesses. Proof that he actually went out and touched sick babies."

The Rivertons continued down the hallway and I couldn't hear them. I pulled off my shoes and was brushing my teeth when Daniel knocked on my door. He looked like he wanted to walk back to London.

"Having a good time, Nicky?"

"It's better than the Ruskin Hotel."

Daniel sat in one of chairs. "What were you and Julia talking about?"

"Culture shock. Coming home after you've been in Africa."

"What do you think of Julia?"

"I like her."

"And Richard?"

"Either he's done too many TV commercials for that bank of his or I've seen too many of them. I can't tell what's underneath the surface. Maybe more surface."

"Richard is a successful businessman. Everything looks good until you notice Billy Monroe standing behind him."

I laughed. "I'm still thinking about that actor and the rental sheep out in the pasture."

"So why is she with a man like Richard? How can she stand to hear him talk about digital cameras and the little moments of drama in a relief camp? People are starving to death and he makes it sound like a goddamn media event."

"The food and the medicine at Kosana were real. He's helping Julia save the world. Not everyone can do that."

"So she stays with him because he sponsors Hand-to-Hand?"

"How would I know? You saw the pressures on her at Kosana. Those refugees were hungry and sick, and she's the one in charge. It must be a relief to come back to England and have Richard take care of everything."

"She's a good person." Daniel spoke slowly, as if he was considering the idea.

"Definitely."

"I couldn't stop looking at her."

"This isn't our world, Daniel."

"I know that." He got up from the chair and walked over to the door. "When the party's over, we're gone."

10   The Hunt

I don't know if the ghost of the dead builder, Mr. Robinson, haunted the manor house, but all that night I kept hearing odd creaks and gasping sounds. Around three in the morning, I switched on a lamp and looked around the room. Nothing. "I don't believe in you," I said firmly, then rolled over and went back to sleep.

Someone tapped on my door around eight o'clock. When I looked out into the hallway I found a laundry basket filled with my kit for the shoot: gum boots, waterproof overalls, a Gore-Tex jacket, and a wool cap. The cap was essential. When I put it on and looked at myself in the bathroom mirror, I felt vaguely British and ready to blast anything out of the sky.

I went downstairs looking for breakfast and Wallace guided me to the morning room. It was a smaller and more comfortable place than the dining room; there was a long mahogany table and sporting prints on the walls. The butler pointed out a serve-yourself meal of fried eggs and sausage on the sideboard, then disappeared through a swinging door. The castle was so large and there were so many rooms that it was difficult to figure out where people were coming from or going to.

I was pouring myself a cup of coffee when George Riverton walked in wearing an identical hunting costume. He didn't look pleased to see me. "Oh," he said. "I didn't think you were going."

"I guess I am."

"This is a rather *English* activity," he said. "It's not like hunting in the States."

"You shoot the birds. They hit the ground. I think I can handle it."

George poured himself a cup of tea, took a muffin, and left the room. Any hesitation I might have felt concerning the shoot disappeared at that moment.

At quarter after nine I walked outside to the stone courtyard in front of the castle. The air was cold and a dark mass of rain clouds was forming on the western horizon. About a dozen men from the village were standing around, smoking and talking to each other. Four women wearing quilted vests and Wellington boots were loading their Labrador retrievers into the back of a Land Rover. They were in charge of picking up the fallen birds.

George and Malcolm were leaning against another Land Rover. They kept glancing at me and muttering to each other, but I ignored them. As I wandered across the courtyard, I saw Richard standing next to a tall man with a reddish beard. "Nicky! Over here! I want you to meet someone!"

I worked my way through the crowd and he introduced me to Mr. Quinn, the estate's gamekeeper. Quinn quickly appraised me, as if I was a new hunting dog.

"Have you shot many times in England, sir?"

"No, I haven't, but I hunted quite a bit in California."

"Mr. Muldoon!" Quinn shouted and an old man emerged from behind a pickup truck. Muldoon had a bumpy face and stained teeth. His rubber boots were caked with mud and it looked as if he had spent the morning trudging through a bog.

Quinn made the introductions. "Mr. Muldoon will assist you today."

"Just do what he tells you," Richard said. "Muldoon has forgotten more than we'll ever know."

"Haven't forgotten a thing," snapped the old man. He jerked his head and I followed him over to the truck.

"Ever shot in England?"

"I grew up in the country. We used to hunt pheasant and quail at my uncle's ranch. Sometimes we drove up to Sacramento and shot ducks."

"This is double-gun shooting from a stand, not like in the States. We don't creep around like a bunch of Injuns." A flat leather gun case was lying in the back of the pickup. Muldoon snapped it open and displayed a pair of double-barreled shotguns. "You just aim and pull the trigger. I'll load for you and keep you from killin' anyone."

About ten minutes later Quinn sent off the young men in two vehicles. Muldoon explained that they were going to work as beaters, driving the birds toward us. Richard, George, and Malcolm got into one of the Land Rovers, and Billy motioned for me to join them. When I slipped into the backseat, everyone stopped talking. Quinn climbed onto an all-terrain vehicle with fat tires. The convoy of trucks and Land Rovers followed him across the drawbridge and turned north onto a muddy road that curved around the hill.

"Well?" asked George. "Aren't you going to ask him?"

"I already told you," Richard said.

Billy glanced over his shoulder. "Nicky, the gentlemen want to know if you're carrying a camera."

"Of course not."

Malcolm gave me a nervous smile. "I don't want any pictures of me with a shotgun."

"What's the problem?"

"An American wouldn't understand, but hunting is definitely not popular in our party. Most of our backbenchers want to get rid of every kind of hunting."

"You could fall down drunk in front of the queen and still survive politically," George explained. "But you'd be in trouble if you were photographed wearing a red jacket and holding a gun."

Our little convoy passed strips of woodland surrounded by haw-thorn and hedge maple. The dense patches of ground cover were de-signed to hide the pheasants from their natural predators, then produce them at the right moment during the shoot. A few miles from the cas-tle, we stopped on a weedy pasture below a hill. Carrying the shotguns, Muldoon spoke briefly to Quinn, then led me over to a peg hammered into the ground. Richard, Malcolm, and George were taken to three other pegs. Quinn stood behind us with the women hired to pick up the birds.

Back in California, my uncle Carl and I would spend an entire afternoon wandering around the stubble of his cornfield with our arth-ritic golden retriever. If we were lucky, the dog flushed five or six pheas-ants, and we killed two of them. The shoot at Richard's estate had a larger sense of order. Quinn muttered commands into his walkie-talkie and I heard a distant clicking sound. The beaters were on the hill above us, tapping sticks together as they drove the birds toward the edge of the cliff.

Muldoon handed me a pair of ear defenders. He loaded both shot-guns and showed me how to exchange them. I was supposed to reach with my right hand for the new gun while handing off the empty weapon with my left. The motion reminded me of switching cameras and I learned the routine quickly. When I glanced down the line, I saw that Billy was fumbling with Richard's guns.

Muldoon jerked his head toward Billy. "I don't know why a man needs a bodyguard in the country. The only thing dyin' today are the birds."

"Are they coming off that hill?"

"Aye. The birds live down there." Muldoon pointed to a thicket of larch and birch trees directly behind us. "But Mr. Quinn feeds 'em up there." He pointed to the hill. "When the lads come through, the birds fly off that rise, tryin' to get back to their pen. Put Big Ben in the sky and shoot between ten and two o'clock." He gestured to the left and right, establishing the firing perimeters. "Whatever you do, don't shoot behind us."

"When I used to hunt in America, we only shot at the male birds. What's the rule here?"

"Shoot what you want, sir."

"What's your rule, Mr. Muldoon?"

The old man gave me a sideways glance. He looked cautious, not sure if he could trust me. "I don't shoot the hens myself. It's more sporting."

"I'll try for the males, but no promises. Sometimes they rise high and fast."

Muldoon chuckled and took out a pack of cigarettes. "Oh, I wouldn't worry about that, sir. Not with this lot."

The clicking sound got louder and we could hear the beaters calling to each other. Behind us, Quinn was chanting into his radio. "Tell them not to get ahead of each other! Stay in the line!"

The cock pheasants began to cackle loudly as the beaters got closer. The birds fluttered up a few feet, then disappeared down into the black-thorn. I felt as if the entire woodland was gathering its strength for one convulsive effort.

A hen flew out of the woods and headed toward the birches. Malcolm fired his shotgun twice and missed both times. He swore and shouted to his loader as a cock pheasant appeared and glided toward us. His red wattles were a precise point of color against the gray sky.

Richard fired and the pellets made a slapping sound as they hit the pheasant's wing. The bird fell quickly and hit the grass with a dull thump like a sack of grain. "Guard the sides! Guard the sides!" Quinn shouted to the beaters.

The birds came over the rise straight at us. I got lucky and brought down two males in a row, took the spare gun from Muldoon, and fired again. The other men were shooting at everything that darted out of the brush. The pheasants dropped before us, the wounded ones twisting and flopping on the grass. Behind us, the dogs strained at their leashes, but the women held them tight.

I saw a white duck come toward us and took my finger off the trigger, but George Riverton fired from a short distance and blew off the bird's left wing. I glanced at Muldoon. Ignoring me, he loaded the second shotgun. Another duck flew out of the woods, then four more. They were flying so low that it was impossible to miss them. Richard pointed his shotgun like a man in a firing squad and hit two in a row.

The gamekeeper blew his whistle and everyone lowered their guns. Bluish-gray smoke drifted through the air and I smelled the harsh, sulfur odor of gunpowder. The women went forward with their dogs to get the fallen birds. A white duck lay about ten feet in front of us. Its blood glistened on the grass like little red jewels.

I pulled off the ear defenders and turned to Muldoon. "What the hell is that?"

He gave me a sly smile. "Looks like a duck, Mr. Bettencourt. Haven't you ever seen a duck before?"

"That one's straight from the farmyard. What's it doing in the woods?"

Muldoon glanced around him, then lowered his voice. "Mr. Quinn trucked a cage of ducks up here and mixed them with the pheasants. They don't know how to fly that well so they're easy to shoot."

I looked down the line and saw Malcolm and George congratulating each other. Richard stood alone, pissing on a beech tree.

"They're not country people," Muldoon whispered. "Weren't raised here. Don't know how to shoot. But they want to kill something, so Quinn fixes it that way."

"Do they know it's not a wild duck?"

"Maybe. Maybe not. Probably don't care."

THERE WERE FOUR different drives that morning before we stopped in a clearing for lunch. The mother of one of the dog ladies had prepared the meal and it was good country food: barley soup and home-baked bread, apple turnovers and strong tea. Now that George and Malcolm knew that I wasn't going to take their photograph, everyone relaxed. I had thought that pheasant shooting was another way for Richard to impress his friends, but I gradually began to understand what was really going on. For George and Malcolm, joining a hunt could hurt their political careers. They probably felt like Richard had fixed them up with a prostitute or taken them to a strip club in Soho. Now there was a secret between them, and secrets implied power and obligation.

There were two more drives that afternoon and Quinn mixed ducks into both of them. I didn't feel compassionate about ducks, but I didn't want to shoot them. The pheasants were used to the woods and they were good fliers, but the ducks didn't have a chance. It felt as fake as a news photographer posing a shot.

It started drizzling on the last drive and then it was raining hard by the time the dog ladies hung up the dead birds in the game cart. My shoulder hurt from the recoil and I wanted a drink. When I gave twenty pounds to Muldoon, he smiled and touched his cap. "A pleasure to load for you, Mr. Bettencourt. You can shoot." It was the compliment I'd been searching for all day, but it didn't make me feel any better.

Everyone got into the Land Rover and Billy drove us back to the house. The windshield wipers slapped back and forth as the Rover skidded a little on the muddy road. Malcolm and George stared out the windows, but Richard kept glancing at me. I wondered if he was annoyed because I didn't shoot at every bird that flew out of the woods.

Billy parked a few feet away from the front door, and Wallace came out with umbrellas. Richard touched my arm and we waited in the car while the other three men went inside.

"Having a good time, Nicky?"

"It's nice to get out of London."

"I was telling George about you last night. You really are a talented photographer. Have you ever thought about putting out a book of your best work?"

"Sure."

"I have some friends in publishing. Assemble a portfolio, then give me a call at the bank when we get back to London."

"Thanks, Richard. I'll think it over."

Raindrops exploded on the ground and rattled on the roof of the

Land Rover. A favor had been offered and I waited to see what it was going to cost.

"I've told Miss Hedges to arrange the place cards for supper. You're going to be sitting next to Julia again."

"Okay."

"Julia likes you, Nicky. You're both in the same kind of business, really, dealing with war and disaster. If you stay in it too long, you get cynical and burned out. Don't you agree?"

"It's that way for some people."

"I'd like Julia to become executive director of Hand-to-Hand. She'd supervise fund-raising and run the office in London. Perhaps you could put in a good word for me. It's a step forward, really. She can't spend the rest of her life acting like a refugee."

Back in my room, I had a long bath, soaking in the hot water until my fingers got all wrinkled. Someone had left a bottle of cologne and a terry-cloth robe on the bathroom shelf. When I returned to the bedroom, Daniel was sitting in the easy chair, looking out at the rain.

"How's it going, Nicky?"

"I'm all right."

"Kill a lot of pheasants?"

"There were some ducks, too." I explained what had happened during the shoot.

"That doesn't surprise me. It's just like Billy said, Richard takes care of the details."

"So how was your day?"

"I borrowed a motorcycle from the garage and started riding around the estate. I bumped into Julia and we went on a tour together."

I could see Daniel's profile as he leaned back in the chair. The absentminded, distracted behavior he had shown on the train had completely disappeared. Now he reminded me of an athlete about to play some sort of game. His body was relaxed, but you could tell that he was ready to jump up and run forward.

"Together—on the same motorcycle?"

"That's usually the way people ride."

"Don't forget, she's Richard's girlfriend."

A bottle of Irish whiskey was on the side table; it was the same brand I had requested before dinner on Thursday night. Daniel stood up and poured himself a glass.

"You're too sensitive, Nicky."

"No one's ever accused me of that before."

Daniel poured me a glass of whiskey. The rain kept falling outside, splattering on the windowsill, and a cold damp smell filled the room. Whatever spirits had clung to the furniture from that house in Kilkenny asserted themselves, and I was aware of several generations of people reading a book in the chair or making love on the bed.

"Julia took me to a cemetery in the village. Lots of old gravestones."

"Sounds like fun."

"We talked until it started raining."

"What about?"

"Her work. My work."

"You talk about Richard?"

"No. Not really."

"Maybe we should get out of here. Go back to London."

He raised his glass and we clicked them together. "Don't worry, Nicky. Nothing's going to happen."

BECAUSE OF THE RAIN we had our evening cocktails in the library. The shelves were packed with old books and there were leather club chairs next to reading lamps. It all appeared very solid and thoughtful until you checked out the book titles. Richard Seaton was interested in lots of things, but I doubt if he spent his evenings reading *British Grain Diseases* or the *1928 Parliamentary Debates*.

I studied the painting by J. M. W. Turner over the fireplace. A brass label said it was titled *Venice Sunset, 1843,* and you could make out the domes of St. Mark's Cathedral. All Turner cared about was light and color, a swirling haze of rose and dark yellow that appeared to glow with its own energy. After my second drink, I wanted to carry it around for inspiration.

George Riverton cornered me near a couch and gave me his theory about the Atlantic Alliance. He believed that America was like classical Rome and that Britain was like Greece. It sounded like he admired the United States, until I started to understand what he was saying. As far as George was concerned, Britain was art and theater and philosophy while America had a large army and good plumbing.

I was placed next to Julia at dinner while Daniel sat at the opposite end of the table between Richard and Digran Petrosyan. Digran didn't talk to anyone. Whenever the servants brought out a new course, he stared at the food as if this was one more wall to climb over. We ate a fairly good pheasant stew, but the vegetables were awful. Some Brussels sprouts must have humiliated the chef when he was a child because he was determined to boil their descendents to a mushy pulp.

Julia wore a pearl necklace and a green silk dress. Malcolm Barthorp was sitting on her left and he told her about a recent by-election in Winchester. He had campaigned there for his party's candidate and now a whole new group of people invited him to their parties. According to Malcolm, politics was about getting the right kind of exposure and playing larger roles; he sounded like a young actor who had just come to Los Angeles to get into movies. Then Malcolm and Jax began to discuss the sexual preferences of a female cabinet minister. Was she gay or straight or just a drab little nun? Julia turned away from them and I stopped buttering a roll.

"How was the shooting, Nicky?"

"Loud. Bloody."

"But you liked it?"

"I've done it once. Now I don't have to do it again."

"Richard was talking about you before we came downstairs. He said you were very perceptive. I'm always on my guard when Richard praises anyone. That means they're part of some plan."

"Richard wants you to become the executive director of Hand-to-Hand. I'm supposed to tell you that it's a good idea."

"Is that what you actually believe?"

"I think it's a waste of time to give advice to other people."

"That's never stopped anyone before."

"What do you want to do, Julia?"

"Ever since I finished my training, I've gone from one emergency to another. I'd like to step back and take a break for a while, but not by sitting in an office and writing grant proposals."

One of the candles went out and a thread of smoke disappeared up into the gloom. They served some port and Julia asked me about the farm in Bracciano. How did I like staying there? What was planted in the garden? Somehow I felt like I was revealing personal details about Daniel's life.

"I went to Italy a few times when I was a student," Julia said. "Then a few months ago Richard took me to Rome on a business trip."

"Bet you stayed at a nice hotel."

"No. Richard hates hotels, so he rented someone's villa." Julia glanced down length of the table. Everyone was listening to Richard talk about terrorism and oil supplies. "Every morning I'd wake up and find my schedule slipped beneath the door. I'd say that I wanted to go to the Vatican and the next day it would be arranged—driver and guide. The Italians would tell Billy what I did, Billy would tell Richard. When I met him for dinner, he'd know what paintings I liked at the museums."

"I wouldn't mind having a driver and guide," I said. "In fact, I'd like two assistants to carry my cameras and open all the doors."

"That's what I thought," Julia said. "It's quite pleasant in the beginning. Then you start to feel like a child with a lot of anxious nannies. When they're around it's difficult just to buy some ice cream, wander down the street, go into a boutique and try on something silly that you know you'll never buy. They're always watching you."

"Why didn't you rip up the schedule and go off on your own?"

"I tried that. It was a complete disaster. I left early one morning and took a train down to Naples. Richard decided that I had been kidnapped by the Mafia. They were talking to the *carabinieri* when I returned."

Billy appeared and gave Richard a fax. Apparently there was some kind of business emergency because they both left immediately. Without the host, dinner ended abruptly and everyone left the table. I saw Daniel glance back at Julia, but he didn't approach her.

"I'll tell Richard that you argued passionately that I should become executive director," Julia said. "He'll be very pleased."

"Richard won't believe you. I've never argued passionately about anything."

We stood together in the hallway. "You think you're a cynical person, Nicky. Sometimes I feel the same way about myself." Julia nodded to the Rivertons as they walked past us. "But we're both amateurs in this crowd."

I WAS RESTLESS that night and didn't feel like going to sleep. The Irish antiques were so carefully arranged that I was tempted to push the furniture into sloppy clusters. I drank two large glasses of whiskey, then put the gum boots and the rest of my hunting kit back in the basket. I decided to go downstairs and give it back to one of the servants. Maybe I would find a lonely maid folding table napkins who wanted to talk.

At night, the hallways were like a real medieval castle: dark and empty with a draft of cold air coming from somewhere. Downstairs, I got lost twice before finding the hallway that led to the library. I decided to take another look at the Turner painting and headed toward a yellowish light that glowed through the glass panels.

I stopped and peered through the glass. Daniel and Julia were at the end of the room, sitting in front of a fire. Daniel was on a small couch, leaning forward with his hands clasped together. There was a direct sincerity, an openness in his manner, that reminded me of our conversations back in Italy. Julia sat on a straight-back chair about four feet away from the couch. She wore the dress from dinner with a black shawl draped around her shoulders.

I saw all this in a moment, a quick glance through a pane of glass. There were two sources of light, a reading lamp near the bookshelves and the fire itself. Although I couldn't see the expressions on their faces, their bodies showed the unity of a single composition. If I had been in the room with a camera, I would have taken the photograph with the orange glow of the firelight slightly left of center. It looked as if Julia was pulling Daniel toward her.

I had always savored the intimate moments of strangers: a man embracing his wife at the Macedonian border, a young woman in Cape Town holding her lover's hand. But I knew Daniel and Julia, and that made all the difference. Like a thief startled by a burst of light, I turned quickly and hurried away.

11 THE PARTY

I left the bathroom light on in my room, but the ghost came back with
his creaks and sighs. Early in the morning I heard a sharp tapping
sound, and I was half convinced that the dead Mr. Robinson was trying to send me a message. When I got out of bed, I realized that the
tapping came from somewhere outside the house. Yanking open the
curtain, I saw men pounding stakes into the grass. They were beginning
to set up tents for the party.

I got dressed and went outside. The grass was still wet from last
night's storm, but there was a sharp breeze and the clouds were moving south. Out in the courtyard it looked like the circus had come to
town. A gang of young Welshmen had already raised one large white
tent and were working on a second. Canopies and portable walkways
connected these two structures to a pair of smaller tents, one for the
cooks and the other for a bumper-car ride.

Trucks squeezed through the main gate where a forklift unloaded
storage containers. A trailer with toilets and dressing rooms had been

set up near the house for a circus troupe—muscular men and women from eastern Europe. I could see some performers sitting on lawn chairs, smoking cigarettes and watching everyone else work. Butchers showed up with cases of meat. There were dance floor installers, liquor deliverymen, and electricians who connected every cord to a thick black power cable that snaked over the wall.

A young woman carrying a loose-leaf binder stood in the middle of the confusion. She was small and trim, with short blond hair, and looked like the kind of person who had done gymnastics as a child. Before I could say anything, she approached me and flipped through her binder.

"Are you one of the comedians?"

"No. I'm Nicky Bettencourt."

She recognized my name and nodded. "Dreadfully sorry. I'm Vivian Hedges. I've hired two comedians and neither one of them is here."

"Are they putting on a show?"

"Not exactly. They're part of the computerized entertainment."

The forklift whizzed past us carrying a portable stove and Miss Hedges hurried after it. I tagged along, peering over her shoulder, and discovered that the binder contained employee names, pager numbers, and a twelve-hour schedule, broken down into five-minute increments. Disasters didn't frighten Miss Hedges. There was even a section marked CONTINGENCY PLANS.

Most men I know dream about movie stars or the airbrushed models in lingerie catalogs. My secret desire was to marry someone like Miss Hedges. There was something irresistible about her meticulous planning and her belief that there was a correct way to do everything. Under her influence, my own sloppy life would become organized.

I raised my camera and got shots of her dealing with a drunken Polish midget who was part of the circus troupe and a French chef who kept poking his finger at the gills of a sea bass. Miss Hedges spoke in a polite but firm voice and pointed to her binder as if it were a sacred text.

In the middle of all this confusion the two young comedians showed up in a mud-splattered sedan. They got out, looked around at the castle, and began to complain about their advance payment.

Miss Hedges smiled at me. "I'm sorry, Mr. Bettencourt. But I need to speak to them privately."

"Sure." I lowered my camera. "Maybe I'll see you later on today."

I returned to the morning room to get breakfast and found Julia drinking tea at the mahogany table. She was wearing a sweater and jeans. No jewelry. The clothes looked far more natural on her than the dresses she had worn at dinner. "Did you sleep well, Nicky?"

"All right. This is a creaky place."

"It's a ridiculous place. Imagine cutting down hundreds of trees and digging up tons of slate just because you liked *Ivanhoe*."

I served myself some scrambled eggs, then dropped two slices of bread into the toaster. "If you have a free hour, maybe you could give me a tour."

"Sorry, there's no free time. I've already been given my schedule. I have to escort Connie and Jax to a beauty salon and then we'll have lunch together. They'll spend the whole day gossiping. First they'll say, 'She's one of my best friends,' then they'll tell you something awful."

"Make an excuse. Don't go."

"It's important that they have a pleasant weekend. They've given political support to Hand-to-Hand. It's maddening to think that being charming and buying the right kind of champagne has anything to do with feeding hungry people, but it's all connected. You saw the refugees and the IDPs at Kosana. The food they were eating was purchased by this silly charity auction we had last summer. People paid a great deal of money to fly to Barbados in Richard's corporate jet."

The toast popped up and I returned to the side table. "I guess it's necessary."

"Of course. But sometimes your activities are so far removed from the result that it all gets rather convoluted. For example, I want to buy four portable power generators for Hand-to-Hand which means"—Julia finished her tea and stood up from the table—"I get my hair done in Cheltenham."

AFTER BREAKFAST, I put on a jacket and went back outside. I walked around to the tennis court and found Digran sitting alone on a bench. The poet wore a new Burberry trench coat that was two sizes too large for him; his body seemed lost in the loops and the buckles.

"How are you, Mr. Petrosyan?"

"Very good, sir. I have just received a letter from your American government." Digran took a fax out of his coat pocket and carefully unfolded it. "It will give me a visa to go to the United States. My niece and her family live in Hollywood."

"A lot of Armenians live in Hollywood these days. It's a nice place, but don't expect to meet any movie stars."

"I don't care about movies. Are there any gardens in Hollywood?"

"Sure. You can grow anything in southern California."

"I will become an old man, sitting in his garden. That's what happened to Dante. Maybe I'll write a poem there. Do you think it's possible?"

"You'll write a lot of them."

I decided not to tell Digran about the Los Angeles smog, the traffic, and the earthquakes. After we finished talking, I crossed the moat and strolled through the sheep pasture. Charlie Drayton, the actor turned shepherd, was sitting on a stump while his rented flock was scattered in front of him. He held a cell phone in one hand and was studying the buttons.

"Good morning, Mr. Drayton."

"Morning, sir. You a guest at the castle?"

I nodded and introduced myself. "So how are the sheep doing?"

"The sheep are fine. All they do is eat and look stupid." He glared at his cell phone. "I'm the one with the problems."

"Phone doesn't work?"

"Me manager left a message on me answerin' machine. Said I'm not gonna be Captain Maslow. You know what I'm talkin' about, sir? Face on the cracker box."

I vaguely recalled a bearded sea captain on a brand of English crackers.

"Company wants a new face so I auditioned. It's only five hundred pounds for all rights, but there are buckets of gravy. I'd get paid extra for TV ads. Paid extra for store appearances. And they were talkin' about a trip to America." Charlie closed his eyes and sighed. "It would be a grand thing to be Captain Maslow."

"But you weren't chosen."

"Didn't get the callback. Don't know why." Charlie resumed dialing. "Now, I can't get hold of me manager."

I continued across the pasture and the sheep shied away from me. "Good luck, Mr. Drayton. I hope it all works out."

"If they hired that wanker Joe Emery, I'm going to be angry. He showed up smokin' a pipe and wearing rubber boots, but he's as much a sea captain as one of these bloody sheep."

I TOOK A LONG walk to the edge of the estate and when I got back a tour bus was trying to squeeze through the barbican gate. Miss Hedges stopped the bus and unloaded the passengers—over two dozen young men and women. "Follow me," she chirped. "Right this way!" Miss Hedges led them into the bumper-car tent where rows of folding chairs faced a large TV monitor. I lingered near the opening while she snapped a cassette into a VCR machine.

The monitor began to play a video that showed a waiter pouring wine and serving dinner. "As you notice, he always takes the plate from the right side," Miss Hedges said, then stopped the tape and pointed at each detail. There was something unusual about the group and I realized that none of them had displayed a mustache, tattoo, or nose ring. The young men and women leaned forward as if they were watching a crucial lecture for their A levels. As the documentary began to show an elderly waitress serving hors d'oeuvres, Miss Hedges hurried over to me.

"Now Mr. Bettencourt. This isn't for your eyes."

"Call me, Nicky."

"Better get dressed, Nicky. The party starts at six o'clock."

"Will you eat dinner with me?"

"I'll be much too busy for that."

"What about a drink?"

Miss Hedges guided me out of the tent and began to close the canvas flap. "It's possible. We'll see."

My shoes had been shined and my new tuxedo had been brushed and laid out on the bed. I got dressed and inspected myself in the mirror, then sat by the window and watched as several helicopters swooped over and landed on the pasture. Richard's guests were arriving. Limousines and black sedans rolled through the barbican and stopped in the courtyard. It was just a party, but I felt like I was walking toward gunfire.

I stepped out into the hallway and saw Julia standing in front of Daniel's door. She wore a red off-the-shoulder dress that rustled when she moved. The floor creaked and she turned toward me, looking surprised.

"I'm looking for Daniel. He's not in his room."

"Sorry. I haven't seen him."

"The man who runs the estate garage said that Daniel borrowed the motorcycle. I don't suppose you know where he went."

"No."

"Do you think he decided to return to London?"

"Anything's possible. But he probably would have told me."

"Yes. He said you were his best friend."

I wanted to ask Julia about that comment, but Billy appeared in the hallway. His muscular arms and chest were stuffed into a tuxedo and he reminded me of a bouncer at one of the London casinos.

"Julia! I've been looking all over for you. Richard wants to see you in his office."

"I'm sorry. I dropped by to see Nicky."

We all smiled at each other, chums forever, then Billy jerked his head slightly. "Better go."

"Why don't you come along and look at the tower office, Nicky? It's quite wonderful."

Julia touched my arm and we followed Billy down the hallway. The hem of her dress brushed against the banisters as we climbed a narrow staircase up to the third floor. Fat little cherubs were painted on the ceiling above us and a cast-iron snake was twined around the railing.

We entered a circular room with three slit windows that overlooked the front courtyard. Halogen lighting fixtures set into the ceiling illuminated a desk with a steel column attached to each end. Both columns had segmented arms with thin computer screens that could be swiveled into different positions. In his dress shirt and black bowtie, Richard sat at the desk glancing at the images on four different monitors. Somewhere in the universe of the Riverside Bank, a research assistant was evaluating a takeover target, a real estate agent was searching for a place to put a branch office, and a man in Tokyo was selling millions of yen.

"There you are, darling." Richard typed something and the monitor screens began to go blank. "We lost track of your location."

"I ran into Nicky. We were just about to go downstairs."

Richard pushed back his office chair and stood up. "Take mental notes, Nicky. I'll be curious to get your reaction tomorrow morning. Julia thinks that the party is nonsense, but you have to make people feel good about giving you money."

"Whatever works."

"Exactly." Richard walked over to a file cabinet, opened a drawer, and took out crocodile-skin jewelry case. "I'm afraid this isn't a gift, Julia. It's just a loan from Asprey and Garrard. I told Billy to take photographs of that dress you're wearing and he e-mailed the images to London. The manager at Asprey thought this would match."

He opened the jewelry case to reveal an emerald necklace and matching earrings. The emeralds were so large that they looked like chips of bottle glass. Richard moved his wrist slightly and the green stones seemed to glow with their own power.

"The big one in the middle actually has a name," Richard said. "It's called *La Dorada*. That's a village in the mountains of Columbia."

"I can't wear that, Richard. We're asking people for donations tonight. Aren't they going to look at this necklace and wonder why we don't sell it?"

"Our guests are going to look at you and this necklace and think, 'How beautiful she is, how attractive.' They don't give money to beggars on the street. They give it to people who look just like them, only better."

He took the necklace out of the box and fastened it around her neck. Julia put on the earrings and touched the dark green stones. They seemed to absorb some of the warmth from her skin. "It does look nice. Doesn't it, Nicky?"

"Yes. It's quite beautiful."

Julia pushed back her hair and turned to Richard. "What happens at the end of the party? Does a little man appear and take it all away?"

"Billy is in charge of the emeralds. He'll make sure they're safe." Richard slipped on his dinner jacket. "Nicky, if you don't mind, Julia and I need to talk about the guest list. A few special donors are coming tonight and I want them to receive extra attention."

"No problem. I'll see you at the party."

I went downstairs and followed a red carpet out into the courtyard. About a hundred guests had already arrived and they were drinking and chatting with each other in the reception tent. A string quartet sat on a platform and played classical music. Couches, chairs, and potted trees from the conservatory had been arranged around the portable dance floor.

The clean-cut young people were serving drinks and hors d'oeuvres. They wore skinny black neckties and white shirts with the Hand-to-Hand logo silk-screened on the front pocket. The staff was inexperienced but cheerful, and one of the women coaxed me to try an egg roll. Miss Hedges had changed into a blue satin evening gown. She wore a radio headset with a tiny microphone and clutched her binder. I grabbed two flutes of champagne off a tray and approached her. "You said you'd have a drink with me."

"That wasn't a promise, Mr. Bettencourt. I didn't write it down."

"Here. Take it anyway." She accepted a glass and took a cautious sip. "These servers look great. Very impressive."

"Yes. Mr. Seaton didn't want professional waiters."

"I didn't know that Hand-to-Hand had so many volunteers."

Miss Hedges scrunched up her nose and giggled. "Oh, they're not volunteers. Hand-to-Hand doesn't have any volunteers. They're a Mormon youth group who wanted to get money for their missionary work." She took another sip. "I tried to hire Jehovah's Witnesses or Seventh-Day Adventists, but they refused to handle alcohol. The Mormons will serve wine, but they won't drink it." A server walked past us and she put her champagne glass on his tray. "And isn't that what you want from a waiter?"

A voice had apparently come over her radio headset. "Of course," Miss Hedges said. "Right away." She left me and hurried over to the bandstand. Bright lights glowed from outside the tent. Richard had let in a TV news crew to shoot the beginning of the party. I was about to get another drink when I saw Daniel entering the tent.

He wore a tuxedo and dress shirt with black jade cuff links. His appearance was quite presentable, but there was a fierce intensity in his manner that made me cautious. If we were strangers, meeting in a bar somewhere, I would have concluded that he was going to start a fight or end a fight before the evening was over. Several women turned their heads, staring at him.

"Where have you been?" I asked. "I haven't seen you all day."

Daniel took a glass of champagne from one of the waiters. "I borrowed the motorcycle and rode west down some country roads. This is a beautiful country, Nicky. Lots of streams and stone bridges."

"Julia was looking for you. She knocked on your door."

Daniel's relaxed manner disappeared. "When was this?"

"About twenty minutes ago. I saw her in the hallway and then Billy came along. Right now she's up in the tower with Richard, talking about donors."

"What did she say to you?" His voice was calm and deliberately neutral.

"She wondered if you'd gone back to London."

"No. I wouldn't do that." Daniel stopped talking when Julia and

Richard entered the tent. He watched Julia intently as people approached her and shook hands.

More guests arrived and the circus performers slipped into the tent. I thought that Miss Hedges would have to tell them where to go, but she had already handled that. Strips of masking tape had been placed on the floor at precise locations. There were no clown acts or flaming torches, but all the performers were talented acrobats. They didn't smile, speak, or play the crowd. Wearing a skin-tight cat suit, a female contortionist got up on a pedestal and began to do her act.

More guests arrived. People glanced at each other, not knowing how to react, and realized that it was sophisticated to ignore the circus performers. A woman wearing spangles did a one-armed handstand on a man's head while the people around them sipped champagne and talked about joining the League Against Cruel Sports. People laughed a little louder. They grabbed for the champagne when the tray drifted by. The woman doing the handstand seemed bored and the man supporting her looked like he was waiting for a bus. It was only when I got closer that I saw the slight trembling of her biceps.

When most of the guests had arrived, Richard climbed up onto the bandstand. He tapped his finger on the microphone and everyone stopped talking.

"Welcome to Westgate Castle. I want to thank all of you for coming tonight and showing your support for Hand-to-Hand. We're going to have a wonderful meal along with dancing, entertainment, and lots of wine. Your only responsibility is to enjoy yourselves so let's get started!"

Miss Hedges raised her hand like an officer leading a charge and the guests followed her out of the tent. Billy emerged from the crowd wearing a headset and carrying a cell phone. He walked up to us and smiled as if he had just won the lottery. "The home secretary is coming here in a helicopter."

"Nice way to beat the traffic," I said.

"They told us he had an important meeting, but now he's on his way. I guess this party is important enough for him to change his plans."

Miss Hedges had placed Daniel and me next to each other in the dining tent. Each of the round tables had a centerpiece of flowers and ferns. Two electric cables fed up from the center of the table and they were attached to a pair of small robots. There was no fake skin—you could see the wires and little electric motors—but one robot was definitely a dog and the other was a cat. I thought they were just for decoration until the dog walked across the table and stopped in front of Daniel's soup bowl.

"Hey, boyo," the dog said with a Irish accent. "You going to eat that soup?"

The robot cat sauntered over, making little buzzing and clicking sounds. "Ahhh, leave him alone. Can't you see the man wants a pint?"

I could see a video camera hidden in each centerpiece and figured that the two comedians I had met that afternoon were controlling the robots and providing their voices. The robot cat wagged its mechanical tail while the young Mormons served sea bass, Chateaubriand, or a vegetarian casserole. They weren't very good waiters, but people felt better about drinking too much and stuffing themselves with food if they were sponsoring such a clear-eyed group of volunteers.

I glanced around the room as people talked and forks clattered against dishes. Julia sat up on the dais between Richard and Digran Petrosyan. The poet was swallowed up by his rented tuxedo, and his shirt collar made a stiff white circle around his neck. I noticed Daniel glancing at Julia as he ate, but she didn't look at him at all.

After the coffee and cognac had been served, a spotlight was pointed at Richard and he stood up with a microphone. "Good evening to my friends and tennis opponents," he said. A few people laughed and the room quieted down.

"I was told by a gentleman who works for the humane society that the best time to ask for money is after the dinner but before the indigestion. Actually, most of you have already contributed to Hand-to-Hand and I expect some spirited bidding during our auction. Although this evening is a fund-raiser, it's also a celebration of Hand-to-Hand's first year of operation. In business, I've never been afraid of trying something new, and I hope that Hand-to-Hand reflects my own philosophy. We have formed an organization without a cumbersome bureaucracy. When an international crisis occurs, Hand-to-Hand will be there on the front line, saving lives."

There was an appreciative murmur from the audience. I heard the Indian woman next to me whispering to her husband. "He's going to run for Parliament. They just have to pick his constituency."

Richard continued. "Some of you might have read an article in the *Times* about our refugee camp in northern Uganda. The success of this effort is entirely due to the dedication and hard work of Dr. Julia Cadell."

Richard turned slightly to Julia and touched her shoulder. The audience applauded, and she nodded slightly. "Julia exemplifies the spirit of our organization. She's knowledgeable and courageous, ethical and innovative. It is for this reason that I am proud to announce that she has decided to serve as Hand-to-Hand's first executive director."

The audience applauded. I watched Julia's face when Richard made his announcement. For just a moment she looked surprised. Then she recovered and smiled graciously. After years of relief work her immediate impulse was to save the food, save the trucks, save the organization. Richard knew that she wasn't going stand up in front of all those contributors and walk out. The most vulnerable people in the world, I thought, are those who feel responsible.

"Dr. Cadell will start work immediately to organize a team that can respond to any international crisis. To do this, we need money, your money. As a businessman, I know that nothing is free, so tonight I'm going to auction off some wonderful gifts in exchange for your contribution."

He pulled a half-dozen index cards out of his pocket and began to auction off a trip to India in his corporate jet with a moonlight dinner at the Taj Mahal. The bidding was loud and spirited. Billy maneuvered around the room with a portable microphone, and several wealthy types made jokes about Richard's TV ads and tennis skills before they pushed up the bid another five thousand pounds.

I looked over at Julia. She looked startled and tense. Finally Richard sold the last item and smiled at his audience. "And now!" he said. "There's only one last thing to do! Let's dance!"

The swing band in the reception tent began to play "Jump, Jive, and Wail." The music blared from speakers hanging from the tent posts. Everyone applauded and a sizable part of the crowd streamed toward the dais to congratulate Richard and try to shake his hand.

Only Daniel and I remained at our table. The robot dog was suffering from a computer glitch. He raised his foot and nodded, over and over again.

"Julia didn't want that job," Daniel said.

"Yes. I saw her face."

"Think she'll do it?"

"Maybe. People like Richard usually get their way."

"He wants to run for Parliament and she's just part of the plan."

"Stay out of it, Daniel. She can make up her own mind."

"I'm just sitting here. I should be doing something, but I'm not."

"Nothing wrong with that. Sitting is an undervalued activity."

We stayed together until I felt like he'd calmed down; then I went to find Miss Hedges. A crowd blocked the entrance to the reception tent, but I wiggled my way inside. Wearing zoot suits and two-tone shoes, the swing band wailed on the platform. Julia and Richard were out on the floor, dancing like a bride and groom while everyone watched them. As the band finished playing, Billy hustled over to Richard and whispered something. I figured the home secretary was just about to arrive because Richard introduced Julia to a group of donors, then left with Billy.

I found Miss Hedges at the opposite end of the tent, still holding on to her binder. Some of her hair had broken loose from her barrette, but other than that she looked as perfect as ever. The band started playing again and I had to shout to be heard.

"Where do you live, Miss Hedges?"

"In London."

"Perhaps I could call you up next week. We could go out and have a drink or something."

Miss Hedges looked as if she'd been presented with a new problem. She glanced down at her binder as if it might provide the appropriate response. "I'm dreadfully sorry, Mr. Bettencourt, but I don't have a great deal of free time these days. I'm getting married in six months and I have to organize the wedding. I still haven't found a caterer that meets my standards."

"Right. Of course. I understand."

I backed away from Miss Hedges and lost myself in the crowd. The rejection didn't bother me as much as the five or ten seconds that she had looked at me and evaluated the entire package. If I had been holding one of my cameras, I could have deflected her attention and taken a picture.

I wandered over to the next tent. A steel floor had been installed on the ground and an electrified wire mesh was overhead. People sat in little cars big enough for two and drove around smashing into each other. It was designed for teenagers at a carnival, but Richard's millionaire guests were clamoring for a ride. Band music blared out of the speakers. Each car had a steel rod touching the mesh and the electricity crackled and sparked whenever someone stepped on the accelerator and raced across the steel floor. It was every man for himself. Whenever they hit another person especially hard, they'd laugh and keep driving.

I went back into the dining tent to find Daniel, but he had disappeared. Only Digran Petrosyan was there, still sitting at his place on the dais. He had a pen out and was scribbling in a little notebook. He could have been writing a laundry list or a new poem.

"Everything all right?" I asked.

"Yes. I'm healthy. But thank you for your concern. I was worried that I'd have to give a speech, but Dr. Cadell told Mr. Seaton that I preferred to remain silent." The poet shook his head. "I'm tired of saying thank-you to everyone I meet."

"Did the crowd make you nervous?"

"Not at all." Digran gestured with his pen at the tables and the flowers and the waiters picking up the plates. "All this is only . . ." He paused for a moment, searching for the right English word. "Decoration."

I grabbed a bottle of champagne from one of the tables and went in search of Daniel. In the courtyard, I stood beside the service tent where the staff had prepared dinner. I could hear the cooks shouting at the waiters, the band playing "Take the 'A' Train," the electric crackle and smash of the bumper cars, someone shouting for a woman named Vanessa, and a power hoist groaning as it lifted a stove back into a delivery truck. The portable sodium lights burned with a cold white power and moths fluttered and bounced against the Plexiglas covering. Suddenly, a helicopter roared over the courtyard with red and green lights flashing. The home secretary had arrived.

Julia passed though the barbican gate and entered into the shadowy light on the edge of the party. She was holding the hem of her dress with one hand but moved with the same confident stride that I had first seen at the refugee camp. Miss Hedges hurried across the courtyard and the two women met beneath one of the lights. Julia nodded and followed Miss Hedges past the reception tent to the castle.

The sounds of the party began to fade as I walked through the narrow tunnel of the barbican gate. I came out onto the bridge, crossed the moat, and followed the driveway down the hill. Daniel was standing by a stone wall and looking up at the sky.

"Daniel. What are you doing out here?"

"I wanted to get away from the noise." A match flared up as he lit a cigarette. For a second I saw him looking excited and happy, then the match went out and his face was absorbed by the darkness. "You okay, Nicky? Having a good time?"

"I guess so. It's not the usual kind of situation for me. Most of the time I'm on the outside, holding a camera. Now I'm on the inside, with just myself."

"What do you think of Billy?"

"A thug in a nice suit."

"But you're not scared of him?"

"No. I can handle someone like that."

I sat on the wall and watched Daniel pace back and forth in the middle of the driveway. From a distance the party tents glowed with a soft white light, like luminous jellyfish floating through a dark sea.

"The *Washington Post* sent me to Brussels to interview a physicist who said that the universe was composed of twenty-three dimensions. One of his graduate students helped me write the article because I didn't really understand the theory. But I figured it out tonight. You can be lost or misguided, then you step off the path, make a certain choice, and you're in a completely different place where all things are possible."

"Sounds good to me. When do I make the choice?"

"It'll happen to you, Nicky. Just keep looking."

Daniel touched my shoulder and headed back to the castle. As I remained on the wall, I heard the faint rustle of something moving through the grass. I thought it was an intruder, someone who had overheard our conversation, but it was only a ram with a broken horn that emerged from the darkness and blinked at me.

12 The London Train

Half asleep, I heard a soft rapping sound that got louder and more insistent. A key rattled. The door swung open and someone switched on the lights. I sat up in bed, groggy, trying to focus.

Billy and Richard entered the room like two detectives raiding a drug house. Richard darted over to the bathroom and glanced inside, as if someone could be hiding there. "Where are they?" he asked.

"What are you talking about?" I exaggerated my confusion, but I knew right away what had happened. Although Billy wasn't pointing a gun or holding a club, the expression on his face made me breathe a little faster. It was the look of malevolent seriousness that soldiers and cops showed right before they started to hurt you.

"Julia and Daniel are gone. They've left the house."

"Maybe they went for a walk or something."

"A six o'clock in the bloody morning?" Billy took a step toward the bed. "Don't lie, you fat bastard."

"I don't know what's going on."

Richard glanced at the armoire, paused a moment, then controlled the impulse to yank open the doors and peer inside. "Last night, Julia told me she was tired. She left the party and went up to her room. I woke up early, slipped in to see her, and she was gone. All the jewelry I gave her was left on the dresser, along with this note." He reached into his shirt pocket and pulled out a sheet of white stationery. "Did Daniel talk to you? Did he tell you where they were going?"

"No."

He unfolded the letter and read it aloud. *Dear Richard. I'm going away with Daniel McFarland. I know this seems crazy and I don't expect you to understand. Perhaps we can talk after some time has passed. I'm very sorry.* Richard stared at the piece of paper as if he doubted its reality. "She's very sorry. What kind of explanation is that?"

"I don't know anything. Swear to God."

Richard raised his forefinger and jabbed it in my direction. "Julia was very important to me."

It's all in the details, I thought. That's what Billy had said. I was glad that Richard hadn't predicted this particular detail, but I knew enough to keep my mouth shut. In a situation like this, it was best to play the role of the plump and bumbling photographer.

"They were talking to each other last night at the party," I said. "But I also saw them talking to everybody else. Daniel just survived this horrible plane crash, Richard. He's different, these days. He's not himself."

"He really won't be himself when I find him," Billy said.

"Where does Daniel stay when he's in London?"

"I don't know. Doesn't Julia have an apartment there?"

Richard began pacing again. "She stays with her friend Laura."

The question of where they might be staying deflected the anger away from me; Richard was a businessman and people like that focus on solutions. He had lost Julia. Instead of asking why, he'd decided to find her.

"If you hear from Daniel, I want you to call me at the Riverside Bank in London. There will be an appropriate reward for doing so."

Richard headed toward the door and Billy followed him. I heard their voices moving down the hallway. "Contact all the village taxi drivers."

"Yes, sir."

"Is there a car-hire office in Gloucester? Find out right away."

"I'll do that, sir."

I splashed water on my face, then pulled on some clothes. I remembered my last conversation with Daniel near the gate. He and Julia had already decided to run away. That's why he had asked if I could handle Billy. I had dodged and shuffled through the initial confrontation, but now I realized I should get away from Westgate Castle before Billy came back to ask more questions.

I slipped out of the room with my luggage and crept down the staircase to the kitchen. Wearing a stained T-shirt and looking very unbutlerlike, Wallace stood near the sink. He filled up a kettle with water and placed it on the burner.

"Good morning, Mr. Bettencourt."

"Morning, Wallace. Look, I need to get out of here as soon as possible. Could you call a taxi?"

"That's easily done, sir."

Wallace went over to a wall phone and dialed a number. It was obvious that he had just woken someone up, but he didn't apologize. "We need a car at Westgate Castle. Right away." He turned and looked straight at me. "Drive round to the back."

Wallace picked up a tin of Yorkshire tea and spooned some into a pot. The kettle began to whistle and he poured the boiling water. "Tea will be ready in a few minutes, Mr. Bettencourt. Would you like a cup before the taxi arrives?"

"If you don't mind."

"Milk? Sugar?"

"Everything." I watched him open up the refrigerator and take out a milk carton. "You know, don't you?"

"Know what, sir?"

"That Julia and Daniel ran away."

Although I'd spent an entire weekend with Wallace drifting around,

I had never really seen him, as a person. Now, he was standing in the middle of the kitchen, studying me with his watery blue eyes. Not a bad man. But not a strong one. Drinking problem, maybe. He needed this job.

"I heard some sounds around four o'clock so I looked out my window at the courtyard. Dr. Cadell and Mr. McFarland came out carrying their luggage and the motion-detector lights went on. They walked through the gate and went away."

"Why didn't you tell Mr. Seaton they were leaving?"

Wallace hesitated, then spoke with a firm, proud voice, heavy on the northern accent. "Because I'm not some bloody fetch dog like Billy Monroe."

A sleepy taxi driver showed up twenty minutes later. As we drove toward the main road, I saw Charlie Drayton climb out of his Ford Fiesta and walk toward his flock of sheep.

I had to wait an hour at the village railroad station, and I kept thinking that Billy was going to show up. I didn't completely relax until I got on the London train and it glided out of the station. In the dining car, I bought a scone wrapped in plastic and a Styrofoam cup of water with a tea bag drowning at the bottom.

For most of my life I had watched other people's affairs like a scientist observing different specimens, but this time it felt different. I realized suddenly how much I wanted Daniel and Julia to get away and create their own version of happiness. They were both solitary, difficult people who seemed to be more comfortable in a war zone than in a living room. Yet if they could come together, then perhaps there was a chance for someone like me. Obviously I wasn't going to end up with Miss Hedges, but there could be somebody else and we could pack our suitcases and walk out the gate and escape from the fear and the failures of the past.

My camera bag was on the overhead rack. I took down the Nikon, loaded a roll, and stared out the window. It was a gray, drizzly morning and fog drifted across the parceled fields.

Julia

13 THE CANAL HOUSE

When I was a child, I was so inspired by the graceful beauty of Olympic ice dancing that I begged my parents for pair of figure skates. The gift arrived on Christmas morning and there's a badly focused snapshot of me tearing the wrapping paper off a cardboard box. The boots were white leather with pink laces; the blades were chrome bright and very sharp. I pulled on the skates in my bedroom, but I resisted using them, sensing that my clumsy performance on real ice would never match the smooth perfection of my dreams.

One evening my father tied the laces together, draped the skates around my neck, and took me to a frozen pond a half mile from our house. I sensed his irritation as he gripped my hand and pulled me out onto the ice. For a cold half hour, I wobbled and slipped and whimpered. I was annoyed with my father for refusing to let me fall, annoyed with my own failure, and I wished a painful death for all the glamorous figure skaters who had ever appeared on television.

I was so frustrated that I pulled away from my father and, with ten or twelve frantic strides, began to skate alone across the ice. Without making a conscious decision, I was moving very quickly toward the edge of the pond. I barely knew how I had started and didn't know how to stop. I should have been frightened, but the relief of breaking away and the elation of finally moving forward was so overpowering that I stood up straight, extended my arms and glided toward the darkness.

AFTER RICHARD WENT OFF to prepare for the home secretary, I circulated around the tent talking to the guests. There was a feeling of comfortable superiority in their conversation, an assumption that we were all in the same little club together. No one asked about Hand-to-Hand and the women kept reaching out to touch the emerald necklace. My tight dress and high heels, the noisy dance band, and the crowd made me feel trapped. I left the tent searching for some fresh air, walked across the courtyard, and passed through the castle's barbican gate.

Alone on the bridge, Daniel looked up at the night sky. I could only see his silhouette at first, the broad shoulders and longish hair. My father would have said that Daniel wasn't a gentleman and perhaps that was true, but there was a sense of grace about him, a resourcefulness and strength that was reflected in his manner. He was everything I feared and wanted, all at the same time.

I walked up to him and stood very close, but we didn't speak. Daniel reached out and pushed some hair away from my face. He leaned forward slowly, and I was very conscious of the choice I was making. I could have run away from him, passed through the gate, and rejoined the others, but I let him kiss me and I kissed him back. When I stepped away from him, I shivered slightly. Daniel removed his evening jacket and draped it over my shoulders. The lining was still warm from his body.

"Let's get out of here," he said. "We'll go to London."

"You mean now?"

"I've got my cell phone and some money. I'll call a taxi. The driver can pick us up on the road."

"Daniel, I can't."

"Because of Richard?"

"No, because of Hand-to-Hand. If I quit tonight and walk away, everyone would know what happened. The donors are here, the home secretary is about to arrive."

"And he expects to meet you?"

"I just need a few more hours," I said. "Give me the rest of the evening."

We kissed again and then lights were flashing in the air and I heard the sound of the approaching helicopter. I left Daniel, and when I passed back through the gate Miss Hedges rushed over to me. "The home secretary has arrived," she said. "Mr. Seaton wants to introduce you."

I thought about the warmth of Daniel's jacket while I talked to the home secretary and his entourage of clever young men. I could still change my mind. No one knew what had just happened outside the gate. If I had been cautious or reasonable I would have postponed the decision, but I didn't feel cautious at that moment. Though I didn't have a clear plan for the future, I knew it was wrong to stay with Richard.

"What a wonderful party," the secretary said. "You've certainly accomplished a great deal in a very short period of time."

Richard put his arm around me and gave me a little hug. "I've had some help."

"Of course. I'm not forgetting Dr. Cadell." The secretary raised his voice so that everyone could hear him. "The prime minister believes that your organization is the perfect conjunction of private compassion and public policy."

We guided the secretary over to the bumper-car tent and our guest squeezed his plump body into a toy police car. The power was switched on and the drivers careened around the steel floor, smashing into each other. I glanced at Richard. He was smiling like an impresario who had just created some elaborate theatrical entertainment.

"Richard, I'm exhausted. Would you mind awfully if I went to sleep?"

"Go on. Get some rest. You were wonderful, darling."

"I hope we raised some money."

"Bags of it. Everyone's very impressed."

Back in my room, I removed the necklace and earrings, dropped them in their case, then shook it slightly. Away from the light, the power of the emeralds disappeared and they rattled about like ordinary stones. I laid my evening gown on the chair, put on my jeans, and packed a suitcase. Richard and I had separate bedrooms at Westgate, but I was worried that he would knock on my door after the home secretary left. Sitting on the edge of the bed, I listened to footsteps moving up and down the hallway.

I waited for hours, trying to control my imagination. Daniel came to my room at four in the morning. We were quiet walking down the hallway and I could hear my own breathing. Daniel opened the front door gently and then we were both outside in the courtyard. As we moved across the flagstones, a motion detector switched on the security lights. I thought there would be an alarm, too, some clanging bell that would wake up the house, but nothing happened.

The party tents looked slack and exhausted, heavy with the evening dew. Smashed glasses and empty bottles were scattered across the grass. We crossed the courtyard with our suitcases bumping against our legs and passed through the gate. The sky was still dark, but the stars were fading away and a faint line of morning light had appeared on the horizon.

DANIEL USED HIS PHONE to call a taxi and it met us on the driveway. We reached Kemble at five-thirty and got on the next train to London. In the car, we sat on opposite seats. Looking at him, I felt as if I had just woken up in bed with a stranger. I didn't know that much about Daniel, but I was drawn to him, even when he'd made me angry. The strength of my emotions, the connection I felt between us, made me wonder. Had my past relationships all been half steps, small commitments held within the boundaries I had created? This was a change, perhaps. I wasn't sure. Would we separate by the time we reached the next station?

Richard would have made an organized presentation at that moment, taking out a pad of paper to list all the reasons why I was making the right choice. Instead, Daniel moved to the seat next to me and slipped his arm around my shoulder.

"Shall we take a plane to Italy?" he asked.

"No," I said. "Not right now. Richard would follow us there."

"What do you think he'd do?"

"I don't want to find out."

"I'm not the sort of person who likes to hide."

"We're not hiding," I said. "At least, I don't see it that way."

Daniel was quiet as the train stopped in Swindon. When we started moving again, he looked out at the flat farmland and the road running alongside the track. "There was a jazz ballad that was popular in the 1950s," he said. "It's called 'Let's Get Lost.' "

"I like that idea. Can you arrange it?"

We checked into a small hotel near Paddington Station and took the lift to the fourth floor. Daniel tossed his bag onto a chair, then closed the curtains. Both of us were exhausted. Still in our clothes, we fell asleep on the narrow bed.

I woke up that afternoon when someone ran a vacuum cleaner in the hallway. Daniel had vanished, and for a few panicky minutes I thought that he had fled the hotel and caught a plane back to Rome. No, I thought. That couldn't happen. If Daniel had changed his mind, he would have switched on the lights, sat on the bed, and told me.

I splashed some water on my face and was ordering tea when Daniel returned. He had been down in the lobby, calling his contacts in London to ask if they knew of an empty flat he could sublet for a short time. After leaving messages on a dozen answering machines, he got a call from Carter Howard, the photo editor at *Newsweek*. Carter told him to ring his lover, Jonathan, who had an artist friend who was running off to California.

"She needs someone to watch her house," Daniel said. "For one week or one year. She's not quite sure. Let's have dinner and go see her tonight."

We ate at an Indian restaurant, then took a taxi over to the Canal House. Amy Pickering was in her late forties, a heavy-set woman known for her silk screens of old news photos and her antiwar politics. One night, as she was waiting for friends at the Sheraton Hotel bar, she'd met an American marine, a young fighter pilot on his way back from a NATO military exercise.

They ended up in bed, which was improbable, and fell in love, which was impossible. Now the pilot had been transferred back to the Air Ground Combat Center in the desert near Twentynine Palms, California, and Amy was following him there. She felt like Marlene Dietrich taking off her shoes to run after Gary Cooper and the other Legionnaires as they slogged through the sands of Morocco.

"I'm crazy to do this. Absolutely insane." Amy gestured with her hands as she gave us a tour of the house. "I hate the army and the navy and the bloody air force. All those stupid uniforms and macho death wishes." Amy had no idea how long she'd be in the States and offered us a low week-to-week rate.

We stayed at the hotel for a few more days while Amy bought her tickets and finished packing. I hadn't earned much of a salary working for relief organizations, but they paid your expenses on a field mission and I had managed to save up a fair amount. Daniel had given most of his savings to Boma Mission and a convent of nuns in Rome, but several German and Scandinavian magazines still owed him payment for articles. Together we weren't exactly rich, but comfortable enough to stop working for a few months. I decided to stay away from Laura's flat and buy a few extra clothes when I needed them. Laura would have asked me for an explanation and I didn't know what I would say to her. Perhaps I was acting like a complete fool and throwing my life away, but I wasn't in the mood to hear that from a friend.

On the day Amy was supposed to leave, we bought bagels and cream cheese and went over to the Canal House. Amy's bags were packed, but she kept changing her mind about her fighter pilot. "He likes sexist video games and McDonald's hamburgers," she said. "But he's innocent about most things and very affectionate." She looked down at her tea cup. "He also has a very smooth stomach."

"Go with the stomach," Daniel said. "You can change the politics."

A taxi came to the door and Amy sent it away. Finally, she gave us the keys when a second taxi appeared. Looking giddy and frightened, Amy waved out the window. The cab disappeared around the corner. Daniel closed the door and we stood in the entryway looking at each other.

When I was a girl on family trips I had always kept the road map beside me, determined to save my parents from the wrong exit and the unknown road. I hated getting lost and refused to go on any journey without a plan. But now I was here, with Daniel, in a stranger's house without a job or responsibilities. I felt as if I was standing on the edge of a dark lake and I didn't know how deep it was or if there were sharp rocks hidden beneath the surface. There were so many reasons to be cautious, but I took Daniel's hand and we jumped together.

WE STAYED INSIDE the Canal House for the next two days, mostly in bed. I remember looking down at Daniel's face and trying to memorize his features: the dark brown eyes and the small scar near his chin. I lay beside him and then beneath him while he lifted me off the mattress. And then I was above him again, kissing his chest and stomach. Silence, then inexplicable sounds, both of us holding on hard, almost desperate, until the ending and the silence again. Sheets pushed onto the floor. Fogged-up windowpanes. And we both started laughing for no reason at all.

Daniel and I finished off the food that Amy had left in the refrigerator, then made our first explorations through the neighborhood to buy food and wine. Returning home, we examined our sanctuary for the first time. The Canal House had been built in the nineteenth century and it displayed all the redbrick confidence of the Victorian Gothic style. It had buttresses on the corners and a brick pinnacle decorating the roof. The Pakistani immigrants who lived in the neighborhood ignored the building, but once I caught an older man with a tweed hat staring at the house with a look of amused condescension.

The house had two stories: one at street level, the other below the street that was supported by the bridge that curved over Regent's Canal. As we returned that day on the canal path, I looked up and saw the arched windows, all of them framed by intricate brickwork. To me, it looked like a Victorian chapel, something staid and industrial that had once blessed the coal barges pulled through London.

Set apart from any other buildings, the house felt like an island in the middle of the city. When you came through the front door there was a small bathroom on the left side and a walk-in closet on the right. After that, you were standing in one long space, divided by half walls into a kitchen and a living room that looked out over the canal. There was a power plant across the way and at night small white lights glimmered on the turbines and towers, like a Christmas display without the star.

The house was filled with a jumble of cast-off furniture, the sort of tables and chairs you bought from friends who got married or took jobs in the States. Everything was saggy and frayed and we never worried about spilling a cup of tea. None of the silverware matched and the dishes were chipped and cracked. The kitchen stove rarely started on the first match and we learned to treat all the appliances like aged relatives that need to be coaxed and coddled to behave. The clothes dryer didn't work at all until Daniel took it apart and discovered that mice had been chewing on the drive belt.

Amy's silk screens and posters hung on the walls, but mainly there were books. Thousands of books. Sometimes I thought that the Canal House was sort of a black hole: when a book passed across the transom it was pulled into the building's gravitation thrall. They were stored everywhere, in heavy oak shelves and board-and-brick improvisations. There had been no attempt to organize them by genre or theme; a romance novel with a lurid cover was squeezed between *Critique of Pure Reason* and *The Practical Apiarist.*

A spiral staircase with a curving banister led downstairs to a bathroom with a claw-foot tub, an artist's studio littered with canvases and half-finished paintings, and a bedroom with old-fashioned wooden blinds. Down there, closer to the water, you could see the brightly painted narrow boats that were moored on one side of the canal. I discovered that people lived on the boats, all year round, using propane burners to cook and little coal stoves to keep themselves warm. In the morning, light was reflected off the water onto the bedroom ceiling. I used to wake up early and lie in bed watching the water light while Daniel moved restlessly in his sleep. Cut into strips by the blinds, the light shimmered and sparkled on the white plaster until a narrow boat approached the house and a dark shadow swept across the room.

BY UNSPOKEN CONSENT, we declared our own private republic and seceded from the rule of time. A digital clock was in the bedroom, but Daniel unplugged it because he disliked the glowing green numbers. "It's too insistent," he said, and that became a code word between us. We decided not to be insistent or nervous about anything. Daniel threw out his last two packs of cigarettes. We went to bed when we felt sleepy, opened our eyes when sunlight entered the bedroom. I'd go upstairs and brew a pot of tea while Daniel made muddy-looking coffee with a French press. We ate simply: I'd make toast or pour a bowl of cereal. Daniel ripped off stale chunks of bread from yesterday's baguette and dipped them in his coffee while he sat at the kitchen table and gazed out the window at the canal.

A pair of swans and a half-dozen sea gulls were usually floating on the dark water. Coal fires burned in the narrow boats, and the sharp smell of the smoke reminded me of the bonfires at Kosana. Plump men in warm-up suits jogged slowly down the canal path, passing old women walking their dogs. While I poured my second cup of tea, the people who lived on the narrow boats left for their jobs or emerged on deck to water their potted plants. As the weeks went by, Daniel made up elaborate stories about these boat dwellers. A bank robber hiding from the police lived in one boat next to a young woman novelist in a green boat who lived next to a bearded man in a yellow boat who had murdered his wife and was removing her body in little parcels.

We went out in the morning, walking a few blocks west to the open-air market on Church Street. Music floated out half-open windows and blared from boom boxes: Sufi chanting, hip-hop, and jazz. Girls with lime green hair searched for cheap shoes and costume jewelry while Muslim women, concealed in black chadors, pushed their wire shopping carts past Jamaican women selling flowers. We bought food and clothes and music CDs from the street peddlers, but we never bought a newspaper. Before he'd gone to Africa with Nicky, Daniel said he'd read three or four papers a day. When I brought home a copy of the *Guardian,* he refused to look at the front page. "It's too insistent," he said, and I gave the paper to the Ceylonese man who sold fish.

We'd return to the Canal House after shopping, lock the door and search through the piles of books. I read *Middlemarch* and *The Woman in White.* Daniel was more eclectic. He read Philip Larkin's poetry for the first time, Joyce's *Dubliners,* and an elaborate book, with blueprints, about how to build your own sailboat.

No television. No radio. Instead we went downstairs and made love in a slow, deliberate way. Daniel recorded tapes of his favorite music and played them when we were in bed together. Sometimes I felt like the music was a liquid and I floating within it. I listened to a John Coltrane solo from a club recording of "Blue Train" and Cannonball Adderley's sad, reflective version of "Autumn Leaves." The clock with the numbers was hidden in the closet and everything we did had a certain languorous quality. I remember Daniel lying naked on the bed while I kissed every spot of his skin. I remember him touching my breasts with the palm of his hand, so lightly that I could barely feel it. One afternoon as it rained I lay on the bed, warm beneath the faded blue coverlet, staring out the window. Daniel held me in the crook of his arm and ran his hand from my shoulder to my knee and back again.

We talked about the past, but not in the usual way. Richard had always been curious about my previous lovers. How did you meet him?

Did you love him more than me? But Daniel never asked these questions and I didn't want to know about his old girlfriends. At the Canal House, there was no one before and no one after.

We had both worked in so many of the same countries that I didn't have to explain everything to him. I could say "I ran a clinic in Sarajevo" and not have to describe the daily sniper fire and the half-starved orphan children rocking back and forth on their mattresses. Daniel would say, "We crossed the border into Liberia, but we couldn't find the rebels" or "It was difficult to travel through Angola that year." And I would close my eyes and see him in a car on a dirt road with hidden land mines, his driver fearful, begging to turn around.

"Sometimes you're lost and scared," Daniel said. "But you can't act that way. You can't show weakness."

"And what do you do when you're lost?"

Daniel drew invisible patterns on my back with his finger. "Always ask for directions from a clever eight-year-old. As people get older, they learn how to lie."

We never talked about the desire for excitement and the sense of mission that had pushed us both into these dangerous situations. For the first time in many years I had truly stepped away from it all and, when I was alone, I tried to assess my life. I had become a doctor to help people and that was still true. Though I didn't want to be famous or wealthy, I was tempted by something even more seductive—that feeling that I was the crucial person, the one who was needed. Perhaps Daniel felt the same emotion. I once asked him why he avoided other journalists and traveled with just a photographer. "Because then it's my responsibility," he said. "I'm the only one who can tell the story."

Sometimes, over a bottle of wine, we'd talk about the plane crash that killed Paul, Tobias, and Joan. Daniel didn't feel guilty about what had happened, but he couldn't believe, as he had in the past, that life was a series of random incidents without implications for the future. He talked about living a life that would justify the fact that he had survived. For years, he'd wandered from one country to another, getting interviews and writing articles, then returning to Bracciano. But the plane crash made him feel that his own existence was a privilege with unknown obligations.

I FOUND SOME COOKBOOKS under the bed and we began to take turns making dinner. One of us would go off alone and come back with surprises in a shopping bag. We offered each other strange foods, expensive foods, pastry and sweets and fruits that we had never tried before. One night, we ate eight kinds of cheeses—a pale yellow Pont-l'Évêque, a wedge of soft Boursin triple crème sprinkled with powdered sugar. Daniel bought fresh mangoes and dipped them in chocolate. I baked a coconut cake and covered it with butter icing. As a medical student I had lived on plastic pouches of food, warmed in microwave ovens. I knew almost nothing about cooking and was constantly burning things or watching cakes go flat for mysterious reasons. But there were occasional triumphs. I made a crème caramel that was perfect, the rich custard surrounded by brown sugary syrup. Daniel ate a spoonful and smiled. "It's delicious," he said softly. And I leaned across the table and kissed him, tasting the sweetness on his lips and tongue.

November turned into December and there were short, cold days with an overcast sky. Ice appeared on the surface of the canal and the sea gulls and swans paced back and forth on the frozen surface like children locked out of their playground. Five days before Christmas, snow began falling, the white flakes clinging to the cables and covering the decks of the narrow boats.

Safe and warm in the Canal House, I realized that I had never really been alone. I had lived in dormitories in college and then shared several flats with friends. In the relief camps someone was always coming into your tent and the clinics were crowded with patients.

But there were enough rooms in the house to keep us from each other for long sections of the day. Daniel would be reading in the bedroom while I sat in the kitchen; then I would go downstairs to take a long, decadent bath while Daniel climbed upstairs to fix the washing machine. When I was with him, making love, there were moments so intense that both past and future melted away. But it was those hours when we weren't together that I fell in love with Daniel, remembering his honesty and intelligence, the way he listened to me and concentrated on my words. It gave me pleasure to sit alone and know that he was near me, in the house. And our love appeared slowly, like a plant growing or the sunlight changing or the warmth from a fire touching your skin.

All this was our life at the Canal House, but the whole time we stayed there both of us knew the same unspoken truth. Hiding behind the brick walls was only a truce in the battle, a temporary respite, and somehow, in some way, it would have to end.

A FEW DAYS before Christmas, Daniel was pouring his second cup of coffee. "I was thinking about Nicky," he said. "Maybe we could invite him over for dinner on Christmas day."

"I'd love to see him. You think he's in town?"

"If he is, he'll be staying at the Ruskin. It's a small hotel over by the British Museum."

Daniel dialed a number and seconds later he was talking to Nicky. "Yes. We're both in London. We've been here the whole time. Can I interest you in a Christmas dinner? No figgy pudding unless you want one." Daniel smiled and turned to me. "Mr. Bettencourt wants the complete Tiny Tim feast, if it's not too much trouble."

"Tell him we'll see what we can do."

We decided to roast a goose and make a pudding. On Christmas morning I put on makeup for the first time since leaving Westgate. Nicky arrived at two o'clock with three bottles of French wine. He immediately pulled out his camera and took a photograph. It made me feel like Daniel and I were an established couple and this was where we had lived for years.

We drank one of the bottles right away, then gave him a tour of the house. Anyone else would have asked about Richard and Westgate Castle, but Nicky never mentioned the weekend party. Nicky was a good friend, someone who would never judge you, but I could feel him watching Daniel and me. He noticed everything—how we touched each other, what we talked about, the books scattered everywhere. When we returned to the kitchen, Daniel started to carve the roast goose while I stirred up the gravy. Nicky stood by the refrigerator and took a second photograph.

After dinner, we pulled Christmas crackers and put on paper crowns. Nicky told us how *Newsweek* had insisted that he photograph an American actress starring in a big-budget action movie that was being shot outside of London. Nicky imitated everyone: the young woman, her unctuous personal manager, the harried West Indian makeup lady, and an Oxbridge type working as a publicist. The American actress was wearing a vial of her boyfriend's blood around her neck and she refused to take it off during the photo shoot. Nicky reenacted the entire screaming argument in different voices and I laughed so hard that I spilled my wine.

Daniel realized that we didn't have any brandy to set the pudding on fire. He went out into the city looking for a bottle while Nicky and I washed the dishes. "This is a comfortable place," Nicky said.

"We think so. Of course, Amy could come back at any time."

"Have you heard from her?"

"Not really. Just a postcard."

Nicky picked up a serving platter and began to dry it. "Two men have been following me whenever I leave the hotel. They're private detectives or something like that. I guess Richard hired them."

"Really? Are you sure?"

He nodded. "It's an older Asian man with a bad comb-over and a younger Brit with a squashed nose. They sit in a blue Ford Cortina parked down the street from my hotel. Whenever I come outside, one of them tags along."

"I'm sorry, Nicky. I don't know why you have to be involved with this."

"But I enjoy it. It's fun." Nicky smiled and I actually believed him. "I have a pretty boring life in London and this makes things a lot more interesting. Besides, these guys are amateurs. If I want to lose them, I just sneak out the back of my hotel. You probably shouldn't tell Daniel about this. If he sees one of these guys, he might get mad and start something."

Daniel bought a bottle of brandy at a Pakistani grocery store. He poured some on the pudding and it flamed up in the dark room. Everything was lovely until we opened a third bottle of wine and Nicky mentioned his recent trip to Kosovo. Suddenly Daniel was very intense, asking about the fighting between the Albanian guerrillas and the Serb militia. He knew the names of obscure political leaders and the commanders of the special police units. He knew who had massacred Muslims in Bosnia and where the killers had been hiding for the last few years. It annoyed him that the *Newsweek* correspondent working with Nicky had refused to leave Priština to travel through the countryside. "Yes, it's dangerous. But so what? That's part of the job. If you don't want to do it, then go back to Washington and write articles about the budget."

When the bottle was empty, Nicky called a radio taxi and ambled out the door. I closed the door and turned to Daniel. "Let's forget about the dirty dishes," I said. We took the candles downstairs and made love in the shadowy light. I felt a greater urgency that night, pulling Daniel closer, as if I could push away the conversation about the war. I wanted it to be just the two of us again, quiet and together, lying beneath the quilt.

The air was cold and our breath came out in puffs of white. Frost made a spidery pattern on the bedroom window. "It sounded like you wanted to go to Kosovo," I said.

"I was curious. That's all."

"You sure?"

He sat up and smiled. "This is where you are, Julia. Why would I want to leave?"

OVER THE NEXT few months we saw Nicky whenever he was in London. With most people, he played the role of a cynical photographer, but I started to see how vulnerable Nicky was and how carefully he protected himself from being hurt. Once he offered to show me his favorite exhibits at the British Museum and I took the bus over to his hotel. His room was a small and dreary place. Cardboard coffee cups and candy wrappers littered the little table near the sink.

"Height of luxury, as you can see," Nicky said. "My regular room, at the Ritz, is being cleaned."

"Where are your cameras?"

"Oh, I wouldn't keep them here. They're at a camera shop." He then described his photography equipment in great detail, as if this implied a more settled life.

Nicky had spent so much time wandering around the museum that he could have hired himself out as a guide. We saw the Sutton Hoo treasures first, and then Nicky led me into an Egyptian exhibit and stopped beside a stone sarcophagus.

"You two seem happy."

"Very much so."

"I'm the last person in the world to give advice about relationships." Nicky walked over to the next glass case and stared at a mummy. "You know, most people think that the Egyptians fished out a mummy's brains with a little silver hook, but that's not true. They forced a tube up the nose, broke through the brain case, and everything dribbled out like custard."

"Go on, Nicky. You were about to say something."

He turned and looked at me again. "So what happens when this woman comes back from California?"

"I don't really know. It will take some adjustments, but we can figure it out."

"Sounds good." Nicky bowed and gestured like a guide. "Now if you'd walk downstairs, Doctor, I'll show you the Shabaka Stone."

DANIEL BEGAN TO glance at the headlines of the newspapers on Church Street. Reading just a few words, he could figure out most of the entire story. As the situation deteriorated in Kosovo, he lingered in front of the racks, reading the lead sentence and then the first paragraph. On Valentine's day, I gave him a box stuffed with newspapers and magazines from five different countries. "Go ahead and read them," I said. "You're starting to annoy that poor woman at the stand."

He read everything in the box, then began to monitor different conflicts around the world. Daniel drank too much wine one night and told me about covering the war in Bosnia with a Polish photographer, Victor Zikowski. Their car hit a land mine as they were driving through the countryside and Victor bled to death while Daniel pressed a folded T-shirt over the wound.

"I was covered with Victor's blood," he said. "When I got back to Sarajevo, I dug a hole and buried my clothes."

He fingered his wineglass. "The one thing I didn't know when I was younger was that terrible images stay with you. They never really go away."

Daniel went out for a walk the next morning and didn't come back until sunset. We didn't talk about Victor again.

As spring approached, the swans broke the canal ice that formed overnight and swam about in their little patch of water. Daniel and I began to leave the house separately to walk through London. I liked to take the canal path to the bridge at Primrose Hill into Regent's Park. I'd pass mothers with old-fashioned baby carriages and businesswomen with leather attaché cases and practical shoes, walking quickly to their responsibilities. I'd always had a strong idea of who I was and where I was going, but now I found myself looking at other women and wondering about their lives.

A boating lake was in one corner of the park with a little island at the center. Gray herons were building nests in the island trees and I spent hours watching them. The herons were large, ungainly birds with white chest feathers. I watched them eat fish and fly around the park with their heads pulled back. Their nests were elaborate constructions of sticks and mud that looked flimsy and vaguely artificial, like something on an opera stage, but the birds fussed over them constantly and guarded their eggs.

I wanted to see the eggs hatch and watch the young birds learn to fly, but that meant I'd have to remain in London. I wasn't so different from

Daniel. We had both been drawn to a life of constant movement, the feeling that every minute was crucial to some larger goal. I was seeing the world—at least, that's what I told my friends—but now I wondered if I was seeing anything at all. If you settled down and stayed in one place, you became aware of the subtleties, the smaller changes around you and the changes in your own life. It was like stopping in front of a painting in a museum, stepping closer and studying the brushwork there.

In the news, the Serbs refused to sign the peace agreement and militia troops in Kosovo started to force the Albanians out of their villages. When NATO started its bombing campaign, Nicky dropped by to say he was off to Macedonia to photograph the refugees crossing the border. I was downstairs, reading on the bed, but the door was open and I could hear Nicky and Daniel talking in the kitchen.

"You should pay me to take your messages," Nicky said. "The *Washington Post* and the *Telegraph* keep calling me to ask about your health."

"And what do you tell them?"

"I said that you had some kind of injury from the plane crash. You're under a physician's care and you're getting better."

"I hope you didn't tell them that Julia was the physician."

"So, is it true? Are you getting better?"

"I guess so." Daniel paused. "After the plane crash, I thought I was going to change my life and do something different."

"You've already given away most of your money, Daniel. What else are you supposed to do?"

"I'm trying to come up with an answer." The floor creaked; water flowed through the pipes as Daniel filled the kettle. "Haven't been too successful."

"Maybe you survived so you could be happy with Julia."

"Yes. That's possible, too." His voice sounded slightly uncertain. "I don't know, Nicky. We're just living here. Not worrying about anything. It can't last forever."

Nicky left the next day. Daniel began listening to news broadcasts on the radio and I used Amy's computer to e-mail people I knew in different relief organizations. I learned that Richard had hired a temporary director for Hand-to-Hand. They'd flown to Skopje, Macedonia, and set up a refugee camp at the airport. The camp was disorganized and undersupplied; there were too many refugees and not enough food. In April, a negative article ran in the London *Times* about Hand-to-Hand. Typhoid had broken out in the camp because of poor sanitation, and several of the refugees had died. The article described Richard as a "billionaire playboy" and said that he'd refused to give an interview. Two weeks later, Hand-to-Hand pulled out of the country and the camp was taken over by the United Nations. I found myself wondering what would have happened if I had been there to run the operation.

On the island in Regent's Park, the heron eggs began to hatch, and the little birds appeared with dark feathers and small crests. I was watching one afternoon when a fledgling stepped out of the nest and was able to flutter safely to the ground. I bought a bouquet of purple irises to celebrate, even though we were trying to cut back on our spending. When I got back to the house, Daniel was in the living room, waiting for me to come through the door.

"Amy called from California. She's argued with her boyfriend about the NATO bombing. Now she thinks he's a fascist and she's flying home."

"How soon?"

"Two days. She's in Los Angeles, staying with some friends."

I walked up to him and we kissed as if to confirm that we were still together.

"We'll go down to Bracciano," he said. "It'll work out. I promise."

"Don't promise."

"I assume—"

"Don't assume."

"I hope."

And there was no answer to that, because I hoped, too.

• • •

WE TRAVELED DOWN to Rome on the train, picked up Daniel's car at the convent, and drove north to Bracciano. The air was warm and the trees along the road showed a green haze of new leaves. Mustard grew in the road ditches and a mass of white morning glories clung to a strand of barbed wire. We passed through a village. Daniel made a hard left onto what looked like a cow path, and we bumped down a dirt driveway past a line of cypress trees. The farmhouse was small, but there was a terraced garden and a grove of olive trees with little gray-green blossoms on the tips of the branches.

Daniel parked on a patch of gravel and a tiny woman in a black dress walked down from the garden. I had already been told about La Signora. I knew a little Italian and had studied a phrase book on the train. *"Buon giorno,"* I said, but she ignored me and began talking to Daniel. It was as if she had spent the last few months composing a very long speech about the farm. As she pointed and explained, we took a tour of the olive grove and the irrigated garden. One of the wells had gone dry and an army of snails had attacked the lettuce. The carrots were sick, but the parsley was triumphant. If something was in good shape, Daniel would say: *"Va benissimo."* If there was a problem with weeds, he'd look sad and murmur, *"Sono spiacente."* I'm sorry.

We stopped beneath the arbor and Daniel introduced me as *l'amica mia, la Dottoressa Julia Cadell.* La Signora stopped talking and appraised me as if I was a farm animal. I could tell that she was satisfied, because she put her arm around me and guided me through the house. She told me that Signor Daniel had been an irresponsible landowner, but now that such a gracious *dottoressa* had arrived, everything would improve.

We were nearly out of money. Daniel contacted the *Telegraph* and some German newspapers and arranged to write articles about the upcoming Italian elections. And for the first time since leaving Kosana, I started working as a physician. The daughter of one of La Signora's nephews was sick and the village doctor had left for Capri. I took out my medical kit and followed La Signora over to a house in the middle of an apple grove. The moment I stepped into the bedroom and saw the feverish child lying on a bed, my doctor self reemerged from hibernation. The girl had a bad ear infection and I prescribed some antibiotics. It was an easy diagnosis, but the parents were grateful and her uncle brought us six bottles of homemade wine.

After that the villagers decided that I was a good pediatrician, and I was asked to examine several children. I had trained myself not to feel an emotional attachment to my patients, but the informality of these examinations made me lose some of my objectivity. I liked to pick up the babies and feel their warm breath on my neck. Sometimes they would touch me and their hands would play with my hair. If I held them tightly, I could hear their breathing and their heartbeats seemed to dissolve through my own skin.

I spent one afternoon with the postmaster's wife and her baby, then returned to the house at sunset. Daniel had cooked roast chicken stuffed with garlic and fresh rosemary. He started a fire in the fireplace, mixed in a few cypress logs with the oak and a faint pine scent filled the living room.

"How's your new patient?" he asked.

"She's getting better. There's lots of pinkeye in the village. That's the third case I've handled this week."

"People don't always wash their hands."

He refilled my glass of wine, but I didn't drink it. "Daniel, I've been thinking. I want to have a baby."

I waited for what seemed like a long time. Daniel looked at me and I felt like he was considering all possibilities—then he smiled broadly.

"Yes. I'd like that to happen."

We never discussed it again. That was all that was needed between us. I was nervous but happy, filled with daydreams about the future. The first month went by and nothing happened, then the second month disappeared with the same result. La Signora sensed what was going on and started bringing me bunches of parsley and bottles of fresh milk from the village dairy, as if these foods would guarantee conception. Daniel and I had a moonlight picnic down by the bridge and we ended up making love on a blanket. Looking up at the stars, I felt as if I had been absorbed into the earth beneath my body. Surely this would be the moment. It must occur, now. But another month passed with no change.

ONE DAY IN JULY, Daniel and I woke up early, when it was still cool and pleasant enough to work. Daniel made French toast with our last two eggs and the bread left over from supper. We ate breakfast outside, with a basket of apricots and a jar of La Signora's strawberry jam.

I drank my tea, he sipped his coffee, and we both read the newspapers. The village postmaster brought us the *International Herald Tribune* and the *Telegraph* three or four days after they were published. I liked the fact that all the urgent stories had lost their shrill insistence. If you were reading about some crisis, it was already fading into the past.

"Looks like a visitor," Daniel said as a Ford sedan with rental plates turned off the road and came down the dirt driveway.

"It's probably another pair of lost tourists, like those Norwegians."

"I liked the woman, but her husband talked too damn much."

The sedan approached the house and I realized that Billy Monroe was driving. Billy parked next to the Alfa Romeo; then Richard got out and gazed up the slope. I had thought about meeting Richard again and in these imaginary conversations we were always polite with each other. Now the real person was here, just a few hundred meters away, and I didn't feel prepared. Perhaps I was a coward back at Westgate Castle, but on the night of the party it felt much easier just to give back the necklace, slip out of the evening gown, and walk away.

I heard a click as Daniel placed his coffee cup back on the saucer. He looked annoyed, but he didn't say anything. Richard left Billy standing beside the rental car and headed up the path. I could see that he'd lost weight in the last few months and that made him look older. As he approached the arbor, Richard's confidence asserted itself and he smiled cheerfully.

"Good morning," he said.

"Hello, Richard."

He nodded to Daniel. "Beautiful place you've got here. Do you own it?"

"Yes."

"Great location. Great investment."

Daniel glanced at me. "Would you like to speak to Richard alone?"

"Oh, no," Richard said. "I must talk to both of you at the same time." He sat down at the table. "Forget about what happened last year. That's over. It's in the past. When you two left I was surprised and upset, but I've dealt with it. Some things don't work out and you just have to accept the reality."

"Then why are you here?" I asked.

"Hand-to-Hand is in trouble. The entire organization is falling apart. I didn't realize how crucial you were," he said, turning to me. "I thought I could hire anyone to do the job. Our refugee effort in Kosovo was disorganized and misdirected. We got some bad publicity."

"I read the article in the *Times*," I said.

"Everyone read that bloody article. Donations are down eighty percent and George Riverton says that the government is reconsidering its support."

"I'm sorry, Richard. I'm not going to be executive director."

"Of course not. I realize that. But I do need your help with a specific situation. I don't know if you two have been monitoring the news from East Timor."

Daniel nodded. "They plan to vote on independence from Indonesia."

"Yes, exactly. When the independence side wins there are going to be refugees, food shortages, and a breakdown of public services. The Indonesian government has armed the local militias and they're already burning down people's homes. This is a crisis situation that will demand an immediate response. It's the precisely the reason why we created Hand-to-Hand. No red tape or committees. Just a group of organized professionals, saving lives. "

"And what do you want me to do, Richard? Go to East Timor?"

"Get us through this deployment while I look for a permanent director." He paused. "Without your help, the whole organization will collapse."

I glanced at Daniel and saw that he had assumed a deliberately neutral expression, the sort of mask he wore as a journalist. It was impossible to know what he was thinking and I felt guilty and boxed in. "I need to think about it," I said.

"Of course. Talk this over with Daniel." Richard glanced at Daniel and grinned as if they were old school friends. "If you don't mind, I'd like to walk around your garden."

Richard hiked back down the hill and Billy approached him. Murmuring to each other, they began to study the hollyhocks like botanists out on a field trip.

"What do you think?" I asked Daniel.

"It's up to you."

"Of course it's up to me. But I still want to know what you feel about this."

"You were right, Julia. I wanted to work in Kosovo. And you know what? I think you did, too."

"I felt responsible, if that's what you mean. There's nothing wrong with feeling responsible."

"I didn't say it was wrong."

"If an organization like Hand-to-Hand is doing some good, you can't just let it go under. You heard what Richard said. It's a short-term problem." I leaned forward and touched his hand. "Daniel, come to London with me. We'll rent a new flat, a place like the Canal House."

"We can't go back."

"You could work alongside me. You know three languages and you've been everywhere. You'd be a great help to any relief organization."

"I'm a journalist," Daniel said. "Not an aid worker. I know how to talk to an editor, travel to a new country and find out what's really going on. We're both professionals, Julia. It's time for us to rejoin the world."

"All this is because of Richard."

"We would have had this discussion, eventually. You're restless, too. It's time to see if we can work at our jobs and stay together. I think it's possible—"

"Hello! Hello, there!" Richard was calling to Daniel. "What are these pink flowers called? They're quite attractive."

"Valerian."

"Yes. Of course. Thank you." Richard nodded, then continued down the slope to the olive trees.

"Do you agree with what I said?" Daniel asked.

I shook my head. "I don't know."

"Then we'll stay here."

"No. That's not right." My voice sounded stronger. "I should take the job."

I TOLD RICHARD I'd return to Britain on Monday. "This is just temporary," Richard said. "Get us over this rough patch. That's all." He praised the farmhouse and the garden again, then got back in the car with Billy and disappeared.

That evening, Daniel boiled pasta and went out to the garden to get the ingredients for a salad. I called Laura to see if I could to stay with her until I rented a flat near the Hand-to-Hand office.

"It's such a shock to hear from you," she said. "You completely vanished. A man named Billy came by looking for you, but I couldn't tell him anything. He was very nice, said he was a friend of Richard's. Paid me your share of the rent, six months in advance. Your room is still here, waiting for you. "

It bothered me that Billy had given her the money last November. Richard had obviously expected to talk me into returning to London. He was right, of course. They had found me and now I was coming back. I had the impulse to hang up the phone and cancel the whole plan.

"So what have you been doing?" Laura asked. "Did you take a new job?"

"I've been traveling," I told her, as if my time with Daniel was a long journey to another country.

It was cold that night and we ate inside with candles on the table. I could feel my practical doctor self returning as I explained how I would organize the relief effort. Daniel nodded and gave a few suggestions, but for most of the evening he was quiet.

We made love that night with new urgency, postponing the moment when it had to end. Afterward, as Daniel slept, I went to the living room and sat on the couch with a blanket wrapped around me. Daniel was right about my growing restlessness. If I had gotten pregnant, if something decisive had pushed us off in a new direction, I would have been satisfied with our new life. But that hadn't occurred. Instead of changing ourselves, we had acted like fugitives, hiding from the world, avoiding our responsibilities.

When I returned to the bedroom, Daniel was lying on his back, breathing slowly, with his right arm lying on the pillow near his head. It looked as if he was throwing a ball or reaching for book or raising his hand to wave good-bye. Stay with me, I thought. Stay with me, forever. But I slipped beneath the blanket and lay beside him and didn't say a word.

Nicky

14 The Lamb

I had planned to fly down to Italy and stay at Daniel's farmhouse for a few weeks that summer. Daniel sent me occasional e-mail about life in Bracciano and the short trips he and Julia took around the countryside, but the messages stopped in July.

It had been nine months since Daniel and Julia had left Westgate Castle and I'd assumed they were still together. Lovers were supposed to break up in the wintertime when the heating failed and the water pipes burst. Lovers fought on Christmas morning, birthdays, wedding anniversaries, and at drunken parties in Hampstead when someone flirted with a stranger in the kitchen. They left each other after the children arrived or the bills came due or when someone's alcoholic father showed up expecting to stay for a few months. It seemed impossible that two people could find anything to argue about at Daniel's farm in Italy.

I had saved up enough money for a holiday and Carter Howard agreed not to call me for two weeks. A normal person would have flown to a tropical paradise where drinks are served with little umbrellas and French girls named Yvette teach you how to scuba dive, but I didn't feel like dealing with people. I had been traveling ever since I became a professional photographer. It feels all right if you keep moving, but the moment your train stops you start to wonder how you got there.

Instead of going to a therapist, I woke up late and watched wildlife shows on television. Richard Seaton had filmed a new commercial for his bank, which ran constantly. The commercial started with this big-necked lad named Shawn saying he never thought he'd own his own place and it ended up with Richard helping Shawn's family move their ugly furniture into their new house. In the final shot, Richard placed a snooker trophy on a shelf and Shawn rearranged it with a smile.

After seeing a documentary about manatees or a family of dingoes in the Outback, I'd walk across the street to the British Museum. I liked to sit in the long hall where they kept the Elgin Marbles. The sunlight filtered through the grayish glass overhead and the benches always felt cool to the touch. The sculptured horses stolen from the Parthenon so many years ago were always galloping forward, the stone centaurs always fighting, while voices of children echoed off the walls.

The Elgin Marbles would calm me down and I'd go outside to the portico. An endless stream of American, Japanese, and German tourists arrived in buses. They carried maps and guidebooks and showed ambition. They would enter the museum and see the Rosetta Stone. They would buy a souvenir for themselves or a gift for their relatives. Then they would leave and travel to another place and then another place after that.

That summer I was jealous of anyone with plans or a destination. Sitting by the Corinthian columns, I watched the tourists enter the museum courtyard. Something about me seemed approachable and couples offered me their cameras to take their picture. If they had given me a camera with an adjustable lens I could have deliberately blurred the shot or messed up the frame, but it was always a cute little device that focused and wound automatically.

I'd hand back the camera, resume my post, and watch my photograph walk away. I envied the people who posed together. Meeting some stranger and falling in love seemed to be the most ambitious thing anyone could do. To seduce another, please another, to enter into another or let them enter into you, to follow or guide another seemed like such a difficult task, and yet so commonplace.

At five-thirty the museum would close and the crowd would flow out through black spike gates. I'd buy two or three newspapers and walk over to the Lamb, a pub near Corams Fields. The original fields had been turned into a playground where no unaccompanied adults were allowed. You could peer through the iron railings and see children running around or riding on skateboards. Some bedraggled sheep lived on a strip of land near the fields. They were kept there for some kind of a petting zoo or as a feeble reminder of the distant countryside.

The Lamb was a cozy pub with a low ceiling and sepia photographs of nineteenth-century actresses and political figures. There was no recorded music, dartboards, or drunken yobs. I liked the pub's padded benches and the wrought-iron tables with a brass railing around the outside edge. If there was an earthquake or a bomb blast the little railing would keep your beer glass from falling onto the floor. After drinking a few pints, I would order supper and the food would come rattling downstairs in the pub's dumbwaiter. I'd drink one last beer, then stagger back to the Ruskin to check my e-mail. No message from Daniel or Julia. No messages at all.

IN AUGUST, THE PHONE RANG at one in the morning and I fumbled for the handset. Daniel was calling from his desk at the Stampa Estera.

"How's my favorite shooter?" he asked.

"I'm fine. Where are you? What's going on?"

"I'm flying to Macedonia to cover the fighting. Julia's back in London, running Hand-to-Hand."

"In London? Is that okay with you?" I asked.

"The organization was having serious problems and Richard said they needed a temporary director. It looks like Hand-to-Hand is going to East Timor."

"Are you still . . ." I didn't finish the sentence.

"Julia and I are doing our jobs. We're still together. Drop by the Hand-to-Hand office. I know she'd love to see you."

I USED MY LAPTOP to go online and find out about East Timor. Four hundred miles north of Australia, it was a small, poor province of Indonesia on one half of a dagger-shaped island. The country had no economic or geopolitical significance. It was notable only for the intensity and duration of its suffering. The Portuguese had once controlled East Timor. They made a profit from the sandalwood trade and introduced the locals to Christianity. After the Portuguese Empire collapsed, the Timorese fought among themselves for a few months, then proclaimed their independence. Indonesia already controlled West Timor. With encouragement from the U.S. government, they decided to invade the rest of the island. Years of fighting between the Indonesian army and the pro-independence guerillas had killed thousands of people.

Now there was a new government in Indonesia and the president had allowed the East Timorese to vote on a possible secession. The Indonesian army wanted to hold on to the province and it secretly organized and armed Timorese militias. When UN observers arrived to supervise the referendum, the militiamen began killing anyone who was in favor of independence.

The next morning I walked over to the new Hand-to-Hand headquarters on Gracechurch Street, down the block from the Leadenhall Market. This was bank and insurance-company territory, the sort of place where businessmen in dark suits carried copies of the *Financial Times*. Most of the other relief organizations in London were housed in converted flats near Russell Square. When you visited them, you found a temperamental copy machine and an electric teapot in the bathroom. Richard must have either owned the entire building on Gracechurch or controlled the property on a long-term lease.

No one was at the reception desk when I got off the elevator so I pushed through the glass door. A tough-looking young woman with piercings in her eyebrows and nose was sitting in an office, talking on the phone. I asked for Julia and the woman pointed me down the corridor. Little slips of paper were taped to the doors. COMPUTER ROOM. STORAGE ROOM. BOOKKEEPER'S ROOM (WHEN WE HIRE ONE). The last door proclaimed DR. J. CADELL: ACTING EXECUTIVE DIRECTOR. Although it was a provisional title, I realized that Richard had won a significant victory. Julia was in his world, sitting in a London office building, rather than making love to Daniel in Italy.

She was on the phone when I walked in and motioned me to sit down. The room was filled with standard-issue rental furniture, bar-code stickers still taped to the edges. The only decoration was a framed poster hanging on the wall, a silk-screen cartoon of a glamorous young woman looking annoyed. GENOCIDE IN THE BALKANS? The caption read. BUT WHAT ABOUT MY CAREER?

Julia finished her call and stepped around the desk. "Nicky! How nice to see you!" We hugged awkwardly.

"Big office."

"We're growing into it." She sat back down at her desk and we both gazed out the window at the wall of buildings across the street. I could just see the spire of St. Peter upon Cornhill.

"Daniel's going to Macedonia," she said.

"Yes. He called me."

"We used to talk on the phone every night. Now, it's down to once every few days." Julia glanced at me, wanting some kind of reaction, then looked away.

"You're both very busy," I said.

"Two more workers start on Wednesday. Three more in a week."

Julia began to explain what she'd been doing for the last few weeks. At established relief organizations, the staff would have written memos and held committee meetings, but she had been forced to make all the major decisions on her own. With help from Richard's bank she had bought relief supplies from wholesale companies in Australia and chartered a cargo ship to carry everything to Timor.

"What do you think, Nicky? I don't have enough time to train idealistic people so it's professionals all the way. That girl outside ran the phones for an out-call prostitution service. She's very good under pressure, doesn't take nonsense from anyone. Our transportation manager can actually repair a truck. I think he used to steal them."

"All this sounds quite revolutionary."

"I can tell them they've made a mistake and they don't burst into tears. It's quite wonderful, actually. No one on the staff has a therapist or a political agenda."

"Maybe they'll get that way later on."

"There's no later on. Everything's happening right now. Most of the other aid organizations are cautious, hoping things will work out peacefully, but I'm not optimistic. The Indonesian soldiers have been giving weapons to the local militia."

"So why are you going? What's the point?"

"We'll distribute food and medicine. I hope we can save some lives."

"But why do *you* have to go? Couldn't someone else handle the problem?"

"Yes. Definitely." She paused. "But I feel like it's my responsibility."

"You've always been responsible, Julia. You've helped thousands of people all over the world. Maybe it's time to retire and go home."

Julia considered the question as the photocopy machine spat out pages in the next room. "I don't have any excuses," she said. "No one depends on me, Nicky. I don't have a child or an elderly parent. I'm not running a business or teaching at a school. So when they show those pictures on television of sick children or people starving, I have to say to myself, 'I can go there. I can help them.' There's nothing holding me back."

"So you feel responsible because you don't have responsibilities?"

Julia looked regretful for a few seconds, then tried to cover it up by checking an order form. "My life could have turned out a different way, but this is the present reality." She tossed the form into a tray and became a surgeon again, disciplined and efficient. "You should always deal with the patient in front of you."

The receptionist walked in with a fax from Australia and placed it on the desk. "I'm sorry," Julia told me. "But I need to make some more calls." She escorted me down the hallway and to the elevator. "What's a stand-up guy, Nicky? That's an American term, right?"

"It's someone who won't turn his friends in to the police."

"Daniel told me that you're a stand-up guy. I guess that means he trusts you."

"I hope so."

"I worry about him. If you two end up working together, please make sure he doesn't do anything crazy." She stepped a little closer and watched my eyes. "Promise?"

IT STARTED RAINING a few days later. Cars hissed down the wet street outside the hotel. I sat alone in my room taking in words and images from East Timor on my computer screen. There had been a brief moment of peace on referendum day. Then the United Nations had announced that a majority had voted for independence. Street fighting started in Dili, the capital, and the entire country lurched into a civil war. After the United Nations pulled out, Indonesia's president asked for a peacekeeping force to take control.

I called the Hand-to-Hand office and the receptionist said that Dr. Cadell and Mr. Seaton had already flown to Australia. My phone at the hotel started ringing, but I refused to answer. I was still on vacation. It was easier to hide at the Lamb, drinking beer and reading the British tabloids. That summer, reporters were running around the country with thermometers looking for the working man with the hottest job in England. So far, it was a tie between a baker in Plymouth and a Jamaican who smeared tar on leaky roofs.

I thought about staying in the Lamb until my money ran out. When the phone rang early one morning I tried to ignore it. *Newsweek* always gave up after a minute or so, but this time the ringing didn't stop. That could only be Daniel.

I picked up the handset. "Forget it," I said. "I'm asleep."

"Hey, Nicky!" Daniel was on his cell phone, driving down to Rome. "Everybody's been trying to contact you. I'm going to East Timor with the UN task force. Julia will be working there, too."

"You don't have to go."

"Of course not. There's always a choice. I've thought about other jobs, Nicky. And I always come up with the same answer. I'm a good journalist. You're a good photographer. It's what we do."

He stopped talking and I could hear tires squealing as the car went around a turn. Daniel didn't beg me to go with him, but I suddenly felt childish for hiding at the Lamb. He needed a friend to come along. A stand-up guy.

"Slow down," I said. "I'll meet you in Australia."

15   DARWIN

I decided to leave immediately and was able to get on a plane going from London to Melbourne. It was a four-movie flight. My legs cramped up and I found it difficult to sleep. After I passed through customs in Melbourne I realized that I had eight hours to kill, so I took a bus into the city and walked down Flinders Street to a pub across from the train station. Young and Jackson's had once been a spit-on-the-sawdust establishment, but now it was slicked up like the rest of the city with a coffee bar on one side and carpets upstairs. Still, it was a pleasant enough place to sit at a corner table and watch the Australians drink. The whole country had a short-sleeve style. Even though some of the executive types at the bar were wearing suits, I felt like they were hurrying home to change clothes as soon as they finished their beer.

I left the bar with a vague idea of crossing the street to St. Paul's Cathedral and lighting a candle for good luck. The moment I reached the curb, the mixture of alcohol and jet lag hit me hard and I knew that I should sit down as quickly as possible. There was a tram stop near the intersection, the green and yellow cars heading out to the suburbs, so I stumbled onto the No. 8 and sat down near an open window.

I was worried about East Timor and the feeling was a bit stronger than usual, something more fundamental than tension about doing a good job. But the moment the tram closed its doors and started moving, the fear began to go away. The evening light softened all the sharp edges of the world. We crossed the Yarra River and there were two rowing shells gliding toward the bridge, the long oars breaking the surface of the water. An old man wearing shorts and black socks got on the tram followed by a group of schoolgirls in checkered jumpers. And suddenly I loved the old man and the girls, loved all the Australians with a drunken benevolence as we started moving again. Tram wheels clicked past a line of massive elm trees in Fawkner Park. Not many elms in America. Gone. All gone. Some kind of fungus. I remembered from childhood how the heavy, gray branches of the trees reached down to the grass, and if you slipped beneath them it was cool and quiet and safe. It was going to be all right, I thought. Relaxed and a little sleepy, I stayed on the tram as it made a dogleg turn at Park Street and clattered toward the gloom of lower Toorak Road.

I RETURNED TO the airport in the dark, ate a burger and some chips, then took the red-eye flight north to Darwin. The sun came up and I could look down at the countryside. There was a vast ocean of red desert, a yellowish flood plain, a dry riverbed slithering across the landscape like a giant snake. As we approached Darwin, the earth became greener, and we passed over lakes and farms, the rectangular fields bordered by roads. Small clouds made separate shadows on the land like little clumps of dark wool scattered across a meadow. Gradually, the trees below us moved closer together, merging in a tropical forest. The plane passed over the mangrove swamps on the edge of Frances Bay, circled over the ocean, then turned back toward the airport.

The runway was bordered with palm trees. It was early in the morning, but I felt the heat the moment I got off the plane. Wet season, the cyclones and the monsoon rains, were still a month or two away, but there was already some humidity in the air, a gathering tension for the storm that was going to arrive. Inside the terminal, I looked out the window at the tarmac and saw that a C-130 transport plane had landed and soldiers were unloading refugees from East Timor.

I left the terminal. A chain-link fence surrounded the airport runway, but I followed three military trucks through the parking lot to a guarded gate. Trying to look like part of the plan, I flashed my *Newsweek* ID card and nodded to the Australian army sergeant in charge of the convoy.

"Is this the right place?" I asked. "They just called me. I'm supposed to meet the refugees."

"Well, they're here," he said. "We're picking them up." The sky was clear, and bright sunlight bounced off every piece of glass and metal. I climbed onto the truck's running board and nodded to the guard as we rode out onto the tarmac. A group of civilian doctors and nurses were there to help the refugees getting off the plane. The Timorese were small, delicate-looking people with high cheekbones and round eyes. They had light brown skin: a mix of Malaysian, a little South Sea Islander, and four hundred years of the Portuguese. The older women had sarongs, but everyone else wore Western-style clothes and rubber thong sandals.

I got a wide shot of the Hercules transport plane, then took a close-up of an Australian soldier holding a little girl. An elderly Timorese woman began to cry, clutching a red cloth bag with all her belongings. When a very blond Australian nurse approached the old woman, I captured a good shot of the two cultures standing together. There, I thought. That pays the rent. Then a military policeman waved me away and I left the area, taking the airport shuttle into town. We rode past banyan trees and Carpenteria palms and climbing ferns with heart-shaped leaves. Some of the plants had shed their foliage during dry season and there was a sparseness in the vegetation like a man with thinning hair.

"Goin' to Timor?" asked the driver.

"Yes. In a few days."

"Wouldn't catch me there," he said. "Lot of shootin' and no sense."

I checked into a hotel on Daley Street and got a message from Daniel saying that he'd be in late that afternoon. Attaching my computer to the phone, I downloaded the digital shots and sent them to *Newsweek*. All my images were turned into bytes of energy, bounced off a satellite and thrown across the world. The blond nurse and the old woman would be sold and cropped and printed, an object independent of their lives.

I left the hotel and walked through Darwin. It was a small, compact city that had been built on a plateau above the harbor. A cyclone had knocked down most of the historical sites in the seventies and the replacement buildings were clean and blandly modern. Aside from a cluster of government offices, it was a tourist town. Big chain hotels that looked like stacks of poker chips stood next to smaller restaurants and hostels set up for the backpacker crowd. September was supposed to be the beginning of a quiet time for the locals, but now Darwin was filling up with journalists and aid workers and soldiers from twenty countries. I could tell right away that the people I passed on the street weren't there to take a tour of the crocodile farm or the pearl-diving exhibition. The United Nations had abandoned East Timor and now an international peacekeeping force was going to invade the country. Everyone seemed to be talking on mobile phones or hurrying down the sidewalk carrying manila envelopes.

I took a taxi to the airport to meet Daniel. Drivers from relief organizations were filling out greeting signs for their workers and a Portuguese army captain paced in front of the gift shop. Daniel's plane arrived carrying business travelers and a platoon of Portuguese soldiers, nice young men who looked like they expected to go snorkeling. The soldiers were followed by a UN contingent, and then Daniel appeared carrying a single travel bag and his laptop computer.

"How's the hotel?" he asked.

"It's small, but okay. The air-conditioning works and the TV has CNN."

"I got a message from Julia before I left Rome. She's in Darwin Harbor, on a boat called the *Seria*."

"And where's Richard?"

Daniel glanced at me and forced a smile. "I'm sure he's on the boat with Billy Monroe and a few Australians."

"Right. They probably hired some local thugs."

"Don't be so harsh, Nicky. Put a necktie on a thug and he becomes a security consultant."

Daniel checked into his room, then followed me down Mitchell Street through the city to the edge of the plateau that rose above the harbor. It was late in the day and the sun was low on the horizon. We could see nine military ships anchored in deep water, seven from the Australian navy, one from Britain, one from New Zealand—all part of the military task force that was going to take control of a very small country.

Stokes Hill Wharf was on one side of the harbor. It was a tourist destination with souvenir shops and restaurants. Fort Hill Wharf was a few hundred feet away. It was a fenced-off industrial area with a massive crane that was unloading twenty-foot-long cargo containers. Daniel and I followed a concrete walkway that led down the slope through some palm trees. We crossed the harbor road to Fort Hill Wharf, passed through a security gate and approached the *Seria*.

The ship was painted dark blue and rust marks trickled down from the scuppers. *Seria* was a city in Brunei, but the ship used an Indonesian crew and was flying a Liberian flag. If I had three or four years to waste I probably could have figured out who actually owned the ship. Later I learned that it was controlled by corporate shells within corporate shells, like a financial *matrioshka* doll.

We walked up the gangplank and an older Indonesian man with a wispy mustache appeared at the railing and spat blood into the water. He reached into a bag hanging from his belt and I realized that it wasn't blood at all, but the brick-red spit from chewing betel nut. Some Indonesians believed *siri pinang* returned the blood of your birth back to the ground, but as far as I could see, it just made your teeth rotten.

"Not permitted," the old man said.

"We're looking for Dr. Cadell."

"Must go way!" He spat again.

"Hello, there! What's the problem?" An older European man with a Dutch accent appeared on deck. He wore leather sandals and dirty tennis shorts. "May I help you gentlemen?"

"We're looking for Dr. Cadell."

"Ahhh, you mean Julia. Pak only knows the first names of our passengers." He spoke quickly to Pak using an island language. The Indonesian spat one last time, then turned and walked away.

"Sorry, gentlemen. Pak is rude as hell, but he's a good first mate." The Dutchman unfastened a rope and allowed us to come aboard. "Welcome to the *Seria*. I am Captain Peter Vanderhouten. You work for Hand-to-Hand?"

"No. We're journalists."

Vanderhouten rolled his eyes. "Please don't mention my name in your articles. I'm neutral about everything. No politics. No opinions. I do a lot of business with the Indonesians and they're angry about East Timor."

"We're friends of Dr. Cadell," Daniel said. "Is she on board?"

"Yes. She just came back from Government House with Mr. Seaton."

Vanderhouten led us down the port side of the ship, past the loading crane and the open cargo bay. I looked into the hold and saw pallets holding sacks of cornmeal and bottles of cooking oil.

"What do you carry when you're not working for Hand-to-Hand?" Daniel asked.

"Coffee beans. Tea. Dry squid. Cloves. We'll go anywhere. Load anything."

"Ever been to East Timor?"

"TimTim? Sure, lots of times. There's a sand bar at the east entrance to Dili Harbor. You have to come in slow through the channel, then turn west toward the wharf."

We reached the starboard side and saw Julia, Richard, and Billy standing near the railing. All of them wore blue T-shirts with the Hand-to-Hand logo. Billy had gotten a sunburn and the skin on his head was red and peeling.

"Good evening," Daniel said. "Anyone want to be interviewed?"

"Daniel! Nicky! Welcome to Australia!" Richard smiled and shook our hands. "When did you get in?"

"Just a few hours ago." Daniel was standing near Julia, but they avoided looking at each other.

"Where are you staying?" Billy asked. "The Carlton or the Saville?"

"The Top End," I said. "It's over by the Holiday Inn."

"Right. I know where it is." Billy didn't look impressed. "That's the one near Lizard's Bar."

"Billy and Richard are staying at the MGM Grand Casino just outside of town," Julia said. "It's a perfectly hideous place with ugly old people tugging at slot machines."

Richard looked amused, as if he had just encountered a child who hated ice cream. "It's quiet, comfortable, and everything works."

"It doesn't make any difference where anyone stays," Julia said. "I doubt if we're going to be here long."

Any sign of government control had vanished in East Timor, and Dili was being looted. After the independence vote the militia began forcing people onto boats to take them down the coast to the Indonesian province of West Timor. Julia described the violence as calmly as a State Department spokesman, but her hand trembled slightly when she pushed back her hair. Daniel began staring at her and that made me nervous. I still remembered Richard bursting into my bedroom at Westgate Castle.

"Well, I better get back to the hotel," Richard said. "Time to catch up on e-mail and see what's going on back in London."

"You'll check at the airport for the next shipment?" Julia asked.

"Of course. We'll go there tomorrow morning."

Billy winked at me like we were fellow conspirators. "Come and have dinner at the casino," he said. "Wednesday is lobster night."

The moment they left the ship, Daniel stepped forward and embraced Julia. "I missed you," he said.

"Missed you, too." They broke apart, still holding hands, and Julia smiled at me. "Sorry for the public affection, Nicky. Haven't seen this one for a few months."

"Don't worry about me. I'm going to look for a cold beer."

Daniel touched his canvas shoulder bag. "I've got the phone. I'll call you tomorrow morning."

I walked around the wheelhouse, heading for the gangplank, then heard footsteps. Julia had followed me. "I'm glad you're here, Nicky. I really am. Daniel said you had some doubts about coming along."

"I still do. But everything's going to work out."

"Of course it will." She gave me a quick hug.

Hiking up the steep walkway to downtown Darwin, I found a group of clapboard houses halfway up the hill. It was the Stella Maris Centre, a low-cost dormitory for sailors coming into the port. There was a bar in one of the buildings—a big open room with ceiling fans and louvered windows. I bought a schooner of Victoria Bitter, sat on the deck and looked out at the sea.

I had always been sensitive to the first signs of weakness in a couple's relationship. When two people were falling out of love, someone would always act sad or a little too happy. Daniel and Julia had come back together without effort, and their separation hadn't changed anything. In some peculiar way, I was involved with what had happened. I was their witness.

WE STAYED IN DARWIN for nearly a week before the UN peacekeepers invaded Timor. Billy hired Tig Collins and Harvey Briggs, two Australian security consultants, in order to get defensive weapons for the ship. Collins was the younger of the two, a blond surfer with a can of beer glued to his hand. Briggs was an ex-cop from the Northern Territory, broken-nosed and broad shouldered; he reminded me of a professional rugby player. Both men strutted around the main deck with their assault rifles, coming up with emergency scenarios. What if Malaysian pirates attacked the ship? What if the Indonesian navy tried to seize all the supplies? I felt like I was listening to two Hollywood screenwriters getting ready to pitch an action movie.

With these two jackaroos, it was easy to see the virtues of Billy Monroe. Billy was calm and confident. He realized that you could anticipate

problems but never predict the outcome. One day, Collins showed up
with a "croc sticker"—a sheath knife with a fourteen-inch blade. Slash-
ing the air with the weapon, he proceeded to tell us how to kill someone in two seconds. "Really?" Billy kept saying. "Is that so?" His right
arm shot out, there was a twist and a leg sweep, and Collins was lying
on the deck with the knifepoint pressed against his neck. "Better keep
practicing," said Billy. "Those crocs are pretty damn tricky."

Every morning, I would leave the hotel and walk down to the coffee shop on Stokes Hill Wharf. As the light changed and the ocean
turned from blue to dark green, I'd order a cappuccino and read the
Northern Territory News, a local tabloid with comforting headlines
like KANGAROO ATTACKS PICNIC or STOUT LOVERS IN A FROTH. By the
time I reached the sports section a large crocodile would inevitably appear a hundred yards from the wharf like a dark piece of wood floating in the water. The croc would drift toward the harbor, looking for
a stray tourist. Daniel would leave the *Seria* and join me for a cup of
coffee.

We would sit there for hours, talking about the stories Daniel had
written during the last few years. I remember a long conversation about
the black-market diamond trade, the pit mines scratched in the red dirt
of Angola and Sierra Leone, and the Lebanese merchants with their secret airstrips. European politicians as well as American intelligence organizations were involved in the business, and Daniel explained how
the diamonds were sold and how weapons were purchased for war-
lords and how a handshake between two men in Paris led to rape and
murder in Africa.

Julia spent her days on the *Seria,* making sure that the emergency
supplies arrived from Sydney. She had to assume that there would be
no electrical power in Dili and that the harbor equipment had been destroyed. Everything carried on the ship had to be taken out of their
heavy cargo containers and strapped onto wood pallets. The job had to
be finished in a few days, but Collins and Briggs refused to lift anything
and Richard was usually back at his hotel. The Indonesian crew hated
taking orders from a woman, but Julia ignored that and acted as if of

course they would obey her and of course this would get done. Wearing a wide-brimmed sun hat, she paced back and forth on the dock. Blankets go there. Tents go there. Please get me some more water bottles. Right away.

Daniel and I offered to help, but Julia turned us down. "You do your job," she told us. "I can do my mine."

Our job was just a lot of waiting around. Early in the afternoon, we'd leave the hotel and meet a crowd of other journalists at Stella Maris. The beer was cheap, and we could have our own table and buy a good lunch for a few dollars. I met several Australian photographers and a Spanish journalist who had spent a lot of time in Rwanda. On the second day, the famous Tristram Müller of *Der Spiegel* arrived from Germany.

Tristram weighed at least three hundred pounds. He carried the bulk well, moving in a slow, steady manner like an oceanliner passing through the water. The layers of muscle and fat seemed to insulate him from the shocks of the world. Tristram's editor kept calling him at five o'clock in the morning. "She wants the German angle to the story," he said. "When we finally get to Dili, I should look for blown-up Volkswagens and militiamen wearing lederhosen."

The German angle to the East Timor story became a running joke at what we decided to call the Stella Maris Social Club. Someone would announce that he was getting the Spanish angle on a new bottle of beer while a young photographer named Mulvaney would come up with complex Australian conspiracy theories that involved the forced consumption of Vegemite. We played pool on the coin-operated table and gossiped about the television journalists who hung out at the bar in the Carlton Hotel. "They've all brought flak jackets and army helmets," a British reporter told us. "Bunch of bloody poseurs. Wartime Charlies. You watch what happens in East Timor. They'll stay out at the airport, get a recording of gunshots, then bleed in fake bang-bang when they do their broadcast."

Daniel sat a few feet back from the crowded table and sipped his beer. He rarely said anything, but everyone knew who he was. Tristram

Müller cornered me outside the men's room and asked if Daniel had cancer or some other serious illness.

"Of course not," I said. "What gave you that idea?"

"He isn't like he was in Sarajevo. He reminds me of my father in the hospital room. Quiet, but watching everything."

Before sunset, Daniel would leave the social club and walk down the hill to the *Seria*. Usually I'd go back to my hotel and watch television, but one night I took a cab out to the MGM Grand and had an expensive dinner with Billy. After threatening me at Westgate Castle, I figured he owned me that much.

"Eat up, Nicky. You're my guest," he kept saying. "Order dessert. Order some brandy. Have some fun before the crucifixion." Afterward we ended up in the casino where I lost eighty dollars playing blackjack. There were no windows in the casino. No clocks or newspapers. Aside from the cricket match showing on a big-screen TV it was difficult to know if you were actually in Australia. Billy said it was a very American hotel, but it was more than that. America was the Snake River or downtown Memphis or the Blue Ridge Mountains—some location that was distinct in my memory. The casino was part of the growing worldwide nation of the Same. You could be in Cairo or Kathmandu, but you could still find the same pastel-colored furniture and piped-in music, the same bottled water and strip of paper on the sterilized toilet seat. No pine trees or fresh-cut clover. No smell at all.

ON OUR FIFTH DAY in Darwin, the *Telegraph* called and said it wanted an article and photograph about Hand-to-Hand. Daniel wrote five hundred words and e-mailed them to the paper while I boarded the *Seria* with my camera. Interfet, the UN military force, was sending the nine navy ships north to Dili. When I entered the cabin, Julia and Richard were trying to decide if they should leave with the convoy. Richard studied a map of East Timor lying on a gray steel table.

Tig Collins stood in the shadows behind Richard and clutched his assault rifle. You couldn't tell that he was a total idiot and that Darwin was as safe as the pope's bedroom. Julia stood on the left side of the chart table. She was beautiful and pale and tired from loading all the cargo. Captain Vanderhouten sat on the right side of the table, his face half buried in his hands. You couldn't tell that he was hung over and annoyed about missing his afternoon nap. Instead he seemed frightened and worried about his ship.

I knelt down on the floor like a true believer and shot upward so that Richard appeared tall and powerful when he made his decision. And it was fake and I knew it was fake, but it was easy and a damn good photograph and I had to take it.

The *Seria* left Darwin that evening. Twelve hours later, my photograph of Richard appeared on the front page of the *Telegraph* and in several other newspapers around the world. Editors were drawn to the image and they believed that Richard was a hero. Because the camera doesn't lie.

16   Into Timor

Like most of the journalists in Darwin, we'd been trying without success to get on one of the first planes going to East Timor. But after my dinner at the casino with Billy, Daniel and I were both moved up on the list and the Australian military command offered us body armor, ground pads, and food rations. We turned it all down, of course—too much weight. I was already carrying my cameras and Daniel had his sat phone and computer. We decided to bring along a change of clothes, a packet of Australian and American dollars, a few drugs and bandages, tropical chocolate bars, and four large water bottles.

"And buy a hat, Nicky."

"I hate hats. I look stupid in hats."

"The heat's going to get you," Daniel said. "Not the militia."

WE WENT TO WAR in a taxicab. Early Monday morning, the driver picked us up at the hotel and took us out to the Winnellie military air base. It was still dark, but the parking lot near the runway was crowded with armored personnel carriers, military Land Rovers, and Australian soldiers bunched up in platoons. The Australians wore green-and-brown camouflage uniforms and combat helmets instead of their usual bush hats. Everyone was strapping on body armor, backpacks, and web belts heavy with supplies. The extra gear made the soldiers appear large and formidable, until you saw their faces. Most of them were no more than twenty years old and Daniel talked to a soldier from Alice Springs who was only seventeen. They looked pale and tense beneath the security lights. Several platoons didn't have enough ammunition and their sergeants ran back and forth, borrowing rounds from other units.

A soldier was crying beside an armored personnel carrier, but when I went over with my camera a captain rushed up and said that he was going to send me back to Darwin. We started arguing, but Daniel slipped between us and spoke with a calm, soothing voice. I'm very sorry about this. He won't take a picture. Daniel took my arm and pulled me away before the captain could change his mind.

"Come on, Nicky. Let's just get on the plane."

"It was a good shot."

"I agree. But I don't want to lose you before we get to Dili."

Just before sunrise, the first transport took off, heading to East Timor. Three more flights left the air base before we followed a platoon of soldiers up the ramp of a C-130 Hercules. The inside looked like the long, ribbed belly of a whale. Canvas benches had been attached to both walls and two other benches ran up the middle. The Australian soldiers sat facing us, each man holding his rifle and a bottle of purified water. I checked my cameras one more time while Daniel studied his flash cards with phrases in Portuguese, Indonesian, and an island language called Tetum. "Stay buckled in!" shouted a sergeant. "If you feel sick, just lean over and spew on your boots!"

Our plane had a few small windows and I twisted around to look outside. The ocean was milky green close to the shore, then cobalt blue as we passed over deep water. We approached Timor from the south and began to fly across the island. There was a flat coastal strip, then tall mountains at the center covered with dense tropical vegetation. Dirt roads followed the ridges like the blurry lines from a brown crayon. The cargo plane reached the north side of the island, banked hard to the right, and flew toward Dili. A gray haze covered the harbor area and black plumes of smoke drifted up from oil fires. It looked as if the entire city was burning.

Our plane landed hard and taxied to the end of the runway. The pilot kept the engines going as the ramp went down and we quickly got off onto the tarmac. It was hot and sticky and there was a bitter smell in the air, as if someone had been burning tires and old cans of paint. The soldiers from our plane jogged over to three military Land Rovers, but when Daniel and I tried to follow them a corporal jumped out of the driver's seat and began shouting at us. "Get off! No room for journos! You're on your own!"

I hesitated, wanting to remain with the soldiers, but Daniel turned and started across the runway. He showed the same lightness, the sense of detachment, that I had first seen in Africa. "You know what, Nicky?" He glanced back at me and smiled. "I like that new hat of yours. It's got character."

"It's just a tourist hat. I bought it at a souvenir shop where they sold fake didgeridoos."

"Maybe it's a tourist hat, but you wear it with a certain flair."

The airport terminal consisted of three small buildings with steep metal roofs that were supposed to resemble the thatched tops of island huts. The red roofs were the first things you saw crossing the runway. They seemed to float above the banyan trees that surrounded the terminal area. Passing through a broken fence, we entered the airport waiting room. Plastic tables and chairs had been kicked over or smashed through the windows. Feces covered the floor and some of it had been smeared on the walls. We stepped carefully through the trash. Daniel motioned to my camera and I took a few photographs.

The hallway out was littered with paper, torn books, and trash. Bullets had chopped holes in the white plaster; it looked as if a madman had attacked the building with a hatchet. The office phones had been stolen; everything else was torn apart or smashed into pieces. Legs had been ripped away from desks and chairs. File cabinets had been pushed over and set on fire. A framed poster of an Australian flight attendant lay on the floor, defaced with bullet holes.

We left the building through a smashed-out door and stood beneath the shaded entrance to the terminal. Daniel lit a cigarette and I asked for one. The burning tobacco helped to overpower the smell that clung to our skin and clothing.

"Who did this?" I asked.

"The militia or the Indonesian army. Both of them were in charge of the airport."

"Everybody's crazy here."

"They weren't happy when the Timorese people voted for independence. I guess they decided to destroy everything before they left the country."

When the UN mission had fled East Timor a few weeks earlier, all the officials had driven to the airport and abandoned their cars in the parking lot. Two weeks later, the vehicles were still there, parked in a haphazard manner. File boxes and half-opened suitcases were dumped on the asphalt as if the drivers had raced to the terminal, then dashed inside to check on a flight.

Some Indonesian soldiers lounged on the back of a cargo truck and watched while a group of Australian army rangers crowded around a passenger van with an Oxfam emblem. The vanished aid workers had taken their keys back to Darwin and the Australians were trying to hotwire the vehicle. Daniel strolled over to the men and smiled like we were all traveling to the same vacation resort.

"Can I help you steal this?" he asked.

A red-haired corporal grinned. "Sure thing, mate. We found the ignition wires, but the steering wheel is still locked up."

Daniel borrowed a commando knife, pried off the plastic covering around the steering column, and began splicing wires together. In a few minutes he'd started the engine. The corporal slapped him on the back. "All right, everybody! Get a rat up yah! We're goin' to war!"

Elbowing each other like a rugby team, we squeezed into the van. The corporal drove around the parking lot. "Where's the bloody map?" he asked. It turned out that someone named Sergeant Malloy had the maps and he was on another plane. Daniel reached into his equipment bag and pulled out a map of Dili photocopied from a tourist guidebook. "Right," he said. "Turn right." And we were on our way.

A quarter mile from the airport, we came to a roundabout with an empty concrete fountain at the center. Five tiered baskets were set inside the fountain and a dozen white angels sat around the rim, all of them kneeling on one knee while they blew trumpets at the sky. Someone had chopped off the angel heads and there were bullet marks on their wings. I grabbed the digital camera and tried to get to my knees, but the bus was crowded with soldiers and a muscular ranger carrying a machine gun was sitting in front of the sliding door.

"No room, mate. Sorry."

"Can we stop?" I asked. "Stop for a second—"

"Not now!" the corporal shouted. "Gotta keep moving!"

We continued past the fountain and turned onto the main road. It was dry season on the island. The palm trees were still green, but the surrounding undergrowth was dead and brittle. In the distance, the ocean shimmered with a bright turquoise color. South of the road a brown ridge rose abruptly to mountains covered with brush and trees. The burning smell got stronger as we approached the city. We crossed a concrete bridge that went over an empty river, then reached a side road that led toward the sea.

"Here?" the corporal asked. "Do I turn here?"

"Keep going," Daniel said. "Stay on the main road."

The muscular soldier let me drink from his water bottle. "I sure hope those militia bastards shoot at us," he said.

"And why is that?"

"If they shoot at us, then we can shoot 'em back. If they don't shoot, then it gets into rules."

A row of concrete houses had been looted and torched by the anti-independence militias. Some of the buildings were still on fire, the smoke rising from charred roof beams and blackened sheets of roofing. The corporal slowed down and everyone was silent. We passed an abandoned school, the Australian consulate, and a small military airport still held by the Indonesian army. The streets were empty and the arson became more systematic: entire blocks of buildings had been torched, leaving a few concrete pillars and piles of blackened rubble. The few buildings that survived looked temporary and fragile.

All the East Timorese men and any women young enough to be raped had fled into the hills. Only the old women and a few children remained. They stood in the street or picked through the rubble. When our van rolled down the street, they stared at us as if we were ghosts that would vanish at any moment. A few Indonesian soldiers wearing oversized tan uniforms were searching for something to steal. They glared at the Australians but kept their M16 rifles pointed down.

"They're not militia?" asked the muscular soldier.

"No. They're regular army. All of them are going home in a couple of days."

"Bet we can't shoot them either. More rules." The soldier spat out the window.

We reached the harbor area and Daniel told the corporal to stop the van. The Australians were supposed meet another squad of rangers up at the soccer stadium, but Daniel wanted to stay near the beach.

"No worries," the corporal said. "Take care of yourself and don't get shot. The whole country ain't worth it."

The rangers turned toward the mountains and the blue van disappeared up the street. Daniel and I walked east past the harbor area. Two inter-island ferryboats were tied to the main wharf and Indonesian soldiers were loading them up with army trucks and all the property from the destroyed houses. I could hear cocks crowing in bamboo cages and singsong pop music from a portable radio. The street in front of us was littered with old mattresses, broken furniture, and the shells of burned automobiles. Pieces of singed paper were everywhere and they drifted across the street like wayward leaves. I took out my digital camera and took a few quick shots, but the smoke and the hazy sky made it seem as if someone had pasted a dirty strip of cellophane on the lens.

I was sweating from the heat and my mouth was dry. There was no real authority in Dili, no clear lines that divided a safe area from the dangerous zone. Daniel was very alert and he walked slowly. Near the Governor's Office, he stopped and looked out at the harbor. The UN fleet was anchored about a mile out and the *Seria* was in the middle of the convoy.

"You think Julia's out on deck?" Daniel asked. "Maybe she has some binoculars and she's watching us right now."

"I hope she doesn't see us. I'm not looking my best today."

As I switched to a wide-angle lens, a convoy of six vehicles came toward us. The transport truck leading the group had an Indonesian flag draped over the hood and militiamen with red-and-white headbands were squeezed into the truck cab. One of the men had an M16 rifle, which he pointed out the window. I stood there, expecting him to fire, but the convoy kept moving. The first two trucks were stacked with stolen property: television sets, refrigerators, a large blue couch. They were followed by three Land Rovers with UN insignia and then an open cattle truck crammed with women and children. They were being kidnapped, taken down the road to West Timor, and when they saw us they raised their hands and screamed for help. A young militiaman with a bamboo stick was standing on the back and he began beating the people next to him. The convoy kept moving, but I was able to get one quick photograph. I was still holding my camera, getting ready for another shot, when two more militiamen drove up behind us on motorcycles.

They were young Timorese men with beards and long hair. One man carried an M16 and the other a shotgun, the weapons dangling from shoulder straps. When they reached Daniel and me, they circled around us with the bikes, revving their engines and screaming in Tetum. The third time around, the man with the shotgun pulled a machete out of his belt. He was trying to cut the strap on my camera bag, but he missed and the tip of the knife scratched across my shoulder blade. I felt a stinging sensation and then they turned back onto the road and raced after the convoy.

Daniel stepped behind me. "Damn, he cut you. You're bleeding."

"How bad is it?"

"I don't know. Let's get out of the sun."

We cut across a patch of dead grass to the Governor's Office. Standing beneath the white colonnade, I removed my shirt and Daniel used it to wipe off the blood.

"It's a three-inch cut," he said. "Let's hope it doesn't get infected." He smeared antibiotic ointment on the wound, then applied some gauze and a bandage. I pulled on my spare shirt. "Does it hurt, Nicky?"

"It's not that bad."

"You're going to get a scar."

"Come on. Let's keep moving."

We remained beneath the colonnade and continued walking. Indonesian soldiers were guarding the building and each time we passed an open doorway they came out and pointed their rifles. Daniel offered a cigarette to one of the men and spoke a few phrases in Indonesian. The man nodded and pointed down the waterfront boulevard. "Interfet," he said. "Turismo."

Daniel glanced at his map. "The Turismo Hotel is less than a mile away. Maybe it's being used by Interfet command."

We reached the end of the colonnade and looked across the street. The Indonesian army garrison was on one corner facing an office building with black smoke coming out of its smashed windows. Someone was honking an automobile horn and sound came toward us. We stepped back as a pickup truck carrying militiamen raced down the road. Several of the young men had machetes thrust in their belts and they all carried rifles. I saw a flash of bright red when the truck passed us. A teenage boy was kneeling in the center of the truck, blood streaming down his face. A militiaman wearing mirrored sunglasses gripped the boy's hair. I started to raise my Nikon, then realized that the militiamen were watching me. I lowered the camera as the truck disappeared into the garrison courtyard.

We returned to the waterfront boulevard and walked on the beach side, beneath a line of shade trees. The army garrison was directly across the street and a young Indonesian soldier pointed his rifle at us. Two of his friends were laughing and shouting. I didn't know Indonesian, but I could guess what they were saying: Shoot them. Kill the foreigners. Suddenly, the young soldier pointed the rifle upward and fired an entire clip into the air. I jerked backward and soldiers laughed.

"Jesus," I whispered. "That little bastard."

"Keep walking, Nicky. Don't look back."

We passed an empty hotel with a smashed television lying in the driveway, then reached a park with the statue of the Virgin Mary on top of marble pedestal. The local bishop's residence was next to the park. Two of the buildings had been burned down, but a few Timorese remained inside the compound. We hurried past the looted International Red Cross headquarters to the Hotel Turismo. It was a rambling two-story building surrounded by a low fence.

British soldiers had taken over the hotel early that morning and the Australians had shown up a few hours later. I could sense the tension right away. Daniel and I approached an Australian captain just as he ordered a British lieutenant to move his Land Rover out of the hotel parking lot. "Yes. Sir," said the lieutenant and there was a space between the two words. It wasn't much of a delay, more like a slight hesitation, but it was enough to suggest a few hundred years of cultural arrogance. The Aussie captain was so angry that his face was turning red.

"Who's in charge?" Daniel asked. "We're looking for Interfet command."

"We're in charge," the captain said, then he glared at us as if we were going to challenge his statement. "General Bates is upstairs, but he probably won't talk to you."

We entered a large courtyard filled with tropical plants. You could see that it had once been an outdoor restaurant, but now the tables were stacked to one side and a soldier was digging a latrine pit. We climbed the stairs to the surrounding balcony and met Major Anthony

Holden, an older Australian army officer with thinning blond hair. He was soft-spoken and comfortably bland, the kind of officer that had spent his career holding the door for generals and carrying their papers around.

"General Bates is quite busy," he told Daniel. "But I'll see what I can do."

A door opened at the end of the balcony. "I hope that makes things clear," said a booming voice, then General Martin Bates, the commander of the UN forces, walked out with three Australian journalists. Bates was a handsome man with spiky gray hair and blue eyes. He shook hands with the Australians but frowned when he saw us. "I just gave an interview to three of our journos and here comes some more. Can't do this all day, Tony. Got a job to do."

Daniel raised his right hand. "Just four questions, General. Four questions in one minute. You can time me."

Bates considered this idea, then turned to Major Holden. "Go ahead, Tony. Check your watch."

We followed the general back into a long room with a bed, a desk, and several folding chairs. There was no electric power and the only light came through the Venetian blinds. A map of Dili and another map of East Timor were taped to the wall, both decorated with pushpins. The Interfet force was here, the Indonesian troops were over there, and the militia was someplace else. I had encountered several pushpin maps over the years. Military commanders loved them, but they had little connection with reality.

General Bates stopped at his desk and glanced at his watch. "What's your name?"

"Daniel McFarland."

"Who you working for?"

"*Newsweek.*"

The general smiled as if he'd tricked us. "You've already wasted ten seconds."

I raised the digital camera and examined Bates through the viewfinder. He had a big head in proportion to his body. Big heads always photographed well. It made Bates look forceful.

"How's the deployment going?" Daniel asked.

"Very well. The Indonesians have been most cooperative."

"How long will it take to secure Dili?"

"We need three weeks to deploy our troops fully, then we'll extend control to the rest of the country. I'm not going to put my men at risk."

"What about the Timorese being killed by the militia?"

"That's most unfortunate."

"But what are you going to do about it?"

"Our soldiers will secure key positions, then we'll begin to disarm everyone."

"What happens to the Timorese who are being kidnapped and taken across the border?"

General Bates looked annoyed. "I've answered your four questions. That's all."

Major Holden escorted us back out onto the balcony and we went back downstairs. "Is it really going to take three weeks to take over Dili?" I asked. "It should only take a few days."

"This is a UN deployment. He's not going to take any risks." Daniel glanced up and down the courtyard. "I'm going to go talk to the Brits, off the record. It's easier if you're not taking their pictures."

"That's okay. I'll wait for you outside."

Back in the hotel driveway, I saw a squad of Asian soldiers wearing dark green berets and camouflage uniforms. It took me a few seconds to realize that they were Gurkhas from the hill tribes of Nepal. The Gurkhas were small, stocky men with smooth skin; they'd fought for England in special regiments since the nineteenth century. Along with the usual army gear, they carried black-handled kukri knives. I tried to think of an easy way to describe them, but the only word I could come up with was *clean*. It wasn't the way the word was used back in the States where clean meant spray the toilet and kill all the germs. The

Gurkhas seemed calm and disciplined, unencumbered with any goals aside from being good at their job.

I switched lenses on my Nikon and a British officer in a Gurkha uniform approached me. He was a big man with the friendly but firm manner of a successful pub manager.

"Can I help you, sir?"

"I'm Nicky Bettencourt. I work for *Newsweek* and the *Daily Telegraph*."

"Well, I thought it was something like that, but you don't need to photograph my men. We're not doing anything important right now."

I lowered my camera and said the first thing that came into my mind. "Why are your men carrying SA80 assault rifles? I heard that they jammed up during combat."

The captain relaxed and stepped closer. He seemed pleased that I knew about the problem. "I've talked to everyone about those bloody things, but I can't get replacements. It's all politics, of course. The Ministry of Defense won't admit it made a mistake."

The captain's name was Terry Jenkins. He had served with the First Gurkha Regiment in Hong Kong until it was transferred back to England. Now he was stationed in Brunei.

"We're there to defend the sultan and his oil wells, but that doesn't bother me. Everyone's got to have their petrol. Makes the world go round." Captain Jenkins watched the Australians set up a roadblock in the middle of the street. "There's oil and natural gas in the Timor Sea. Maybe that's why we're really here."

"The Indonesians are stealing everything and the militia are out of control. Someone has to come in and establish the peace."

Jenkins plucked off a red blossom from a bougainvillea bush and twirled it between his thumb and forefinger. "That's what my men could do. But the Australians are in charge and they want us on guard duty. It's like using a lorry to carry a six-pack of beer. Waste of good machinery, wouldn't you say?"

Daniel came out of the Turismo looking annoyed. I liked Jenkins and decided to keep him out of trouble. "This is my partner, Daniel

McFarland. Be careful, Captain. He's a journalist. If you say something foolish, he's going to write it down."

Jenkins stood a little straighter and spoke like a schoolboy giving a recitation. "The Royal Gurkha Rifles are proud to be serving in East Timor. We'll do everything we can to restore order."

"No, you won't," Daniel said. "You're going to waste your time guarding this hotel."

DANIEL PLACED HIS LAPTOP on the wall in the parking lot. Standing beside an armored personnel carrier, he wrote a quick article and sent it off to London with his sat phone. When he was done, I sent off digital photographs of General Bates and the kidnapped women and children screaming in the back of the truck. We were safe at the hotel, surrounded by soldiers, but I could tell that Daniel wasn't satisfied. He ate a candy bar and drank some water, then packed up his equipment.

"Let's go, Nicky."

"Go where?"

"I've already got the general's quote. Now I've got to find something real."

We left the Turismo and headed west on a side street. It was about two o'clock in the afternoon, but it seemed much later. Smoke was smeared across the sky and the sun looked like a hazy disc of fire. With all the haze it was difficult to gauge distance and aperture. The ash particles in the air diffracted the light and the leaves on the shade trees turned a darker shade of green.

Gunshots echoed in the distance, then we heard the whoosh-bang sound of a rocket-propelled grenade. A few blocks away, an off-key car horn kept bleating loudly. We discovered a street littered with smashed computer monitors and another street covered with spilled rice. Someone had ripped up a plastic shower curtain and little shreds of neon pink were scattered over a five-block area. A pickup truck raced toward us near the ruins of the teacher's college and Daniel pulled me into a doorway. Two Indonesian soldiers were in the truck cab and two more sat in the back guarding a goat and an exercise bike. I had the feeling that all the valuable property had been stolen weeks ago and now the Indonesians were blindly grabbing whatever remained.

Around four o'clock we returned to the harbor and accompanied an old woman on her way to the Igreja Motael church. Daniel thought that a priest or a doctor might be there—someone who could give him a quote and tell him how many people had been killed. A low white wall surrounded the church grounds and hundreds of people lay on the dirt beneath banyan trees. No one moved or spoke to us when we passed through the little gate. The people looked too exhausted to show any emotion.

More refugees were inside the church, sleeping on the floors or leaning against the walls. Some feeble light oozed through the stained-glass windows and a single candle burned near the altar. The building smelled of urine and smoke. Only two girls were crying and that was a bad sign. It meant that the other children were weak and dehydrated.

I stepped carefully around people as I walked up to a side altar. Someone had shot off the head of the Virgin Mary. The plaster chunk that contained her eyes watched me as I crouched down and tried to take a picture of the ruined statue. I didn't want to use the flash on my camera. It felt wrong. I took a few pictures with the digital, then opened up the f-stop on the Nikon and hoped for the best.

When I turned back around I saw Daniel kneeling beside a small, elderly woman lying on the floor. I thought he was trying to interview her, but he motioned for me to help. "Give her some water, Nicky."

"We only have two full bottles."

"Give her my bottle. You can keep yours."

I handed him the larger bottle and he helped the old woman drink. Some of the water dribbled down the side of her mouth.

"Got any food, Nicky?"

"Just some candy bars."

"Give me one."

I passed Daniel a chocolate bar. He broke it up and gave a piece to the old woman. "A lot of these people are going to die."

"We're not medical workers and we don't have any supplies. Come on, Daniel. It's getting late. Let's get the hell out of here."

Daniel had distributed the rest of his water and three more candy bars before I finally got him to leave. The sun was going down as we hiked back to the waterfront area. The smoke from the destruction had created a beautiful sunset of pink and scarlet. I switched to a wide angle lens and got a shot of the UN fleet outlined against the luminous sky. We met two Dutch journalists who were going to spend the night out at the airport, guarded by the Interfet troops, but Daniel didn't want to leave the city. A two-story hotel was just across the street from the Governor's Office. When we entered the hotel restaurant, a skinny Timorese man peered out from the kitchen.

"*Jornalista?*" he asked in Portuguese.

"*Sim. Jornalista,*" said Daniel. "*Queriamos quarto.*"

The skinny man nodded and used most of his English vocabulary. "Australia dollar, good. America dollar, good. No rupiah."

Our hotel had no electricity, no phones, no water, and no bed linen, but we paid 150 Australian dollars for two mattresses in an empty room. The moment we closed the door, I felt a little calmer. We weren't exactly safe, but it was better than being on the street.

I downloaded my photos and sent them directly to London. While Daniel typed up articles and sent them off, I paid ten dollars to fill up our bottles from a bathtub of water in the hotel manager's room. I dropped purification tablets into the bottles, then drank as I ate a candy bar. The taste of iodine and chocolate always reminded me of war.

As it began to get dark, more journalists straggled into the hotel. The manager sold us candles and bowls of rice mixed with bits of dried fish. I was trying to decide if a rubbery strip of tissue was actually food when the Portuguese cameraman knocked on our door. "*Há incêndio,*" he whispered. There's a fire. We followed him up a ladder to the roof. Other journalists were already there, looking out at the city. Houses were burning in the west section of Dili. Flames glowed bright orange in the darkness and there was the faint popping sound of someone firing an automatic rifle.

"Lot of jumped-up crazies," said a journalist from New Zealand. "Can't have the bloody country so they're going to burn it down."

Daniel stood on the edge of the roof and watched the destruction. It bothered me that he had given away his food and water at the church. In Africa, he'd been selfish and single-minded, but I trusted his instincts. Nowadays he seemed a lot more vulnerable. I wondered if I should have left him at the convent garden back in Rome.

"Look at that fire! The world's burning down!" a Portuguese journalist said. Something exploded inside one of the houses and sparks rose up to the sky. I moved my shoulder when I took out my camera and the cut on my back felt like it was burning, glowing in darkness.

AT DAWN, DANIEL LEFT our hotel room and returned with a pot of tea and two bowls of plain white rice. He prodded me in the ribs and I decided that everything was going to be all right.

"Wake up, Nicky. Time to get going."

"I'm not asleep. I'm resting my eyes."

"How was your mattress?"

"Better than the Ruskin."

He gave me some chopsticks and poured a cup of tea. It was hot and strong and the steam had a flowery scent. "I just hired a driver who says he can find a car."

"How'd you do that?"

"When everything is falling apart, look for the man wearing a clean shirt. A clean shirt means he's either disciplined or resourceful."

"Or maybe he just stole it from a laundry."

"That's the resourceful part."

Daniel replaced my bandage and we left the hotel. The fires had died out in the center of Dili, but a charred smell still lingered in the air. We saw several other journalists on the street, then Tristram Müller ambled out of the hotel holding a coconut.

"Nicky! Daniel! Did you stay here last night?"

"Up on the first floor."

"I've got a room on the ground floor, near the back. I paid some extra money and got a chair." Tristram held up the coconut. "You're Americans. You rope cows and slaughter Indians. So how do you crack this open without a hammer?"

"Go to one of these churches and drop it off the bell tower."

"That's way too much effort." Tristram looked exasperated. "What this town needs is some Chinese merchants. If the Chinese had stayed around I bet we could buy a bottle of cold beer and a decent meal."

Daniel glanced up and down the street, looking for the man with the clean shirt and a car. "What's the latest rumor?"

"Some militiamen chopped off the head of a priest and impaled it on a stick in the middle of the village." Tristram gave us a sly smile. "Of course, no one knows the location of the village or the name of the priest or even if it really happened."

Tristram waddled off to crack his coconut and we remained outside the hotel. While we waited for the car, I watched how the rumor of the headless priest gained substance and then an air of reality. Journalists told each other the story, then scurried around like ants that had just heard about a crumb of blueberry pie. People insisted that a Japanese TV crew had actually photographed this incident, but then we were told, no, a Swedish cameraman filmed it. The Swedes announced that no one had actually seen the head, but they were going to the village in southwest Dili later that day.

There was great excitement when a fourteen-year-old boy named José appeared and offered to sell directions to the dead priest for ten Australian dollars. Daniel watched this transaction for a few minutes, then took the boy's hand and made him touch the crucifix hanging from his neck. "*Não há cabeça,*" Daniel whispered in Portuguese.

José panicked for a moment, then relaxed like a witness who was finally allowed to tell the truth. "*É verdade, senhor.* No head."

Daniel gave the boy three cigarettes as a tip and walked over to where I was sitting.

"Waste of time?" I asked.

"You noticed Tristram didn't go for it. Usually the rumors are about a crucified priest. This was a new variation."

Most of the other journalists were gone when a Honda Accord with blown-out windows turned the corner. It stopped a few feet away from us and the driver got out. Silverio Fernandes was a thin, jittery young man with oily hair. He didn't look very reliable, but he did have a clean shirt.

"Good morning, gentlemens. Please to be in my automobile."

We pried open the door and got into the backseat of the sedan. Someone with an automatic weapon had fired into the vehicle. It looked like a madman had attacked the upholstery with a hatchet and the back door on the left side was tied to the doorframe with rope and twisted wire. Dried blood covered the driver's seat and the rubber mat under the gas pedal. The blood was dark red, like rust, and little specks of it clung to the back of Silverio's jeans.

"Where are we going?" I asked Daniel.

"A suburb called Becora. It's a pro-independence neighborhood where there's been a lot of fighting."

Silverio got back into the car and gave us a big smile. "Gentlemens, I am ready to serve you."

"*Leve-me a Becora,*" Daniel said in Portuguese and pulled out a wad of Australian dollars.

Silverio shook his head rapidly. "No. No. This is *muito dificil.*"

The money disappeared back into Daniel's pocket and he forced open the door. "Get out of the car, Nicky. We're done with Mr. Fernandes."

"*Com certeza,* I can take you there. I only say it is *dificil.*"

"It's always difficult," I said. The car jerked forward, then shivered and backfired up the street. Although the Honda was wrecked, Silverio acted like he had just bought it from a car dealer. Whenever we encountered a burned-out vehicle or a pile of rubble, he hit the turn signal and made a wide curve around the obstacle.

I had both my cameras out, looking for a shot, and I focused on the few things that had survived the general destruction. A small red flower. A jacaranda tree. Two straight-back chairs and a white refrigerator.

We drove up into the hills that surrounded the city and found the smoking ruins of hundreds of houses. A few old women were dragging away sheets of collapsed roofing, then searching through the ashes. They watched us warily, like the deer you might encounter on a country road. Silverio announced that we were in Becora and Daniel told him to stop. We got out, walked through someone's backyard and approached a bare-chested man.

"*Boa tarde, senhor.*"

The man had come down from the hills to look for his lost daughter, Gabriela. "Are you Australians?" he asked in Portuguese. "Are you from the United Nations?" Trying to act invisible, I focused on his thin, exhausted face. "I think they killed her," he told us. "But I pray."

Silverio looked nervous. He combed his sideburns, then glanced up and down the streets. "Gentlemens," he pleaded. "*Se faz favor.* We go back now."

"*Mas lento,*" Daniel said. "I need at least one more interview."

We got back into the car. When we drove past a house that was still burning, I asked Silverio to stop for a minute. A framed photograph of some saint with rays coming out of her head was still hanging on a scorched wall. Nice colors, I thought. Half a page in the magazine. I jumped out and crouched down in the ashes for a shot.

A dump truck came up the hill, its gears grinding. Men wearing red-and-white headbands stood on the truck bed and gripped the frame. When they saw us they shouted and began firing their assault rifles. It didn't sound dangerous, more like the crackling sound of a string of firecrackers, until a bullet ricocheted off the Honda's back bumper. Silverio leaped out of the car and sprinted across the road as Daniel ran toward me.

"Go!" he shouted. "Let's get out of here!"

We scrambled over a wall, ran between two houses, and cut through a garden filled with bright red peppers and tomato plants. Why would anyone kill us when people were growing zucchini and honeybees were buzzing around some morning glories? The fast-breathing, dry-mouthed terror that had taken over my body found no confirmation in the pleasant scenery. We heard more gunfire in the distance as we cut across a dirt road and began to climb a ravine.

We reached a grove of thatch palms at the top of the ravine and I collapsed on the dead leaves that covered the ground. I was sweating and breathing hard, but I felt exhilarated. Still alive.

Daniel lit a cigarette, then buried the match in the dirt. "Lost my phone. Left it in the car."

"Yeah."

"Lost the water bottles."

I nodded.

"Lost the chocolate bars."

I lay on my back and gazed up at the sky. "Now that's a real crisis."

Julia

17 DILI

I stood on the bow of the *Seria* as we followed the UN convoy into Dili Harbor. The city was burning. Columns of smoke from different fires rose up into the sky and combined into a hazy gray cloud that drifted across the water. Small particles of ash—very light, very fragile—fell on the deck of the ship. I could hear gunshots and a single alarm bell that rang loudly at first, then weakened and died.

Everyone came out on deck and stared at the burning city. Richard had some binoculars and we took turns using them. Columns of gray smoke came from looted buildings while the black smoke came from burning cars. Billy nodded solemnly like a theater critic watching an impressive performance. "The Indonesians would burn down the whole bloody island if they could," he said. "They don't want to leave anything behind."

The *Seria* was filled with tons of food, water, and medicine, but Interfet command had ordered Captain Vanderhouten not to move the ship without permission. As the day went on and the smoke kept rising, Billy played cards with Collins and Briggs. The crew slept on deck or fished for shark with chunks of rotten meat. Richard sat in his cabin with his sat phone and told executives how to take control of a Scottish bank. We had traveled thousands of miles to come here and now we weren't helping anyone. I kept pacing from the bow to the stern and back again.

Different patches of fire flared up that night. They grew larger and merged together. I watched the wind push the fire north, extending its bright orange fingers through the darkness. When I woke up the next morning and went out on deck, I could smell a harsh chemical odor that reminded me of melted plastic. The flames were gone, but smoke drifted from the ruins. Using the binoculars, I watched Indonesian soldiers carry looted furniture and television sets down to the wharf where two ferries were waiting. On the radio they were saying that UN troops had landed at Dili airport and were beginning to take control of the city. If the soldiers had arrived, that meant Daniel was probably with them.

I locked the door of my cabin and lay on the narrow berth. In my mind, I saw Daniel at Bracciano digging out the roots of a dead olive tree. Sweat glistened on his skin, and his shoulders shifted and moved as he raised an ax and swung at the earth. I remembered him walking down Church Street on a rainy afternoon. Then he was standing in the bedroom of the Canal House on the first night of snow. He opened the window, took a knife from the dresser, and held it out into the cold darkness. Silently, he turned and walked over to our bed, a single perfect snowflake resting on the blade.

Now we were just a few miles apart, but there was no way to see him or know that he was safe. When I left Bracciano, I had wished for the sort of fantasy that appears in the Sunday supplements: together, but apart, the modern couple who manages to have a relationship even though she's lecturing at Harvard and he's directing operas in Bayreuth. It was all nonsense, of course. If you loved someone, you tried to stay with them, and yet somehow we had thought that it was the right choice to go off in different directions.

The burning city was dangerous, even for an experienced journalist. The radio reported that groups of anti-independence militiamen were starting the fires and killing people. And there were other dangers, too: the chance that Daniel would be lured back to the solitary life. It was easier being alone and unencumbered, like having fewer bags to carry to the train.

THE CREW ON THE *Seria* owned a video collection of karate movies and Indian musicals, but the VCR had jammed. As the only woman on the ship, I was the next option for entertainment. Pak, the first mate, and his friends spent their free time staring at me and chattering to each other in Indonesian. Occasionally, Captain Vanderhouten translated their comments so that I learned that they were discussing which T-shirt best showed off my breasts. Vanderhouten was an alcoholic who kept asking me to look at his hernia and the fungus growing beneath his toenails. Collins and Briggs were convinced that I wanted to sleep with them. They were each drinking ten to twelve cans of lager a day until Richard restricted them to three. Now they consumed their quota with great ceremony during dinner, then secretly drank more when it was dark.

Billy had assumed more power ever since we'd left Darwin Harbor. The day that we sailed, I discovered that someone had stolen a case of chloramphenicol and some infant dysentery medicine. I mentioned this to Richard, and then Billy showed up at my cabin.

"It's probably somebody in the crew," he said. "Although it could be Vanderhouten. I've never trusted that bastard."

"You don't have to start a war over this, Billy. Just search the ship. You'll probably find the medicine hidden somewhere."

Billy smiled at me like I was a little girl who still believed in Father Christmas. I realized that he wanted a confrontation and would make it as threatening as possible.

"I don't want anyone beaten up," I said. "This is an aid organization and we're supposed to be helping people."

"I'm not going to hurt a fly," Billy said. "All I need is a prop."

"What are you talking about?"

He rummaged through my medical bag and pulled out a piece of plastic tubing. "Don't worry, Julia. This'll do."

Billy called the entire crew up on deck and lectured them about the theft, all the while playing with the plastic tube, snapping it in the air and whipping it around his fist. Billy never said what the tube would be used for or if it would even be used at all, but there was something frightening about his performance.

"I want the drugs back by tomorrow," Billy told them, then had his remarks translated into Indonesian.

The stolen medicine was stacked neatly outside my cabin door the next morning. After I had sorted through the boxes I realized that the thief had held back 10 percent, accurately gauging the amount of loss I would allow without complaint.

"Good job," Richard said to me when he saw the boxes. "All you need is a clear statement about consequences. Of course I couldn't do it and you couldn't either. In this particular area, Billy has credibility."

In London, Richard and I had managed to establish a professional relationship. He'd drop by the office once a week and we'd communicate through e-mail and faxes. When we flew to Australia, Richard sat two rows in front of me and tapped away on his laptop. He never mentioned Westgate Castle or the fact that we had been lovers. He was polite, but not overly personal, and I began to relax around him.

But the moment we'd left Darwin, everything changed. Richard started to touch my shoulder or arm when we were talking. I would step back slightly when this happened and yet it continued. He wanted us to eat every meal together so we could discuss our supplies and the messages we received from the United Nations. Gradually he stopped talking about cooking pots and asked more personal questions. Did I sleep well last night? Did I like his shirt? Should he run for Parliament when he returned to Britain? In the past, when I had separated from men, I had taken another job and never seen them again. Now Richard was standing next to me and acting as if nothing had changed.

OUR SECOND NIGHT in the harbor, I asked Richard if I could borrow his phone to call Daniel. "Sure. Give it a try," he said. "But for all we know they could still be in Australia. Maybe they never got on the plane."

I dialed Daniel's phone three times and kept getting a recording. There was no electrical power in East Timor and I decided that he was keeping his phone switched off to spare the battery. Early the next morning I called Laura, just to hear a friendly voice.

"I've become East Timor Central here in Islington," she said. "I'm buying all the newspapers, listening to the radio, and watching television. There was a nice photo of Richard and you in the *Telegraph*. He's pointing at a map of Timor and everyone's staring at his finger. You seem a bit tired, but Richard looks good. His hair always has that little wave."

"Nicky took the picture."

"Yes. I saw his byline. Daniel sent out three articles from Dili. It does seem rather"—she paused for a second, trying not to sound worried— "rather difficult there."

"The whole city is burning down."

"Where's Daniel?"

"I don't know. Probably walking around Dili."

"Where's Richard?"

"On the ship with me."

"God. And I thought I was the one who had complex relationships."

"I'm here to do my job, Laura." I tried to sound confident, as if the future was already planned. "I'll hand out the food, Daniel will cover the story, and then we'll go back to Italy."

The Indonesian soldiers set fire to their barracks, then marched down the boulevard to the wharf. Using the binoculars, I watched them board the ferries and saw the deck crews cast off the lines. The soldiers waved their rifles and stomped their boots on the top decks of the ferries while their friends honked the horns of the stolen trucks. Then both ferries turned slowly in the water and headed north. The soldiers were taking their loot and going back to Indonesia.

Soon our radio started squawking with military commands and two navy ships pulled into the wharf. The Australians were running the operation, but they were under the command of the United Nations. Although the Timorese were starving, the military action had top priority and we were told that the *Seria* would be the last ship to dock. I wanted to get on the radio and yell at the Australians, but Richard ignored them and called UN headquarters in New York. He chatted with someone in the secretary-general's office and got transferred to someone higher up in the organization. They discussed apartment rentals in Manhattan and ski holidays in Canada before Richard nudged the conversation around to East Timor.

"You know, we have a fair amount of supplies on our ship," he said. "Lots of journalists are in Dili and they're looking for a positive spin on the story. It would make the UN look good if we could reach the wharf fairly soon."

Messages ricocheted back and forth between New York and Canberra, and suddenly we were allowed to jump the queue. Richard grinned like a football player who had just scored the winning goal. For a second, it looked like he was going to embrace me, but something in my expression kept him back. Instead, he placed his hands on my shoulders.

"Did you hear that? They're going to let us dock."

"That's wonderful, Richard. You handled it perfectly."

"Take a look around you." He motioned to the ship and the crew and the supplies stacked on the deck. "All of this happened because the two of us were working together."

"It's not over yet. We've got the food. Now we've got to distribute it."

The main wharf was on the right side of the bay, a concrete ledge built out on pilings. Although he looked hungover, Vanderhouten maneuvered the ship to the wharf with confidence and flair. Water surged from under the stern as the propellers went into reverse and the ship shuddered like a living thing. It looked as if we were about to smash into the concrete, but Vanderhouten spun the wheel around at the last moment and we drifted up against the wharf in perfect position. There were three buildings on the wharf that looked like warehouses. I saw a burned car and the rotting carcass of a dead pig and remembered Laura once asking me how I was able to deal with the sort of things I witnessed during relief work. I told her that it wasn't Julia looking at the famine victims or the sick children; it was Dr. Cadell. Usually that protected me, but sometimes it was hard to play the role.

There was a short drop from the ship to the wharf. The crew jumped down and tied up the boat while Pak shouted directions. I told Vander-houten to get ready to unload the supplies and left the ship. Not know-ing what do, I walked toward the warehouses, then Billy caught up with me. He was wearing a flak jacket and carrying an assault rifle.

"Be careful, Julia. We don't know what's going on."

"That's right, Billy. So don't run around pointing that rifle at people."

We went down a concrete ramp to a tarmac area where there were stacks of shipping containers, all of them torn open and looted. The wharf was surrounded by a fence topped with barbed wire, but the entrance gate was wide open. I stepped around an abandoned refrig-erator and looked down the street. Australian soldiers were on patrol, moving toward the Governor's Office, but there were a few civilians, too. From a distance, I could see only the color of their clothes—a bright green shirt or a red shawl—but as they came closer I saw the faces of frightened women and children and crippled old men. Some-how they knew our ship was carrying food and water and this knowl-edge passed between them like a magnetic force, pulling them forward.

I HURRIED BACK to the ship and told the crew to place four cargo containers on the wharf. Using rope, I marked off the evaluation and distribution areas, and within minutes, the first people arrived. I greeted them in Tetum and tried to see if anyone was seriously ill. The first group was strong enough to walk to the harbor, but most of them were suffering from malnutrition and dehydration. I took their names, marked their arms with a red felt pen and Richard distributed packets of supplies: a cooking pot, a spoon, three water bottles, a sack of corn-meal and a sack of rice, a bottle of cooking oil, and a length of blue plastic sheeting. Using some phrases from a Portuguese travel book, Richard told everyone it gave him *muito prazer* to meet them. The Timorese were cautious and polite with me, but everyone smiled at Richard. I was evaluating them and he was giving out food.

The first group left the wharf area and spread the word throughout Dili; within hours, thousands of people were heading toward us. We needed extra help and I wandered through the crowd, hiring a young woman who had once worked for the Red Cross, another who was a Jehovah's Witness, and a schoolteacher who knew the island languages. Some young men introduced themselves as freedom fighters and suggested they be in charge. I looked at the people standing around them and I sensed their fear. *Não necessário,* I said and kept moving.

The *Seria's* crew used a power winch to lift the plastic-wrapped pallets of supplies out of the hold and place them on the wharf. Collins and Briggs guarded the food while Billy slashed open the pallets. It was very hot now, but people kept coming. Hundreds of them passed through the broken gates and went up the ramp to the wharf. There was no fighting or pushing; they were all too exhausted. The children were hungry and some of them couldn't walk. If I had been looking down on the crowd, I would have felt overwhelmed by the situation. Instead, I concentrated on whoever was standing directly in front of me. I had ten seconds to decide if he or she was strong enough to get food or if that person needed immediate medical attention. The real division in the world wasn't race or culture or language, but food. You were either hungry or you were fed. Hunger was the acid that could dissolve all those moral qualities we felt were basic to mankind. Hunger destroyed beauty, pride, and cleverness; it made philosophy and ethics seem like luxuries.

Billy spoke loudly to the Timorese as if the increased volume would help them understand his English. That morning he had his sleeves rolled up to show his biceps. Richard stood next to him with his expensive sunglasses and a Hard Rock Cafe baseball cap. I wondered what the people on the wharf thought of us. Perhaps we seemed as strange as a group of space aliens that had suddenly landed. The Timorese were starving, but most of them acted with a quiet formality that suggested a gentler culture. They never said, "I'm hungry," in Tetum but instead, "Excuse me for being hungry," as if the war and famine were somehow their fault.

I looked over my shoulder and saw Daniel and Nicky coming up the ramp to the wharf. My body relaxed for a moment and I breathed deeply. I wanted to run over and embrace Daniel, but I knew that was inappropriate. It was easier to do my job if I didn't give in to emotion. Daniel nodded as if we'd met at a garden party several years ago, but then we shook hands and that was a mistake. Neither one of us wanted to let go.

"Here you are." Daniel looked tired and on edge, not as calm as when I had first met him at Kosana. Nicky stood behind him, anxious, forcing a smile.

"Here we all are," I answered.

Nicky raised his camera. "There's a bottleneck at the airport and no other organization is bringing in food. Looks like you're the only game in town."

"Daniel! Nicky! Good to see you!" Richard said, striding across the wharf. "How long have you been in Dili?"

"A day and a night," Daniel said.

"I really have to thank you, Nicky. You're an incredible photographer."

"Sometimes I get lucky."

"Remember that photograph you took in Australia? The one where I'm standing in Julia's cabin and studying the map? People have been calling me from all over. The damn thing's appeared in at least forty newspapers."

Nicky didn't answer. He switched cameras and began to take pictures of the people receiving their food. Richard fell in behind him, listing the different papers that had published the photograph.

Daniel let go of my hand. "The militia have burned about half the city. There's no government, police, running water, or electricity. General Bates is going slow on deployment. He's cautious about everything, although this area seems fairly safe in the daytime. The militia are still active in the villages."

"Where are you staying?"

"A hotel near the government building. No electricity or water, but we have a room. I'll come back for you around sunset."

I heard angry voices. An old woman was quarreling with Billy. "No! Only one bag of rice!" he shouted. "We follow rules around here!"

"Be careful," I told Daniel. "And come back whenever you can."

I left him and went over to the food line. As the argument got louder, one part of my mind remained quiet and separate, remembering the Canal House. Daniel and I were alone together. It was dark outside. Lying on the red couch, I placed my head on his chest and listened to his heartbeat.

THE CROWD GOT A little smaller, but it never disappeared. People began to arrive from the outlying parts of the city. An afternoon breeze came off the ocean, but the smell of ashes remained in the air. Now hundreds of people were camped on the beach or in the courtyard of the Igreja Motael across the street. People began cooking the food we had given them or made shelters with the blue plastic sheeting. I walked over to the church and watched women loan bowls to one another, then barter for spices and salt.

When the first television crew appeared on the wharf, Richard pretended to ignore them as he passed out food. The cameraman and the reporter with the microphone were blond and sunburned. Germans, I thought, but they turned out to be Dutch journalists. With the refugees shuffling forward in the background, Richard stopped working and gave his first interview. He had learned years ago how to deal with a camera; there was nothing dramatic about his voice and posture. He was your television friend, relaxed and sympathetic, looking directly at the lens.

He must have given over twenty interviews that afternoon. Reporters and photographers lined up next to the refugees while Billy told them, "You're next, then you're after him." The television crews all seemed to take the same shots: the city and the ship, Richard talking, a family receiving their food and cooking it in the churchyard across the street. The cameramen had already walked through Dili and photographed death and destruction. Hand-to-Hand's activity was a positive ending to a negative story.

Think of the good, I said to myself. I knew that the publicity would help Hand-to-Hand as well as the other aid organizations coming here. Richard was the perfect spokesman, modest but confident, and I could tell that the reporters liked him. "This has nothing to do with me," he kept saying. "It's a gift from the people of Britain to the people of East Timor."

Think of the good. I had, after all, accepted the contradictions of famine relief many years ago. People donated money for tax reasons or to get their name in the paper; aid workers were there to play hero or victim; and the aid itself was often questionable. Sometimes the food was used for political reasons and it destroyed the people you were trying to save.

I knew all this, had experienced it directly, but watching Richard with the television cameras made me angry. Had this always been the goal for him, even when we had first met in Cambridge? Was Hand-to-Hand just an elaborate way for him to help his political career? As I watched, Billy raised a piece of cardboard behind a French cameraman, cutting down the glare and shielding Richard's face from the sunlight.

Think of the good. I spoke to my helpers, making sure that they understood my instructions, then packed my shoulder bag with medicine and headed for the church across the street. As I left, a Timorese nun approached me. She wore a brown cotton skirt and blouse and a white head scarf. Her body was small and delicate, but her face was severe.

She spoke to me in Portuguese, then switched to English with an Australian accent. "I'm Sister Xavier. Do you work with the United Nations?"

"No. We're a private organization. Most of the UN staff are out at the airport."

"I just walked here from Liquica, on the coast road. In the last few days, the militia forced everyone out of their houses. A boat was going to take us to West Timor, but it never arrived. Now maybe four hundred people are on the wharf. The children are dying from sickness and lack of water. Someone must help them as soon as possible."

"We've got food here, but no transport." I looked over at the churchyard. "If I can get a truck, we can go to your village this afternoon."

"You'll need soldiers, too," she said. "The militia has been killing anyone in favor of independence. Their leader Cristiano is an evil man and the others are scared of him. One of my students was guarding us last night. He let me run away."

"How long will the people survive on the wharf?"

"Two days. Then everyone will die."

GETTING DIRECTIONS FROM the Australian soldiers, I walked with Sister Xavier down the waterfront boulevard to the military command post at the Turismo Hotel. A colonel told us that General Bates was the only person who could send troops to Liquica, but he was out at the airport talking to some UN officials. The colonel got us onto a truck going there to get supplies.

The Interfet camp was on a dirt field about a half mile from the airport. Soldiers were setting up a barbed-wire fence, tents, and an electric generator. Military Land Rovers and armored personnel carriers roared in and out of the camp, stirring up red dust that drifted through the air.

General Bates had already left, but we met an American named Larry Stans who had some mysterious job with the UN force. He wore a baseball cap and a bush jacket with epaulets and sat in the shade of a large tent talking into his portable radio. Apparently they were driving around Dili inspecting the area. The radio buzzed and hummed, and Larry's team kept saying "I copy that" and "Over" like they were bad actors in a television police show. The population of Dili was reduced to Friendlies, Possible Unfriendlies, and Bad Guys.

"Sorry you missed the general," Larry said. "Great guy. Strong leader. Knows how to prioritize."

"We need his permission to send soldiers and a medical team to Sister Xavier's village."

Larry smiled at Sister Xavier. "Are you a community leader, ma'am? We're making a list of community leaders."

"I'm just a nun."

"That qualifies." Larry wrote down Sister Xavier's name.

"Perhaps you could contact General Bates on your radio," I said.

"Well, I could, but I can't. Got to save my ammo for the big bears in the woods. All this pacification stuff takes time. Bates will start deploying troops in about four or five days. Can't save the world overnight."

Sister Xavier shook her head. "I just want to save my village."

"We're wasting time here," I said. "Let's go back to the city." I turned from Larry and headed for the road.

"Want some water bottles?" he asked.

I stopped walking. "Go back to America, Mr. Stans. You're a bloody fool."

"Calm down, Doc. We're all on the same team."

We stood by the entrance to the camp, then hitched a ride on an APC with some Australian soldiers, young and happy to be in control of an armored vehicle with a large machine gun. They were elaborately polite when we climbed in and kept making sure we were comfortable. With the hatch open, we sped down the road. Hot air roared around us; the sun burned down and the sky was painfully blue.

"Here's our theme song," said a corporal named Trevor and he played a tape on his portable stereo. It turned out to be something called "Highway to Hell" and the young soldiers sang along.

General Bates was back at the Turismo Hotel, but he was very busy and Major Holden told us to wait. Sister Xavier and I sat down on a saggy couch in the lobby and watched Australian officers hurry down the hallway carrying faxes. They were tan and fit and ready for action. "Timor is the big show," one lieutenant told me. "If you're going to be in the army, you've got to be here."

I tried to talk to Sister Xavier, but she was like a smooth granite wall.

There weren't any cracks or soft places in her personality, nothing to hold on to in a conversation. Everything was reduced to a single desire: we must save the village. I wanted to resist this single-mindedness, but I knew she was right, that we had to keep everyone from dying.

It was almost five o'clock when Major Holden ushered us in to the general's office. Bates sat behind a desk studying a fax and making notes. I introduced myself and Sister Xavier, trying to keep the desperation out of my voice as I explained the situation.

"Hand-to-Hand has enough food and medical supplies," I said. "What we need is transportation and a military escort. We should leave immediately, before it gets dark."

As I tried to make the journey sound quick and easy, the general kept glancing at the map of East Timor taped to the wall. I knew what he was thinking. Loo-key-sah. Where on earth is this village?

"Thank you for telling me about this problem," Bates said. "We've received similar reports of people having trouble with the militia." He picked up a water bottle and tore off the plastic safety seal. "Right now we're completing Stage One, the process of inserting our forces and taking firm control of Dili. Stage Two will begin in a few days. We'll secure Liquica and the other nearby towns."

"But we can't wait for Stage Two," I said. "These people are dying right now."

"It's just like building a bridge, Dr. Cadell. First, you construct a solid foundation. Then you extend yourself inch by inch to the other side."

"You don't need a bridge," Sister Xavier said. "You can drive to my village in thirty minutes."

"Yes. But what if there's an ambush waiting for us? Roadblocks? Land mines? You've already told me that these militiamen are dangerous. What we need is a fully organized military operation."

I shook my head. "If you can get me a truck or a Land Rover, I'll take the risk and go there alone."

"I'm sorry, Doctor. In order to protect you and other civilians no unauthorized vehicles are being allowed out of the city."

Major Holden seemed to have a natural instinct as to when a meeting was over. Suddenly he reappeared carrying more bottles of water. "I'm afraid that the general has a conference call in five minutes," he told us.

"The militia will run away the moment you send in soldiers," I said.

Bates tapped his finger on the desk. "That's what the Americans thought during the UN action in Somalia. And it was a disaster. They had unacceptable casualties."

"East Timor isn't like Somalia. If the Australian government didn't want to risk its soldiers, then it shouldn't have sent them here."

"We're fulfilling our obligations."

"Yes. Of course. But I think that you need to be a bit more aggressive."

"These troops are my responsibility." Bates paused dramatically as if the room were filled with young Australian soldiers and their mothers. "I'm going to make sure that no one gets hurt during this operation."

"But what about the hundreds of civilians who are going to die because you didn't go twenty-four miles down the road."

Looking angry, Bates picked up a pushpin and walked over to the map on the wall. "Good-bye, Doctor."

"I'm sorry, General Bates," I said. "I apologize. But don't you see that—"

"This conversation is over." Bates turned away from us and forced the pushpin into the black dot that marked Liquica.

WE LEFT THE HOTEL and walked down the boulevard toward the wharf. I saw Nicky standing next to an Australian APC. Someone had wired a white plastic skull to the machine-gun bracket and Nicky was taking a photograph of this decoration.

"Hey, Julia. Hand-to-Hand was the news story of the day. No competition."

"Where's Daniel?"

"We lost our phone. He's back at the hotel using Tristram Müller's gear."

I introduced Sister Xavier and told him about the meeting with

Bates. The nun reached out to shake Nicky's hand, but he raised his camera and took a picture.

"You're an American, Mr. Bettencourt?"

"I guess so."

"Could you talk to the United States Army? Perhaps the Americans would go down to my village."

"Our army's not involved in this. The only Americans here are UN officials and the pilots flying the planes."

Sister Xavier looked at me. "Then we need British soldiers."

"The British are part of the Interfet forces," I said. "General Bates is officially their commander."

Nicky lowered his camera. "I've met the man in charge of the Gurkhas. He's all right. Maybe you can talk to him."

He led us back to the hotel. A British army captain was sitting on the grass in the overgrown courtyard, eating rations with some of his men. All I wanted was a few words from Nicky, perhaps a suggestion that going to Liquica was a good idea, but he acted as neutral and uncommitted as ever. Nicky was always the man watching, no matter what was going on. He made the introduction, then stepped back and fingered his camera.

"It's a pleasure to meet you, Captain Jenkins. Where are you from in Britain?"

"Dorset," he said. "But I don't give a damn about the place. I'm here, doing my job. That's good enough for me."

I began talking, but I could see that Jenkins didn't care if all the people in Liquica died. Their lives were an abstraction to him, a useless number. He ate a spoonful of canned peaches, then scratched a mosquito bite on his hand.

"Perhaps this isn't your direct responsibility," I said. "But nobody else wants to get involved."

Jenkins nodded politely to show that he was listening. Then he scratched his neck.

"You know that protecting these people is the right thing to do. That's why we've been sent to this country."

I looked hard at Jenkins, willing him to listen to me. The captain nodded again, but this time he appeared a bit more interested. Doing the right thing was something he could understand.

"I'm sorry to put this in your hands," I said. "But I can't travel to the village alone. You can stay here and do—whatever. Or go down the coast road with us and save some lives."

Jenkins didn't look at the grass or the trees or the canned peaches anymore. He faced me directly and I knew that he had made a decision. "All right. You've made your point, Dr. Cadell. Let me go talk to our senior officers. There aren't a lot of British here so the chain of command is a bit more informal."

"Thank you, Captain. You can find me at the *Seria* on the wharf or . . ." I glanced at Nicky.

"Or at the Resende Inn. Room 212."

"I can't promise anything of course, but I'll give it a try. My men feel a bit useless guarding the people at this hotel."

Sister Xavier was still worried as we left the hotel. "Perhaps the British will also say no," she said.

"It's possible."

"Maybe we should talk to the Portuguese."

"Forget about that," Nicky said. "It's late. We need to get off the street."

Sister Xavier went to the bishop's compound to search for some nuns from her order. Nicky and I turned toward the wharf. The sun was dropping toward the mountains and orange clouds glowed on the horizon. Night was coming and I could feel a wave of fear spreading through the city. Everyone started walking a little faster. Tires whipped through the trash scattered across the pavement as a Land Rover raced back to the airport. People wanted to find shelter before the sun went down.

Nicky stopped to take a photograph of the Igreja Motael. "The first day we arrived, Daniel and I went to this church together." As he switched lenses on one of his cameras, he told me how Daniel had given all of his water to a sick woman.

"You make it sound like a mistake," I said.

"He shouldn't do things like that."

"You won't lose your license if you occasionally got involved, Nicky."

"Helping people is your job, but that's not what we do. If Daniel keeps crossing the line, he's going to get into trouble."

The food line on the wharf had disappeared. Richard was back on the ship and Collins was standing guard with his rifle. I paid my helpers with triple rations and was just about to leave when Billy came down the wharf carrying his rifle. "Where'd you go with that nun?" he asked.

"Out to the airport and back. Then we saw General Bates. Sister Xavier needs some soldiers to take control of her village."

Billy rolled his eyes as if I'd told a bad joke. "You're a very helpful person, Julia. Too bad you weren't wearing the Hand-to-Hand shirt."

"Where's Richard?"

"He's giving an interview up in his cabin, talking to reporters from the *Guardian* and the *Times*. Daniel's going to miss out on the big story and that's us. Everything's working out perfectly."

DANIEL, NICKY, AND I ate dinner that night at their hotel with Tristram Müller and a journalist named Peter who worked for a French wire service. Tristram had bought two large pineapples and Nicky cored them with his Swiss Army knife, the juice dripping onto the floor. The hotel manager served us pancakes for fifty Australian dollars each and I ate two of them before I realized that I was dining on food made from Hand-to-Hand supplies. Someone had already sold his cornmeal and cooking oil to the manager. I had to smile. One way or another, we had helped restart the local economy. Tristram produced a tin of strawberry jam and this was smeared across the pancakes. There wasn't any alcohol for dinner, but the sugary meal surged into our bloodstreams and made everyone feel giddy.

Tristram insisted that Peter tell us about his hobby. It turned out that he spent his spare time taking photographs of different women baring their breasts in famous locations. He had scrapbooks of photos back at his apartment in Paris, the nipples appearing at the White House, the Kremlin, and Buckingham Palace. Daniel had once gotten Peter and his girlfriend into the Vatican garden and now he wanted Daniel to sneak him into the pope's bedroom. For an hour or so, I forgot about Sister Xavier and her villagers. I sat on the floor next to Daniel, his arm wrapped around me, and laughed when Peter described bare breasts at Napoleon's tomb.

We left them as Tristram ordered another round of pancakes. Nicky was talking about a Florida millionaire who had offered a hundred thousand dollars to anyone who could take a photograph of a soul leaving the human body.

Peter looked amused. "That's very American."

"Hey, the money's real. So how we going to get it?"

"I don't believe in soul or spirit or *inneres Licht*." Tristram said. "It's all just flesh and Coca-Cola. Isn't that right, Julia? We need a medical opinion."

I could have easily sat down and resumed the conversation, but now I wanted to be alone with Daniel. "I'll give my prognosis tomorrow," I said, slipping out the door.

We stumbled upstairs in the dark, fumbled with the key, and finally got into the room. Daniel closed the door and locked it. A breeze came through the open window and the curtains flapped like tattered flags.

"I missed you," Daniel said and put his arms around me. I closed my eyes and felt his body pressing against mine. Lying down on the bare mattress, we kissed each other and then I touched his face. I had thought about Daniel so often, his nose and mouth and eyes; now that we were back together I had to make sure that he was real.

"You look tired," I said.

"And you look beautiful."

"I don't quite believe that. I thought journalists were supposed to tell the truth."

"I am telling the truth." Daniel embraced me and I felt the muscles of his back and shoulders. Both of us moved slowly, lingering on each sensation, as if we were back at the Canal House, with all the time in the world.

We made love as the final light disappeared, then lay together in the dark room. It was colder now and I pulled the scratchy blanket over my body. Daniel stood up, walked over to the window, and pushed back the curtains. I could see part of the moon and thousands of stars. Someone was firing an automatic rifle in the distance—two short bursts, then silence, then a longer burst that exhausted the clip.

"Victor Zikowski was always teasing me about being an American," Daniel said. "He said we were a cheerful culture, obsessed with happy endings. That's why America stayed so long in Vietnam. We didn't want to win the war. We just wanted to feel good about leaving."

"Happy endings aren't always possible," I said.

"No. Time keeps pushing us forward. You might be happy at one particular moment, but the world keeps changing." He came back to the mattress. "No matter how much we wanted, we couldn't stay in Italy."

Daniel kissed the palm of my hand and lay down beside me. He went to sleep a few minutes later. I drank some water from one of our bottles, then watched a moth as it fluttered in through the open window. Oh God, I thought. Protect us, please. Daniel's legs twitched and his hands reached out as if he was fighting demons in some dark place.

THE NEXT MORNING Captain Jenkins came to our room with one of his Gurkha soldiers. Sergeant Santbir Gurung had a broad, smooth face and carried his kukri knife in a custom-made sheath. Gurung looked tough and disciplined, but there was an alert intelligence in his eyes. He stared at Daniel and me as if judging us, searching for our weaknesses.

"I spoke to my senior officers about your situation," Jenkins said. "We all agree that the UN could be a bit more aggressive in a situation like this, but we're supposed to obey General Bates."

"And you can't just drive to the village on your own?" I asked.

"I'm sorry, Doctor. We can confiscate weapons, return fire, things like that, but military escorts need to be cleared through Interfet."

"So you can't help us."

"We can't officially escort you to Liquica. Nevertheless, I've been ordered to take a platoon down the coast road, on a reconnaissance mission. We're supposed to evaluate the situation and see if anti-independence forces are in the area."

"And what if we followed you?" I asked.

Jenkins nodded slightly, like a teacher who had been waiting for the right answer. "Your actions would not be authorized by Interfet and we couldn't provide you with a vehicle. However, no one would stop you from coming along."

"When do you plan to go?"

"We'll drive past the Igreja Motael at fourteen hundred hours," said Gurung. "Perhaps you'll be there and perhaps we'll travel together. As I said, it would just be a coincidence and not an official decision."

Jenkins nodded to the sergeant and they got ready to go. "Have a very pleasant day, Dr. Cadell."

"Thank you, Captain."

"There's no need for that, ma'am. We came here to do our job, not sit around a hotel like a bunch of wankers."

I closed the door and Daniel began to pull on his shoes. "So Jenkins is going to Liquica and you have an unofficial escort. It's all very diplomatic."

"I think it's quite brilliant, actually."

"You've got just five hours to find a vehicle and fill it with supplies. I'll help you."

"Nicky doesn't think you should get involved in relief work."

"It's a news story with good photographs," Daniel said, looking up at me. "Even Nicky can't argue with that."

DANIEL LEFT THE HOTEL to find Sister Xavier while I returned to the wharf. My helpers had already shown up and one of the women had brought along her cousin. Pak and the crew unloaded pallets of food and we divided everything into different piles. I told them how it should be distributed: people who had a red ink mark on their arm could get additional food and water while anyone showing up for the first time received the basic supplies. Cooking fires were burning in the churchyard and a bluish-gray haze drifted through the air. A man was building a shelter with blackened pieces of roof sheeting while a woman braided her daughter's hair. It was a small moment, but it made me feel hopeful.

I hadn't seen Richard and Billy all morning. Perhaps they were exhausted from the interviews. As we began to hand out food, Collins and Briggs came down onto the wharf. They seemed happy to sit in the shade and watch the Timorese do the work.

"So where did you go last night?" Briggs asked.

"I stayed with friends."

"Your *special* friend," Collins said.

"That's right."

"I'm special, too. You just don't see my good side."

I left the wharf and walked down the street to the bishop's residence. Inside the gates, there were several white buildings with red-tile roofs. The militia had looted all the buildings, smashed every window, and set the main house on fire. The bishop had fled to Australia, but hundreds of Timorese had come down from the hills and were living in the compound. There was a safe feeling about the area; it was home, a refuge. Everyone believed that the bishop would eventually return to his people.

I kept saying, *"Ando à procura de Sister Xavier,"* and finally a boy led me to a patch of dead grass behind the house. Nicky and Sister Xavier were both there, watching Daniel work on the engine of a Toyota pickup truck. The Indonesians had tried to steal the church truck, but the bishop's servants had removed the alternator, the battery, and the carburetor. Now Daniel was trying to put it back together with a screwdriver.

"It's going to work," he said.

Nicky shook his head. "Twenty minutes ago, you said it wasn't possible."

"God will help us," Sister Xavier announced.

"I'm sure he will," Nicky said. "But perhaps you could ask God to fix the carburetor."

DANIEL MANAGED TO GET the truck started though it wouldn't go past second gear. That was good enough. I drove us back down to the wharf and bought petrol from some Portuguese soldiers. Food distribution was going on in a slow but organized manner while Collins and Briggs drank beer. I told Daniel and Nicky to load the truck with water bottles and emergency food rations, then climbed back onto the ship. In my cabin, I quickly gathered up medical supplies. The villagers in Liquica would be dehydrated and there probably would be cases of infant diarrhea. I needed IV tubes and needles and sealed bags of saline solution. I needed syringes. Two boxes. No, three. Tinidazole. Bactrim. Surgical gloves.

I had filled one bag and was starting on the second when Richard came in. He looked as calm as if he were back in England. I felt frantic and disorganized. We had to load the truck and meet Captain Jenkins in just twenty minutes.

"Where are you going?" he asked.

"Down the coast road to a village called Liquica. The militia is holding four hundred people on a wharf there."

"They'll kill you, Julia."

"I hope not. A platoon of Gurkhas is traveling with us."

"And you arranged this?"

"Basically." I broke open another box of saline packets.

"You should stay here and do your job."

"Everything is going quite well here and there are four hundred other people who need some immediate assistance." I pointed to the felt pens on my desk "Yesterday, we put a red mark on people's arms. Today, it's blue. I recommend green for tomorrow."

"Are you angry because you weren't interviewed?"

"You know I don't give a damn about that."

"I'm helping our organization. You know how it works."

"Yes, I know. Would you move to one side, please. There's another box of saline packets beneath the table."

Richard stood back as I ripped open the box. "I'm sorry about yesterday," he said. "You're the one who got us here and made all the major decisions. I'll hide from the press. I'll do whatever you want. You're in charge from now on."

"All right. Then I'm ordering you to stay here and hand out food. I hope to be back by nightfall."

"That isn't what I meant."

I opened another box and scattered its contents on the bed. "When you came to Bracciano, you told me that our relationship was over. I believed you and that's why I took this job. So why are you always hovering around, waiting for something to change?"

"I can't help it, Julia. I still love you." Richard shrugged his shoulders as if his emotions were a peculiar disability.

I finished packing and picked up the canvas bags. When I turned around, Richard was standing a few feet away, blocking the open doorway.

"I'm sorry, Richard. But I don't feel the same way. When we're finished with our work here, I'm going back to Bracciano."

I brushed past him and left the cabin. I jogged across the deck, slung the canvas handles of both bags around my neck like bandoleers, then lowered myself down onto the wharf. The medicine was heavy, but I moved fast, eager to get away from the ship. When I reached the warehouse, I glanced over my shoulder and saw that Richard was standing on the deck, watching me.

Nicky

18 INTO LIQUICA

It's common for journalists to travel with relief workers; you get a story and they get publicity. But this time I felt uncomfortable about Daniel and his motives. Instead of remaining an observer, he had fixed the church truck and loaded the supplies. He actually seemed to care about the people in Liquica and I was worried that I'd catch the same disease.

We drove across the road to the churchyard. Captain Jenkins and a platoon of Gurkhas met us there a few minutes later. Jenkins had gone out to the airport and found three Land Rovers abandoned by the United Nations. One had been set on fire and a second had a jagged line of bullet holes on the side. The third was in good condition, but someone had nailed a dog's skull onto the hood. Sergeant Gurung pried off the head with his kukri knife, but there was still a smear of blood on the metal.

The seventeen men in the platoon were commanded by a second lieutenant, Colin Mitchell; he was a young officer with wire-rimmed glasses who looked like he should be supervising basketball games at a parish hall. Jenkins split the platoon into three groups. Lieutenant Mitchell would take the point position while Jenkins commanded the reserve. Sergeant Gurung and four other Gurkhas were responsible for everyone riding in the church truck.

"You'll have about three hours in Liquica," Jenkins explained. "Most of the platoon will continue down the road for another forty kilometers, then we'll come back and pick you up before nightfall."

I could see that Julia wasn't satisfied with only a few hours in the village. "Would it be possible for your soldiers to spend the night there?" she asked Jenkins.

"General Bates is so bloody cautious that"—the captain saw Daniel take out his notepad and decided to be more diplomatic—"Interfet command isn't ready to extend the range of the pacification effort. This is only a reconnaissance mission. We're not holding ground."

Sergeant Gurung introduced us to the four men in his squad. Corporals Battis and Mainla were in their thirties, but the two privates, Thapa and Rai, looked like teenagers. Thapa was shy and polite around strangers. Rai seemed more confident. He wore his beret at a sharp angle. "You are English?" he asked me.

"Dr. Cadell is from Britain. Mr. McFarland and I are Americans."

"New York. Chicago. Texas. Hol-ly-wood," he said, rolling the last word around in his mouth.

"Yeah. That's about it."

Lieutenant Mitchell and his men led our convoy, followed by Jenkins. Sergeant Gurung was twenty feet behind them, driving the half-burned Land Rover. The church truck carrying the relief supplies was to follow the soldiers. We were in a fairly safe position unless the militia had mortars or rocket-propelled grenades. I doubted that they'd stop shooting if I showed them my *Newsweek* ID.

Julia drove the church truck and Sister Xavier sat beside her. Daniel, Corporal Battis, and I sat in the back with our legs dangling over the side. The corporal was a stocky man with a shaven head who smoked cheroot cigars. He told us that the Gurkhas had invented nicknames for the three UN Land Rovers and tried to translate the Nepalese phrases into English. "Sergeant Gurung is driving the fire Land Rover and the lieutenant has the wounded Land Rover," he said. "It's wounded because someone shot it with a machine gun."

"What's the captain driving?" Daniel asked.

"The dog Land Rover. You can still see the blood." Battis puffed on his cigar and stared at the hills. "The dog Land Rover is bad luck. We should have taken another one."

The convoy passed through an Interfet roadblock near the airport and headed west on the coast road. A steep hillside was on the left of the two-lane road, the ocean on our right. The water was clear enough so that even from the truck I could see the coral beds and rose-colored seaweed clinging to the rocks. A pelican circled in the sky, swooping down over a line of whitecaps formed by a hidden sandbar. If I turned my head and ignored Battis and his assault rifle, I could pretend that we were tourists, on our way to the beach.

"I need a rum drink with a little umbrella," I told Daniel.

He smiled and leaned back against the boxes of water. "Sounds good, Nicky. But first let's go scuba diving."

The road went inland a few hundred yards and passed through a small village. Several of the huts had been set on fire and I didn't see any stray dogs lurking in the underbrush. You could take the pulse of a war zone by evaluating what was going on around you. We had a kind of running list; as you moved down it, the situation got more dangerous. At first, you saw villagers who looked cautious. Then they automatically ran away when they heard a car approaching. Then all the people disappeared. Then you saw burned huts and dead animals. Then dead villagers. And finally, the bodies of soldiers that had been left there by their friends. The road west wasn't that bad yet, but there was enough to be concerned. It looked as if a powerful virus had spread across the island and destroyed everything but the palm trees.

We passed the turnoff that led south to the mountains and traveled across a mud flat bordered by mangrove bushes. The bare ground was dotted with clay mounds. I had seen the same kind of mounds on the coast of Mozambique; they were ovens, used to boil down ocean water and turn it into salt. Near the drainage ditch the road had collapsed and someone had placed palm fronds across a pothole; it was a typical way to conceal a land mine. Lieutenant Mitchell stopped the lead vehicle and everyone got out. I jumped off the truck, hustled up the road, and took a few photographs of a Gurkha sweeping the area with a mine detector. When I came back, Daniel was talking to the two corporals.

"You know why Mainla is our best shot?" Battis asked.

"No. Why?"

"Six children! He never misses his wife!"

Corporal Mainla was a thin, quiet man. He drank from a water bottle while Battis giggled. "Now you have proof that you're alive," Mainla said. "Battis tells that joke to anyone who is breathing."

A faint tapping sound came from a mud-wall hut near one of the salt ovens. Battis and Mainla raised their rifles and Gurung ran forward with the two younger soldiers. The sergeant whispered something in Nepalese and pointed with his forefinger. You go left. You go right. He crouched beside the road ditch, ready to fire, while his men split up into two groups and flanked the hut. They darted around to the back, then reappeared a minute later.

"Nothing to worry about," Mainla said. "The wind pushed a sheet of roofing against the wall."

There were no land mines and the men kicked the palm fronds away. Lieutenant Mitchell drove a little faster and we reached a flat area where the road moved inland from the sea. Our convoy slowed down again as we crossed a bridge and reached the outskirts of Liquica. The village *mercado* was on the left side of the road. It had once been an open arcade with merchant stalls, but someone had blown up the water tank and set the stalls on fire. All that remained was a few pieces of charred wood and white columns. It looked like the ruins of an ancient city.

We crossed a second bridge, then stopped on the outskirts of Liquica. Jenkins ordered most of his men to get out of the Land Rovers and dispersed them on both sides of the road. The vehicles stayed back as the platoon moved toward the center of the village. Most of the buildings in the village had been burned down a few days earlier and the soot-covered walls provided cover. Standing on the back of the pickup truck, I leaned my elbows on the roof of the truck cab and peered through my telephoto.

Just past a graveyard, the road ended in a T. Two burned-out cars formed a roadblock in the middle of the intersection and a group of about twenty militiamen stood behind the barrier. Even from a distance I could see they were nervous. The young men kept shouting at each other, waving rifles, and running back and forth. They looked like a street gang getting ready to defend their territory.

Jenkins parked sideways in the middle of the road and the drivers got out of their vehicles. Daniel, Julia, and Sister Xavier took cover behind the pickup while I remained on the truck bed.

"You're too exposed, Nicky. Get down," Julia said.

"Just a second."

"Hurry up, Nicky," Daniel said. "Take the picture and come over here."

Jenkins stood behind the dog Land Rover and wiped the sweat from his face with an olive green handkerchief. "Remember what I told you this morning!" he told his men. "Only fire your weapon to protect yourself or a civilian!"

Mitchell was farther up the road, crouched behind a concrete wall. "Excuse me, sir. But it looks like they want to fight."

"I bloody know what they want to do," Jenkins said. "But the rules of engagement require that we—"

A young man wearing a blue T-shirt raised his rifle and fired in our direction. He emptied the entire ammunition clip, then screamed something and jabbed his right fist like a boxer. The other militiamen crouched behind the burned cars and began firing. The gunshots had a quick, flat sound like someone beating a rug.

"Hold the point and keep them busy," Jenkins told Mitchell. "Gurung, get the Parker and take care of those bastards. Make sure you don't hit any civilians."

"Yes sir."

Jenkins led his squad through the burned-out houses on the side of the road. I figured they were going to circle around through the deserted village and flank the intersection. I jumped off the truck and crouched down beside Daniel. We were probably too far away to get picked off by a sniper, but over the years I'd seen several people hit by random bullets.

"That's the Red and White Iron militia," Sister Xavier said. "Some of the people are from Liquica. Others come from the villages south of here. They are young men who liked to sit in the square at night and talk about politics—then the Indonesians took them to the police station and gave them rifles."

Daniel was taking notes. "And they started killing people?"

"First they set up a roadblock to look for guerrillas, then they shot a man who was trying to protect his daughter. After that first killing, the devil entered their hearts."

"Why did they force the villagers down to the beach?"

"They're hostages."

I left the truck and joined Gurung beside the Land Rover. Opening the back, he took out a sniper rifle with a telescopic sight. I followed him as he sprinted up the road to the concrete wall. Mitchell and his men were crouched down, coming up occasionally to fire their rifles.

"Start with that man wearing the blue shirt," Mitchell said. "He really is quite annoying."

Gurung placed his elbows on top of the wall and chambered a round. "I can see him, Lieutenant."

"Go ahead then."

Gurung peered through the sight, waited a few seconds and squeezed the trigger. The rifle made a cracking sound and the man in the blue T-shirt was hit in the chest. There was a flash of blood and then he fell backward. The militiamen stopped shooting for few seconds, then blasted away at the same time. A bullet ricocheted off the road and smashed through the Land Rover's windshield. Gurung chambered a new round, moved the rifle slightly, then killed a second man.

I peered over the wall and got two quick photographs as the militiamen panicked and ran toward the beach. Gunfire came from Jenkins's squad and a third militiaman was hit. A bullet spun him around and he collapsed like a marionette that had just been dumped into a box. Lieutenant Mitchell ordered me to stay behind the wall as he ran forward with his soldiers. I drank some lukewarm water from a plastic bottle as Sister Xavier came up the road with Daniel and Julia.

"We're supposed to stay here," I said.

"Why? There's no danger. The militia has run away."

We followed Sister Xavier past the burned-out cars to where the three dead militiamen lay sprawled on the road. Corporal Mainla and Private Rai picked up the abandoned rifles, then dragged the bodies over to the grass, leaving three ribbony streaks of blood on the asphalt. The shrill brightness of the color startled me.

Mainla pointed down the hill at the beach. "There are many people there," he said to Julia. "No water. No food. It's very bad."

Liquica had once been a resort town for the Portuguese and there were still a few remnants from that era. An elaborate wrought-iron fence surrounded the local Catholic church, and banyan trees spread their branches and shaded the street. Weeds had overwhelmed a cobblestone road that led down a hill to the ocean. Looking across the beach, I could see the remains of a pagoda, changing rooms, and an outdoor restaurant. Everything had been destroyed by grenades.

Near the edge of the beach, the Portuguese had dug into the hillside and built a tennis court. Retaining walls ran along two sides of the court and the rest was marked off by a chain-link fence that had once captured wayward tennis balls. I could imagine Portuguese children darting back and forth with their rackets while their parents sat beneath striped umbrellas and watched them play. Now the militia had turned the tennis court into an enormous cage to hold their prisoners. Hundreds of women, old people, and children sat on the court. Some had taken plastic tarps and constructed open shelters to protect themselves from the sun. The Gurkhas stood near the fence and stared at the

villagers, but no one approached the crowd. There were too many people. It was too big a problem. Even Captain Jenkins looked intimidated.

The villagers didn't move until they saw Sister Xavier. People shouted
her name, pushed through holes in the fence, and surrounded her.
Standing in the middle of the crowd, Sister Xavier tried to find out what
had happened in the last twenty-four hours. Some of the information
was confusing and there were arguments about who was dead and who
had run away. An old lady began to weep about her missing grandson;
another person shouted about the lack of water. This man was shot,
that girl was raped, the militia had set the school on fire.

Sister Xavier explained the situation to Julia and Captain Jenkins.
The leader of the militia, a man named Cristiano, had been waiting for
Indonesian ferryboats to come up from West Timor and land on the
beach. He hated the independence movement and wanted the villagers
out of the country. All the hostages were going to be shipped to special camps organized by the Indonesians. After a few people ran away,
no one was allowed to leave for food or water. Most of the villagers
were suffering from heat stroke and dehydration.

"Where are Cristiano and his men hiding?" Jenkins asked.

"Somewhere up in the hills."

"Can they walk to the border?"

"It would be very difficult. The pro-independence guerrillas hate the
militia. They'll kill everyone if they catch them on the road. That's why
Cristiano was waiting for the boats."

Jenkins told his radioman to send a message to Interfet; then he went
over to talk to Sergeant Gurung. "Form a defensive perimeter around
this area. We'll continue down the road a bit farther. When we've finished the reconnaissance, we'll come back here to pick you up."

"Yes, sir."

"As far as I'm concerned, we followed the rules of engagement. If
you see anyone with a weapon, kill the bastard right away."

I watched Jenkins, Mitchell, and the rest of the platoon disappear
down the coast road. Sergeant Gurung and his four men had been left
behind to defend us. While the sergeant and Corporal Battis remained

on the beach, Corporal Mainla and the two younger men were told to patrol the village. Mainla retied his bootlaces, then carefully checked his assault rifle, knife, and grenades before leaving. He reminded me of an electrician about to rewire a building.

Daniel went up the hill to get the church truck while Julia and Sister Xavier walked around the crowded tennis court. Julia did a quick triage of the villagers. This person was dying. This person can be saved. This person is sick, but can drink water. I took a few photographs, then put my camera away as Daniel drove the pickup truck down the cobblestone walkway. Daniel didn't say anything when I started to help him. He kept glancing at Julia and Sister Xavier.

"They won't want to leave when Captain Jenkins comes back."

"You're probably right. I can't see Julia walking away from a lot of sick people."

"It'll be safe as long as the Gurkhas stay here. Cristiano is probably up in the hills, waiting to see what we're going to do."

Julia came over to the church truck and gave directions to everyone. It felt like she was in an operating room, picking up a scalpel and cutting through someone's skin. "This is going to be difficult," she said. "I didn't bring enough saline solution."

"What do you want us to do?" Daniel asked.

"Help Sister Xavier and start distributing water bottles. Nicky, go talk to Sergeant Gurung and see if he can find some sticks to hang the IVs."

Daniel ripped open a cardboard box and began handing out bottles of water while Sister Xavier told her parishioners to swallow one mouthful, count to two hundred, and swallow another. I went off with Sergeant Gurung to look for sticks and we came back with lengths of steel rebar pulled from wrecked buildings. After Julia inserted a needle into someone's arm, I used a brick to hammer the rebar into the cracked tennis court, then hung a bag of saline solution.

An old woman lay on a quilt, moving her lips as if in prayer. Julia knelt beside her with an IV needle. She tapped the woman's arm with her forefinger and tried to make a vein appear. No luck. She moved over to the other arm.

"You feeling okay, Nicky?"

"I'm fine."

"Keep drinking water. You don't want to get sick."

A young woman in a flowery dress sat a few feet away from us hold-ing her four-year-old daughter in her arms. The little girl was barely breathing and her body was limp. Without really thinking about it I knew that the child was going to die. The woman pressed her daughter against her body as if her own life could filter through cloth and skin. The child's open hand and faded red dress, her mother's hopeless ex-pression, created a perfect photograph. I would like to say that I cared about them, that I felt compassion, but at that instant my only thought was, Don't move until I get the shot.

I pulled out my camera, switched on the auto-advance, and placed mother and daughter in the middle of the frame with the blue sky as a background. I moved forward a step. The click-clicking of the shutter sounded like an obscenity.

Julia looked angry. "Put the camera down, Nicky."

"I'm sorry."

"Stop being a photographer for five minutes. We've got to help these people."

"Dr. Cadell!" Sergeant Gurung shouted. "Please! I must talk to you!"

Gurung stood over an army radio, adjusting the knobs. "One of the vehicles has broken down and they're trying to fix the engine. If they don't come back for us, we need to return to Dili."

"These people need a doctor," Julia said.

"You can't stay here alone. We must go back to the city."

Ten minutes later Gurung called us back to the radio. The reception was bad and the radio voices had to contend with static and a popping noise. Lieutenant Mitchell was doing most of the talking and he spoke in a clipped British manner that barely concealed his tension.

"Command, this is Delta One. There's a sniper here. Possibly two snipers. We're under fire."

• • •

I STAYED NEAR the radio and listened to the sporadic conversation between Jenkins and UN command. The British had taken cover in the ruins of a power station and were trying to find the sniper. Jenkins asked for helicopter support and was told that there were logistical problems. All the messages back and forth were short and full of military phrases, but Jenkins sounded angry. The Interfet officer in charge of the UN radio kept saying, "You were informed there was resistance in the area," as if this one phrase absolved General Bates of any responsibility. Jenkins was told that the logistical problems would disappear the next morning. If the British forces had been foolish enough to leave Dili, then they could spend the night sleeping in the rubble and swatting mosquitoes.

Sergeant Gurung listened to this final message and switched off the radio. "It's politics, Mr. Bettencourt. Very much politics." He said the word as if politics was in the same category as an earthquake or a hurricane.

All five soldiers came down to the beach and stood guard. The sun was just a hand's width above the horizon. A light breeze made the tops of the palm trees sway back and forth. Daniel, Julia, and Sister Xavier returned to the pickup truck and we all drank some water. Julia was still wearing her surgical gloves and splotches of blood were on her khakis. If human souls have weight—some vague but perceptible mass—then she was carrying an immense burden.

Gurung came over to the truck and said it was time to leave. "Corporal Mainla didn't see any of the militia, but they could still be in the area."

"I counted three hundred seventy-eight villagers," Julia said. "Twenty-five to thirty of them are in critical condition. They might die tonight."

"It's dangerous to stay here."

"Yes, it's dangerous. But we can't just abandon them."

She looked over at the villagers as if someone might be dying at that exact moment and she wasn't doing anything to save them. Daniel touched her arm, then spoke to Sergeant Gurung. "Did you receive an order to return to Dili?"

Gurung hesitated, then shook his head. "It wasn't a direct order. Captain Jenkins told us to protect you and shoot anyone carrying a rifle."

"Could you decide to stay here?"

"I can't speak for the others, Mr. McFarland. We must have a conversation."

The sergeant led his men across the beach to the ruins of the pagoda. They sat on chunks of concrete with their rifles cradled in their arms. Battis passed around his cheroot cigars and everyone had a smoke. The Gurkhas discussed the problem and I felt like I was watching a village meeting in Nepal. Everyone got a chance to talk, even the younger men.

The western horizon was a luminous gold ribboned with red light. Waves came in with a soft hushing sound and the pebbles on the shore tumbled and clicked against each other. I hiked down the beach a few hundred yards and took a silhouette shot of the sunset and the palm trees and the walls of the destroyed restaurant. During the moment that I was taking the photograph, I forgot about the villagers; there was only light and shadow. When I got back to the tennis court, the Gurkhas had made a decision. Rai and Thapa began to open their field rations while Sergeant Gurung approached Julia.

"We will stay here tonight, Dr. Cadell."

Julia relaxed slightly and she touched Gurung's arm. "Thank you, Sergeant."

"Battis and Mainla said that you would stay here without us and it's our job to protect you. Private Rai said that he isn't frightened of the militia and we would be cowards to run away. Private Thapa said that if the people at his village were sick he hoped a doctor like you would help them. And I said"—Gurung shifted his rifle around and looked embarrassed—"I said we must do this."

The sun disappeared behind the hills and a cool breeze came off the ocean as the stars and sliver of new moon appeared in the night sky. Julia had brought along a flashlight and she borrowed another one from the Gurkhas. She and Sister Xavier moved among the refugees, paying special attention to the children. The two light beams came together for a few minutes, then wandered off in different directions.

Daniel finished unloading the supplies, then sat on the tailgate of the church truck. I went over and joined him. "Corporal Mainla said we could eat some of their rations," I said. "One packet has deviled ham, crackers, and applesauce. The other has processed cheese and canned peaches."

"Maybe later, Nicky. I'm not that hungry right now."

I sat down beside him. The steel truck bed was still warm from the sun. "Julia would have stayed here without the soldiers."

"I think so."

"And Sister Xavier would have stayed because this is her village. And you would have stayed because of Julia."

"What about you, Nicky?"

"I would have stayed because I'm a damn fool."

"You're a better person than you think you are. For some reason, you keep telling yourself that you're not good enough."

"Maybe that's true."

"Nobody is good enough, but we can still hope."

Daniel began to talk about his farm at Bracciano. He wanted to plant some peach trees near the house but La Signora insisted that the trees would die. Did I know anything about peaches? If peaches could grow there, why not apples? I didn't know anything about gardening, but I began to argue about winter frost.

A Timorese woman began screaming. The two flashlight beams, now weak and yellow, moved toward the sound. "Daniel!" Julia shouted. "Bring the truck down and turn on the headlights! Hurry!"

Daniel drove the truck down onto the beach and aimed the headlights at the villagers. The two beams were so bright and unexpected that the refugees shielded their eyes. Trying not to step on anyone, we walked across the tennis court and found Julia bending over the little girl in the red dress. The child was dead, but her mother refused to accept it.

"Ajudar-me!" the mother shouted. *"Por favor, ajudar-me!"* But we couldn't help her. It took almost an hour to get the girl's body away and cover it with a towel.

Some of the old people began to weaken. Julia hurried to each one, trying to defeat death with a few medical supplies. As we helped her I thought of the sand castles my sister and I used to build on the beach every summer. We'd guard our creations all afternoon from the attacks of other children, but then the tide came in and the relentless waves pushed over our walls, destroyed our towers.

Two more people died. Our flashlights began to weaken. The pickup truck was low on gasoline. Daniel talked Sergeant Gurung into driving the Land Rover down on the beach so that we could use the headlights. "Only for a short time," he said. "If snipers are around, it's not safe to shine a light."

Moths and mosquitoes swarmed around the Land Rover's headlights, bouncing against the glass. Julia moved into and out of the light as she tried to help an old man who was having trouble breathing.

"Is there enough petrol to drive the truck back to Dili?"

Daniel nodded. "What do you want to do?"

"I'll stay here with Sister Xavier and the soldiers. I want you and Nicky to put six or seven of these people into the truck and get them to the airport."

As she led us over to a sick old woman, a rocket-propelled grenade came out of the darkness and hit the Land Rover. All three of us fell to the ground, shielding our heads with our arms. When I glanced up the Land Rover was burning and three of the Gurkhas were lying on the sand. Private Rai was on his knees, his face covered with blood. Gurung was bending over as if someone had punched him in the stomach. He raised his rifle and fired down the beach.

There was a booming sound and a second RPG hit the Land Rover. The vehicle split apart and bright fragments of burning metal went spinning into the night. Gurung was knocked off his feet by the concussion. Gunfire. Bright flashes. And then the militia ran down the beach and came toward us. A man stood over Sergeant Gurung, pressed the muzzle of his rifle against the wounded man's neck, and fired.

Some of the militiamen went over to the tennis court and shot a refugee woman who tried to get away. People were screaming. I raised my hands to surrender. A boy with braided hair swung his rifle and hit me in the face. I started to go down, but another man grabbed my arm and dragged me toward the burning Land Rover. I could taste blood in my mouth as Julia, Daniel, and Sister Xavier were pushed up beside me. A young man carrying an M16 approached us. He had a scraggly beard and wore a white yachting cap with a plastic brim. The other men were waiting for his orders and I realized he was Cristiano, the militia leader.

Cristiano screamed at us in Tetum. I glanced to my left. Private Rai and Corporal Mainla were lying on the ground. Both of them moved slightly, but the other three Gurkhas were dead.

In the light of the burning Land Rover, I could see Daniel's face. He watched the militiamen fire a few more bursts at Sergeant Gurung's body. I knew that he was considering every option, trying to figure out some way to save our lives. Daniel began to say something, but the boy with braided hair punched him in the mouth. Cristiano shouted a command and two men forced Julia to her knees. One of them took a long knife and slid the tip inside her T-shirt, ripping through the cotton fabric. Her shirt fell away, exposing her breasts and stomach.

The militiamen laughed and I realized what was going to happen. I tried to make my brain retreat to a safer place, to be the observer one step back, looking for a photograph. I watched the smoke and flames rising from the Land Rover, the dirty orange light, and the shadows moving across Julia's bare skin. Her face was rigid and defiant as she willed herself to be brave, but her eyes kept jerking around, showing her fear.

"I must talk to Cristiano," Daniel said to Sister Xavier. "Translate for me." He took a step forward. "I have something you want, *comandante*. I have something."

Sister Xavier translated the words into Tetum. Cristiano made a joke and the men laughed again.

"Cristiano says that you can't trade this woman because she already belongs to him."

"But I can give him the thing he really wants." Daniel's voice was urgent, pushing hard. "I can protect him. I can save his life."

Again the translation and this time Cristiano looked uneasy. He said something in Tetum and his men pulled Daniel and Sister Xavier across the tennis court. Cristiano followed and they began to talk.

Julia stood up, covering her breasts with her arms. The knife blade had scratched a line down her neck and upper chest. Blood trickled across her skin. She ignored the wound, ignored everything but Daniel standing in the shadows with Cristiano.

Five minutes went by. The burning Land Rover had lit up the area, but now the flames were dying down. Militiamen pulled doors and cracked window frames from the destroyed restaurant and used the wood to build a bonfire. A man with a flashlight searched through the crowd. He avoided the children and focused on the elderly villagers. I assumed that he was looking for a particular person to kill.

Cristiano shook his head and began to walk away, but Daniel followed him, speaking with a soft, coaxing voice while Sister Xavier translated. Finally, there was some sort of agreement and Daniel returned to us. He unbuttoned his cotton work shirt and gave it to Julia. Daniel's blue undershirt was dark with sweat. When he embraced Julia, she closed her eyes and shivered as if a spasm of pain was passing through her body.

"It's going to be all right. I think we've got a deal."

"What do they want?" I asked. "More guns?"

"They need a way out of here. Cristiano knows the guerrillas will ambush them if they take the road to West Timor. So I offered them a boat ride."

"What kind of boat? Indonesian?"

"Anything that floats. We can use the *Seria*. The big argument was about weapons. But Cristiano agreed to disarm before they go on board."

"What about the villagers?" Julia asked.

"You have to get them out of here tonight. You and Nicky put the weakest people in the truck and lead everyone back to Dili."

"What about you?"

"I'm going to be a hostage. They'll kill me if a boat doesn't show up by sunset tomorrow."

"You can't do that." Julia looked frightened. "It's too dangerous."

"This is our only option. We don't have anything else to offer them."

"What if we can't get back to Dili?"

"It'll be difficult, but you can make it. When you reach the port, go immediately to the *Seria*. Don't waste your time with General Bates or anyone else at Interfet."

"He might want to send in troops," I said.

Daniel nodded. "That's the one thing that could get me killed. Just tell everyone to follow the plan. Captain Vanderhouten can get the *Seria* down here in a few hours. We'll keep the boat in deep water and ferry the men out. There's a rubber raft on the stern. It's big enough for five or six passengers."

Julia tried to argue with Daniel, but one of the villagers started screaming. We turned around and saw the man with the flashlight holding an old woman while his two friends knelt beside her. One of the militiamen pulled a machete out of his belt, gripped the woman's jaw with one hand and forced her mouth open. He swung downward with a quick motion and smashed the machete handle into her mouth. She spat blood out, lay on her side and moaned. The man with the machete stood up with his prize—a gold tooth.

Sister Xavier turned to Julia. "Come and help me, Dr. Cadell. We'll get them ready to travel." The two women moved to the middle of the crowd and the nun spoke to her parishioners. Julia kept glancing over Daniel. I knew that she was worried. Over the years, she had dealt with looted food shipments and dust storms that grounded all the supply planes. Trucks broke down. Nurses caught malaria and returned home. The only reliable expectation was that nothing ever followed the plan.

Daniel started the church truck. The wheels spun around, digging up sand as he drove onto the cobblestone walkway. When the truck was pointing up the hill, I reached into the back and grabbed a cardboard box. We tore it into strips, covering the three dead soldiers, then went over to the wounded men. Corporal Mainla had been hit in the back with shrapnel and his shirt was wet with blood. He was unconscious and breathed with a wheezing sound. Private Rai had a dislocated shoulder and a gash in his forehead. Looking dazed, he knelt by Mainla and spoke softly. Julia returned with her medical bag. She cut off Mainla's shirt and covered the wound with a wad of gauze and a bandage. "That's all I can do," she told Rai. "There's not enough time. Not enough light."

Daniel and I picked up the corporal and laid him in the back of the pickup. Private Rai climbed into the truck and crouched beside Mainla. "Keep his head to one side so he won't choke on the blood," Julia said. "Good. That's good. Now put your hand on his chest and try to feel his breathing."

Private Rai touched Mainla's chest. "He has a wife and six children. A man with so many children should not die."

Daniel and I loaded the weakest villagers onto the truck bed, pushing them up against Mainla's body. Small children went on the tailgate or were squeezed into the truck cab. Julia found an old man who could drive and he got into the truck with the frightened children. "*Espere, por favor,*" she said in Portuguese. Wait. Please. Don't start the engine. A little girl began crying and Julia hugged her, whispering softly.

Daniel wrote something on a sheet of notepaper. "Take this, Nicky."

"What is it?"

"My will. Julia gets the farmhouse. You get my car."

"No."

He stuffed the paper into my shirt pocket. "Take it anyway."

"We'll get the *Seria* down here as fast as we can. Vanderhouten will do anything for money."

Daniel smiled as if we were back in Rome together. "That's the lovely thing about greedy people. They're predictable."

Some of the villagers were arguing with Sister Xavier. She turned away from them and returned to the truck. "They won't go, Dr. Cadell. They think we'll be killed at the bridge near the *mercado*. Four years ago, the Indonesians murdered nineteen people there and threw their bodies into the river."

"It's their choice to stay here, " said Julia. "We can't force them to come along with us. If we just start walking—"

Cristiano screamed and waved his rifle. The bonfire was getting bigger and the shadows of his men glided across the bodies of the dead soldiers. "He says we have to go now," said Sister Xavier. "He says we are traitors and he wants us out of his sight."

Daniel kissed Julia on the forehead and the lips, then they held each other for a few seconds. I turned away from them, toward the fire, but the image stayed with me. We were caught in a flood with Daniel in the water and Julia on land. She was holding him, holding tightly, so that he wouldn't be swept away.

"Let me stay with you," she said.

"That's not part of the agreement."

"We shouldn't have come here at all."

He shook his head. "You had to do this and I had to be with you."

Cristiano shouted again and the old man started the truck. "I'm sorry," I told Julia. "But we need to leave."

Daniel let go of Julia. "Don't worry. I can handle this. Just talk to Vanderhouten and get the ship down here."

The old man shifted into first gear. The engine made a metallic screeching sound as it began to move up the cobblestone walkway. The crowd of villagers held back for a moment, then began to follow Sister Xavier. It was like watching a jellyfish, pushed back and forth by the currents, until it flowed off in a new direction.

Daniel smiled and waved good-bye. A little boy started to fall off the tailgate of the truck and Julia reached forward to catch him. When I looked back at the bonfire I couldn't see Daniel anymore.

THE WALK BACK to Dili is not a coherent memory. None of the refugees spoke and the noise from the truck seemed more real than our bodies. If the truck had stopped, if the engine had failed, our group might have dissolved into the darkness that surrounded us.

I remember the first bridge and the second bridge, the tidal flat and the dark mounds of the salt ovens. At some time during the journey I picked up a little girl and started carrying her. Her body was tense and rigid; she clung to my shirt with both hands. Eventually she went to sleep and I slung her over my shoulder like a sack of rice.

Julia seemed to be everywhere, her worried face moving in and out of the shadows. "Everyone's so tired," she whispered. "I don't know if we can make it." And then she would hurry over to encourage someone who had stopped walking. More bodies were loaded into the back of the pickup. People sat on the roof of the truck cab with their legs on the windshield and others lay facedown on the hood. The truck looked like a moving sculpture of limp bodies; there was so much weight that the tires flattened and squeaked as they rolled across the asphalt.

We lost eight refugees during the journey. I still don't know if they died or if they lay down in a road ditch and went to sleep. The night seemed to go on forever, but when we stopped to place one more body onto the truck I noticed that most of the stars had vanished. The sky had turned a dark purple and a faint strip of light glowed on the horizon. Still holding the little girl on my shoulder, I maneuvered the camera out of my bag, stepped across the road, and took three quick photographs of our weary procession.

We reached the section of road close to the ocean and I could hear the waves falling on shore. The old man driving the truck stuck his arm out the side window. "*Acabou a gasolina,*" he said in Portuguese. Out of gas. The needle had fallen well below the last line on the gauge, but the engine didn't stop and we kept going. I don't know if a deceptive fuel tank rivals the loaves and the fishes, but it felt miraculous at that moment. We kept walking, a little faster now, and Venus appeared — a clear point of light in the sky.

We stumbled past a thicket of bamboo, came over a hill, and saw two Australian armored personnel carriers parked in the middle of the road. A few soldiers jumped down and stood there with their rifles, but they didn't approach us. We probably would have marched the last four miles into Dili if the old man hadn't stopped the truck and switched off the engine. The refugees sat down in the middle of the road. An old woman appeared and took the little girl from me as the soldiers approached Julia.

"I'm Dr. Julia Cadell. These people are from the town of Liquica."

"That's a bit of a distance," a sergeant said. "You walk all the way here?"

"Yes. And they can't go any farther." Julia's voice was raspy, but she spoke with a brisk, formal manner. "I want you to get on your radio and contact the UN medical team out at the airport. Tell them that you have over three hundred fifty refugees and they need to come here with food, water, medical care, and transport."

"No worries, ma'am. We can do that."

"Two wounded soldiers are on the truck. Load them onto an APC and we'll get them into Dili right away."

They carefully lifted Corporal Mainla out of the pickup and placed him inside the armored personnel carrier. Private Rai sat on the floor next to his friend as we roared down the road to the Interfet camp.

Some tents had been set up as a hospital. An army medical team ran out with a stretcher and the wounded soldiers were taken away. It took over an hour to find the Australian colonel who was the commanding officer at the camp. Julia explained the situation in Liquica, warning him not to send troops into the town until the militia was gone.

It was about eight o'clock in the morning when we left the camp with some Portuguese soldiers on their way into Dili. They dropped us off at the Governor's Office and we hurried to the wharf. Julia was exhausted, but she spoke quickly. Make a deal with Vanderhouten. Yes. That was our first objective. Did a ship's engine need to be warmed up? Did I know anything about engines? She had a car when she was a medical student that had to be warmed up in the morning. But it was cold in England and warm in East Timor. Did that make a difference? It must make a difference. Can't waste time for an engine.

She took a took a deep breath and squeezed my hand. "Sorry, Nicky. I'm talking nonsense, aren't I?"

"It's okay. We're both tired."

"We've got nine or ten hours to get down the coast to Liquica."

We climbed up the *Seria's* gangplank and found Richard and Billy eating breakfast near the stern. Julia spoke to both of them in a flurry of words, describing the situation and insisting that the ship leave as soon as possible. "Of course," Richard said. "We'll do everything we can." Then he took two steps back and let Billy get the details.

"They'll give up their weapons," Julia said. "Daniel worked out a deal. Tell them it's safe, Nicky. We just have to get there as soon as possible."

We walked up the deck to the wheelhouse where Captain Vander-houten stood drinking coffee. The captain's face formed a sympathetic mask while Julia and I described the problem. Vanderhouten nodded and mentioned the *Seria's* owners, a mysterious group of men who had warned him not to risk their property in dangerous activities.

"If it was up to me, I'd go right away," he said. "But of course I have a responsibility to my shareholders."

"What shareholders?" asked Julia. "You don't have any sharehold-ers. You're a smuggler."

Vanderhouten put down his coffee cup and tried to look offended. "Dr. Cadell, I am a graduate of the Rotterdam Shipping and Transport College. I placed third in a class of eighteen."

"I don't give a damn what you did! Get this ship moving! Right away!"

"We'll pay for this service," I said. "Perhaps we could negotiate a price while the ship gets ready to leave the harbor."

"The *Seria* can't leave, Mr. Bettencourt. You haven't been listening to me. As much as I wish to help, I must not violate the trust of my shareholders."

Julia took a step toward the captain. "If we don't go, they're going to kill Daniel."

"Nicky, take Julia out on deck." Richard spoke in a bland manner, as if he was talking to the cleaning staff at his office. "Billy and I will talk to the captain."

I glanced over at Billy and he nodded his head slightly. Holding Julia's arm I coaxed her out of the wheelhouse. The ship's cook brought us coffee and two bowls of rice, but Julia refused to eat anything. When Collins and Briggs appeared on deck I told them what was going on.

"Sorry, pal. Can't go. Won't go." Collins said. "Playing nursemaid to a mob of militiamen is definitely not in our contract."

"To hell with your contract," I said. "Take your gear and get off this ship."

"You didn't hire us," Briggs said. "We don't answer to you."

"If you did, I would have fired you two weeks ago. You're both cowards."

Briggs flexed his shoulder muscles. "This little ratbag just insulted us, Tig. I think he needs a lesson."

They both came toward me, but I was ready. I wanted to hurt someone —kick, gouge, and bite like a crazy man. I had to do something that would release the furious energy in my brain.

Billy stepped out on deck and realized what was going to happen. "That's enough of that," he said.

"This has nothing to do with you," Collins said.

"Sure it does. Now get out of my sight before I break every bone in your grubby little hands. You know how that's done, Tig? I know how it's done. Because I've done it. A couple times."

Billy took a quick step toward them like a boxer moving across the ring and they retreated down the hatchway to their sleeping area. Billy smiled at me. "Jesus, Nicky. I can't believe it. You were going to fight 'em."

"What happened?" Julia asked. "What did Vanderhouten say?"

"He's going to do it. We had to give him all the money in our pockets and now the little bastard wants Mr. Seaton's personal check."

Billy walked to the wheelhouse and returned with a leather checkbook. He went back into the cabin and Richard came out a minute later. "Okay. We've got an agreement," Richard said. "He'll transport everyone for twenty thousand English pounds."

"Thank you, Richard," Julia said. "I'll pay you back."

"Don't worry about that." Richard touched her arm, then turned to me. "You got film in your cameras, Nicky?"

"Sure. Everything's working."

Richard smiled, thinking about a seat in Parliament, maybe even a cabinet post. "Take lots of pictures when we get to Liquica. It's going to be a dramatic day."

CAPTAIN VANDERHOUTEN SLIPPED Richard's check into his money belt, then came out on deck and started giving commands. The ship no longer carried much cargo; it had been unloaded during the last two days. When the engine started up, we could hear a hollow, vibrating sound. The crew cast off the lines and Vanderhouten backed the ship away from the wharf. The *Seria* turned in the water like a large, slow creature, then pushed its way through the waves.

I picked up the uneaten bowl of rice and brought it over to Julia. She stood near the bow, staring at the coastline. Now that the ship was moving she was calm and focused on the next part of the plan.

"You better eat something, Julia. It'll make you feel better."

Julia took the bowl and picked at the food with some chopsticks. "It was wonderful how you carried that little girl, Nicky. Every time I looked around, I saw the people on the truck and that child in your arms."

"I hope she's okay."

"When we return to Europe, you and Daniel are going to be my special projects. First, I'm going to teach Daniel how to sing. He loves music, but he's a terrible singer."

"We'll take group lessons. Start a chorus."

"I've planned something different for you. I'm going to fix you up with a girlfriend."

"Stick with Daniel's singing," I said. "That's a realistic goal."

"We can put your photo up in the London underground. Wanted: a suitable partner for an American photographer who's brave, loyal, and kind."

"What about plump and stubborn, yet sexy?"

"You can write your own ad, Nicky. I'll get all the letters and pick out the most promising."

A thumping sound came from inside the ship. It wasn't particularly loud, more like a hand slapping the base of an overturned washtub. The hatch cover was pushed away and four crew members scrambled out, followed by a plume of black smoke. The *Seria* shuddered and stopped moving. Captain Vanderhouten burst out of the wheelhouse and began screaming at the Indonesians.

"No power!" he told us. "The engine just stopped!"

Billy climbed down the ladder into the hold, then came up a few minutes later holding on to Pak. The first mate's skin and clothes were black with smoke. He lay on the desk, gasping for air. Billy coughed and spat onto the deck. "Something's on fire," he said. "It's down in the engine room."

Captain Vanderhouten kept shouting orders. Two crew members started a portable water pump and dropped its intake hose into the ocean. The pump coughed and sputtered like a sick lawn mower. Salt water leaked from the brass couplings. The crew caught the water in buckets and poured it down the hold. Gradually, the smoke subsided and we climbed down to the engine room. Everything was hot and covered with soot. Black marks appeared on our hands and clothing.

Pak stood close to the engine and examined the destruction. It looked like he was trying to communicate with some deeper essence of the machinery. He shook his head and spoke to the captain.

"Pak thinks the fuel line burst," Vanderhouten said. We were pushing the engine when we left the harbor."

"Can you fix it?" I asked.

"It's going to be difficult. We don't have any parts."

"We need to get back to Dili right away," Julia said. "We'll have to talk to General Bates."

"My shareholders are going to be very angry," Vanderhouten said. "Who's going to pay for this damage?"

Billy reached out and grabbed the captain's throat with one hand. Vanderhouten tried to pull himself away, but Billy tightened his grip.

Terrified, the captain stopped struggling. His face turned pink and spit drooled from his mouth.

"Listen up," Billy said. "I could snap your neck right now and no one would give a damn. We'll talk about money later, but right now we want off this bloody ship."

The crew found the rubber raft, but its outboard motor wouldn't start and Pak had to put in a new spark plug. Now it was almost twelve noon. As each minute passed, we moved closer to sunset and Cristiano's ultimatum. Richard switched on his sat phone and called his contacts at the United Nations. Although General Bates didn't control the fleet in Dili Harbor, neither the Australians nor the British would allow their ships to be moved without a formal request from Interfet. Richard continued using the phone while we rode the raft back to the harbor. "Bates will see us," he told Julia. "Just let me do the negotiation."

We landed on the beach and ran up the waterfront boulevard to the Turismo Hotel. Interfet headquarters was being moved to the airport, but General Bates still had an office there. Julia wanted to go upstairs immediately, but the Australian soldiers held us in the lobby. Young men in camouflage uniforms walked around carrying manila folders and I heard a short-wave radio playing the kind of bouncy pop music you'd hear in an exercise class. Bottles of water were stacked against the wall and the sergeant standing behind the hotel desk told us, "It's free, mate. Take as much as you want." I had a fantasy of water bottles and cans of diet cola and all the other products of the industrial world being tossed out of airplanes flying over East Timor. There were no parachutes in my fantasy. Nothing to slow the fall. And television sets and personal computers and lounge chairs and enormous bales of snack crackers were tumbling through the air and exploding on the ground.

Major Holden came downstairs and guided us to the general's new office on the first floor. A portable electric generator was chugging away down in the courtyard to power the general's air conditioner. We walked into a pocket of cool, dry air and found Bates sitting at his desk with a stack of Australian newspapers.

"We need a transport ship," Julia said, then started to explain what had happened.

"Why don't you sit down, Dr. Cadell."

"We need—"

"I'm quite aware of the situation." General Bates looked annoyed. "My office has already contacted naval command and requested that the cruiser *Botany Bay* be sent down the coast to Liquica."

I took Julia's hand and got her to sit down on a bench facing the general. "When will the ship leave the harbor?" I asked.

"The order has to go through the appropriate chain of command."

"Tell them to do it right away," Julia said. "A boat has to get there by sunset."

"We're following the correct procedure, Dr. Cadell. Obviously, you didn't care to obey the rules and that's why you got into trouble."

"It's unfortunate that all this happened." Richard's voice was soothing and respectful. "But there is a deadline here. Perhaps the Australian ship could be heading toward Liquica while the order is being processed."

"I don't like to be ordered around, Mr. Seaton. Especially by a bunch of misguided do-gooders who have deliberately disobeyed my instructions. Everyone involved in our effort here seems to be part of the program except the British. I told Captain Jenkins he could lead a reconnaissance patrol. Without my permission, he took along a group of civilians."

"We're sorry for the confusion," Richard said. "But right now we need to help Mr. McFarland. My Australian friends have told me that you're the kind of man who can cut through all the clutter."

Bates smiled at Richard. "Interfet is handling the problem, Mr. Seaton. Now go outside and my staff will keep you informed about the situation."

We sat on the wicker furniture in the hotel waiting room and more people offered us bottled water. Around three o'clock Major Holden told us that the *Botany Bay* was leaving for Liquica. I went outside with Julia and we walked across the waterfront boulevard to the beach. One of the Australian cruisers that had been anchored near the wharf was already gliding out of the harbor. "That's got to be the *Botany Bay*," I said. "They'll get there in time, Julia. Don't worry."

I ran into Tristram Müller and he let me go to his hotel room to use his phone and computer. I downloaded the disc of photographs from Liquica, then called the *Newsweek* office and gave the story to John Scofield. Around five o'clock, I called an editor working for the *Telegraph* and told him about Daniel.

It was close to sunset when I went back to the Turismo and found Julia and Richard in the hotel lobby. General Bates and Major Holden had left for the airport, but a neatly dressed Australian lieutenant knew about the situation and was monitoring the radio reports from naval command. Now it was getting dark outside, but none of us wanted to admit that the deadline had passed. Billy showed up an hour later and said that the *Seria*'s crew had gotten the engine started. Using a fraction of normal power, the ship had drifted back to the wharf.

Julia sat on the couch in the lobby with her elbows resting on her knees. Although her eyes were open, she didn't seem to be looking at anything. The lieutenant went upstairs for a few minutes and returned with a sheet of paper. His face had been so confident, so assured of his mission, that I had felt relaxed watching him. Now he looked embarrassed and ashamed.

"We just received a radio message from the *Botany Bay*. The ship reached Liquica at approximately nineteen hundred hours. The captain sent a landing party to the beach, and when they arrived no one was there. I guess the militia went up into the hills with your friend."

Richard tried to call his military contacts in Australia, but everyone had left their office for the day. The lieutenant said he would radio General Bates out at the airport and ask for instructions, but he doubted that anything could be done until morning. Billy escorted Julia back to her cabin on the *Seria* and I walked through the dark streets to the

Resende Inn. The hotel manager sold me a bottle of warm beer and a bowl of rice for twenty Australian dollars and I went upstairs to the room. I fell asleep almost immediately, then woke up in darkness. The cut on my back was burning as if the skin had been touched with a white-hot piece of iron. Lying on the mattress, I listened to the sound of my breath, my heartbeat, my awkward prayer.

19   SANTA CRUZ

Someone pounded on the door of my hotel room early the next morning. I was sure it was Daniel. He had probably spent the night listening to Cristiano and then manipulated the young man's vanity. *And now you must let me go, comandante. So I can write your story and tell the whole world about your struggle.*

I pulled on my pants, opened the door, and found Captain Jenkins standing in the hallway with two of his Gurkhas. "The Australians picked us up with their helicopters," he said. "Now they're sending their soldiers down to Liquica."

"We told Bates not to do that," I said, getting worried. "The militia might kill Daniel if they're attacked."

"It's not my idea, Mr. Bettencourt. I don't have any transport so I'm riding in one of the Aussie vehicles. Thought you might want to come along."

I finished getting dressed and grabbed my cameras. Julia had spent the night on the *Seria* and I knew she was planning to meet with General Bates as soon as he returned to his office. I scribbled a short note on the back of a chocolate-bar wrapper and gave it to the hotel manager's nephew. Using a lot of gestures and a smattering of Portuguese I told him to take the message to the woman doctor living on the boat with the Indonesian crew. The boy ran off to the wharf and I followed Jenkins over to the Turismo Hotel.

The Australians had assembled a convoy of Land Rovers. The officers bustled about carrying their Steyr assault rifles, talking to Interfet command on their radios. The lieutenant driving us to Liquica was a friendly young man. I watched his Adam's apple bob up and down as he drank from a water bottle.

"You want to hear some music?" he asked.

"That's not necessary," Jenkins said.

"It's nothing loud, Captain. I brought my own tape cassettes along. We could listen to country western, jazz guitar—"

"I don't want to hear any bloody music."

"No worries, sir. Suit yourself."

Our convoy left the city. By now most of the fires had gone out. I could still smell burned rubber and oil whenever we passed a wrecked car, but the sky was clear and blue. We went through the airport roadblock, then traveled down the coastal road. Sitting in the front passenger seat, Jenkins swiveled around to talk to me.

"They flew Corporal Mainla back to Darwin. It looks like he's going to be all right. Private Rai is at the airport medical facility. He's still a little shaky, but he told me the basic story. I thought you might give me your version."

I tried to explain what had happened, but the palm trees and the sunlight and little white waves on the ocean challenged the darkness of my story. The Land Rover we were traveling in was new and comfortable and the lieutenant kept offering us bottles of purified water. Three Black Hawk helicopters roared over us and continued west.

"That's our rangers," the lieutenant said. "They're coming in first."

By the time we reached the first bridge on the outskirts of Liquica the helicopters had landed and a platoon of rangers was fanning through the town. I could see them checking the wrecked buildings as we drove past the churchyard and down the cobblestone road to the beach. Everything in Liquica had become larger in my memory, but now it appeared small and shabby.

The front Land Rover stopped at the end of the road and soldiers jumped out, ready for action. As the drivers switched off the engines all I could hear was the sound of waves and the screech of sea gulls circling over the dead bodies. I led Captain Jenkins down to the tennis court. The blown-up Land Rover was still parked on the sand near the ashes of the bonfire. Sergeant Gurung, Corporal Battis, and Private Thapa lay near the vehicle, covered with the cardboard strips. Five dead villagers were scattered across the tennis court along with bundles of cooking gear and clothing that had been left behind. The steel rods I had hammered into the ground were still there attached to the IV bags. The empty bags fluttered back and forth in the ocean breeze, dragging their plastic tubes across the concrete.

Jenkins looked down at the dead soldiers and shook his head. "Who covered up the bodies?" he asked.

"Daniel and I."

"Thank you, Mr. Bettencourt. That was a decent thing to do."

I stepped through a hole in the chain-link fence and wandered across the tennis court. A rolled-up blue blanket lay near a suitcase. I assumed that the blanket was wrapped around a quilt until I saw a tuft of black hair. It was the girl who had died while I took her picture. The girl's mother had covered the body before she followed the church truck to Dili.

Standing in the bright sunshine, I realized that I had never come back to any of my photographs. I had become an absurd American movie, cutting quickly from one image to another, but never stopping to focus on one thing. For the first time I had looped back—and here was my old photograph, wrapped in a blue blanket while the gulls spiraled overhead.

Wearing medical gloves, Jenkins and his men picked up Gurung's body and slipped it into a black plastic bag. "Careful. Careful," Jenkins whispered as if the sergeant was asleep and Jenkins didn't want to wake him.

The young Australian lieutenant got a message on his portable radio and then walked across the tennis court. "Mr. Bettencourt, would you please come with me."

"Why? What's going on?"

"We found something."

"Found what?"

"Something that concerns Mr. McFarland. It's up in the village."

The lieutenant and I got back into the Land Rover and he drove me over to the destroyed village *mercado*. We walked through the concrete columns, ashes all about us, clinging to our shoes. A concrete drainage ditch surrounded the *mercado* and three Rangers stood near one section of it. They stepped away as we approached them and then I saw Daniel lying on his back in an awkward posture. His face was unmarked, but he had been shot at close range in the chest and stomach. A pool of blood had formed beneath his body and some of it had trickled down the slanted ditch. His socks and shoes had been stolen.

"Is that your friend?" the lieutenant asked.

"Yes." My voice was a harsh whisper. It didn't sound like it was coming from me.

"I'm sorry, Mr. Bettencourt. Bad luck all around."

Without thinking, I raised my Nikon and took a picture of the body. The click of the shutter ended something, as if I'd cut a taut string with a very sharp knife.

WHEN I WAS COVERING the earthquake in Turkey, I met a woman whose husband and children had been crushed inside their apartment building. Instead of weeping and tearing her clothes she wandered around Adana looking for her lost cat. I thought she was crazy when I took her photograph, but now I understood. When there's too much grief to handle, part of your brain clicks off and you concentrate on the small details that surround you. At the end of time, when Judgment Day finally arrives, a great many of us will be rearranging the cereal boxes in the pantry or cleaning out the shower stall.

CAPTAIN JENKINS AND his Gurkhas appeared at the *mercado* a few minutes later. They knelt beside Daniel and placed him in one of the bags; Jenkins tied up the cords. I was watching Daniel disappear, but there was something false about the moment. I could still hear his voice and see his face in my mind. All those memories had a greater reality than the body in front of me.

The four bodies were loaded into an armored personnel carrier and we followed it back to Dili. There weren't any civilian hospitals or funeral homes in Dili and so we took the bodies to the new Interfet camp near the airport and lay them on the wooden floor of an army tent. When the job was done, Jenkins snapped to attention and saluted the three dead soldiers. He glanced at me, then walked over to Daniel and saluted him as well.

"Don't worry about the bastards who killed your friend," Jenkins said. "We'll track them down before they reach the border. There's no justice in this world unless you make it yourself."

Jenkins left me alone. I sat down on the floor of the tent and stared at the body bag. It was my responsibility to tell Julia what had happened, but that demanded more strength than I had at the moment. For most of my life I had avoided having any kind of friend. I had been a coward with my heart, preferring to watch the pain or happiness of others. Daniel had ignored my defenses. Our friendship had occurred before I was even aware of it. You think you're on a separate journey but then you suddenly realize that you're traveling together.

I don't know how long I stayed in the tent. Sunlight came through one of the mesh windows and I watched a patch of brightness move slowly toward Daniel's body. When the light touched the body I told myself I was going to do something—stand up, leave, go back to the *Seria*—but the moment passed and I remained on the floor. Motes of dust were in the air and I watched them float upward and downward like wayward atoms.

All of a sudden, I heard Richard's voice outside the tent. "Is this it?" he asked. "Is this the one?"

Richard pushed back the canvas flap and entered the tent, followed by Julia. Billy and Major Holden were with them. Someone had already told Julia that Daniel was dead, but I could tell that she didn't believe it. I jumped up as she came toward me with a frantic intensity; if she could find Daniel, just find him, then everything would be all right.

"Nicky, they told me that—"

I didn't say anything, just nodded and motioned to the body. Julia knelt down beside Daniel, hesitated, and looked away. I watched her struggle with the pain, then gather her strength and untie the top three cords. She hesitated again, pushed back the heavy plastic and exposed Daniel's face.

No one spoke. Richard and the others stood there, watching. Julia raised her hand to her lips and kissed her fingers, then touched Daniel's lips.

"This is all my fault, Nicky. I shouldn't have let Daniel go with us. We shouldn't have gone at all."

She stood and I held her and felt her grief pass through my body. Then Richard touched Julia's shoulder and coaxed her away from me.

"Stay here and help," he told Billy. "I'll call you when we get to Australia." Major Holden pulled back the tent flap and I saw that Collins and Briggs were waiting outside. "This way," Richard said softly. "This way."

And then she was gone.

Major Holden drove them over to the airstrip and they were given seats on the first flight out. I found out later that a doctor met the plane in Darwin. Julia had became hysterical and was given a strong sedative. Richard chartered a plane to Singapore, then another plane to London.

THE DEAD GURKHAS were flown to Nepal in three sealed coffins and transported to the hill country west of Kathmandu. It was a minor news story, with photographs. Gurkhas from the London regiment played the bagpipes during the funeral.

I REMAINED IN East Timor and tried to arrange Daniel's burial. None of the publications he worked for knew how to find his family. I had to work backward through his various jobs until an editor at the *Seattle Times* searched their old personnel records and found the name and address of his father. Sergeant McFarland had left the air force; it took a dozen more phone calls before I got a number in Tulsa, Oklahoma. A woman answered and I wondered if McFarland had remarried. "Ned! It's long distance!" she shouted and Daniel's father came to the phone.

He didn't seem surprised when I told him the news. "I knew Daniel was doing some dangerous things, but he wasn't going to stop. When he called me up two years ago, I told him he should come back home and get a job with an American newspaper."

"Daniel was a great journalist. Everyone respected him."

"Respect don't help you when you're dead. He spent too much time writing about foreigners and people don't care about foreigners. Daniel wouldn't listen to me."

The conversation wasn't going the way I had planned. Daniel's father seemed slightly pleased that his opinion had been vindicated. "What kind of person was Daniel when he was younger?" I asked.

"Well," he said and paused for a few seconds. "Daniel never played sports, never joined a club, spent all of his time walking around town, looking at things. After his mother got the cancer he said I didn't take care of her. That is an outright falsehood. Completely untrue. I was always at the hospital when I wasn't busy."

There was a tightness in his voice and I wondered what had happened when Daniel's mother died. I could picture Sergeant McFarland in a clean kitchen with a white tile floor. He had a short haircut and military posture. A woman stood in the background, mixing a pitcher of iced tea.

"I don't know what to do with his body," I said.

"You could ship him to Oklahoma. Or you could bury him there. I'll pay for everything. You just call me back and tell me what it costs."

I hung up and decided I would never talk to Sergeant McFarland again. The confusion I had felt over the last few days had evaporated and left a residue of anger. It didn't seem fair by anyone's faith or morality that Daniel had lost his life in this place. I blamed every person that was connected to the murder. I blamed Daniel himself for the choices he had made. I still remembered our conversations after the airplane crash and his desire to live a good life. Perhaps that was possible in a safe society where people respected each other and obeyed the traffic signs.

I considered a funeral at Bracciano but rejected that idea. If Julia wanted to live there, then the death would always be with her. If she sold the place, strangers would own Daniel's grave. After walking around Dili for a few hours, I decided to buy a plot at the local cemetery. I dropped by the *Seria* to tell Billy about my decision; he was packing up to fly back to London.

"Thanks for your help," I said. "I can handle it from here."

We stood on the bow of the ship and gazed out at Dili. The landing craft the Indonesians had used to invade East Timor so many years ago were still rusting on the beach where they'd been abandoned. UN Land Rovers and army trucks moved slowly up and down the waterfront boulevard.

"Take care, Nicky. Still a lot of crazies running around."

"I know."

I held out my hand, but Billy pushed it aside and gave me a bear hug. When I turned away, I saw that Pak was watching us. The old man nodded and winked as if we both knew the punch line to a private joke.

I hitched a ride on the back of an army truck and went to Santa Cruz Cemetery in the southeast part of the city. A concrete wall surrounded the grounds. Its spiked entrance gates had been ripped off their hinges and dumped into the street as if a thousand evil spirits had burst out of their coffins and escaped. Most of the tombs were narrow boxes of blue tile or limestone with a stone cross at one end. Families were buried together, each name painted on the stone. The first names on the family memorials were large and significant, then more deaths had been added in smaller print. Over the years, the names and dates pushed up against each other, as parents and children had been killed in successive waves of arrests and executions.

The cemetery was overgrown with creeper vines and stalks of bamboo and there was a sloppy, haphazard feeling about the place. I was just about to leave when a young boy approached me. He made a digging motion with his hands. I nodded and he came back with the chief gravedigger, a barefoot old man called Afonso. *"Posso ajudar?"* he kept saying. May I help you? When I told him that my *amigo* had just died, he showed me two narrow patches of ground, surrounded by tottering crosses. *Errado,* I told him. Wrong. Very wrong. I'd look for another graveyard. Afonso nodded his head and took me to a space by the wall surrounded with hibiscus. Even in the dry season, there were red flowers and lush green leaves. It was better than a municipal plot in Tulsa, with half-dead grass and some guy on a tractor mower.

Jenkins and four Gurkhas picked me up at the hotel the next morning. We drove out to the Interfet camp, placed the body in a coffin, and went to the cemetery. Other journalists in Dili had learned about the funeral, and a crowd of reporters, photographers, and television cameramen was waiting beside the broken gates. I got out of the truck and everyone clustered around for an improvised news conference. Tristram Müller asked me the first question; then everyone else had their turn. How was he killed, Mr. Bettencourt? Did they catch the guys who did it? What was the last thing you heard your friend say? They asked me if Daniel was married and then seemed annoyed that I didn't know his age. "Give me a rough guess," said an Australian reporter and I made up a number. All the journalists glanced at one another as if to say, Do we agree on this? before writing it down.

Afonso and the boy approached us carrying their shovels. They guided the truck down a dirt pathway to a hole dug near the wall. The Gurkhas pulled Daniel's coffin out of the truck, then lowered it into the ground. I heard the rapid click-click-click of an auto-advance and saw a Dutch photographer working. I had done the same thing countless times, crouching down and snapping in a new lens, bending and jumping and twisting my body around for a good shot.

Jenkins cleared his throat and glanced over at me. Obviously, he felt that the Official Best Friend should say something. When I remained silent he took a step toward the grave. Clods of dirt and a few white pebbles dribbled down onto the top of the coffin.

"I talked to Private Rai before he flew home. He told me what happened after my men were attacked in Liquica. The militia was going to kill everyone until Mr. McFarland stepped forward. He saved the lives of hundreds of people. God bless him. He was a brave one. That's all I've got to say."

Jenkins stepped back and gave me another look. An American television cameraman zoomed in on my face and his soundman extended the boom. I knew that I should say something about my friend's death, but I felt like shouting insults. I hated the reporters and the photographers. I hated the tropical sun and the burned-brown hills and the ragged palm trees.

"Good-bye, Daniel," I said. "I wish we hadn't come to this place."

A group of children ran toward us and I turned away from the grave. Sister Xavier was leading her parishioners into the cemetery. They were clapping and singing hymns in Portuguese. First the women would sing a phrase, then the men, and then everyone would join together for the chorus. The crowd flowed around the tombs and gravestones like a brightly colored wave.

Sister Xavier took my hand. She smiled shyly as if we had just met again after a long separation. She raised her hand and the crowd stopped singing. The refugees from Liquica had plucked flowers from the bushes and trees as they marched in from the airport. Each person stepped forward and said something in Tetum or Portuguese, then tossed their flower into Daniel's grave.

CAPTAIN JENKINS TOLD me that the Gurkhas had begun to search for the militiamen who had been at Liquica; every soldier in the regiment had volunteered for the assignment. Jenkins had picked two teams of eight men and hired local guides at the airport refugee camp.

The Gurkhas found one of the killers right away, then tracked down the others as they tried to reach West Timor. Some people said there was a final shoot-out near the border. Others heard that Cristiano's militiamen surrendered and begged for mercy. Each story had the same conclusion: there were no prisoners.

All I know is Captain Jenkins showed up at my hotel room five days later looking like he'd been sleeping in the jungle. He opened an envelope and dumped out Daniel's wristwatch and passport.

"We also found your friend's shoes, but they were covered with blood. I dug a hole and buried them."

"Thank you, Captain."

"The suspects died resisting capture, but we managed to interrogate one of them before he bled to death. You know what that little bastard bragged about? He'd raped nine women."

According to Jenkins, the militiamen had waited near the wharf for a transport ship to appear. Daniel talked to a few of them and took a nap in the shade of a banyan tree. When the ship didn't arrive by sunset, Cristiano became worried about a counterattack and told Daniel they were going to hide. A large plane with lights on its wings passed over the town as they were walking past the *mercado*. It was probably one of the C-130 transports returning to Darwin, but Cristiano assumed that the plane was carrying paratroopers who were going to land in the darkness and capture them. He ordered Daniel to stand beside the drainage ditch and told his followers to shoot. It was over in a few seconds.

LATER I HEARD a different story about Daniel's murder when Sister Xavier wrote me from East Timor. In her version the transport plane passed over Liquica and Cristiano become frightened. He told his men to take Daniel over to the ruined marketplace. Daniel looked calm when he was ordered to stand beside the ditch and the improvised firing squad became nervous. They whispered among themselves that this killing was bad luck and it would cause them to be punished by the island spirits. The men lowered their weapons and Daniel extended the palm of his right hand, as if he was offering them a gift. Furious, Cristiano grabbed a rifle and fired the entire clip.

"THIS STORY'S OVER," announced a British reporter in the hotel hallway. The foreign journalists were sending out their final sum-it-all-up articles, then flying home. Julia was gone, Daniel was buried, and I still remained. I felt like one of those windup toys that marches across the living room floor and hits a wall.

The wet season was only a few weeks away and the air felt stagnant and heavy with moisture. Interfet command had transferred out to the airport and I moved over to the Turismo Hotel. Water began to dribble out of the faucets. It was enough to take a shower, but you had to keep your mouth shut because of typhoid. The UN shipped in four electric generators and power flowed through the city. I touched a switch in my hotel room and a lightbulb went on. The ceiling fan above me squeaked and shivered, then spun around with an awkward, wobbling motion as if the wooden blades might break off. I stayed up late that night and woke up when a soldier knocked on the door.

"Mr. Bettencourt? I'm sorry to bother you." It took me a few seconds to recognize the young Australian lieutenant who had taken me down to Liquica.

"What's the problem?"

"We're cracking down on people selling stolen property. This morning we found this old Indonesian selling a lot of expensive medicine down by the harbor. We told him to hand it over, but he was as mad as a cut snake. He said you gave it to him."

I leaned against the door. "I don't know what you're talking about."

The lieutenant swallowed and looked embarrassed. "He's a bad-tempered old man. He just said 'Nicky, Mr. Nicky.' Then he pretended to shoot a camera."

I pulled on my socks and shoes, then grabbed my camera bag. "All right. I'll talk to him. Let's go."

We got into a Land Rover and drove through the city. More Timorese had come down from the hills in the last few days and they drifted around the city staring at the destruction. None of the burned-out buildings were being rebuilt, but women had started to sweep up the ashes with homemade brooms.

Out at the Interfet camp, the Australians had built a jail using an empty cargo container and a chain-link fence covered with razor wire. Two young militiamen sat beside the open container and drank from water bottles. They looked like schoolboys picked up for throwing rocks. Pak squatted near the fence and guarded a cardboard box filled with antibiotics and chloramphenicol tablets. Globs of red spit were splattered on the dirt in front of him. Pak reached into his leather bag to get some more betel nut, then grinned when he saw me. The guard let him out of the cage and we shook hands.

"Morning, Pak. What's going on?"

"Hello, Mr. Nicky." The old man glared at the Australians and gestured to the box of medicine. "Small trouble. They no believe me."

I crouched down and the lieutenant left us alone. "What don't they believe?"

"You and Mr. Billy are good friends."

"Not exactly friends. What does that have to do with the medicine?"

He nodded at the box. "Pak did what Mr. Billy said. This is what you pay me."

I felt as if I'd been carrying my camera all day long, dealing with bad light and missed opportunities. Suddenly the world had rearranged itself and if I took one step, just one more step around a corner, the right image would appear. Look away, I thought. Act like you don't care. I scratched a mosquito bite on my arm as if it was the most interesting problem in my life.

"Yeah. I was wondering about what happened. Did someone help you?"

"No! It was just me!" Pak made a fist and tapped his bony rib cage. "When the *Seria* goes out of the harbor, Mr. Billy comes down and tells me. 'Break the engine.'"

"Right, and then there was an explosion."

"No explosion. That was me. I take a beer bottle, fill it with petrol, and attach a rag. I set it on fire and bang!" He slapped his leg with the palm of his hand. "It looked very bad."

I smiled as if I was pleased. "And you told us that the fuel line had burst."

"Yes. That was easy to do. Mr. Billy was happy. Captain Vanderhouten get the money. I get the medicine."

I wanted to make Pak repeat his statement in front of witnesses, but I knew that the old man would sense trouble and deny everything. Even if a police force and a judicial system had existed in Dili, no one would have arrested Pak and prosecuted him for a crime. Pak hadn't killed anyone. He was the first mate on a ship. Everyone knew that the militia had murdered Daniel McFarland.

I pulled out my camera and took the old man's picture. He gave me a black-toothed smile as if we were fellow conspirators, then I stood up and walked over to the lieutenant.

"So you know him?"

"Of course. Thank you for your help, Lieutenant." I turned away from him and headed back to the road.

"But what about the medicine? Do we confiscate what's in the box?"

"No," I said. "He earned it."

20 LIGHT

I boarded the plane to England filled with rage and elaborate plans of revenge. I would hold a news conference, demand that Richard be prosecuted. Perhaps I'd write a defamatory article and force him to sue me. Most of my fantasies involved courtrooms and barristers and people pointing fingers at each other. Of course, it was all nonsense. By the time the plane passed over Pakistan and Central Asia, I realized that I had no options at all.

I couldn't hurt Richard or demand his arrest; he was too wealthy and influential, protected by lawyers and his political friends. East Timor was a long way from Britain and it would be difficult to prove Richard's involvement in what had happened. Even if I could have figured out some kind of legal strategy, I didn't have the confidence to push it forward. Daniel would have known what to do, but now I was on my own.

Back in London, a cold autumn rain was falling and wet leaves filled the gutters. Alex, the night clerk at the Ruskin Hotel, said a Mr. Seaton had left several messages asking me to contact him as soon as I arrived.

He wanted to know if the caller was the famous "I Bought My Home with Richard" Seaton, and when I nodded he hummed the tune that went with the TV commercial.

I slept for about ten hours, then woke up and ordered some toast and a pot of tea. When the breakfast-room waitress showed up with the food, I searched through my pockets for a tip, then rummaged through my camera bag. Tucked in a side pocket was a single roll of black-and-white 35mm film. I had attached some medical tape to it and written the words *Canal House*. This was ancient history, shots I had taken of Daniel and Julia the first time they invited me there.

I didn't want a stranger touching the negatives so I went out that afternoon and bought developing chemicals, photographic paper, and three plastic trays. I sealed off the cracks around the bathroom door with duct tape, processed the film in the darkness, and hung the negatives from the shower rod. After the film dried, I covered the light over the sink with a sheet of red cellophane. I taped the negatives to a sheet of photographic paper, then gave the paper a burst of light with a desk lamp held in my hand.

Kneeling on the bathroom floor, I pushed the paper into the developer and the photographs appeared. The pictures were small, the size of the film itself and I took one of my lenses and turned it over to magnify the images. I saw Daniel and Julia standing at the front door of the Canal House, Daniel working in the kitchen, the two of them together, sitting on the couch, his arm on her shoulder as they looked at my camera. I stared at Daniel's face, looking for an answer. Had he known that he was going to die in East Timor? Was there a hint of sadness, a deeper knowledge, in his smile?

I HID IN MY ROOM for two days, then finally called the Riverside Bank. Some people think that power is revealed by the number of layers protecting you from the outside world. By that standard, Richard Seaton was a very powerful man. I had to talk to a series of receptionists, secretaries, and special assistants until Richard's voice finally came on the line.

"Nicky! Glad you called. We lost track of you after you left Dili."

"Where's Julia?"

"In Bracciano." Richard said. "Staying there just brings back a lot of bad memories. I'm flying to Italy this weekend in the jet. Maybe you could come along with me. We need to talk her into returning to England and resting. For a long time."

"Maybe she doesn't want to leave."

"Yes. That's why I need your help, Nicky. Where are you?"

"In London, at the Ruskin. Maybe we could meet later on this morning."

"Of course. Right away. Let me send a car over."

"It's not necessary. I'd rather walk."

"Whatever you want. Pick a time and I'll be here."

He gave me the address of his office and I said I'd drop by in two hours. Sitting on the edge of my unmade bed, I ate a candy bar and wondered what I was going to say. The only real decision I'd made was not to bring along my camera.

The Riverside Bank, Ltd., was in a large office building near the Strand. A security guard wearing a blue blazer was sitting in the central foyer. When I gave him my name, he picked up his phone and dialed a number. Another guard appeared and escorted me to the twenty-third floor where an older woman with a clipboard was waiting. Modern art decorated the office, geometric shapes on white canvas that were easy on the eyes. My guide escorted me past several determined-looking people staring at computer screens, pushed open a burnished steel door, and told me that Mr. Seaton was waiting.

The office was immense, four times bigger than the breakfast room at the Ruskin. It had glass walls on three sides and a spectacular view of the River Thames. Richard was sitting at a massive desk that looked like it had been molded out of concrete. He was looking at two different computer screens and typing on a keyboard. There was a phone on his desk with lots of buttons and a framed photograph of Julia standing on the tennis court at Westgate Castle.

"Nicky!" He jumped out of his chair and gave me a hug. I felt his hand pat me on the back a few times as if I was on his team and we had just lost a game.

"It's wonderful to see you again. I still can't believe all this happened. Daniel's death is such a loss."

"A big loss." I said. My voice was all wrong, cracking a little, not confident.

"Please. Sit down," he said and led me over to a conversation area. Framed photographs were on the wall: Richard talking to two American presidents, the prime minister of Britain, and the Dalai Lama.

"Can I get you anything? Coffee? Tea? Or maybe something a bit stronger? Anything you want."

"That's okay." I sat down on a black leather couch. He took a heavily upholstered chair. Magazines were on the coffee table—some going back several years—but all of them had Richard's face on the cover.

"What happened after Billy left East Timor?"

"We buried Daniel in a cemetery. A lot of people came to the funeral."

"Is there a gravestone?"

"Just a wooden cross."

A pad of paper lay on the coffee table. Richard picked up a silver fountain pen and scribbled a note. "I'll get a memorial stone carved here in London and have it shipped to the cemetery. We can just put his name on it—or anything else you want."

"That's a wonderful thing to do for the man you killed."

The words just came out of my mouth. I didn't even think about them. I felt like a little kid who had just leaped into the deep end of the pool. Now I had to start kicking or I was going to drown.

"I beg your pardon?"

"I talked to Pak, that old man on the *Seria*. He said you paid him to fake an engine breakdown."

Richard looked like a cyclist who had been rolling down a smooth boulevard when suddenly the pavement disappeared. "That's insane," he sputtered. "Completely untrue."

"I know what happened."

"Calm down, Nicky. Just calm down. Daniel was your closest friend. His death must have been an enormous shock."

"I don't know how you can justify killing another person, but I'm sure you have an explanation. Maybe you tell yourself that everything was crazy in Timor and now you're back in London and everything's normal again. People do that a lot, Richard. Blame it on the Third World. Blame it on the weather. There's a million excuses and none of them are true. I think it was all about power. When Daniel ran off with Julia, he took something from you. And nobody does that to Richard Seaton."

Richard pushed one of the buttons on the table phone. He stared at me, not saying a word, then the steel door popped open and Billy charged into the room. This was the London Billy, wearing an Armani suit and gray cashmere shirt.

"What's the problem?" he asked, then recognized me and grinned. "Hey, Nicky! When did you get back in London?"

"This isn't a social visit. Nicky is acting a bit strange."

Billy shrugged and tried to make a joke. "Well, he's never been completely *normal*. Isn't that right, Nicky?"

"He says we paid Pak to sabotage the ship's engine."

Richard and Billy glanced at each other. They didn't play leader and follower at that moment; it was something much more complex. At that moment I wasn't sure if killing Daniel was Billy's idea or if Richard had actually given the order. Perhaps Richard only provided the desire, the need, and Billy made it real.

"What are you talking about, Nicky? You saw the explosion yourself."

"You probably came up with the idea when you were negotiating with Vanderhouten. You paid him off and Pak threw a gasoline bomb."

Richard stood up and looked down at me. "You think you understand the world because you've photographed a few starving babies and bribed your way around some roadblocks, but you're an innocent, Nicky. You don't know anything."

"I know that you killed Daniel. That's enough."

"You can't prove that. I don't care what that old man told you. It's not true and no one's going to believe him."

"That doesn't make a damn bit of difference to me. All I have to do is spend some time here in London, buying drinks for journalists, and telling them what happened. Then I'll fly over to New York and do the same thing. The story would leak out. It always does, these days."

Billy stepped forward and jabbed his finger in my direction. "Doing something like that would cause some very negative consequences."

"Tell Billy to shut up. I didn't come here to talk to another murderer."

"Watch your mouth!" Billy shouted.

"I want him to be quiet because I'm about to explain the only way you can get out of this."

Everything changed the instant I said that. Billy glanced at Richard. His fists became hands again and he returned to the door. Richard smiled slightly, then decided that it didn't look dignified. He went over to the concrete desk, sat down, and flipped open a thin leather binder that contained rows of blank checks. "I'll pay you one hundred thousand pounds, Nicky. Take it or leave it. I won't negotiate."

"I don't want your money."

He looked startled. Over at the door, Billy shifted his weight around like a boxer getting ready to attack.

"What I'm telling you is this—you will never see Julia again. You will never talk to her. You will never inquire about her. You will stay out of her life forever."

Richard stopped writing the check and sat there with a pen in his hand. "You can't order me around."

"You're wrong about that. That's exactly what I'm doing." I stood up and headed for the door. "You're not going to talk to Julia and you're not going to talk to me. I've already written out a statement and left it in a safe place. Keep away from me or the world is going to learn that you killed Daniel."

"Stay here," Richard said. "We're not finished with this conversation."

"Everything you say about me is true. I'm not rich or successful, I don't have a home or a family, and now I've lost my best friend. But that's an advantage in this situation. I'm like one of those suicide bombers with nothing to lose."

Feeling tense and sweaty, I passed through the outer office and stood in front of the elevators. I expected the phone to ring downstairs in the lobby and waited for the security guard in the blazer to give me that "Step this way, sir" routine. When I made it out to the sidewalk, I started breathing again.

I bought a pad of paper and a manila envelope at a stationery store and sat in a pub. I wrote down exactly what had happened on the *Seria* and described the confrontation with Richard. When that was done, I signed the statement and placed it in the envelope with a roll of film that included Pak's photograph.

It had rained that morning, but patches of sky were starting to appear when I took a cab over to the *Newsweek* offices. Ann and Carter were checking the color levels of some photographs on a computer when I walked in. They both looked surprised to see me.

"Nicky! When did you get back?" Carter said.

"Yesterday."

"It was just terrible what happened to Daniel McFarland," Ann said. "It's been in all the papers. The magazine ran a half-page, boxed, with his picture."

"I haven't read any of it."

"Have you seen this?" She handed me a copy of *Newsweek* from a few weeks ago while I was in Dili. My shot of the mother with her dying child was on the cover. Inside were four pages of my photographs with the headline AGONY IN EAST TIMOR. I had even gotten a reporter's byline for what I explained over the phone.

"New York loves you," Carter said. "They're going to nominate you for the Pulitzer Prize."

A few months ago I would have dragged them down to a pub and bought drinks for everyone. Now I didn't care. "It's stuffy in this office," I told Carter. "Let's get out of here and take a walk."

We used the pedestrian passageway to Hyde Park. The statue of the falling lovers was still there, but the cherubs had been wrapped in plastic sheeting. Carter and I headed down Lovers' Walk, trying to avoid the patches of mud. A cold wind tugged at the flap of his trench coat.

I handed him the sealed envelope. "Take this and keep it in a safe place. If I get killed in some idiotic accident, it's probably not an accident. Open it and show the statement to everyone you know."

"Okay." Carter stared at me. "You all right, Nicky? How you feeling?"

"Tired."

"Listen, I could authorize payment for fifteen sessions with a psychologist here in London. Sometimes people need to talk to a therapist after they've been through a difficult experience."

"That's not what I want to do right now."

Carter stopped walking and we stood between two beech trees. A few dead leaves still clung to the branches. "If you want another assignment, that's easy enough. New York just called me about your availability."

"Where do they want to send me?"

"Three blind people, including the son of Senator Bob Rawlings, will attempt to climb Mount Everest this January. You wouldn't have to go all the way to the summit, just to one of the base camps."

"The whole thing sounds completely pointless."

"Of course it's pointless, but you could get some good photographs."

"Who knows? I might get lucky. Someone might die."

Carter's voice was calm and sympathetic. "You really should go see that therapist, Nicky. I've used her myself to deal with a few issues."

"I need to take some time off."

"Of course. No problem. You've earned it."

We stood there for a few minutes with our hands in our pockets. A gust of wind made the dead leaves shiver.

"I guess Daniel was your friend," Carter said.

"Does that surprise you?"

"People work together for years, but you never really know what their relationship is until . . ." Carter looked embarrassed. "Until something happens."

• • •

I FELT AS EMPTY and fragile as a paper cup, too tired to sleep or eat or do anything but wander around London. If I had been left on my own, I probably would have returned to the Elgin Marbles at the British Museum. Sitting on one of the benches, I could have spent the rest of my life watching thousands of strangers stroll in and view the sculptures, make the circuit around the room, stop and examine the angry centaurs, then walk out the doorway.

But I couldn't stay in London. I had to see Julia. A plane flight seemed too immediate so I took a train to Paris, then booked a ticket on the express going down to Rome. I sat alone in a first-class compartment with a fold-down bed, table, and a little steel sink. Everything was clean and in the right place. The young porter smiled and told me that the dining car was open for supper. Chrysanthemums trembled in a fluted vase as we rolled past cornfields and clattered over bridges. Later that night we stopped at a train station near the Italian border. I lay in the lower bunk and peered through the half-opened curtain. Fluorescent light. An empty train platform. And it seemed so lonely, like a way station to a shadowy, awful place. Wheels squeaked, the train shuddered as another car was added, and then we were moving forward.

The little nun at the convent recognized me from the time I visited Daniel. I told her that I wanted to see the mother superior and she led me up a stone staircase to an office that overlooked the garden.

The mother superior was a large woman with a broad face. She looked like someone who owned an Italian corsetry shop. She listened intently as I described what had happened in East Timor. When I told her that Daniel was dead, she looked startled and sat back in her chair.

"We prayed for Mr. McFarland's safe return."

"I guess it didn't work."

"Excuse me. I must tell the others."

The mother superior stood up suddenly and left me alone in her office. I sat there for a few minutes and listened to footsteps moving up and down the hallway. Staring at a faded photograph of a dead pope, I had a vision of an enormous prayer machine hidden down in the convent basement. It had pedals and lights and looked like a cross between a slot machine and an old-fashioned concert organ. Now they were removing Daniel's soul from the device, the little tag that listed his name.

When the mother superior returned she was very brisk and efficient. She questioned me about Daniel's funeral and seemed relieved that he had been buried in a Christian cemetery. I took Daniel's improvised will out of my shirt pocket and placed it on her desk. The nun unfolded the crunched-up sheet of notepaper and studied it as if it was a fragment of the Dead Sea Scrolls.

"He wanted you to have his car," she said.

"Yes. Is it still here at the convent? Will the engine start or do I need to get a mechanic?"

"A mechanic is not necessary. When Mr. McFarland left Rome, he gave me the key and asked me to check the car occasionally. This became a source of tension among us until I decided that we would all take turns, oldest to youngest. Every night, after dinner, one of the sisters got to sit in the car and run the engine for a few minutes to keep the battery alive."

"Thank you."

"We would have done anything to help Mr. McFarland. Everyone here respected him. He was a very generous man."

"That didn't help him either."

"I don't understand what you're saying, Mr. Bettencourt."

"The fact that you prayed for him and the fact that he was a good person didn't stop this from happening."

The nun folded up the will and handed it back to me. "I'm sorry you lost your friend," she said. "It must be very painful."

THE CAR STARTED the first time and I drove north to Bracciano. The autumn rains hadn't arrived and the days were still warm. A herd of goats scrambled through the road ditch. Farmers were burning the stubble off their fields and there was a smoky odor in the air.

I opened the gate near the cottage, then drove slowly down the dirt driveway. La Signora was digging up onions in the vegetable garden.

When she saw me, she thrust her shovel into the dirt and walked down the terraces to the patch of gravel where Daniel had always parked the car.

"*Buon giorno, Signor Nicky.*"

"*Buon giorno, signora.*"

The old lady touched the red hood of Daniel's car, then started crying. She said a few things in Italian that I didn't understand.

"*Dov'è la Signora Julia?*" I asked, and my question transformed the old lady. She stopped crying. If Billy Monroe or any other threat had dropped out of the sky, she would have chased them away with her shovel.

La Signora pointed down the slope to the ravine, and when I hesitated she gave me a little push forward. As I crossed the field to the dirt pathway, I inspected the cherry trees I had planted last year. All of them had lost their summer leaves, but their trunks were straight and their branches reached toward the sky. The Monterey pines Daniel had planted still looked like saplings, but the eucalyptus trees had taken root and were peeling off strips of bark like a snake shedding its skin.

Julia sat on a boulder, facing the ruins of the Roman bridge. She wore a long cotton skirt and a wide-brimmed straw hat to protect her from the sun. When I came closer through the grass I saw that she had walked down the hill to pick blackberries, but the basket was only half full.

She stood up when I approached and we both looked at each other. Just my presence there reminded her of Daniel and I could see that she was struggling to control her grief. I felt damned forever, responsible for what had happened.

"Good to see you, Nicky." Her voice was strained, but she wasn't going to cry.

"Maybe I should come back later."

"No. I'm glad you're here. I left messages at your hotel in London."

We sat down on two chunks of marble while a hawk drifted across the sky. "Tell me what happened after I left Timor," she said. "Even the smallest thing."

I told her about Daniel's funeral and the crowd at the cemetery. I told her that Jenkins and his men had tracked down the militia and that Daniel's wristwatch and passport were in the car. I didn't mention Richard's betrayal. Some other time, I thought. Not this afternoon. "And what happened to you?" I asked. "Did Richard take you to Westgate Castle?"

"No. They put me in a private hospital in West London. It was the sort of place where the staff wears pink T-shirts and you call the doctors by their first names. I saw a cabinet minister and a rock star shuffling down the hallway in their pajamas."

"What did they do to you?"

"Drugged me for a week or so, then brought me out of it. A psychiatrist came into my room twice a day and we had these bizarre conversations. He kept asking me to visualize my grief. Was it an animal? What kind of animal? Nonsense like that. When I told him to go to hell, they changed my medication."

"Could you leave?"

"No. It was a lockdown facility and I had actually signed myself in. After another week of being in a haze, I faked swallowing the pills and became a bit more coherent. I borrowed ten pounds from the woman who served the meal trays and slipped out the back entrance. Then I took a cab to Laura's apartment, borrowed some more money, and flew to Italy. I kept crying the whole time, in the airport lounge, in the women's room, in the back of the taxicab. When I finally got here, La Signora put me to bed and I slept for two days. She's been wonderful."

Julia bent down and picked up a smooth white pebble. She rubbed the surface with her thumb, then tossed it away. "I'm going to stay in Bracciano. I'm not going to leave. I feel like Daniel is here. Sometimes he's right beside me. Sometimes he's in the house or up in the orchard. And there's another thing, too." She looked up at me and smiled for the first time. "I'm pregnant, Nicky. La Signora seemed to know before I did. I think she's a bit of a sorceress."

"That's wonderful, Julia. Congratulations. Daniel would be very happy."

"I plan to have the baby here. I'll run out of money in a few months, but I've applied for a special certificate to practice medicine in Italy. They need a doctor in the village so everyone is fairly positive about the idea."

We were both silent for a moment and I thought about the child. Then we looked at each other and we both remembered Daniel and the pain came again.

"I better go."

"Please don't, Nicky. I'm glad you're here."

"We remind each other of what happened."

"And it did happen. When I was in the hospital, I pretended that he wasn't dead, but of course that's not true. We were all on that beach together. Cristiano was going to kill everyone there and Daniel saved our lives. No matter what happened afterward, he made the right decision at that moment. I don't think he'd take it back."

"No. He wouldn't. But that doesn't make it any easier."

"God, I wish I knew all the answers or just a few of them. But I don't, Nicky. All I know is that I'm still in love with Daniel. That hasn't changed."

We sat quietly. The sun was warm and a light wind made the grass sway back and forth. A few yards down the slope, a brown finch was pecking out the seeds from a sunflower. I forgot about myself, who I was and what I wanted to do.

La Signora shouted something in Italian. I looked up the hill and saw the old lady standing beneath the arbor on the patio. There were plates of food and loaves of bread on the table and she waved her right arm, summoning us to the feast.

Julia glanced at me and smiled. "Are you hungry, Nicky?"

"Sure."

"La Signora wants me to eat all the time. She says it's good for the baby."

We walked up the hill together. "So?" she asked. "Will you stay for a while?"

I nodded. "For a few days."

Julia seemed pleased. "Wonder if it's a boy or girl. I bet La Signora knows, but she's not telling."

"Maybe she'll tell me."

I glanced at Julia; she held her head up slightly and looked forward as if she was about to start a long journey. And the world felt larger, it seemed to expand around us so that I was aware of the farm and the bridge and the distant hills. I pulled out my camera and raised it to my eye, then decided not to take the picture.

WHEN I FIRST became a photographer, I was only aware of the sun over my shoulder and the flash on my camera. Then I got older and began to notice the shadows that touched all of us. Now I realize that every object in this world reflects and absorbs light. We are created by light, shaped by light, and we burn our image into the hearts of others.

Reading Group Guide

1. How does Nicky's profession as a photographer affect the way he sees the world around him? How does his job influence his perspective on Daniel and Julia's relationship? Do you trust Nicky as a narrator?

2. Why is Nicky drawn to Daniel? What does Daniel possess that Nicky realizes he himself lacks?

3. In chapter 15, when Nicky takes the photo of Richard and Julia leaning over the map of East Timor, he demonstrates the photographer's ability to reconstruct reality. To what extent is this a turning point for Nicky?

4. Why is Julia involved with Richard? Is he a shelter from a stressful life? Or does she see how he can serve a greater cause?

5. Did Richard acquire Julia only for her usefulness? In what way might he have loved her?

6. When we first meet Daniel, he's having an affair with an Italian aristocrat. How does Julia challenge Daniel's attitudes and expectations?

7. Daniel is a journalist with a commitment to the truth. In chapter 3, he worries that he will turn into someone like the cynical editor, Matthew Vickery. Contrast his actions in Uganda with those in East Timor. Should journalists become involved with their stories? Is it possible for journalists to stay detached from what is going on around them?

8. The airplane crash radically changes Daniel's view of the world. Why does this event—more than any other he had witnessed or endured—become a turning point? How does his time at Boma Mission confirm his new attitude? In chapter 7, Father Lokali connects love for God and the love for another. Can emotional love ever bring one closer to spiritual knowledge?

9. In chapter 9, Richard makes a crucial speech about relief aid during the dinner party. How are his attitudes also indicated in the pheasant hunt and in the setting of Westgate Castle? Is the manipulation of the truth ever justified in order to help others?

10. Why do Julia and Daniel have to retreat to the canal house? How does their relationship to each other—and to the world—change during their retreat? Why do they decide to leave the farm in Italy?

11. Is Daniel's sacrifice foreshadowed by the author? How does the tension build during the sequence in East Timor? Did you wonder if Richard might betray Daniel?

12. What is Daniel's legacy for Julia and Nicky? Do you think both characters reach the same level of understanding and acceptance? How does the final paragraph show how Nicky has changed?